A Question of Precedence

A Question of Precedence

and other Middle East Stories by Marmaduke Pickthall

Edited and Introduced by
Peter Clark

BEACON BOOKS

Published by Beacon Books and Media Ltd
Innospace
The Shed
Chester Street
Manchester
M1 5GD
UK

www.beaconbooks.net

ISBN 978-1-912356-02-7

A C.I.P. record for this book is available from the British Library

Cover design by Bipin Mistry
Cover art by Si Muhammmad Bin Saalim Fes, Morocco

The Pickthall Novels series:

A Question of Precedence -
and other short stories by Marmaduke Pickthall

Saïd the Fisherman

Oriental Encounters

The Children of the Nile

The Valley of the Kings

Knights of Araby

The Early Hour

House of War

Veiled Women

House of Islam

Contents

INTRODUCTION

Marmaduke Pickthall (1875-1936) is remembered best as the translator of the Holy Koran. He embraced Islam during the First World War and his translation was undertaken under the patronage of the Nizam of Hyderabad. His was the first translation by a believing Muslim who had English as his mother tongue. But he was also an accomplished writer. He was a prolific campaigning journalist, a writer of sermons but also a writer of fiction. He published fourteen novels and three volumes of short stories. A fifteenth novel was unpublished. Eight of the novels were located in Syria, Egypt, Turkey or Yemen. Twenty-seven of his short stories were located in the Middle East.

Pickthall came from a solid English middle-class family. His father was a Church of England minister who died when Pickthall was a boy. He was close to his mother who had spent twenty years with her first husband in India. Educated as a day boy at Harrow, he went to Jerusalem when he was still a teenager and spent two years travelling in Palestine and Syria, learning fluent Arabic and living not as a detached European tourist but in village inns and houses. He returned to live a conventional middle-class life in England as a compulsive writer. The summation of his years in Greater Syria was the publication of his novel, *Saïd the Fisherman*, in 1903. This was his best-known novel and went through many editions for twenty-five years. It also received much critical acclaim.

In the following years he produced novels set in England and, after a prolonged stay in Egypt, novels based in Egypt. His first volume of short stories, *Pot au Feu*, was published in 1911. It includes one story first published in a magazine in 1899. In 1913 he spent six months in Istanbul, learned Turkish and wrote articles expressing his support for the Young Turkish Ottoman regime. His sojourn also led to his later writing of a novel based in Turkey, *The Early Hours* (1921). Meanwhile in 1914 a second collection of short stories, *Tales from Five Chimneys*, was published.

During the First World War Pickthall wrote extensively, expressing sympathy for the Ottoman point of view. When the two Empires, the British and the Ottoman, were at war with each other he tried to arrange a separate peace. He was regarded by the authorities with great suspicion. In 1917 he further alienated many of his fellow-countrymen by announcing that he was a Muslim. His scholarship, his Arabic and his reputation put him at the forefront of the British Muslim community. He led prayers at the London mosque, delivered sermons and wrote extensively about his faith. After the war he was unemployable in Britain and Indian friends found a job for him as editor of the *Bombay Chronicle*. His third collection of short stories, *As Others See Us*, was published after he had left Britain, in 1921, For the last sixteen years of his life India was his base, first Bombay and then, from 1925, Hyderabad. He returned from India ten years later, dying in Cornwall in 1936.

As a writer of fiction Pickthall had no models, but he was clearly influenced, consciously or not, by the works of Walter Scott, Charles Dickens, George Eliot and Thomas Hardy. He has the circumstantiality and the care for authentic detail of Scott. His imaginative compassion, like that of Dickens, reaches out to the marginal people of society, the bandits, and the desperately poor. There is a moral passion that reminds the reader of George Eliot. And in creating a discreet world with his habits and language he is like Hardy.

Indeed his use of language is remarkable. In his Middle East fiction, novels and stories, he uses an archaic English, comprehensible but unfamiliar. It is as if the world he is reproducing is alien, and needs to be clothed in words and phrases that take the reader right away from his or her world. It is an artificial creation. He is similarly affected (in a positive sense) in his use of dialogue. Frequently a Syrian or Egyptian is given English words that are a direct translation of the colloquial Arabic equivalent. It is interesting to note that he is just as painstaking when he gives lower class Suffolk or Sussex characters authentic dialect. Pickthall had an excellent ear for language – he was a skilled linguist. In his middle class English characters he does not use dialect but has the appropriate expressions that identify the speaker in terms of age and class.

There is a development over the quarter of a century during which he wrote fiction. In his pre-war fiction he is observing, recording and reproducing. In the earlier stories his style is naturalistic, his stories are the productions of a verbal cine camera. After 1914 there is a harsher tone, a growth of a very definite point of view. His novel based in medieval Yemen, *Knights of Araby*, published in the year he declared his Islam, has no non-Muslim characters. His post-war novel about the Young Turks, *The Early Hours*, reflects much of his pre-war journalism. His last English novel, *Sir Limpidus,* is a black satire about everything in England he rejected and deplored – cosy self-satisfied sentimental parochial liberalism. And in his short stories, there is a similar progression. In his last collection, *As Others See Us,* the stories located in Turkey have an edge to them, with Muslim characters presented as noble and liberal, and Christians drawn as fanatical – a reversal of conventional wisdom. In the introduction to the last collection, written in 1922, when he was already committed to exile (as his fellow-countrymen would have seen it) in India, he acknowledges a "progress towards disillusion as illustrated in the Eastern stories here." He thought Britain had been dragged into a war against the Ottoman Empire by Russia. "Goodwill and geniality," he wrote, "towards Eastern peoples could hardly flourish in the shadow of the Czardom which still lies over England's Eastern policy." Passionate words written five years after the fall of the Russian Empire.

What is the relevance of Pickthall's fiction to the twenty-first century? Just as he had no models, so he had no obvious successors? His migration to India cut him off from contacts and networks of literary Britain. But in his independence he was curiously very contemporary. He anticipated post-colonial literature and it has been argued that he was a pioneer feminist writer. As these stories show, many of his feminine characters, in social circumstances stacked against women, show an assertiveness and independence that defies expectations.

Pickthall is a wonderful story teller. He brings us straight into the narrative, with sharply drawn personalities, dealing with dilemmas to which we can relate. He builds a picture of the physical environment – buildings, flowers, the landscape – that is convincing.

He also presents us with the environment of ordinary people in the Eastern Mediterranean world, with realism and lack of sentimentality, His central characters may be rogues and cheats, religious fanatics, bandits or hypocrites, but they are all drawn as the result of acute observation. We see the world from the perspective of an Egyptian soldier, a Syrian peasant, an Ottoman official. There is historical value in his recording of small social changes in language, in dress and in habits in the generation before 1914, changes that may elude the conventional historian. His readers from outside that region are obliged to disengage from their own prejudices and values and to see the world "as others see us". This is an odd imaginative exercise for all of us, especially if it gives us an understanding of other people, other worlds.

The lands in which Pickthall's stories are set have, since his time, undergone changes that have been violent and unprecedented. Wars, revolutions displacement and emigration, voluntary and forced, have been the lot of Syrians,

Palestinians, Egyptians and Turks since Pickthall's time. These people are the grandchildren and great-grandchildren of the men and women among whom Pickthall travelled, whom he loved and whose lives he has reconstructed for our enlightenment and delight.

PETER CLARK

GREATER SYRIA

A BIT OF HISTORY

This story first appeared in Pickthall's first collection of short stories, Pot au Feu, published in February 1911. Like other of his stories of Greater Syria, it turns on the barely suppressed antagonism between the confessional communities. One small incident can cause riots in which people are killed. The story is told coolly, without sentimentality of censure.

The central character, Leylah, a Jewish courtesan, is a strong personality, economically independent and indeed having others dependent on her. She is amoral, having to survive in a cruel world. She has travelled around the Levant, having been born in Damascus and lived in Egypt.

This is the only story in which a Jew takes a leading role. She is clearly an Arab Jew rather than a recent Zionist immigrant. It is not a positive portrait of the Jews of Beirut, but nor do Christians or Muslims come out well.

Leylah the courtesan was of so fierce a temper that other women of her sort could not put up with her; so from the outset of her career she had lived alone, at first as the guarded pet of a rich notable of Damascus, then at Beyrout as a singer and dancer, and afterwards at Cairo and Alexandria in the same capacity. A Jewess of Damascus, which is enough to say that she had native wit and vigour; trained to charm men as carefully as hawks are trained; she found lovers everywhere, and little wonder, in lands where women usually are of almost bestial stupidity. She was travelled and fairly educated, could recite Arabic poetry, and sing to her lute distractingly in the husky heart-broken voice which drives every son of the East to the verge of madness. Yet, despite fatigues and vigils, she preserved her freshness, thanks to a cat-like indifference to the embraces she provoked; which indifference proceeded from a pure attachment.

From some obscure instinct of race she loved, and loved only, an invalid and ugly Jew, whom she supported. Him she saw seldom and by stealth, but all her toils inferred him; and the motive of unselfish kindness kept her young. In the towns of Egypt she had maintained this man in comfort near her, and, now once more in Beyrout, had hired for him three rooms in the heart of the town, while she herself inhabited but one room with a balcony on the first floor of a newish and red-roofed house in a back street running up towards the country.

On the night of my story she was sitting in her room at business, making talk and music for the entertainment of two visitors, a Muslim and a Christian; the one the son of a great notable of the town, the other a man of forty who had lately returned from America with five thousand pounds. It was a duel between these two which should outstay the other; but while the Christian showed politeness, even deference, in his rivalry with a professor of the dominant faith, the Muslim, with knit brows and grinding teeth, grew more and more insulting in his muttered reflections, making no attempt to hide his disgust of the other's presence.

Leylah felt furious, and could not keep from showing some displeasure in her manner towards him. She had no wish to be alone with either of them; but, having experienced both men, she preferred the Nazarene[1], who, besides being generous, was polite in his approaches; such politeness being grateful to a woman who detested the fatigues of passion. The Muslim was a cub of savage breed, against whom she would have shut her door had it not been for his father's high position in the city.

At length, after midnight, he pulled out a revolver and toyed with it lovingly. His opponent then withdrew, surprised, it seemed, to find the hour so late; a little comforted by Leylah's despairing shrug to him, and the glance of contempt she levelled at the boorish victor.

No sooner was he gone than the Muslim flung himself upon the courtesan, who, hating roughness, fought with him and pushed him off. The anger in her eyes was unmistakable. Taking offence at that, he hurled reproaches at her, cursing her religion and ancestry; till, finding these of no avail, he relapsed to pleading. When he seemed tame, she let him approach once more; but at her touch, her perfumed breath, he lost his head again and became violent. He swore to pay her out for tantalising him, her born superior, who with a word could have her whipped and cast out of the city.

---

[1] Christian; the word meaning, a man from Nazareth.

"Think not that I am blind," he told her, mouth to mouth. "I saw thee smiling at that base-born Nazarene – low, Jewish sow!" With a snarl he swore to kill her, slowly, and with all cruelty.

Enraged as Leylah was already, his insults and the pain his grasp inflicted made her mad. She bit his wrist and forced him to let go; then, whipping out a poniard from her breast, she stabbed him again and again, hissing:

"Take that! – and that! – and that! – O son of a dog!"

The youth on his knees beside her flung up both his arms; his eyes turned up their whites, while his body, in the act of falling backwards, seemed suddenly to change its mind, and collapsed sideways. She towered over it with set teeth and blazing eyes, intent to catch the slightest sign of life and strike it out. Satisfied at last that he was dead, she turned away with a smile, and went to fetch a live coal for her narghileh, which had gone out. Returning from the brazier, holding the bit of fire with pincers, she felt the after-chill of rage, and shivered slightly; then, sitting down beside the corpse of her admirer, regarding it thoughtfully, she carried the tube to her lips, and smoked to regain composure. The murmur of the water in the bowl as the smoke passed through it made a chuckle in the room, whose air was thick with perfumes burnt and sprinkled.

Once she leant forward and with one hand drew out the dead man's cloak so as to save the blood from running on to the floor.

"Thou art a dangerous inmate," she apostrophized the dead, in thought. "Thou art the darling of thy father, and he is great among the dogs, thy co-religionists. There will be vengeance for thee, that is certain; and I would not have it fall on my poor head. I must keep thee here much longer. I shall bear thee forth, God helping me, and leave thee at some neighbour's door. Thou art not very big, to be so fierce. I fancy I could carry thee without much trouble. God forgive me the defilement!"

Coiling the tube of the narghileh round the bowl of it, she set to work to try. But when she stooped and strained to lift the corpse, it fell back with a thud, proving too heavy. To obtain better purchase, she grasped the hip with both hands, and strove to turn the body over, heaving with all her might. A great weight struck her face and stretched her on the floor, half stunned. The dead hand!

The hand which lay so limp upon the ground had swung up like a weight of lead and hit her. She cowered down by the body, staring wildly. The dead hand!

Her Jewish blood ran cold with superstitious horror. The corpse, she thought, had risen up against her; perhaps had set its mark upon her face indelibly.

Rubbing her cheek, she fancied she could trace a clear impression of the thumb and fingers. What was to be done?

To learn the time, she pulled aside a curtain, opened the window, and looked out. She could hear a muezzin calling up the dawn, a slender trill of sound enhancing silence; then a cock crowed. In another hour mankind would stir, and she would be unable to purge her room without discovery.

Turning back from the window, she imagined – nay, could swear – the thing had moved. Paralyzed with fear. She stood and gazed at it. Moved, nay, it was still moving – floating towards her – or was her sight deranged? She could not bear its presence there a minute longer. Care for her own skin, cunning, native caution were overwhelmed by need to cleanse the place of it. Nerved by abject terror, she seized both the feet and dragged the body out on to the balcony. She heard a clip of slippers on the cobblestones, someone was moving in the street beneath; but determination to be rid of her ghastly inmate was stronger than the fear of detection. Calling on God for strength, she caught the corpse around the waist and, lifting, leaned it against the railing of the balcony; then picking up the feet, she tipped it over. It fell with little noise. She wished it might have fallen on the head of the owner of the talking slippers. Then, startled by a cry: "Ya Muslimin[2] – a Muslim – murdered – dead!" she stepped indoors with haste and shut the window.

The dead hand, when it struck her, must have numbed her brain, for ever since the blow she had been acting madly; nor could she now think connectedly and devise a plan of escape, though her mind was set to do so. She sat and rocked herself and laughed and wept by turns, while conscious of the danger closing in.

At length she realised the need to fly at once, unless she desired to be killed like a rat in that room. Having stowed her bag of money in her bosom, she threw a coarse cloak over her tinselled gauze, a shawl over her head, and stole out down the stairs. At the house door she paused and listened, hearing angry voices:

"From that balcony he was flung." "A harlot dwells there." "Let us hale her forth!"

Then, with as little noise as could be, she slipped out, and was gliding off by the wall. When the group of men around the body saw her, for it now grew light.

"Stop!" they cried, running after her; and she obeyed them, praying to her Maker for protection, shrinking close to the wall.

"Murderess!" "Daughter of a dog!" "Abandoned harlot!" "Stinking Jewess!" "Thou shalt die for this." "Kill her now at once, a dog's death, for she has slain a true believer!" Four or five pair of hands had hold of her, dragging this way and

---

[2] O Muslims!

that. The shawl was plucked from her head, the cloak from her shoulders; she shivered in her robe of tinselled gauze, which showed the limbs beneath it as in mist. A red flower in her hair seemed laughing at her tears, her death-like pallor.

"I slew him not!" she shrieked. "Another slew him, and I grew frightened at the corpse and cast it out. By Allah, I am most innocent!"

"Swear by thy father's bones!"

"I swear by them. Listen, O my masters, O generous men, and I will tell you the true story. Two men courted me, a Muslim and a Nazarene; they were rivals. Last night they quarrelled in my presence. Allah knows how I strove to separate them! But one struck me on the cheek here – you may see the mark – and when I recovered from the blow, the Muslim lay dead at my feet; his foe had fled."

"The name of his foe, the Nazarene? Quick, this minute, or we strike you dead!"

"Shukri Suleymân, surnamed El Amerikâni[3]."

"His dwelling?"

"At El Mazra'eh[4]."

A man who, disturbed by the din, had come to a lower window of the house, here cried assuringly:

"It is true, Shukri was here last night; he and the Muslim also, for I saw them on the stairs."

"Swear by thy wretched life that this is true."

"By God, I swear it!" answered Leylah, weeping bitterly.

"Had we not best detain her till the full inquiry?"

"No, let her go, poor thing. There will be no inquiry. This is not a question for the cadi[5]. This is all men's business – a religious matter. We have too long endured the insolence of these accursed Nazarenes."

Resuming her cloak and shawl in haste, with praise to God, Leylah glided off down the street and made haste to hide herself in the populous heart of the city.

Down in the maze of dim and dirty markets, overarched and narrow, the breath of daybreak roused the stench of festering offal. Threading tunnel after tunnel, she at last turned in at a squalid entry and knocked at a door which did not fit its doorway. Upon the lintel was a red device – the conventional presentment of a hand – with which the poorer sort of Hebrews protect their dwellings from the evil eye.

---

[3] The American.

[4] A Christian suburb to the east of Beirut.

[5] Loosely used, it can be a judge, or more simply a legal adviser official.

The door was opened by a lanky, shambling Jew just roused from sleep. Two locks of hair like ram's horns framed a face of that excessive, deathlike pallor, which, with the lack of courage, makes the Arabs name the Jews "sons of a dead woman." The face was sheeplike, with pale blinking eyes. A long and very dirty sort of dressing-gown clung like a shroud to the attenuated frame. Coughing painfully, with hand against his mouth, this youth inquired:

"What brings thee, O my dear?"

"A Great misfortune, Eleazar. I have killed a great one of the hogs, the Gentiles, and must hide here till the cry is past."

"Welcome, O thrice blessed; enter! Is it not thy house? I am proud to receive thee in it as a second Judith. Would to God that others of our race possessed thy bravery; then should we soon destroy the race of scorners who oppress and set at nought God's chosen people. Now I myself cannot endure the thought of killing. It makes me think of being killed, and turns my stomach. But thou art heroic; nothing earthly daunts thee. Now sit down on that cushion there and tell me how it happened."

His speech concluded in a fit of coughing.

"Thy cough is worse this morning," exclaimed Leylah, losing sight of her own worries. "How careless to expose thy throat like that. Wrap something round it! I will buy thee a warm shawl. In the meantime take this one."

Doffing her own head-shawl, she draped it warmly round his neck and shoulders before proceeding with her story. For her the murder was no more than a vexatious accident. She had stabbed the Muslim as naturally and inevitably as a cat will scratch in certain circumstances. She spoke of it with a shade of annoyance, but indifferently, growing animated only when she came to tell of her escape.

"He, he, he!" sniggered Eleazar, exhibiting great yellow teeth and whitish gums. "That was capital – to tell them that the other Gentile did it. Thy dagger slew but one hog, but the arrows of thy wit, please God, will slay a thousand. For the Muslims will go for vengeance to El Mazra'eh. There will be a fight, a massacre. I must repair at once to the house of the father of the dead – there is certain to be a concourse round the door – and try to learn for certain what is being planned."

"Wrap thy shawl much closer then; the air is chill! And forget not to loose it when the sun's rays get full strength."

"Fear not, O angel from heaven, I shall obey thee."

Eleazar clapped a shapeless hat upon his head, and went forth, chuckling and coughing.

In his absence, Leylah changed her evening robe of gauze for coarse clothes from a bundle which she always kept there; then she set to work to tidy the room, which lacked nothing in the way of modest comfort. Ever since she had found the youth Eleazar penniless and dying in a Jewish lodging-house at Jaffa, it had been her pleasure to maintain him in a life of ease. Sometimes he worked a little at his trade, which was the fabrication of false antiquities, coins, medals, gems, and so on; but his state of health forbade continued effort, and she was glad, liking to think of him as hers entirely.

Having removed the rose from her hair and the paint from her cheeks by the time he returned, she presented the appearance of a common woman of the country, black-browed, heavy-jowled, and not exceptionally good-looking.

"Well, what hast thou learnt, O Eleazar?" she inquired. "Have they killed the Nazarene Shukri yet, or is the matter to be tried before the court?"

"I found the yard of the house filled with a great crowd shouting for vengeance. I dared not go in, nor seem to linger at the gateway; but I passed and repassed in the street, employing my eyes and ears. A man in the turban and habit of a religious doctor presently came out of the reception-room into the courtyard, and addressed the throng. Then I heard a great shout: 'Dîn Muhammad[6]! To-morrow, at El Mazra'eh!' Beloved, there will be a mighty vengeance, a slaughter such as has not been seen for many years. Ere all is done thou wilt have slain as many of the infidels as the sword of David counted of the Philistines. For the people of El Mazra'eh are not unwarlike like the ruck of Christians. They are turbulent, and will fight fiercely even though taken by surprise. He, he, he!" Eleazar bared his teeth in glee! "I have a friend, a Hebrew, dwelling on the outskirts of El Mazra'eh, who is such a quiet and obliging man that the Christians of that quarter make a friend of him and tell him secrets. I will go to him this evening and learn all there is to know on their side."

"Aye, do so, O my soul, for it concerns us nearly. Please God they will kill the Nazarene Shukri at first sight, without question; for he alone can certify my guilt."

The rest of the day was spent in loving converse; Leylah waited on Eleazar hand and foot, he showing his unsightly teeth for pleasure till his face with its lovelocks resembled nothing so much as the skull of a horned sheep. Then, in the dusk, he sallied forth as he had promised, while she cleaned out the room and spread the beds of both of them. It seemed long before she heard his cough outside the door.

---

6 The religion of Muhammad.

“Ha, ha!” he chuckled as she opened to him. “Great news, O beloved! My friend says that the Nazarenes of El Mazra’eh have been warned of the attack to-morrow. A renegade, Abdullah by name, who was of their faith and is now a Muslim, felt compassion for his former comrades and sent word to them. To-morrow is the first day of the week. The assault is planned for the third hour[7], when most of the inhabitants are wont to be in the church at Mass. The door of the church is very low and narrow; it was built against disturbance from without; but its structure tells both ways, obliging those within to come forth one by one and in a stooping posture. Two or three of the Muslims could deal with the congregation, while the rest sacked and burned the quarter. It was well planned. But now the Christians know, they will not go to Mass to-morrow. From dawn their men will line the cactus hedge before the church, which bounds the quarter in the direction of the pine-woods.”

“And what of Shukri Suleymân, the alleged murderer?”

“Hallelujah, he has fled to the mountains.”

“I thank the Creator. That is all I wished to know. Now thou art tired. Thy cough is worse. Wrap thyself up warmly in these coverings, and lie close to me.”

Next morning, no sooner had Eleazar yawned and knuckled himself awake than he began to snigger: “He, he! It is the great day, O beloved. In mercy let us walk out towards El Mazra’eh and see the fun.”

“If it would give thee pleasure, I am willing. But there may be danger; and to walk much makes thee ill.”

“For the love of Moses and of Ezra, I entreat thee, let me go and look!” Eleazar coughed and chuckled, sneezed and choked in one.

“First let us break our fast then,” she replied, indulgently.

Having eaten a little, they set out together towards El Mazra’eh. Every man they saw had his face turned in that direction – this with terror, flying from it, chin on shoulder; that with fierce eagerness, advancing hotfoot towards it.

“The slaughter has begun!” exclaimed Eleazar, quickening step, though Leylah kept imploring him to save his strength. “What news, O sheykh?” he inquired of an aged Nazarene.

“They fight, my son. Our young men fight like heroes. They have driven back El Islâm on to the plain beside the pine-woods. And there they fight, two thousand men at least, and will fight on till not one man is left alive. O, woe is me, to live to see this day.”

---

7 That is three hours after sunrise, about 9 am.

Carriages kept passing, filled with wealthy Nazarenes, men, women, and children, all with frightened faces, driven furiously by coachmen maddened by the repeated promise of bakhshîsh in the direction of the Lebanon frontier.

Going a long way round to avoid collision with the fighters, Leylah and her beloved approached the scene of combat from the further side, by a sandy path through the pine-woods. At length they could plainly hear the din of battle and see the struggling forms beyond the tree trunks.

"It is enough," said Leylah, pulling her companion's arm. "I fear the excitement for thee, and there might be danger."

Eleazar pleading, "Just a little nearer!" they advanced to the end of the grove.

There, on an open plain between the pine-woods and some flat-roofed houses, outposts of El Mazra'eh, the battle raged. On the skirts of the fray, men fired off guns and pistols; but in the centre it was hack and thrust with daggers, biting, wrestling chest to chest, strangling with the bare hands, trampling with the feet – an undistinguishable mass of humanity, striving, crawling, which seemed as senseless to the two onlookers as a swarm of insects. There was no hope for anyone there in the thick of it, and yet fresh men kept rushing in on either side, as if in love with death.

"God has maddened them. Hallelujah!" cried Eleazar. "See how they haste to the slaughter, like bees when one beats upon a tin. Surely this is the battle long foretold, when the Gentiles shall annihilate one another, and so cleanse the world for the dominion of the chosen people, the coming of the Son of God! Praise be to God!"

He laughed aloud; but the excitement brought on so severe a fit of coughing that at the end of it he leaned against a tree trunk, appearing more dead than alive.

"O my dear!" cried Leylah in an agony. "This is what I feared for thee. Come away from the fighting and the folly, which will last till sunset. Take a sip from this flask; it holds good wine of Rischon[8]. Now walk slowly; lean on me. I knew it, thou art much too weak for sight-seeing."

---

8 Rischon was an early Zionist settlement near Jaffa, now a large city of Israel, still well-known for the production of wine.

A CHAMPION OF CHRISTENDOM

This story first appeared in the collection of stories, Pot au Feu, published in February 1911.

In the early 1860s, Lebanon was divided administratively. Under pressure from European powers, the predominantly Muslim coastal cities – Beirut, Sidon and Tripoli – remained under Ottoman control, while the rural mountainous areas to the east, mostly, but not exclusively, Christian, were semi-autonomous and under a Christian governor. The story is best understood in the context of this division of authority, political and jurisdictional.

It shows the intense strength of religious identity. Pickthall empathised with the Muslim and Ottoman authorities and Muslims in the story appear as victims of Christian fanaticism. The only other Muslim is a saintly figure. The central Christian, Yuhanna, is a murderous fanatic.

Pickthall has another strong-willed female character, Amîneh, who does not accept or approve of her fiancé's boasts.

He also defines people by their dress and even hair styles. Yuhanna is "fashionably dressed in European clothes beneath the red tarbush". Amîneh wears "a flowered gown and a broad-brimmed Frankish hat" and her "hair carried up to the top of the head in the mode of Europe, allowing a glimpse of the nape of the neck, which to every son of the East is ravishingly indecent". This defines them as non-Muslims, as Christians looking for inspiration to Europe. But nonetheless Yuhanna has to help his father in arduous toil for weeks.

There had been a murder in a back street of Beyrout, an event of such common occurrence that those who gathered in the morning before the house of the victim discussed it in the tone of common news. The crowd were Christians, and they named a Muslim, one Muhammad, as the murderer.

A young man, fashionably clad in European clothes beneath the red tarbush, happened to pass that way, inquired of the matter. A noise of women screaming in the house announced the reign of death, but such a throng about the door appeared unusual. He put his question to a burly fellow in a long striped robe, who wore a dirty rag bound round his fez by way of a turban. Having ascertained by a glance that the inquirer was a co-religionist, this person spat on the causeway, then raised both hands up towards the shining sky, before replying:

"It is a poor good man, our neighbour, killed last night. He was shot in the street as he came home late – a little drunk, it may be; none can say with certainty. Turning a corner in a narrow place, he chanced to run against a certain Muslim. The Muslim cried out 'Pig!' and, whipping out a revolver, fired three shots into his body. Three persons saw it done."

The listener was by nature excitable; and he had been brought up at the college of the Jesuits[9] to love our holy religion single-mindedly, execrating all others as vile abominations of the prince of darkness. With tearful eyes and a trembling voice, he exclaimed:

"O Lord, can such things be? Can the heathen kill baptized people as if they were dogs, yet go unpunished? Surely punishment must follow on the slayer. If he has fled, he will be caught directly, seeing there is nowhere to flee to save our Lebanon, where the majority are Christian, praise to Allah! There is a law, a court of some kind, in the wilâyet[10]; and he will be punished, since thou sayest there are witnesses."

The man in the striped robe laughed.

"It is well seen thou art of the mountain[11]," he rejoined sneeringly. "Here, in the wilâyet, there is no justice for the likes of us. The murderer has not fled; why should he? He has nought to fear. He opened his shop this morning, doubtless, and sits there as usual. Moreover, for our three truthful witnesses he would produce a hundred liars, who would swear that the poor, dead, righteous man attacked him first with violence. Would to Allah that we dwelt within the bounds of Lebanon! Only there is no money to be earned yonder. When the

---

9 St Joseph University was founded by Jesuits in 1875.

10 Province.

11 Between 1860 and 1914 administrative arrangements differed in the coastal towns from those in the mountainous areas to the east of Beirut (Beirout). Beirut and the coastal cities were predominantly Muslim. The rural areas were predominantly Christian and had a Christian governor.

High Government, pushed by the Franks, gave the Mountain its liberties, it took care to destroy every hope of prosperity for the inhabitants by walling their freedom in with a prohibitive tariff. Poor men must eat, so we come into the city here, and get maltreated."

"O Virgin Immaculate! O Allah!" cried the youth in a frenzy. "Why – why not rise and slay them, every one, or die in the attempt? Is there not among you one great soul, one hero to take vengeance for Christ's people? Behold, I am a youth, not bred to fighting; yet I swear by the sword of St George, by Allah and all of you here present, that I will kill two for every one they kill of us from this day forth, by Allah's help. In the name of the Father, and of the Son, and of the Holy Ghost. Amin[12]." The young man crossed himself devoutly.

The men who heard him, however, only chuckled at this outburst.

One said: "Go away, young hothead. Mix not in quarrels which do not concern thee. Vengeance is taken always, never fear; but subtly, in the way of wise men, not asses. Go back to the mountain, and leave us to manage things."

Their unbelief so mortified the would-be hero that he left them straightway, weeping bitter tears, and asking Allah to destroy their dwelling-place. Alas! How perfect was the degradation of the people of the cross! His vow might be, in fact, impracticable; but, as an example of religious fervour, it should have won their admiration; instead of which they smiled and gave advice as to an infant. And was it so impracticable? Might it not, conceivably, be performed without much danger? If only one among the host of trampled Christians could do some gallant deed to rouse the others, the triumph of the Faith would surely follow. Still vibrant from the strains of his heroic utterance, with brain inspired thereby, he imagined the task easy.

He saw in mind a place which he had passed that morning, a lane between high walls without a window; against one wall a stall containing vegetables, and, on a bench behind it, two old Muslims. Not another soul in sight! What was there to prevent his taking those two lives, in God's name, for the fulfilment of his vow? He stopped in imagination and said good-day with the air of a would-be purchase; he asked the price of a melon or a cucumber, and when their attention was for a moment diverted from his movements, flashed out his small revolver and shot the nearer in the ear. Then, before the other could recover from surprise, he had entered a second chamber into his gaping mouth; and was running fast away, as if in terror, crying to the people whom he met that there had been a murder.

[12] The Arabic form of Amen.

A shout of "Oäh! Oäh! Look where thou art going, madman!" and a bump from a donkey's load, recalled him for a moment to the passing scene; but failed to spoil his elation. He beheld himself the avenger of the murdered Christian, a religious hero of the breed of saints and prophets; he had done a deed that would dismay the caitiff Muslims, had inaugurated a crusade whose end seemed nothing other than the reign of Christ on earth. Then arose a crying need: he must confide in someone, or his head would burst. But where could he find a man to keep his secret? A priest, under seal of confession, might be trusted; but his own priest was in a village of the mountains four hours distant; and, being a mild man, might impose a heavy penance. Then, as he threaded in a dream the crowded streets, the remembrance of a kinsman of his own occurred to him – a black-bearded, black-browed priest with small fierce eyes and a noiseless laugh, who served the Maronite cathedral of the city in some slight capacity. The man had spent one summer in the mountain, at his father's house.

At once he bent his steps towards the cathedral, and, making inquiry for his relative in the adjoining shops, soon found his lodging. The priest was at home, and welcomed his distant kinsman when he recognised him, which was not at the first glance.

"O our father!" the young man cried out, "I am in trouble, and to whom in Beyrout can I turn for help except to thee?"

"Hast thou killed? Are the avengers of blood on thy tracks?" asked the priest with a certain gusto, stroking his paunch. "Fear nothing. I will hide thee safely."

"No, abûna[13], I am not pursued; I come here of my own will, unmolested. But I have killed, and I desire to know the measure of the guilt attaching to me. Not an hour since, walking in a certain street, I saw a crowd and asked the reason of it. A man informed me how a good Christian, of our own communion, was killed last night by a Muslim wantonly. The same man told me there is no redress; the Muslims slay the followers of Christ like dogs daily. At that my heart became a roaring fire, the world was blackened in my eyes, and I felt madness. Passing thence, in that state, I saw two Muslims sitting in a lonely place, and, producing my revolver – here it is!" (he showed the little deadly weapon in his pocket) – "I shot those two before I was aware; and went my way, well pleased. But then I thought I might have sinned, so ran to thee, a priest, to hear thy judgment."

The priest embraced him fondly. "Thy sin, O my son, is light. Pay me four mejîdis[14] to be spent in intercessions, and behold thee spotless!" Having pouched

[13] Our father, the normal way of addressing a priest.

[14] Ottoman currency.

the silver coins, he continued: "I see no sin in thy behaviour more than in that of Mûsa[15] the prophet, when he slew the Egyptian who oppressed God's people. Nevertheless, since there is foulness in the act of killing, perhaps I had better shrive thee to make sure."

Having given the absolution, he again embraced the young man, saying: "In sh'Allah[16], thou wilt prove as Mûsa proved, a prince and deliverer of God's chosen! A scourge and consuming fire to El Islâm. Would to Allah every Christian had the readiness to strike without fear, for the Faith! Farewell, O Yuhanna! Remember me to the old man, thy father."

The young man answered nothing, hardly hearing for the throbbing in his ears. His heart was full, he trode on air, and seemed surrounded by a heavenly radiance. He had been compared to Moses, called the predestined conqueror of El Islâm, and full of ardour, must begin God's work at once. He[17] went straight to the lonely place that had been shown to him in his vision, found the two old Muslims sitting at their stall of vegetables, and drawing his revolver, shot them both, unwitnessed. Then, running for his life, he told all those whom he encountered of the horrid murder, so that they ran also, but away from him.

He went on running till the town was left behind, and he found himself in a region of scattered huts and one-roomed houses among gardens and mulberry orchards, with tall reeds feathering the boundary ditches, and here and there a palm-tree or an umbrella pine standing out sentry-wise in the great sunlight, its shade drawn close around it, like a mantle. Here he left the road and went leisurely, crossing some ploughed land beneath pollard mulberry-trees till he found another track leading back to the town. Courage returned with his breath; he experienced the tremendous exultation of one really chosen of God, for, regarding his escape this minute as miraculous, he concluded that he bore a charmed life.

In a narrow, sandy way between high cactus hedges, he saw a man with a small child hanging on his neck, riding towards him astride of a shambling jackass. Yuhanna glanced behind him and saw no man. He listened sharply with either ear, but caught no sound indicative of human neighbourhood. Grasping the revolver in his pocket, "A happy day!" he called to the donkey-rider. "Art thou a Muslim, O my uncle?"

"Praise be to Allah. There is no God but God."

---

15 Moses.

16 If God wills, a prescription for Muslims when they say anything about the future, in accordance with Surat al-Kahf, 23-24, adopted also by Christians.

17 This and the next sentence are unusually odd for Pickthall.

"And is this thy son? Ma sh'Allah[18]! A fine boy."

"Praise be to Allah, yes, he is my son."

It was the Muslim's last word. As he gazed fondly down upon his son, Yuhanna fired in his face; his hands went up, his eyes turned over in his head, the donkey sprang aside, and the corpse fell off, the child still clinging to it, shrieking horridly. Yuhanna shot the child, placing the muzzle of his revolver close to the back of its head, and ran on till he spied a gap in the cactus hedge, when he took to the fields.

It seemed so easy: why had no worshipper of Christ ever thought of it before? It might be because he alone could do it easily, being the chosen. Already the murder of that Christian had been thrice avenged. But Yuhanna, exalted, looked beyond mere vengeance, contemplating nothing less than the gradual extermination of El Islâm. At any rate, he would put such fear in them that every Muslim would go in dread of every Christian, lest he might prove to be the unseen killer, the redoubted scourge of God. He saw himself shooting a notable through the open window of his house – a muezzin from the roof of an adjacent building. Then, when their terror had become disabling panic, Yuhanna would stand forth as the Deliverer, and, cross in hand, would gather all Christ's people to the final carnage.

Thus prophesying in his mind, he sauntered back towards the city by a frequented road. Nine out of ten of the people he encountered were Christians or Druzes, natives of the mountain villages, and the tenth, the Muslim, he was forced to spare through lack of privacy. In the city he found an eating-house, and ate, and drank, and smoked before proceeding. It was late in the afternoon when he resumed his prowl; but he was now in no hurry, feeling that the fullness of his morning's work entitled him to take his ease in wait for a safe shot. At length he happened on a blind beggar sitting in the doorway of an empty house. At the noise of steps approaching, this creature sent up piteous cries to God. The pious terms employed announced a follower of Muhammad.

"Look up, O poor man!" said Yuhanna kindly; and, as the wretch obeyed, he fired point-blank into one of the sightless eyes. The human form collapsed and lost significance. Yuhanna walked away, without fear this time, feeling safe in Allah's favour. Content with his day's work, he repaired to his khan[19] to supper and to sleep.

In the morning he remembered his deeds of yesterday almost without belief, they seemed so strange to him. He felt a little diffidence at going out, expecting

18 As God wills, said to appreciate something of value.

19 Hotel, lodging place, caravanserai.

to find the town in tumult, clamouring for the punishment of the author of so many murders. Foremost in his mind now was the original object of his tarrying in Beyrout, which was far from bloodthirsty. His cousin and betrothed, Amîneh, was to leave the convent-school this day for good; for weeks he had looked forward to the four hours' journey with her in the public carriage.

That carriage was full to start with, so that, when it pulled up by appointment at the French convent, Yuhanna, who was in his cousin's place, got out, prepared to hang on somehow by the box. But Amîneh forced him to resume his seat, protesting that she was slender and could squeeze in nicely. The drive, thus pressed together, was a long embrace. But Yuhanna could not thoroughly enjoy it till they had passed the frontier of the Lebanon, being haunted by vague terrors of a hue and cry. Then, as the crazy overladen vehicle jolted on over a road in need of mending, the driver plying his whip, the sorry horses galloping convulsively, ringing bells whose merriment derided their sad plight, the passengers gossiping and jesting. Yuhanna forgot his late adventures, his high destiny in the rapture of close contact with his beloved. Amîneh wore a flowered gown of chaste simplicity, and a broad-brimmed Frankish hat, beneath whose shade her eyes seemed wells of joy, profound yet sparkling. She wore her hair carried up to the top of her head in the mode of Europe, allowing a glimpse of the nape of her neck, which to every son of the East is ravishingly indecent. He could have loaded her with ornaments of gold, have filled her lap with precious gems, had he possessed them. Then he remembered he had something to bestow, something that would make his love more valuable; for was he not the deliverer of the land, the destined hero of all Christendom?

Having assured himself that their fellow-travellers spoke no French, he told the story of his mission in that language, leaning close to her ear, as the carriage crawled and jolted slowly up the first slopes of the mountain. To his dismay, she cried:

"I call it horrible! Thinkest thou that I wish to wed a fighting-man, a kind of brigand? On the contrary, I would have thee shine in commerce, and grow rich. Then we can live in the city there, a life worth living; can mix with cultured people who give soirées and observe the mode of Paris."

"But listen, darling!" he entreated. "Once my mission is accomplished I shall govern the whole country from Tarabulus[20] to Saida[21]; and thou, my bride, wilt be a queen."

---

[20] Tripoli, north Lebanon.

[21] Sidon, south Lebanon.

"Say 'in sh'Allah!'" she commanded, laughing. "Thou art boastful in thy mood to-day! What ails thee, dear? Am I a child that thou shouldst tell me fairy stories?"

Though he swore by things most sacred, she refused to hear him; and, curious to relate, her scepticism revived the frenzy of his heaven-sent vision, which, while he deemed her credulous, had almost left him. Since words could not instruct her, she must learn from deeds, from his warlike reputation from the mouths of all men. He swore to return at once to Beyrout and pursue his task there till its grandeur was apparent.

But, reaching home, he found his father had much work for him to do – field-work which could not wait – and it was weeks ere he could find the pretext for another outing. All through those weeks of expectation his zeal was kept inflamed by the continual scoffing of the girl Amîneh. At church on feast-days he was conscious of peculiar sanctity, and whenever the name of David, or of Samson, or of Moses, or of Gideon was pronounced by the priest, he kissed the pavement in an ecstasy of self-devotion. He held himself at the devotion of the Most High, awaiting only his call and opportunity; but sometimes he prayed for that chance, and sometimes feared it. When it came at length, he felt elated. Saying farewell to Amîneh on the eve of departure, he begged her not to tell his father what she knew concerning him.

"Fear not; I shall not tell a soul, O foolish boaster! I would not have the whole world laughing at thee. Now confess, before we part, that thou art lying."

"No; by Allah Most High, it is true, every word!"

"Then it is finished. I will not speak to thee again till thou canst talk of something else but silly fables. Thou art mad, I tell thee! If thou hast killed innocent people, as thou sayest, thou art a malefactor! But it is not so, for thy character is mild and good. Thou art a fool merely, and a most dreadful liar."

"By to-morrow night I shall have slain a score of Muslims, in the power of Allah."

"Go, go! And be ashamed," she cried disdainfully.

The public carriage started before the dawn. At sunrise Yuhanna could look down upon the beautiful, accursed city, by the red seashore, its suburbs reaching out across the plain to the foot of mighty mountains starred with villages. Two hours later he alighted in the square. He broke his fast, then went in search of business. All day he wandered through the less frequented streets and beheld many solitary Muslims, yet performed no deed of valour. Somehow his power seemed gone. His hand, his arm, refused to make the needed gestures. He meant beforehand, even prayed, to kill; but when the game appeared, it was is if some devil touched his arm, and froze it. Where were the twenty he vowed to kill ere night? Already the sun was sinking towards the west. There remained but two hours at the most; he must do something. Clenching his teeth, he swore by the Blessed Sacrament to slay the next follower of Muhammad – were it man, woman, or child – whom he met alone in the way. No sooner had he made the oath than the streets seemed fuller; people appeared in groups of two and three, which, as if of purpose, moved in sight of one another. At last he reached an alley quite deserted, and stood there in the hope of someone coming. But the hope failed him; he was moving on, despondent, when a Muslim came out of a garden gate in front of him – a tall man in the prime of life, the texture of whose cloak and turban spoke high rank.

Yuhanna clutched his revolver, giving praise to Allah, but as the man approached his arm grew nerveless. He let him pass; then, fearing for his own salvation, turned short round and fired. The man had also turned. His gaze disconcerted Yuhanna – spoilt his aim. He fired a second time, more wildly, seeing death before him, and then took to his heels, but too late; the Muslim had already made the spring to catch him. He was caught and held. He turned to face his assailant, revolver in hand, but the Muslim knocked his arm up, and he fired in the air. At that moment men came running from the garden whence the Muslim had emerged – one, a negro, flourishing a great staff.

"They have fired on our lord the Bey. A hog – a Christian – fired a pistol. Praise be to Allah, our good lord is safe. He holds the miscreant. What wickedness to assail so kind a man! No death is bad enough for such a devil. I will bash his head in with my staff this minute."

The black came running to perform his threat, but his master stopped him by a gesture. He had just succeeded in wresting the revolver from Yuhanna, who cowered, half-dead with fright.

"It is a poor madman, O Hoseyn," explained the victor, coolly. "See, now his fit is over, he is weak and harmless. Help me to drag him there inside our garden. If people came it might go badly with him, for he is a Christian, and the vulgar are fanatical; they may not regard his very evident madness. Now that I have his weapon, there is nothing to fear."

Yuhanna was pulled into the garden, and the gate made fast behind him.

"Shall I fetch soldiers?" asked the negro, eagerly. "He must be put in prison to await the judgment."

"Talk not to me of judgment!" sneered his lord. "He is mad, I tell thee. Did I send him up for trial, being who I am, they would condemn him at a glance, to fawn on me; they would think my intercessions mere hypocrisy – the vice I chiefly loathe. No, let him go. No human court has power to judge his motives. And besides, where I alone am aggrieved, I recognise no judge save the Most High."

"The praise to Allah, for thy mercy!" cried the gardeners. "Wallah[22], thou art an example to the age."

But the black still pleaded: "O my dear lord, let me beat his back a little. They say it is the medicine for some kinds of madness."

"No; let the poor man be!"

"He may kill others."

"Not immediately. His future is the care of One Above. I have his pistol, which was all his strength. Look at him only! He is helpless as a babe."

"Well, ask his name, in mercy, that we may know him and inquire if he is really mad. He is well dressed, like a student of the college."

"If he is mad, he will not know his name; if sane, he will answer falsely. Let him go! Is the street clear, O Hoseyn?"

"Yes, O my lord!"

"Then I will walk with him a little for protection. His shots must have disturbed the neighbours, and there may be roughs abroad."

The Bey took Yuhanna's arm and led him by the least frequented ways till they reached a quarter far from the scene of disturbance, when he said:

"May Allah heal thee! Go in peace!"

Yuhanna made a few steps, reeling like a drunken man, then fell at the foot of a wall, annihilated. The shade was black around him, for the sun was setting.

He was not the chosen of Allah, the appointed deliverer of Christ's people. He owed his life to the generosity of a Muslim – such generosity as surely never had been shown by man since Jesus, on the cross, forgave his murderers. He wished now that he had confessed the whole of his guilt to his preserver, believing the confession, though it had entailed a cruel death, would have made his plight less bitter than it was at present. For now those people he had killed might rise from the dead and claim his punishment. Such miracles had been known in the land. He longed to resort to a priest, but feared to be misunderstood. The sly-eyed Maronite, who had incited him to murder, would deride his present feelings; and the French priests, his instructors at the college, would be stern with him. His tale would seem too horrible to foreign ears. As the Muslim had said, he was indeed a madman, whose case could be judged only by the Most High.

Rising at length, he tramped through all that night, and at dawn of the next day saw his native village. As he climbed the path up the terraces, the branching

[22] By God!

trunks of the olive trees alone seemed black and solid, a part of earth; their foliage had the hue and texture of thin moonlit cloud. Women were descending to the spring, to fill their pitchers. Among them came Amîneh. She turned her face away from him, still quarrelling.

"I confess," he whispered. "They were lies I told thee. Never, I swear by Allah, never will I tell such lies again."

A QUESTION OF PRECEDENCE

This is one of Pickthall's earliest stories. It first appeared in Temple Bar in January 1899 and was later included in Pot au Feu, published in February 1911.

The story is about the consolations of Islam for a vulnerable poor man. As a poor man but the servant of God, he is superior to the servant of the Pasha, who is below God. Frequently Pickthall talks of the humble people, in contrast to the struggles and vanities of the great people.

Pickthall was twenty-three when it was published. He shows his sharpness in observation but there is little in the way of story line or character development.

As in his 1903 classic, Saïd the Fisherman, a romantic description of the city is offset by prowling and menacing dogs.

There is no hint of the location of the story. Both Beirut and Damascus, seats of Pashas, depended on stone for construction.

In the shadow of an archway sat, or rather squatted, Abdullah the merchant. He was not really a merchant, but he loved so to style himself, and those who wished to please him addressed him by that title.

In reality he was but a seller of sweetmeats and iced drinks, one upon whom the real merchants – those who had stalls of their own in the big bazaars, those who dealt in rich stuffs, perfumes, or jewellery – looked down as upon the dirt of the roadway. But Abdullah was proud.

As he squatted in his archway, his long white beard hanging almost into the lap of his many-coloured robe, and his white embroidered turban – concealing the time-honoured dirt of his tarbush, he seemed the very soul of dignity. Before him was a stall, a rude structure – neither more nor less than an inverted packing-case – bearing three full-bellied glass bottles, each with its ball of snow instead of a stopper, and a tray of basket-work piled up with a pyramid of oleaginous sweetmeats.

He would have seemed lost in meditation, save that from time to time he gave vent to a dreary, monotonous chant in praise of his wares; at the sound of which chant sundry yellow, wolf-like dogs lying curled up in the sunlight beyond the archway would raise their heads to blink and yawn, and the pigeons would rise with a flutter of wings from their researches in the roadway, uttering a soft coo of protest.

From Abdullah's corner the minaret of a small mosque, round which the pigeons loved to wheel and coo, was to be seen tapering white against the blue sky. Thence at the appointed hours came the cry of the muezzin calling the faithful to prayer.

But it must not be supposed that dogs and pigeons were the sole companions of Abdullah the merchant. There was a constant going to and fro of people under the archway – veiled women and turbaned men, passing on different errands to fulfil their destinies – many of whom would stay to drink a cup of iced syrup at Abdullah's little stall. At the mosque door stood a blind beggar, whose eternal whine – half plaintive, half peevish – had become part of the atmosphere of the place. Mules, packhorses, and even camels were occasionally led through the archway. These sometimes troubled Abdullah.

Once a camel came by, laden with stone, so that the stone scraped the wall on either hand. Then the aged merchant was driven to beat a hasty retreat to save himself and his stall from destruction. Ever since then he had hated camels, and never failed to curse them when they passed.

Business had been slack on the day in question, and Abdullah was dozing peacefully behind his wares, when a guttural shout aroused him. From the direction of the mosque a camel was drawing near, laden with stone. He screamed to the driver to wait, but the man paid no heed. Abdullah cursed him from his heart, and hastened to move his goods to the other side of the archway. Then, to his horror, he beheld another camel, also laden with stone, approaching from the opposite direction.

"Each striving to pass the other, they care not what becomes of Abdullah!" he moralised. "Sons of swine that they are! But I will teach them the respect due to a merchant!"

"Sons of a pig!" he cried aloud. "Stay your steps lest evil befall you! Abdullah the merchant is rich, and he has many friends. It is a sin to offend such as he."

But the men paid no heed. Already the first camel was entering the archway with its long swinging steps, and the other was close at hand. Abdullah sighed.

He had hoped to impose upon the drivers. Alas! They must be men of the city who knew him well. He lay down flat on his face against the wall and awaited, with bated breath, the upsetting of his stall.

But no! The camels stopped nose to nose. Their burdens scraped the wall on either hand. The archway was blocked for both, and Abdullah's stall was between them.

"Go back, fool!" shouted the first camel-driver, he who had approached from the direction of the mosque. "My master, the great merchant, Kheyr-ud-dîn, is waiting. He will slay thee for hindering me, he that is the bosom friend of the Pasha."

"Go back thou!" retorted the other. "My master the great judge builds a house. He has need of this stone. He is as the Pasha's own brother. He will destroy thee and all thy unclean race for daring to delay me."

One of the camels, bending its head to take a sweetmeat from Abdullah's stall, overturned two large bottles, so that a stream of snow-cooled fluid poured down the merchant's neck as he lay upon the ground.

Abdullah sprang to his feet. "Sons and grandsons of a dog!" he cried. "Know that I whom you have insulted, whose stall you have all but overturned, whose wares your beasts have defiled, am Abdullah the merchant, beloved of both your masters! Know that the Pasha is but as wax in my hands. Withdraw forthwith, or I will have you slain for your insolence and presumption. Lo! The archway is blocked. Many people are waiting to pass! And you pigs dare to keep them waiting!"

"It is that rascal's fault, old man!" said the first camel-driver, pointing to his opponent. "Make him first withdraw and I will withdraw also. His master is but as a slave to mine. It is for him to withdraw before me."

"Yon fellow is a liar and the son of a liar, old man!" cried the other furiously. "His master is not worthy to wash the feet of mine. And yet he dares to hold the passage against me. By Allah, I shall tell my master of his insolence, and he will tell the Pasha, and the man will be slain and his house destroyed by fire!"

"Make way, O people, make way!" came a loud voice from the direction of the mosque. "Make way for the harîm of his Excellency the Pasha, who return from the bath. Make way, I say."

"You hear that voice?" cried Abdullah wildly. "Make way for the harîm of his Excellency the Pasha, who return from the bath. How dare you – malefactors, thieves, scoundrels! – how dare you bar the passage with your wretched quarrel!"

("Make way, make way, curse your fathers!")

"Do thou withdraw," said the first camel-driver to his rival. "It is thy place, for thy master is as dirt compared to mine."

("Make way, I command you, in the name of the sultan's Majesty!")

"Liar! Child of all obscenity! Do thou withdraw, and that quickly! Dost thou not hear them crying to make way? We are both dead men, an thou make not haste to withdraw."

"We shall both be ruined by thine obstinacy, foul father of disgusting sins! How darest thou linger thus? A curse on the religion of thy camel! Draw him back at once, madman, and let me pass on my way."

"Draw back your camels at once!" cried a soldier who had crept up under the load of one of the beasts. "Are we, the servants of the Governor, to stand aside for curs like you? Make way, I say!"

"It is for him to withdraw," cried both the camel-drivers.

"Here, Ali! Do you seize these curs while Ahmed and I back the camels," cried the soldier.

The camel-drivers being taken in charge, the archway was speedily cleared. But in the confusion Abdullah's stall was overturned, the bottles broken in a thousand pieces on the cobblestones, and the sweetmeats scattered far and wide, a prey to the urchins of the quarter.

"Mercy, O my master, I am a poor man, and I am ruined!" cried the merchant, wringing his hands. "I have sat under this archway every day for thirty years, and never have I been treated thus before. Let the rogues of camel-drivers be well punished, O my masters, for indeed they are the worst of criminals."

"What hast thou to do with it, old man?" said the foremost soldier. "Stand aside for the Pasha's harîm, and dare not to howl in this unseemly manner in a public place."

"What hast thou to do with all this tumult?" he continued, when the veiled women had swept past them with their escort.

The camels stood a few yards away in the sunlight, under the charge of a negro. The dogs that had slunk away snarling at the unwonted disturbance were resettling themselves in their former lairs; the doves, which during the tumult had been wheeling excitedly round the minaret, began to resume their old researches in the roadway, and cooed reassuringly to one another.

"Nothing, efendim[23], nothing; by Allah, I had nothing to do with it," cried Abdullah the merchant.

"He lies!" said one of the camel-drivers sullenly. "He was, in truth, the cause of all the trouble. He told us that the Pasha was as wax in his hands, and promised

---

[23] A Turkish term of respect.

to have us punished for our insolence. So when we heard you crying to make way for his Excellency's harîm, we thought fit to stay and finish our quarrel, since we were to be punished anyhow."

"Good!" said the soldier grimly. "Then he also shall taste the bastinado. What is thy name, old man?"

"Men call me Abdullah the merchant."

"Merchant, sayest thou? Then it is not seemly that a man of thy position should go to prison with these dogs. Give me but two mejîdis[24] and go free."

Now Abdullah the merchant had but four mejîdis in the world, and it seemed hard to have to part with half his fortune through the fault of others. Nevertheless, he produced the required sum from some hiding-place under his robe.

"Go thy way in peace, old man," said the soldier. And Abdullah went his way in an agony of rage and grief, to gather together the wreckage of his stall and count his losses.

The camel-drivers looked at each other, and as if by agreement felt under their robes. The one produced a single mejîdi, and the other a handful of small coins.

"Let me also go free, I pray thee," said the one to the soldier who held him.

"It is all I have in the word, efendim," said the other to the guard.

The soldiers took the money greedily and stowed it away among their clothes.

"Sons of crime!" they exclaimed. "What is this? Do you presume to bribe the servants of the Pasha? Your wealth is insufficient to excuse such impudence. Forward! The judge awaits you."

The doves were cooing softly, wheeling round and round the minaret, which tapered, warm with sunset, on a sky of amethyst. The dogs, missing the sunlight, prowled hither and thither wakefully in search of offal. Merchants passed under the archway, hastening homeward after the toil of the day. But Abdullah squatted still upon his bit of carpet, stroking his beard and looking sadly at the ruins of his stall.

It became quite dark under the archway, though a glow still lingered in the western sky behind the minaret. Then arose a wild chant without time or tune. It was the call to prayer.

Abdullah turned towards Mecca, knelt and performed his devotions. Then he gathered up such of the remains of his stock as might yet be of some use, and turned his steps homeward. He considered:

---

[24] Ottoman coin.

"I am greater than the camel-drivers, but the smallest servant of the Pasha is greater than I. The Pasha is greater than his servant; but Allah is above us all. If the Pasha's servant is greater than I, Allah's servant must be greater than the Pasha, for who can count the greatness of Allah. I am Allah's servant, therefore I am greater than the Pasha. O Allah, get me back my two mejîdis."

THE TALE OF A CAMP

This story first appeared in Cornhill Magazine, in February 1911 and was included in his first collection of short stories, Pot au Feu, published in February 1911.

Pickthall's first experience of Palestine was through missionaries, when, not yet twenty he was the guest of the chaplain of Bishop G F P Blythe. He spent two years travelling around Palestine and Syria, sometimes with an off-duty dragoman, Suleyman, a great raconteur, from whom he may have heard this story.

The journey from Uganda to Britain before (and for long after) the First World War was by ship via the Suez Canal. Travellers often took time off for a visit to the Holy Land.

Pickthall, in his youthful wanderings in Palestine and Syria in the mid-1890s, encountered a similar missionary tourist to the one in this story, telling the tale in Oriental Encounters, chapter 10, 'The Parting of the Ways'.

The story shows the British exclusively from the point of view of the Syrian/ Palestinians.

"What is thy opinion of them?"

"The chief one, the big hypocrite, is very filthy."

Ibrahîm the cook questioned Shibli the dragoman in the kitchen-tent where they squatted while the dinner was a-cooking. Outside, a level space with rocks and tufts of grass extended to a ruined arch, within which gushed a spring; beyond that was a graveyard, then a flat-roofed village, and then a barren hill quite black against the twilight sky. Smooth stones in the foreground still gleamed wanly; the air immediately around their fire seemed tinted violet; the flames leapt up, deep orange, like a flower. The camp had come out three days from Jerusalem; yet the dragoman and the other attendants were still uncertain what kind of people were the tourists whom they served.

"Filthy – a true word!" said Amîn, the waiter.

"I knew what to expect," the dragoman pursued with scorn. "Jûnas always gives me filthy ones for the last of the season, that they report ill of me, and so he may avoid paying me the ten pounds extra promised if I do well. I have had enough of him. I shall apply for work with Kûk[25]. To-day the big hypocrite made me leave the straight road twice vexatiously, in order to visit places of no interest, with the result that we came late to the camping-place, and the horses are half-dead."

"And when you did arrive," put in the cook, "he made us move the tents just twenty yards for caprice merely. May there spring up a gale in the night and lay them flat, since he spurned the place of shelter which we had selected!"

The muleteers came in from baiting and watering their beasts. Having deposited their sacks of chaff and barley, they squatted down and joined the conversation. "He is one of those whom you can never please," observed their sheykh. "In his madness, this morning when we started out, he made me loosen the girth of a packsaddle, with the result that, after a bit, the load slipped round and nearly killed the mule. May Allah grant him endless pain hereafter!"

"What is his profession?" asked Amîn the waiter.

"Hast thou no eyes nor ears? He is a priest, though in disguise," said the dragoman.

"Aye. I guessed that. But there are different sorts of priests among the English. Some are rich and generous, others filthy."

"Well, he is of the filthiest – a missionary from Uganda. I overheard the ladies saying so."

"Ugh!" came in disgust from all the circle.

"Then there will be no bakhshîsh," observed the cook with a wry face. He clicked his thumbnail on his two front teeth, and therewith spat disconsolately.

"Yea, he is a missionary," pursued the dragoman. "And, having dwelt among the savages of Africa, believes he knows the way to manage us poor Syrians. We are the same as blacks, it seems; we live and learn! We must be kept in perpetual fear; we must never be allowed to do anything right; lest the knowledge thereof should breed complacency, which in such base natures is the same as impudence; we cannot know anything; we must defer to our white master. He says repeatedly to the three ladies and the stout khawâjah: 'Let me manage – I understand these beeble.' May his house be destroyed!"

---

[25] Cook

"Could anything be filthier?" the cook suspired. "What are we to do, O Shibli?"

The dragoman hung his head as one world-weary. "I must think," he said.

He thought, with knees drawn up to meet his chin, while the cook and Amîn were busy with the dinner of the tourists; and the swarthy muleteers looked on concernedly. But when the council was resumed, he had invented nothing.

"What are we to do?" sighed Amîn. "Just now, when I started round the table one way, he cried in wrath, and made me go the other. The curse of God on the religion of his father!"

He too assumed the posture of the dragoman, lowering his brow and drawing up his knees to meet his chin.

Silence ensued.

For every son of the Arabs it is the first necessity, whether by fair means or guile, to win the favour of his employer for the time being. Where all means fail, his limbs refuse their motion, and he sits and scowls, forlorn. The alternatives then presented to his understanding are either to deceive the blockhead and to get the laugh of him, or else to run away. The whole assembly in the cook's tent, from the resplendent dragoman to the most ragged muleteer, were now upon the horns of this dilemma; and, flight all together being quite impracticable, were seeking how to make sport of the English missionary from Uganda.

"He is mad; may his limbs all wither!" muttered Shibli the dragoman, first to break the silence.

"May Allah balk him of his heart's desire!" exclaimed the cook.

The muleteers each added to the curse.

All of a sudden, as they growled dejectedly, Amîn the waiter lifted up his head, and laughed:

"Ha, ha, ha, ha!"

"What is it, O Amîn?"

"Oh, ho, ho, ho!" Amîn slid down upon his back, and lay convulsed. The others flung themselves upon him, smote him, questioned him, endeavouring to drag him up and learn the matter. It was some minutes ere they heard distinctly:

"Ha, ha! He, he! Let us be all he thinks! For the love of Allah, let us be the filthiest of human idiots! Oho! He is accustomed to bad servants – ah, I see it! – he does not know good servants when he finds them. He must be teaching everyone. O Shibli, O 'brahim, O every Muslim, every Christian present, for the love of my old beard, be fools henceforward! . . . . O Lord of heaven and earth! O Holy Miriam!"

The laughter became general as the thought grew clear in every mind. Amîn's intelligence was praised on all hands.

"By Allah!" exclaimed the cook, "I am absolutely ignorant of Frankish cooking. I am his Honour's poor disciple. He must teach me."

"And I," gasped Amîn between spasms of creative mirth, "shall be so nervous – O, so nervous! – when I wait at table. I shall appeal to him for instruction at every turn."

"Behold me such a stricken fool!" laughed Shibli, "as not to know when I am not wanted. In sh'Allah, I shall spoil his courtship of the fair young lady."

The chief of the muleteers, a dirty greybeard, here laughed out. "As for me," he declared, "I swear by the Prophet, they shall have no sleep this night."

The three superiors – dragoman, cook, and waiter – had their beds in the kitchen tent. They slept peacefully; but the muleteers, who lay among their beasts, kept wide awake. Among the baggage animals were several donkeys, which the rascals by a trick compelled to bray at frequent intervals. At length the voice of the big hypocrite was heard calling from the mouth of the tent which he shared with the stout khawâjah. At once the five muleteers sprang up and ran to him, knuckling sleepy eyes, and talking all together. He had no Arabic to speak of; they no English. After a deal of altercation, they perceived his meaning suddenly, and all rushed headlong on the only donkey which happened at that time to be performing. It is the simplest feat to stop a donkey's braying; you have merely to pull his tail down hard and hold it, and the brazen voice dies instantly in sobs. To hang a weight upon the tail is to secure silence.

But no sooner had the clergyman gone back to bed than the noise broke out afresh. Four times did the hypocrite come forth with shouts of anger, while voices from the ladies' tent called out in anguish; and at each fresh call the sleepy muleteers experienced the same difficulty in understanding. At length, towards dawn they thought it best to rouse the upper servants. Shibli, heavy with sleep, could not at first comprehend the matter of complaint. Amîn stepped in before him, asking:

"What the bother, sir?"

"Can't they find some way to stop that awful noise – those donkeys braying? None of us have slept a wink. The ladies will be quite unfit to ride this morning."

Amîn conferred a moment with the chief muleteer. "He say he cut their tongues out, if you order, sir! He your serfant, same as all of us. He kill those beasties dead to gif you bleasure."

"No, No! The foolish man! Tell him on no account to be so cruel!"

Shibli, by this time awake, here thrust Amîn aside, exclaiming:

"Dear sir, I'm fery sad you woke this night. It will not habben again. They make such noise all account of one dam little herb grows in this blace."

There was some delay in setting out that morning. Though the tents and baggage had been some time loaded up, though the travellers had finished breakfast and were ready to mount, the train of mules still waited; whereas their custom was to gain what start they might, their rate of progress being slower than a horse's pace.

"What are they waiting for?" shouted the big hypocrite, his large, rosy face, with red moustache and prominent grey eyes devoid of lashes, shaded at the moment by a solar topee and a puggaree[26]. Shibli the dragoman hurried up with suppliant mien.

"The muleteer, he wish you see the loads all right; he say you know his business better than what he do. He only wish you habby and be blease with him." Shibli was half ashamed with his own impudence.

"Oh, yes. Quite right," the Frank replied. "I'll come at once." He went over to the line of mules and examined every load with seeming care.

"You been a muleteer, sir?" Amîn could not forbear the sneer as he looked on.

"Ha ha! No, not exactly; but you'll find there isn't much I don't know when it comes to travelling in these countries."

The heaven-sent fool received the insult as a compliment. His simplicity was clearly seen even by the muleteers, who, though ignorant of English, had no difficulty in interpreting the cook's broad grin.

The dragoman thought Amîn had gone too far. To counteract the rudeness, he kissed the hypocrite's hand, then pressed it to his brow, exclaiming:

"I'm your serfant, sir. You tell me what to do, I do it. At first I thought you was a common traf'ler, I done wrong. Now I see you know a thing or two, I'm broud to serf you!"

When Shibli had performed his part, Amîn did homage in like manner, so did Ibrahîm, and then the muleteers with shouts of acclamation. The fool beamed on them; there was even a glisten of tears in his eyes as he exclaimed:

"There, there, my men! Now we understand each other. No shirking, no deceit! Be fair to me, and I'll be fair to you."

He strode back towards the other tourists with pride, announcing: "I've got them into shape. We understand each other. They'll give no further trouble."

---

[26] The muslin cloth hanging from a topee hat at the back to shelter the nape of the neck from the sun.

The ladies of the party were a tough old maiden, sister to the stout khawâjah; a widowed lady, who travelled in a palanquin between the two mules, and regarded the tour in the light of a dangerous illness; and the daughter of this last, a pretty, fair-haired girl, between whom and the big hypocrite there was attraction. They and the gentleman all wore white, as if in duty bound, making the dragoman's gorgeous clothes the more conspicuous. Shibli had two objects on that morning's ride: to let the missionary do the work of guide and general servant to the party, and to interrupt all talk between the lovers. In both he succeeded with a colour of the greatest innocence.

When they reached the spot where Amîn was waiting with the luncheon-hamper, they found that he had not yet unpacked anything.

"I wait for you, sir," he informed the missionary from Uganda, "to see if you like this blace. We easy change it."

"Oh, hang it all!" exclaimed the stout khawâjah, who was ravenous. "Why can't you, Pearson, leave the men alone? They did all right till you got meddling with them."

Amîn and Shibli exchanged lightning glances. It was almost the first utterance they had heard from the stout khawâjah, and it gave them a respect for his intelligence. But the missionary ignored it, smiling on Amîn.

"That's right," he said. "Quite right to wait and ask before unpacking."

Amîn bowed low in gratitude for this approval; and then, in the simplest manner, with a mien of great abashment, beguiled the simpleton into setting out the lunch himself, while he, the waiter, watched as one instructed.

That night, around the camp-fire, the servants waxed uproarious, their laughter spreading to a group of ragged, staring fellahîn[27]. "He likes it! By Allah Most High, he loves us as pure idiots! Go on! Go on! He will feel foolish in the end."

But though on each succeeding day fresh tricks were played, some of them so bold that Shibli trembled in his riding-boots, the big hypocrite continued well content. It was the stout khawâjah who grumbled; seeing which the men took care that he should have nothing to complain of.

"By Allah, he alone has intellect!" Amîn declared. He says 'damn!' where 'damn!' is needed. But the ladies scold him. What shame, they say, to curse kind Mr Bearson, who takes such trouble to make things go right."

Even when, by the contrivance of a muleteer, his luggage was precipitated down a rocky slope, two hundred feet, into a torrent-bed, the missionary, arriving

---

[27] Plural of fellah – peasants, farmers. Pickthall elsewhere often lengthens the a.

on the scene, said only: "Dear, dear! How annoying!" The muleteers were all in tears; they had been waiting an hour for the treat of watching his behaviour.

"It's your own fault, Pearson," growled the stout khawâjah, "for interfering with the way they load. The men know their own business. Why can't you let 'em alone?"

The missionary cast about for some way to recover his two portmanteaux, and his Gladstone bag; which last had burst open in its passage down the rocks, scattering its store of personalia. He declared it would be easy to get down and fetch them. The servants swore by Allah it was quite impossible. Egged on to prove his point, that prince of fools at length himself descended, collecting his belongings as he sprang from rock to rock. It was quite easy, he called up with pride, and scrambled back, the bag upon his shoulder. Reassured by his performance, two muleteers leapt down like goats and brought up the portmanteaux.

"Where there's a will, there's a way!" panted the missionary, mopping his brow and gazing round him with complacency.

"How brave of you!" the ladies cried. "In this terrific heat!"

Amîn the waiter leaned to Shibli's ear. "I shall go mad," he whispered. "It is more than flesh can bear. O Lord, have mercy on me! My brain aches!"

When they halted for the night he repeated aloud his statement that he must go mad or expire immediately.

Then, with a creative laugh, he changed the tense, exclaiming:

"I will go mad – like Neby Daûd, when he wanted to deceive his enemies! I must have the freedom of apparent madness for an hour, or die this night."

The others gaping on him, he enlarged his meaning.

"Well, do it thoroughly," the dragoman enjoined. "Give not a hint of sanity, or we are ruined."

Amîn allowed a strangeness to appear in his demeanour while waiting on the travellers that night at dinner; and then, as soon as he had cleared the table, he tore off all his clothes and, shrieking, danced stark naked round the fire. Shibli ran for the missionary.

"O sir! O sir! Come, bray! We're in such trouble. Something dreadful habben to Amîn. He's mad, sir!"

The fool rushed forth. "Back! Back!" he cried to the ladies, who pressed after him. The stout khawâjah went to help should strength be needed. They held the madman, who soon gave up struggling. He seized an end of the missionary's red moustache, and tweaked it, as a slobbering baby might, grinning insanely in its owner's face. He was carried to the missionary's own bed, and there attended.

The camp was at Mejdel-esh-Shems, below Mount Hermon. There was no doctor within twenty miles. The travellers were in despair, till the cook assured them:

"That soon bass ofer, sir. He's kind of boisoned, sir, by eatin' of a little thing what grows about here. I tell him not to, but he will. The madness only last an hour or two. Blease God he soon be well, sir."

"He's fast asleep now," the stout khawâjah, coming from the tent, reported.

"He will be all right to-morrow, neffer fear!" said Shibli cheerfully.

But when the next day came, Amîn was found too weak to move a limb. After a long discussion, it was arranged that he should occupy the palanquin, the widow lady, in the strength of pity, consenting to affront the perils of a donkey-ride. The dragoman scowled at the decision, but his lips were sealed before the English. He cursed Amîn's religion and parentage as he passed the tent where he lay; and pinched him spitefully when helping bear him to the litter. More than once upon the morning's march he rode back as if to ascertain the sufferer's state; really to mutter:

"Out, O ancient malefactor! Are we here to wait on thee, O child of devils?"

A sweet voice answered:

"Allah! I am comfortable. How sweet to take one's ease while others labour."

The boy in charge of the mules which bore the palanquin fed the invalid with chickpeas and with monkey-nuts, in return for mirth-provoking grins between the curtains.

"But arise, O evil joker! This cannot go on. While thou art ill, I have to do thy work as well. By Allah, thou hadst better get well quickly, or I will take a stick and beat thee near to death," cried Shibli, past all patience, in the afternoon.

"In mercy, O my dearest, be not wroth with me," the rogue replied. "Repose is sweet, and I am deep in love. The old one, the widow, trembles when I kiss her hand in gratitude. O desire! O rapture! As for the work, beloved, do as I do! Persuade a horse to kick thee, and go lame. The big hypocrite is such a filthy ass, he will believe thee!"

There was no way of making Amîn work again, short of beating, to which Shibli did not wish to have recourse, for they were friends. He took the rascal's hint, and limped that evening. The missionary asked what ailed him.

"Oh, it's nothing, sir!" His face was wrung with pain while he thus spoke. "That dam' horse of mine – he's fery naughty, sir – he kick my shin, that's all."

The ladies cried out in compassion; the stout khawâjah went into his tent and fetched some ointment. Shibli was forbidden to wait at dinner. The missionary himself laid the table and took the dishes from the cook's hands. Next day Amîn was still extremely weak, and Shibli's lameness was evident the minute he set foot to ground. The cook then discovered something, "which blayed hell in his inside," and made it an excuse for working languidly. The muleteers too started ailments, and were lazy; but still the missionary smiled on them all, since they deferred to him. It was a tribe of invalids that brought that party of tourists into Damascus, where the camp broke up.

The muleteers, the cook, and the waiter were paid off. Shibli the dragoman alone remained on duty, it being part of his service to escort the travellers to Beyrout, where they were to take ship. A single visit to a doctor in Damascus had, he assured them, quite dispelled his lameness. Amîn and the cook, the former likewise whole again, went down in the same train to Beyrout, on their way to Jaffa. Shibli joining them in their compartment, there was much laughter as they reviewed the wondrous journey.

"But all is not yet complete!" Amîn insisted. "He does not know how daintily we fooled him. We must not tell him plainly, I suppose. But let us devise a parting speech of such absurdity, that, hearing it, he may see cause to doubt our previous gravity. By Allah, we must sow misgiving in his mind, for a farewell blessing."

"Aye, why not?" agreed Shibli with a shrug. "I care not though he take offence, for my part. He will complain of me to Jûnas, that is all; and Jûnas will withhold from me the ten pounds he promised. He would find a pretext to do that in any case; he is such a rascal, and he hates me so. I will not work for him another year. He gives me all the refuse of the travellers. Come, let us set to work at once, and compose the speech."

They put their heads together and devised the following:

"Great sir, we grief to say goodbye to you; you are so cleffer. We think you are the clefferest man was effer seen. If we not know for sure God made the world, we think you made it, sir; you're such a cleffer deffil! We thank you fery much for showin' us our business; that safed us lots of trouble. You'd make a good cam'-serfant, sir; you take such bains combared with what we do. Amîn he soon forget to wait at table; the muleteers they soon forget to load the mules. You come back soon, sir, and Mr Fenner and the ladies. We neffer had such a jolly good time in all our lifes."

This oration was delivered in due course by Shibli, as spokesman of a deputation which approached the travellers as they sat in the spacious upper hall of Bassoul's Hotel in Beyrout. The audience, to the speaker's grief, appeared enraptured. Only the stout khawâjah, Mr Venner, looked strangely on the servile trio; and he seemed not displeased. He hated Pearson. As for the missionary from

Uganda, that amazing simpleton rose up solemnly and replied to the address. There were tears in his eyes.

"Thank you, my men," he said with voice half-choked, "and may God bless you! We've had a pleasant time together; and I, for one, am never likely to forget it; since I must tell you I have won a bride since we set forth" - Amîn here cried "Hooray," and clapped his hands – "Yes, I have won a charming bride, and shall look back always on this tour through Palestine with affection, at the time when I received God's greatest blessing. You have behaved very well. A few little differences we had at first. You thought me just a common tourist who could be deceived. You found out your mistake, and then we understood each other. All went smoothly after that. I am highly gratified by this free expression of your goodwill. Once more, God bless you – and – goodbye."

He dwelt upon the last word mournfully. Then there was giving of bakhshîsh by all the party. The stout khawâjah said in Shibli's ear: "You're a cheeky rascal. But I must say he deserved it. Here's something for you."

The sums received were greater than could have been expected, judging from the appearance of the party. Even Amîn's hard heart was a little mollified by this circumstance. "Allah is greatest!" he remarked to Shibli with a shrug. "Fools have their uses: may our Lord increase them!"

TRA-LA-LA

This story first appeared in the collection Pot au Feu, published in February 1911.

Free education at the foreign missionary schools in Greater Syria gave young people from the Maronite villages of the mountains the opportunity to enter Beirut's new commercial job market, requiring among other skills, knowledge of French or English. After the British occupation of Egypt in 1882 and the Anglo-Egyptian taking of the Sudan in 1898, these countries provided bright young professional and trading Syrians (including Lebanese and Palestinians) opportunities for careers and for making money.

The story plays on the tensions of Druze and Christian and also the class differences, with the poorer classes dependent on serving the rich and powerful.

It also includes the fatuous character of the philosopher whose referenced authorities all have the names of items of popular Lebanese food. Pickthall rarely indulges in such slapstick humour.

So many charitable and religious foreign agencies have, of late years, opened mission schools in the Lebanon, attracted by its fine scenery and agreeable climate, that any Christian native of those parts whose children are not educated free of charge has only his own bigotry to blame. The youths, thus trained, betake themselves to Egypt, to western Europe, or to America, and return with money in the pockets of their foreign clothes, and strange ideas disturbing to their parents. Time was, within my memory, when children of the Mountain mocked at Frankish trousers, shouting: "Hi, O my uncle, you have come in two!" But to-day all that is changed. Young native Christians wear cheap German slops to show their progress; they doff their fez when entering a house, an action formerly esteemed the greatest rudeness; they wear loud creaking boots, which are the mode out there, to advertise the difference from old-fashioned slippers; they decipher the Latin character more easily than the Arabic, and corrupt their mother-tongue with French and English; so that one forebodes that, in a few years' time, the ancient dignity of these people and their individuality will be found only among the Druzes and the Mohammedans.

A poor peasant of the province of Kesarawân, in Mount Lebanon, a Maronite of the Maronites, and fanatical in that faith, nevertheless contrived to have his children taught by English Protestants. The boy, Selîm, then completed his education at the Jesuit college in Beyrout, while the girls, Afîfeh and Zeydeh, returned to their village, to the faith and practice of the Maronites. Every Christian in Syria at that time looked to Egypt as an Eldorado. Selîm resorted thither, his studies finished, and obtained a clerkship in a good commercial house then opening operations in the newly conquered Sûdân[28]. For three years he had worked there, in a trying climate, when tidings of his father's illness reached him; and he journeyed home, only to find the old man dead and buried. His sisters being averse to village life, he sold the inheritance for a little ready money, and took a lodging in Beyrout – a single room at the top of a tall new house in a decent quarter, which boasted a small balcony overlooking the street.

The girls – big, white-skinned, black-browed beauties, each with a profusion of dark hair plaited in a solid tail behind – were enraptured with the sojourn in the city, home of culture and of elegance. In the mornings they performed the housework in the intervals of their toilette, pouring their slops superbly off the balcony; in the afternoons they sat out, gracefully attired, and watched the carriages full of fashionables go jolting and swaying down the ragged street beneath; they cooked the mess of rice or lentils for their brother's supper; and then all three sat out under the stars and sang together, choosing Frankish airs for fashion. The frowning mountains seen above the roofs seemed to the girls a prison-house from which they had at last escaped.

But Selîm was not so happy. He could get no work, and was loth to return to the Sûdân, which, now that he was back in Syria, appeared a perilous and very distant country. Moreover, he adored his sisters, and would not entertain the thought of leaving them. He prayed to Allah and the saints continually, and neglected none of those superstitious observances which have been proved conducive to good fortune. Yet none came to him. Each morning he set forth with hope renewed, but every evening saw that hope demolished.

One morning he was starting, light of heart, singing "Tra-la-la!" in the Frankish manner, as his sister had been doing overnight, when his foot slipped on the top step of the stairs and he sat down suddenly. The stone was hard. "O

[28] Sudan was taken over by an Anglo-Egyptian army after the Battle of Omdurman, September 1898. Many Syrians flocked to Sudan as merchants or in the administration.

Lord!" he cried, and crossed himself, striving to rise; but the effort came too late. Again he bumped a step, again he crossed himself and called on Allah; and so on down the flight of fourteen steps.

A philosopher, who lived on the floor below, looked out of his doorway at sound of the first impact and ejaculation, and watched with interest at the subsequent descent, in appearance so deliberate, and yet involuntary.

"Allah is merciful!" he asserted gravely when Selîm finally landed at his feet. "Another time thou wouldst do well to name the Name and cross thyself before descending and then look well to thy going. Now enter my abode and rest awhile with praise to Allah. Thou mightiest have broken a limb or even killed thyself. Of a verity we sons of Adam are extremely fragile; our life is at the mercy of a sudden fall, a shot, a spark. A poisonous wind." So saying, he led the dazed young man into his room and shut the door again.

The room was most untidy, being strewn with sheets of newspaper, most of which showed signs of having been cut with scissors. Under the window was a little pile of books.

"Behold, my son, the scene of labours which will benefit posterity," remarked the owner with a flourish of his hand. He was an elderly man, clad in a tattered silken robe and a soiled tarbush. The skin of his face was almost coffee-coloured and seemed very dry, as if its vital moisture had all gone to fertilise the grey moustache, which was bushy, drooping, and extremely prominent. A pair of gold-rimmed spectacles lent to his deep-set eyes mysterious wisdom. He smiled self-consciously. "Know, O my son, that I am engaged upon a mighty work – no less than a comparison of all the nations of the world, their manners, customs, laws, and form of government, compiled from Arabic authorities. For this cause do I study all these journals, sent to me weekly by a friend in Egypt, since they often give strange facts concerning foreigners. Now eat some leben[29] and some bread. It is a known specific where the nerves are shaken. As the learned Abu Kûseh[30] has it in his golden verse:

A modicum of soured white juice of cow or goat in association with the
produce of the oven,
Engenders in him who engulfs it tranquillity of mind and equilibrium.

[29] A yoghurt drink.

[30] The names of the philosophers and poets to whom Hasan's neighbour refers are all items of popular Lebanese food: kûseh is a courgette; marcûc is flaky pastry; camr-ed-dîn is dried apricot rolled into a sheet; adas is lentils; fustuc el Halebi is pistachio; dibs is molasses; bedinjân mahshi is stuffed aubergine; kiteh is meat-balls and batîkha is water-melon.

Selîm accepted gratefully and ate with gusto, sitting on the divan, at his learned host's right hand.

"What is thy name; thy business?" cried the latter suddenly.

Selîm told his story briefly, and complained much of the difficulty he experienced in finding work.

"Well, return to the Sûdân to thy former post!" counselled the philosopher. "Here there is too much Frankish education such as thine. Only the Muslimîn still study Arabic. Return to the Sûdân therefor; thou hast no chance here."

"I cannot, O my uncle. The climate of the Sûdân is most insalubrious. I suffered much from boils – a great calamity. It is health before all things here below, since Allah only grants to us one life."

"Well said," applauded the philosopher. "Thy wisdom is beyond thy years. Alas, how many do we see in this world who barter health and virtue for the chance of gain? Now look at me! I have here in this room a priceless book, hand-written, which contains the true secret history of the world from the burial of our father Adam till the crucifixion. Were I to show that book to the Doctor Adisûn of the American college[31], he would cover me with gold to let him have it. I do not show it; I despise the dross of this world . . . . Then why not go to America?" he added after some reflection.

"How can I leave my sisters here defenceless? Besides, my soul abhors the thought of foreign lands. I suffered much from boils when in the Sûdân."

"Well, hast thou no rich friend whom thou canst flatter? As the homely proverb puts it: 'Kiss the dog on the mouth, till you have got what you want from him.'"

"There is one to whom I would attach myself – a young chief of the Drûz, by name Hasan Bey Abdul Melik, who leads a gay life in the city here. He lets me feed with his servants and follow in the train of courtiers, but has paid no heed to me."

"Ha! It is plain we must devise some stratagem. Hast thou any gift of wit or comicality? The learned and polite Marcûc, that best of poets, having failed to gain preferment by his poetry, one day made laughable grimaces in the presence of his lord, with the result that the monarch filled his mouth with gold and flung on him a robe of honour. Thou mightst do likewise with thy young Druze. Fear not, I will give thought to it; we must devise some stratagem."

"With thy permission, I must now be going," said Selîm. "May Allah reward thy kindness to a stranger. Deign to honour our poor dwelling in the evening. My

---

[31] The Syrian Protestant College, later the American University of Beirut, founded in 1866.

sisters are well-educated and conversable. They sing most rarely in the Frankish manner."

"Be sure that I shall do myself the honour. Go in peace, my son."

Out in the street, in the sunlight, the Frankish tune once more recurred to Selîm, and he sang "Tra-la-la-la!" from a restricted throat. Not everyone could make a noise like that; he felt flattered by the stare of passers-by; but when he had been refused employment at three likely places, his spirits sank and he remembered the bad omen of his fall downstairs. It was with relief that, towards noon, he approached the town house of the young Druze sheykh. There, at any rate, he was sure of getting what he went for, which was food.

It was a tall house with a roof of scarlet tiles, walls painted a rich blue, and monstrous plate-glass windows which flamed at sunset far across the sea. Twelve orange-trees in tubs adorned the entrance court; in which and in the entry lounged a crowd of suitors – youths of the town in Frankish clothes and fezzes, who aspired to be companions of the great man's pleasures, and Druzes from the Mountain in striped cloaks and snowy turbans, who had business with the chieftain or his steward. Selîm waited to kiss the hand of Hasan Bey as his lordship crossed the courtyard on the way to lunch, before he joined the servants at their meal.

Hasan Bey Abdul Melik was eighteen years old, generous, high-spirited, and beautiful. The hair that showed beneath his fez was black and curly, his complexion a clear olive readily suffused, and his dark blue eyes were quick to answer any challenge. He had come to Beyrout on purpose to enjoy himself; and the aged steward of his house accompanied him to restrict his enjoyment to the bounds of decency. For the Druzes are so prudish as a nation that the least taste of wine or arac in the mouth, the smoking of a single cigarette, disqualifies a man from entering their secret councils. As yet Hasan had done nothing obnoxious to their scruples; and it was hoped that he might live to be initiated, which great nobles who indulge their lust can never be. At present his chief amusement consisted in walking in the streets, instead of riding, attended by a mob of sycophants whom he treated with good-natured contempt.

That afternoon, as he strolled by the sea-shore, Selîm was in the crowd escorting him. The young Maronite suddenly espied his sisters. Alarmed at encountering so great a crowd of men, the two girls had shrunk close to the wall, and were trying to hide their faces with their black lace head-veils. He stopped to speak to them, and was amazed when they moved on to find that the whole procession had stopped likewise. The voice of Hasan Bey cried:

"Who is it? Tell me quickly!"

And one replied: "It is Selîm the Maronite, a son of nothing."

Then obsequious hands seized hold of the astonished youth and thrust him forward till he stood before the young Druze chief.

"Thy face is known to me, but not thy story," said the latter kindly. "They tell me that thou art poor, and dost support thy sisters – a good action. Is it true?"

"It is true, O my lord the bey[32]."

"What is the name of the taller of the two?"

"Afîfeh, O my lord the bey."

"Well, O Khawâjah[33] Selîm, I have an offer to make to thee. I love the lady Afîfeh with an urgent love. I will pay thee a hundred pounds, and keep her in luxury. What sayest thou?"

Selîm could say nothing for a minute, for the rush of blood to his head. At last he managed to articulate: "It is a sin – against my honour," and walked off in dudgeon.

"Thy honour! What hast thou to do with honour?" exclaimed the nobleman in pure amazement.

"Art mad, or what, to reject unheard-of fortune?" whispered a lickspittle at Selîm's ear.

But, in spite of all his urban affectations, Selîm remained a native of the Mountain, and averse to infamy. He went home, divided between shame and anger, ascribing the outrage to which he had been subject chiefly to his fall downstairs that morning.

He found his sisters seated on the tiny balcony, the philosopher behind them, squatting just within the room. The last-named rose upon his entrance, observing:

"I have already made acquaintance with these ladies, as thou seest."

"What luck, O Selîm?" inquired Zeydeh.

"None at all," Selîm confessed dejectedly. "And you, have you not heard of anything?"

The sisters had been to visit some English missionary ladies to whom they had obtained an introduction. They had been charmed by the respect with which those ladies treated them, giving them dignities in Arabic to which, being low-born, they were not entitled; and otherwise fulfilling every detail of the most extravagant Oriental politeness; but, in fact, had gained nothing by the interview.

Owing to the multiplying of mission schools and colleges, there were now too many educated women seeking posts as teachers.

32 A literal word for word translation of the Arabic.

33 Christians were often addressed by non-Christians as khawâjah.

"It is the same story always. Things are bad," Selîm suspired. "Our money is almost spent. Allah help us, for I know not what to do."

"Despair not, O my son!" said the philosopher. "I have thought on thy business since our talk this morning, and have gathered certain stories from the old for thy instruction. Here is one of them: –

"It is related of the clever Camr-ud-dîn, who became king of a country among the islands of Sind and of Hind, that, being in his boyhood destitute and at the same time ambitious, he devised the following stratagem. He stole a saucepan from his neighbour's house and sold it; then, with the money – which was very little – in a purse, he repaired to a certain merchant famed for absent-mindedness, and begged him to take charge of a purse containing two dînârs. The merchant at once consented, flung the purse into a box with other moneys, and called on the bystanders to witness the deposit. Later that same day the clever one returned and demanded his purse containing two dînârs. The merchant flung it to him. He opened it; it contained but three dirhems. Then he cried so loudly that he had been robbed, that the merchant, though he saw the fraud, made up the money for the sake of his reputation. With the gold thus obtained, Camr-ud-dîn purchased merchandise, which he sold again to such profit that in a week he had returned the saucepan to its owner, the gold to the merchant, yet kept much in hand. Thus, by force of cleverness and bold invention was laid the foundation of a splendid fortune."

"Capital!" cried the two girls. "Our brother too is clever. He could deal as wisely. Tell us some more strange stories, O khawâjah."

The philosopher complied with a store of anecdotes, which grew more and more facetious as the day wore on, till Selîm himself was lured from his despondency to join the laughter which those tales provoked. The philosopher shared their supper of rice and olives, after which the girls sang Frankish songs, "Tra-la-la!" ogling the stars above the Beyrout roofs.

Next day Selîm went out to look for work as usual. He avoided the palace of the young Druze sheykh. When he returned towards evening, Afîfeh called to him:

"I have seen thy friend. He rode past here on a splendid horse, and smiled up to me especially. By Allah, he is lovely as an angel."

"He is no friend, but an ill-wisher. Never speak of him again," he answered sternly.

Afîfeh turned away as one sore wounded.

The little store of money was exhausted; their credit would not last a week; and still there seemed no prospect of employment. Selîm became morose and very irritable; he often wept at night. His friend the philosopher tried to cheer him, saying:

"The man who possesses his own soul is a great proprietor; the lord of great possessions is a slave. That is the opinion of the learned Ibn Adas. Look at me! I have here a book that, if but shown to Doctor Adisûn at the American college, would bring me a hundred pounds, perhaps more. Yet, if deprived of it to-morrow, I should not be downcast. Be patient, O my son, devise some stratagem!"

Selîm tried hard to obey, but could think of no scheme more hopeful than that related of the clever Camr-ud-dîn. He determined, in despair, to try its efficacy. Descending the stairs one morning, he found the philosopher's door wide open, his room empty. He entered and, searching through the pile of books below the window, abstracted the rare manuscript so often shown to him, and hid it under his coat. He was going to show it to Doctor Edison of the American college; and, if his luck but equalled that of Camr-ud-dîn, would return it to its rightful owner in a week. Running down the lowest flight of stairs into the street, he knocked against the philosopher, who was carrying a bowl of leben.

"Curse thy father!" cried the sage, exasperated, seeing half the curds were spilt. He added when Selîm was almost out of earshot: "Haste is from the devil."

Selîm walked as far as he could to the American college, and there craved audience of Dr Edison. After an hour's delay he obtained it quite by accident. The doctor was pointed out to him by one of the students, in the act of flying from one building to another. Selîm ran and intercepted him. The doctor cried: "No, no! I have no time!" and was going to push him aside when, spying an ancient manuscript, his face softened. He took the book from Selîm's hand and turned the pages.

"What wouldst thou with it?" he inquired.

"I would sell it now at once."

"It is worth a pound at least; I have not that sum with me. Come to my house in an hour."

"A pound only!" gasped Selîm. But by then the doctor had fled out of hearing.

The homeward way seemed long and tedious to Selîm, deprived of the hope which had inspirited his going out. He carried the book in his hands, in sight of all men, forgetting he had ever thought to steal it. With alarm he saw a little crowd before the doorway of his house, surrounding the philosopher, who gesticulated like a madman. Hurrying to learn the cause of his commotion, he found his throat seized by the sage's bony hand, the book snatched from his grasp.

"So thou art the thief, O accursed, O unnatural malefactor – thou whom I befriended, whom I loved and cherished! Come with me before the judge, this minute. Thou shalt be cast into prison for this shameful crime."

"But the book is in thy hand; it is not stolen," wailed Selîm. "I did but show it to the Doctor Adisûn. He says that it is worth an English pound."

"He said that! Dost thou tell me he said that? – the miscreant, the traitor, the unblushing liar! But he did not value it fully – say, now did he? Come to my room and tell me all that passed."

Alone with the sage, Selîm fell down at his feet, confessing:

"Allah witness, I am at the last gasp. I know not where to find enough to purchase daily bread. So I bethought me of thy story of the clever Camr-ud-dîn, and took the book, hoping to sell it for a hundred pounds, and with that money speculate upon the Bourse and make a fortune. Allah witness I intended to restore it to thee in a few hours' time. Moreover, thou has assured me more than once that it would not grieve thy soul to be deprived of it – "

"I meant by some cataclysm or calamity, as of fire or flood or war," put in the philosopher reproachfully. "The hand of God is one thing, the hand of man another; bear in mind."

"O, my uncle, I implore thy forgiveness. Behold me destitute, with two dear angels trusting to me. O Allah, take my life, for it is useless."

"Tush, O my son! Be patient! Think but a minute; let us devise some stratagem. What of that sheykh of the Drûz of whom thou once didst speak to me?"

"I have forsworn his company these many days. He made a proposal which impugned my honour. He wished to buy my sister for a hundred pounds."

"Ah, did he so, the libidinous wretch, the devastator? That explains why he rides by each day on his thoroughbred horse, passing and repassing this house a score of times . . . . nevertheless, O my son, a hundred pounds is hard to come by openly; and love is credulous and easily beguiled. By giving him hope and placing obstacles, thou couldst, perhaps, extract the money without harm to thy sister. Thou hast a precedent in the case of the learned Fustuc el Halebi and his wife Dibs. A certain merchant of the richest loved this Dibs and pursued her. She complained of his persecutions to her husband, who, instead of getting angry in the way of fools, sought to turn the matter to his own advantage. By means of his wife he lured his merchant to his house and there played merry tricks on him, involving his discomfiture in divers ways as well as nearly half his substance. In the end, the woman having wrought him to the verge of madness and got from him a heap of priceless gems, I recollect he squirted benj[34] into his nostrils, and while he slept, departed with her husband. The knowledge of benj is lost to us degenerate, but at any pharmacy thou couldst obtain a soporific to still the rascal if he got too dangerous."

"But, O my uncle, is it not dishonourable?"

"Honour," sings the poet "Bédinjân el Mahshi, is the rose-water of the opulent. The hungry cannot stop to wash their hands. Return to-day to thy patron, as one repentant. Say thou thyself art willing, but the girl is very shy. Entreat him to do nothing to alarm her modesty. Lay stress upon thy poverty. And thy obedience to his will in all things."

"It shall be as thou sayest," exclaimed Selîm with bitter resolution; and went out from the conference with teeth set. Weeping, he turned his face towards the southern quarter of the city, where towered the blue-walled, red-roofed palace of the Abdul Meliks. Its plate-glass windows were already flaming in the sunset. The people at the door, impressed by his wretched appearance, which seemed to bespeak grave tidings, procured him an immediate audience.

Hasan Bey was lolling on a divan in his private rooms, consulting with the aged steward, who sat humbly at his feet. At sight of Selîm, he asked his cause of grief.

"My errand is a private one," the suppliant murmured.

"I have no secrets from the Sheykh Muhammad. He is my soul," remarked the boy with dignity. "Hast thou changed thy mind with respect to thy sister, the lady Afîfeh? By Allah, in that case we will dry thy tears with benefits."

"Allah knows my shame!" Selîm blubbered. "Only most pressing need has brought me to it. O my lord, if thou canst win her consent, then take her. But she is very shy, and must be wooed politely. Honour our poor dwelling when it pleases thee. O Allah Most High, forgive me!"

He buried his face in his hands.

"Give him ten pounds!" the bey commanded his major-domo. "I will visit thy house privately this very evening, O khawâjah."

The Sheykh Muhammad shook some gold coins out of a silken purse, and counted ten of them into Selîm's palm. That old grey-bearded sheykh, black-coated and white-turbaned, then put questions, shrewd and searching, to Selîm concerning his sister's education and accomplishments, her age, her previous conduct; till the young Christian marvelled at the depravity, thus evidenced, of a man so respectable in appearance.

---

[34] The leaves and flowers of cannabis, in this case the juice. Known as bang or bhang in India.

"It is well," he said in conclusion, "now go in safety, for our lord is busy."

Selîm, thus dismissed, returned through the twilight streets. "Alas," thought he, "to what vile depths can poverty degrade the righteous." But with ten pounds in his pocket he felt much more comfortable.

On his way upstairs he looked in on the philosopher, announcing:

"All goes well. My one misgiving arises from the presence at his lordship's ear of a wise counsellor, the Sheykh Muhammad, steward of his household. The sheykh is wily, and his lordship hearkens to him. I fear he may suspect our purpose and defeat it."

"Fear nothing," rejoined the sage with a transcendent smile, "seeing that thou also hast a counsellor. With all the wisdom of the ancients at my beck and call, am I not more than a match for an astute barbarian?"

Selîm pursued his way upstairs, and told his sisters of the stratagem he had devised.

"This sheykh of the Drûz desires thee," he informed Afîfeh; "he has offered to buy thee from me – O the insult! Now we will be avenged on him, and at the same time obtain much money for our needs. I pretend to accept his offer; he comes here to-night; show him a little favour, make his love grow. And thou, O Zeydeh, help to get things ready!"

"Be certain I will do my best to charm him," said Afîfeh, laughing gaily. "O the wretch, to plan such wickedness, with that angel's face! Ah, we will punish him!"

Selîm gave then one of his gold pieces, wherewith to buy choice sweetstuff for the entertainment, and also candles to light up the lodging. Zeydeh went downstairs to do the shopping, while Afîfeh decked the room and donned her best apparel, all the while singing "Tra-la-la" in the best Frankish manner, seeming light of heart.

Hardly were the preparations finished ere the young Drûz knocked at the door. Selîm opened to him, and performed the introduction. His Honour was conducted to a throne of cushions placed in readiness, where the two girls plied him with sweetmeats, of which he ate but little, seeming very nervous. To put him at his ease, Selîm then bade his sisters sing a Frankish song; but the effect of the performance upon Hasan Bey was unexpected. When the two girls flung their heads back and began their "Tra-la-las" from tightened throats, his Highness strove at first to keep his countenance, he gulped, he pressed a hand to his mouth, but at length exploded, fairly rolling on the floor for stress of laughter. The singing stopped in horror.

"Pardon! I ask pardon!" the young bey gasped out, trying with all his might to summon gravity. "But, by Allah, never in my life heard I a noise one half so funny."

"It is the music of Europe, O my lord!" Afîfeh pouted.

"There is no music in it!" the bey chuckled. "Leave it, O queen of beauty, to the Europeans, to professional jokers. Sing thou sweet love-songs of our native land."

Directly after coffee had been served, he rose to go.

"So soon!?" exclaimed Afîfeh and Selîm together.

"With your permission, I will come again to-morrow. I am not well this evening." The truth was he still wrestled with a wish to laugh.

"Thou hast beheld his rudeness, his contempt for us – this heathen! By Allah, he is no better than a wild beast!" said Selîm when he was gone.

Next morning, at the housework, there was no more "Tra-la-la!" The sisters cooed soft Arab songs while they were dressing. In the afternoon the young bey reappeared, this time with less embarrassment in his demeanour. Afîfeh sat down near him, temptingly. To give her a chance to play upon him, Selîm went out and leaned upon the railing of the balcony. Two Druzes, whom he recognised as of the young chief's household, sat out on stools before a coffee-house across the way. Here and there, all down the street, appeared white turbans on the heads of idlers. At least a score of Druzes loitered within call. With a shudder, Selîm turned back into the room. Young Hasan held Afîfeh in his arms, his lips were glued to hers. The world was blackened in her brother's eyes. The malefactor, the young brute, was growing dangerous. The benj, the soporific, must be bought at once.

As his shadow fell across the room, they sprang apart. Afîfeh's face was red, her eyes downcast. Her aspect stabbed Selîm to the heart. It seemed a mute reproach of him, her brother, for compelling her to play a part so ignominious.

The cause of all this grief was unabashed. "I shall sup here, O khawâjah. Of thy kindness, go and buy provisions of the best," he said as to a servant, at the same time tossing to Selîm a piece of gold.

The master of the house could not refuse, for had he not promised to obey in all things the will of this abandoned bey; and though loth to leave Afîfeh at the young dog's mercy, he was glad to be spared the spectacle of her martyrdom. Zeydeh at least was with her, and he felt a crying need to speak with the philosopher. So he went quickly.

"Tell me, O my more than father," he cried as he burst into the sage's room, "where I can buy the drug of which thou spakest! It is time I had it, for the beast grows violent."

"I will come with thee. We will make inquiry of the pharmacy." The philosopher, who had been reading in a book, rose up and joined him.

At the street-door they brushed against a man, whom Selîm recognised as the Sheykh Muhammad, steward of the household of the Abdul Meliks. He clutched the philosopher's arm, and whispered:

"Look around thee! See how many of the Drûz! They guard the house while he is here. Did anything befall him they would take immediate vengeance. How then can he be drugged without discovery?"

"Fear nothing! Has not our house two doors? As the eloquent Abu Kifteh sang of old: 'Two doors are of the essence of good building as for human kind, for vice and virtue call in opposite directions, and no man living but is swayed by each in turn.' First ascertain that the young lord has money on him, then drug him and escape with that money, thou and the ladies with thee, by the back-door. He will not pursue you hotly, since the laugh will be against him, the shame his."

Thus conversing, they arrived at the pharmacy, where, under colour of a friend who could not sleep for headache, they inquired the properties of divers drugs, and at length bought one adapted to their purposes. They were returning with this treasure, when Selîm remembered the errand with which Hasan Bey had charged him to provide choice food. He turned back, therefor, his friend with him, to a cookshop, where there was more delay; the philosopher insisted upon tasting every dainty that the place afforded and discoursing learnedly of its effect and history, quoting poetry in support of is assertions; so that it was more than an hour from the moment of their setting forth ere they again drew near the house. Selîm felt gravely anxious for Afîfeh. Scarcely hearing the philosopher's remark, with praise to Allah, that the street was purged of Druzes, he dashed up the stairs in advance of his friend, who, having seen the dainties purchased, intended to go up and help to eat them.

He found Zeydeh alone, in tears.

"She is gone, O Selîm!" cried the young girl distractedly. "No sooner didst thou leave the house than he took her down to a carriage. An old man of his people got in with her. They drove towards the mountain. He went to join his horses and attendants; by this time he is at her side. He told me not to weep; no harm should come to her. He seems to love her truly. She went willingly."

Selîm had staggered back against the wall, letting his parcels fall. He stared at his sister stupidly, repeating:

"Willingly . . . ."

The philosopher, who had come up, puffing and blowing, in time to catch the gist of Zeydeh's story, now observed: "The proper course for thee to take is doubtless that which the learned Ibn Batîkha adopted when they stole his wife. He went to a place of concourse and there cried aloud till the whole city was commoved with his distress, and rose to help him."

"Curse thy religion!" Selîm flashed on him suddenly. "Thou, and no other, art the cause of all my shame. How can I cry in public, when my conduct has been criminal?"

"Control thy temper, O my son; though I can make allowances for one placed suddenly in such a plight. What thou sayest is quite true; we must avoid publicity. Our project has recoiled upon our own heads. As a poet of old has well said: 'My dagger is the light of my eyes when inserted in the belly of my enemy; but when it pricks my hand I curse its parentage.' By the life, I know not what to advise save patience."

He continued in this strain through half the night, partaking with Zeydeh of the dainties they had brought home with them, while Selîm kept moaning, little heeding what was said or done. When he retired at length, it was with the promise to return early in the morning to resume his consolations. In this respect he proved as good as his word. By the second hour after sunrise he was again at Selîm's ear, sermonising; and at the third hour after noon he was still declaiming, citing learned instances of bitter grief, when there came a loud knock at the door.

Zeydeh opened it. An old Druze entered it, making reverence. Selîm sprang to his feet, and stood glaring at the intruder, teeth and hands clenched, quivering in every limb.

"Curse thy father! Art thou not ashamed to come here, to the house thou hast dishonoured?" he said huskily.

"Nay, nay!" cried the philosopher, as one much scandalised. "Curse not a man who has saluted thee with courtesy. For what is the first rule of politeness: 'Return a compliment with interest, and then to converse.'"

He might have spoken to the air. The Sheykh Muhammad had his eyes fixed on Selîm. He answered proudly:

"Why speak of dishonour, when thou hast greater honour than ever fell to the lot of a dog like thee. My lord exalts thy sister, and has deigned to write to thee with his own hand. If we abducted the girl, it was only because we saw thou hadst a mind to trick us. She came like a bird to its nest. I served my lord in this affair, when I had ascertained the girl was modest and of good report. He loved her, and I saw that she would keep him good, while many strive to lure him into evil courses. For what dost thou revile me, O khawâjah?"

Selîm found no word to reply. The sheykh then took from his girdle the letter of Hasan Bey, handed it to Selîm, and withdrew.

> Having heard the nice game thou didst think to play with us, we wish never to see thy rascal face again; so give thee money enough to keep thee all thy days, to wit: two thousand French pounds, which we have this day ordered to be placed in thy name at the Imperial Ottoman Bank in Beyrout: and bid thee shun our sight for evermore – From our castle of Jedeydeh, in Mount Lebanon.
>
> HASAN ABDUL MELIK.

Selîm stood staring, wild-eyed, at that cruel letter. The philosopher, finding his questions concerning its import furthered nothing, finally snatched it from the dreamer's hand and fell to reading. "Praise be to Allah!" he exclaimed as one demented. "O Selîm, awake, rejoice with me, for we are rich. Knowest thou what we will do – it is the dream of my life – we will found a newspaper and teach men wisdom and morality."

THE WORD OF AN ENGLISHMAN

This story was published in ***Temple Bar*** *in July 1898 under the nom de plume, Y Greck. It is thus Pickthall's first publication on the Middle East (and second story ever published). He was just twenty-three at the time. It was reprinted in his second collection of short stories, Tales from Five Chimneys, in June 1915.*

While it has all the descriptive power and lack of sentimentality of his mature fiction, there is a touch of cultural smugness. The people of the Palestinian village have no redeeming features. The sheykh's wife is captivating but her personality is not developed in the way his female characters often were in later novels and stories. There is a touch of unwonted melodrama in the way the English doctor turns up in time.

In the rich plain of Sharon, midway between the mountains and the sea, lies the village of Sulfoon. Its houses are built of mud, not unmixed with stone, but mud predominates. Here and there among the hovels and strange conical mud-huts – which last serve as granaries, storehouses, and the like – date-palms rise, each tapering shaft crowned with a noble plume of wide-spreading leaves and pendant fringe of reddening fruit. To the east and south a vast grove of silver-grey olives stretches without a break into the blue distance as far as Lydda and the white mosque of Ramleh, and away to the foot of the mountains. To the north and west is the wide plain, swelling seaward with gentle undulations, a dark-green streak in the distance marking the line of the orange gardens of Jaffa. The men of Sulfoon were till lately of evil repute in the land. They were robbers and, of course, liars. They were fanatics, Muslims in name, but in nothing else save in their hatred of unbelievers. Worst crime of all, they were inhospitable. A good man may be a robber – by robbery one may come to riches and great honour. And he who will not tell a lie for his own advantage is a fool, and the son of a fool. But for any man to send a stranger hungry and thirsty from his door is an unpardonable crime.

But a change, hard to understand, has taken place in the men of Sulfoon. Formerly no European could ride past the village unstoned; now he can hardly avoid being feasted. The reason of this strange enthusiasm for people formerly regarded as detestable is this: –

It was the third hour of a spring day. The season of the latter rains was past, but the land was still green and flowery. The sun beat down upon the village, making the palm-leaves high in air quiver in a swimming haze of heat. The children of Sulfoon, both boys and girls – half-naked, brown-skinned, dusty, with blue beads strung round their necks as a charm against the power of evil – were playing in the narrow pathway which meanders through the village, serving at once the purposes of roadway, dust-heap and general gutter.

The game could hardly be called scientific. It could not be said to have a beginning, a middle, or end. They were pelting each other furiously with dry camel's dung and other refuse, shouting and screaming all the while as if their very lives depended on it. Now and then a dismal howl of pain would be raised as some well-aimed missile struck one of the players full in the face, blinding him or her for the moment; and the friends of the victim would attempt a strong reprisal.

Foremost in the fray was Ahmed, son of Mustafa. Being nearly nine years old – the oldest boy engaged in the skirmish – he showed his manhood and superiority by smothering every girl who came within his range with dirt. His father had ridden away to Jaffa at sunrise, upon an ass, together with a load of tobacco leaves to be sold to the Régie[35]; his mother and his elder sister were at work in the fields; and Ahmed had begun his holiday by kicking his little sister, Lulu, aged three – it was lucky that Mustafa was far away at Jaffa, for Lulu was the apple of his eye – until she roared with pain, then rolling her over and over in the dust and refuse of the roadway and filling her mouth with offal just to stop her noise. Some neighbours coming to her rescue, he had fled to the maize-fields, and there lay hidden till the storm was overpast.

The present game was very much to Ahmed's mind, for, being bigger than the rest, he could torment them freely. He had just succeeded in making one little girl cry by a well-aimed blow on the mouth, and was in the act of throwing

[35] The Ottoman government had a monopoly on the production and marketing of tobacco, organised through the Régie Company. The company had collection points in towns near where tobacco was cultivated.

a great clod of filth at a very small boy, naked, save for a battered and tasselless fez, who had ventured to remonstrate with him for so doing, when the clatter of approaching hoofs alarmed the swarm of them, and the clod fell from his hand. Two Frankish horsemen were just entering the village.

"Dogs of unbelievers!" muttered Ahmed, with clenched teeth.

The other children fled in terror, every one to his or her own doorway, but Ahmed stood his ground. He was almost a man, he considered, and knew well how a man should act at such a juncture.

The horsemen were both clad in white coats, white riding-breeches, and brown top-boots. The one wore a pith helmet and a puggery[36], the other a broad-brimmed felt hat. Ahmed had seen their like once before when he had been to Jaffa with his father. They were Franks, unbelievers, and accursed.

He of the pith helmet held a white rag to his nose as he rode. Ahmed, who knew nothing of the use of a pocket-handkerchief, saw something sinister in this behaviour. The two were chattering together in an unknown tongue, and their voices sounded deep down in their throats, not in their mouths like those of human beings.

"Surely," thought the boy, "they utter cruel spells against us, and the rag which he holds up to his pig's snout is an evil charm."

He shrank close up to the mud wall to let them pass, his bare feet finding a soft warm cushion in the sun-baked refuse, and clutched at his blue beads for protection. Then he stooped and, picking up a large stone with jagged edges from the pathway, flung it after them, murmuring the proper curses for such heathen dogs.

The stone struck one of the two horses; and the rider – he of the pith helmet – had for a moment all that he could do to keep his seat, and at the same time save his legs from being crushed against the walls, as the horse kicked and plunged in that narrow place. Ahmed grinned with delight, and was just bending down to seek another stone more useful for his purpose, which was their destruction, when he was aware of the horseman in the broad-brimmed hat riding towards him threateningly with whip upraised. The boy stood still; his arms hung helpless with dismay. Could the dog, the unbeliever, who only existed in the world by sufferance, be about to whip him, a good Muslim, in his own village, in a Muslim land? – to whip him for vindicating the honour of his religion in the orthodox way? The mere thought filled him with such horror

[36] Otherwise puggaree, as spelt in the story *The Tale of a Camp*. A muslin scarf hanging from the back of a pith helmet to shelter the nape of the neck from the sun.

and disgust that he began to howl and scream, "Ya Muslimîn[37]!" even before he felt the wicked lash curl lovingly around his bare brown limbs. It stung like ten thousand hornets.

At the first touch of the whip Ahmed threw himself face downward upon the ground, writhing, and shrieking in an ecstasy of pain – the pain he was going to feel. And he lay there still writhing, howling, and cursing, long after the Frank had made an end of thrashing him. The music of his anguish brought out haggard, slovenly women and a few old men from the hovels, and penetrating even to the maize and tobacco-fields, caused the workers there to throw aside their tools and hurry to the place of torment in alarm.

A crowd barred either end of the narrow way, and a sound of muttered curses filled the air. The stranger took in the position at a glance, and motioned to his friend, who seemed much frightened, to draw close to him.

"That will teach thee to show some courtesy to strangers, son of a dog!" he cried, in much better Arabic than Ahmed was used to hear. Then, turning his horse, he rode up to the larger and more angry crowd of villagers.

"Bring hither the sheykh of the village," he commanded.

The men glanced furtively at one another. This was certainly some great one by his tone, perhaps even a consul – one with whose doings it is not well to meddle. He spoke as if the world belonged to him. Yet none was found to answer or obey.

"Bring hither the sheykh of the village, and that quickly, sons of a dog, or it shall be the worse for you!" the Frank insisted sternly, without anger.

This was indeed a great one. Nobody who had not the security of high position would dare to call men "sons of a dog" in their own village, and he alone with but one follower. No doubt he had armed servants – soldiers – close at hand.

An old man in a long and ancient cloak of camel's hair, and a turban conspicuous by its extreme filth, stepped forward.

"I am the sheykh of the village," he said gruffly. "What may your Honour want with me?" His eyes were bold.

"Come hither, then, and hold my horse's bridle," said the Frank.

"Your Honour wishes to dismount here? He is welcome," said the sheykh, with a short laugh. "We are much ennobled. Here, some one hold the bridle for his Honour!"

---

37 O Muslims.

"Dog! Darest thou disobey me? Come quickly and hold the bridle in thine own hand," cried the Frank, in a voice of thunder, at the same time grasping the revolver in his belt.

The sheykh obeyed, cringing, and the stranger dismounted with a sigh of vast relief.

"We've won the day!" he shouted to his friend in English. "Bluff goes a long way in this land."

He glanced disdainfully at the downcast faces of the villagers – one of whom rushed forward with extreme servility to help the other stranger to alight – and proceeded quietly to fill and light his pipe. There is nothing which so awes an ignorant, half-savage people as perfect self-possession, and that state of quality is best exhibited in the deliberate filling and lighting of a briar pipe.

"Bring two stools and some water. My friend and I are tired and thirsty," he remarked at length superbly, when his pipe was going.

The order being given to no one individual, at least a dozen men sped upon the errand. The number of stools and pitchers brought was overwhelming. When the strangers had made their choice and seemed contented, two of the fellâhîn led the horses off to a shady place. While the rest of the villagers stood round at a respectful distance, whispering together, with eyes intent on the unlooked-for guests.

Little Ahmed, who had retired to his own doorway for safety, was receiving condign punishment at the hands of his mother. His monotonous wail – there was none of the luxury of pain now, for the situation was far from romantic – caused two lean pariah dogs to howl in sympathy.

"Quite a concert – eh, Jim?" said the self-possessed one, removing the pipe from his mouth for a second.

"I must say I think you were rather too hard on the little rascal," answered the other, a little reproachfully. "You needn't have leathered into him quite so hard. He's catching it pretty hot at again this moment, I fancy, and two hidings in ten minutes is a bit too strong for such a little chap."

The self-possessed one gave a most portentous wink, and went on smoking placidly in face of the villagers, now and then giving his moustache a twirl to add to the ferocity of his appearance. The fellâhîn were chattering together in low tones, and seemed to be getting excited, though no longer in a manner hostile to the Franks.

At length the sheykh stepped forward, bowing almost to the ground, and laying hand to heart and lips and brow. Would his Excellency, whose mere presence in the house was of more value than many medicaments, before whose face disease was wont to flee affrighted – a doubtful compliment to the Frank's mind, this last – deign to look upon his little son, who even now, alas! was lying at the point of death?

"What does he say?" inquired the stranger in the pith helmet.

His companion translated. "In these out-of-the-way villages," he explained, "almost the only Europeans they ever see are medical missionaries, so they look upon us all as doctors, more or less."

The sheykh's shifty little eyes, meanwhile, were wandering from one to the other anxiously.

"I am no doctor, old man," announced the stranger of the broad-brimmed hat in Arabic. "Of what use could it be that I should look upon thy sick child?"

The villagers looked at each other, upon that, and smiled. "The great are ever thus," they murmured knowingly. "They must be bathed in a very sea of flattery ere they will grant a poor man's boon. Now we know in truth that he is a very great physician."

"I know well that I and all my people are as dirt before your Excellency," whined the sheykh in servile ecstasy, tears trickling down his cheeks. "Trample on us an if please thee. We are all thy servants. Yet it is but a small thing that I ask. Do but honour the ground by treading on it so far as to the doorway of my house, do but look upon my son and speak one word of healing, for one word from the mouth of such an one is worth all medicine."

"Thou art an ass and the son of an ass," replied the Frank, after a moment's silence. "Yet, since thou needs must have it so, I will look upon thy child that is sick. But I have told thee I am no doctor but a plain man, the words of whose mouth have no power or authority more than thine own."

The villagers indulged in shouts of "Praise to Allah". The sheykh girt up his loins and ran to show the way.

"You don't mind stopping where you are and keeping an eye on the horses, do you, Jim?" the supposed doctor called back to his friend of the pith helmet.

The house of the sheykh was larger than the other hovels of the place and its walls were almost entirely of stone. It stood at the north-west corner of the village, with its face towards Carmel. A giant palm-tree, a landmark for miles round, rose before the door.

In the low door-way, sheltered from the sun's glare, a young woman was sitting kneading dough in an earthen pan. She was dirty like the place, but quite good-looking, though her eyes were tired and anxious. She rose, drawing her veil across her face, as the sheykh, her husband, bade her praise the Highest for his mercies. Bade her look with thankfulness upon the greatest doctor upon earth, who with a word was going to heal their son. The crowd of villagers – men, women, and children – which had followed to the house, gathered by the threshold watching with eager curiosity the movements of the Frankish doctor.

It was some time before the stranger's sight became accustomed to the shadow of the room. The wooden shutters of the window were fast closed. A single bar of light, shed from the open door, seemed from without to traverse solid darkness.

But by degrees he saw the four walls, the cooking utensils scattered here and there about the floor, a heap of dirty cushions and coverings in a corner, and – in the darkest nook of all, on a rough couch, of which the squalor and discomfort made him shudder – the sick boy.

He drew near and bent over the child. A cloud of flies rose from around the bed as he did so. It was evident that they distressed the sufferer, for he moaned and tossed continually, as they settled here and there upon his face and body. The air of the room was foul, compounded of a thousand stifling odours.

The Frank stepped to the window and flung apart the crazy wooden shutters with a bang. A draught of warm sweet air refreshed the room. Then he turned to the sheykh.

"Listen, O man," he said. "Thy son will die, unless thou move him quickly to some cleaner place. The foulness of this village would bring sickness even to an ox."

The sheykh shrugged up his shoulders, spreading out his hands in deprecation.

"The village is your Excellency's – that is known! – to do with it even as he shall think fit. If it is his will that the whole place be destroyed, it is destroyed, and that immediately. All that is understood. Only let him speak the word of healing for my son!"

The stranger turned away with an impatient gesture.

"O thou ass!" he said. "I told thee at the first that I was no doctor, yet will I speak one word of power for thy son's health. Send thy child at once to Jaffa, to the English hospital there, and his life may yet be saved."

"To hear is to obey," bowed the sheykh, with evident insincerity, "but I am a poor man, and hospitals are for the rich. Moreover, it is a long way and my son would die upon the journey. Let your Excellency but name some medicine for the boy, and he will be cured without trouble or cost. It is an easy thing to do, for one like thee."

"Aye, medicine, it is medicine that he needs – and charms!" came in chorus from the group about the threshold."

"I have spoken," said the Frank severely, making towards the door. "It is my last word, and I repeat it. Send thy son to the hospital at Jaffa if thou hast a mind to save his life. It will cost thee nothing."

He was already at the threshold, and the villagers had drawn aside to let him pass, when the woman of the house, who had till then been crouching down beside her child, sprang after him and stopped him, clutching at his raiment. As he turned in anger, she flung herself upon the ground and clasped his feet.

"O Khawâjah, save him! Save him!" she implored. "He is my only child!"

The Frank stood still a moment, looking down at her. The girl's face – she was but a girl in years – was as the face of an angel pleading with him. Conscious of something like a lump in his throat he turned back into the room and once more confronted the sheykh. "As I have told thee many times already, I am not a doctor," he repeated. "But hear what I shall do. I go hence direct to Jaffa, and I will send a doctor hither to attend thy child this evening ere the sun sets."

"But your Excellency may forget!" the sheykh objected. "He has many weighty matters in his mind. It is a small thing. Let him but speak."

"I shall not forget. I have given my word as an Englishman," said the stranger, stepping forth into the sunlight. As he turned the corner of the house, the agonized shrieks of the woman filled his ears. She was calling down curses on his head, because he had refused to cure her child.

"It is a pretty place," he said, five minutes later, turning in his saddle for a last view of Sulfoon. The two horsemen were crossing a dry wady some five hundred yards from the foot of the knoll on which the village stands.

"A filthy, dirty place," said his companion, "and a nest of scoundrels into the bargain."

But the supposed doctor had forgotten the dirt and squalor. He was thinking of the face of the woman as she lay at his feet; and his backward glance found the village fair enough, with its grey-brown dwellings and its tapering palms, standing out against a background of blue distant mountains.

"One touch of nature!" he remarked, half to himself. "If these people were not such confounded humbugs one would feel more inclined to do things for them. That woman's grief was genuine at any rate. Lucky there happens to be a medical man staying at the hotel with nothing to do. You should take a general view of things, Jim," he added, with a laugh to his companion, "and of people too, for that matter. Details are apt to be disheartening."

The day wore on, and the dark shadow of the palm-tree before the sheykh's house lengthened slowly eastward. The sick child tossed and moaned upon the squalid couch within. And his every moan struck as it were a blow upon his mother's heart.

"A curse upon the Frankish unbeliever!" said the sheykh to his cronies, as they squatted in a circle on a grassy mound, a stone's throw from the village, shaded by an ancient carob-tree. "Would we have stoned him when he beat the boy Ahmed – the poor, ill-used one! – with his whip. My son – my only son, the hope of my house, will die. And he could have saved him with a word – may his tongue be plucked out by the roots."

"He promised to send a doctor from Jaffa, before the hour of the sun's setting," said a young man, who was leaning with his back against the gnarled trunk of the tree. "It is possible that he may keep his word."

"Thou art a fool, O Abdullah, and devoid of judgment!" quoth the sheykh contemptuously. "Never since thy birth hast thou shown any intellect. I tell thee that the sun will sooner forget the hour of his setting than a rich man will remember his word, pledged to one that is poorer than he."

"But," Abdullah persisted, "I have heard men say in the city, even in Jaffa, that the word of an Englishman is not as the word of the son of an Arab, or as the word of other nations of the Franks."

"Be silent," roared the sheykh. "Thy talk is folly. The people of the city are all liars, and invent such stories to make game of countrymen. Their fathers were like that before them – all defiled prevaricators! Abu Nabbût has said – and the words are written up above his fountain, at the entering in of the city, among the gardens – 'Cursed is the man that chooseth him a friend from among the men of Jaffa'. And thou, Abdullah, puttest faith in their inventions! The promise of a rich man to a poor is the same all the world over. Why should this Frank keep his word, more than another? He merely said the thing. He did not swear by any of his idols. Is it his son that is ill, I ask you all? No, he is gone – may the curse of God pursue him! – and the matter has passed from his mind. He is not a fool that he should burden his thoughts with the sorrows and concerns of strangers. My son – my only son – will die, when a word might have saved him! Allah! Allah!"

So the day wore on, and sun hung lower and ever lower over the western sea, and the hues of the land grew warmer and more ruddy, and the shadows ever longer to the eastward. And men shouted cheerily one to another, for the time of toil and heat was past, and the coolness of evening was on all the land.

A noise of hoof-beats sounded in the village.

"It is Mustafa, the father of Ahmed, who returns from the city," said the sheykh.

"Perchance it is the Frankish doctor," said Abdullah, the pig-headed.

An ass, staggering beneath the weight of two sacks, and its master appeared in the narrow way between the hovels. Abdullah was proved wrong, for it was Mustafa's ass, and Mustafa himself, clothed in his striped cloak of camel's hair, brown and white, and the portentous turban he had worn for twenty years, was seated sideways on it, with his bare legs dangling almost to the ground.

"Didst thou pass any Frank on the way, O father of Ahmed?" cried Abdullah, running down to greet him.

"What have I to do with Franks?" retorted Mustafa, dismounting, and preparing further to unburden the much-burdened beast. "And as for passing one of them – they ride upon horses, and that furiously! It is not an easy thing for one that rides an ass to pass them in the way."

"Is it not even as I said?" cried the sheykh, when Abdullah returned to him. "Thou art a fool. Thou wast born and thou wilt surely die in the pursuit of folly. The word of a rich man to one that is poor is the same all the world over! That is known. Behold! It is the hour of sun-set, and the physician has not come! My son will die!"

Even as he spoke the sun's rim dipped below the western horizon, and an amethyst hue suffused the eastern sky. One-half of the village glowed as red as fire, the other was in shadow, black as night.

"It is the hour of the evening meal," said the sheykh, and he rose with intent to go to his own house for supper.

One-half of the sun's disk was below the horizon. The shadows of the palm-trees stretched far away towards the mountains.

"I hear the sound of hoofs," exclaimed Abdullah.

Even as he spoke, a European horseman came in sight, followed by a native servant with two laden mules.

"Where is the sheykh of the village?" cried the new-comer, "he whose son lies at death's door? Show my servant some good place where he can pitch the tent. Where is the sheykh, I ask you? Does his son yet live?"

The Frank poured forth his stream of mingled question and command, with the rapidity of one who has no time to waste.

A great awe took possession of the fellâhîn. Here was a strange thing indeed, a rich man in a hurry! Still more strange, he was in a hurry on another's business. They stood staring at the prodigy, with mouths agape.

"I cannot wait here all night," said the physician irritably. "I am an English physician, and I have come to tend the sheykh's son who is sick. The Englishman who was here to-day has sent me. Guide me to the house of the sheykh, one of you!"

The word "physician" roused the sheykh out of the state of torpor into which the awful energy of the stranger and the rapidity of the latter's speech had plunged him. "The western sky is still red with the sun-setting," he shouted, waving his arms wildly. "A rich man has kept his word to me that am poor! Surely the end of all things is at hand!" And he ran before the doctor to the door of his own house.

Late that night, when the great stars were beating in the sky, and the sick child was peacefully asleep upon a camp-bed in the doctor's tent, the men of the village sat and spoke together at the foot of the tall palm-tree before the house of the sheykh which looks towards Carmel. And they swore a mighty oath that they, and their sons, and their sons' sons would never suffer a Frank to pass by Sulfoon unchallenged, and, if he proved to be an Englishman, unfeasted.

And, at this day, when the men of Sulfoon wish to bind themselves to some performance solemnly, they swear by the "Word of an Englishman," which is as the word of Allah – "faithful to rich and poor alike".

THE JUST STEWARD

This story first appeared in Tales from Five Chimneys, published in June 1915. In his early wanderings Pickthall had travelled around the Shuf area of Lebanon, lying south of the Damascus-Beirut highway and homeland to the Druze. Indeed, according to Oriental Encounters he nearly bought a property there. He knew the Druze chieftain, Jumblat, and his home in Mukhtara and the description of the Druze chief's reception room could be based on his memories of that.

"Go to thy house, O sheykh! Return not hither till I send for thee."

His lordship's steward heard the order as a thunder-clap. The words reverberated in his brain and deafened him, while lightnings came and went before his eyes. His stupefaction was reflected on a hundred bearded faces, for the hall was lined with dark-cloaked, turbaned Druzes come to celebrate their chief's rare visit to his mountain home. The note of water falling in a basin of the court without, heard through the doorway, rang of impish laughter. For a space of heart-beats it remained the only sound, its small shrill pipe engrossing the last hall of audience; while all men stared in wonder at the chieftain, who, lolling in the seat of honour, kept his face averted.

The steward had not moved.

"Dost hear me? Go! And give thy books to Câsim!"

It needed that! His books, the pride of his existence, kept so lovingly that not an ill-formed figure or erasure could be found in them, were snatched from him and handed to the town-bred favourite, whose fat, sly face, as he received them, wore a servile grin. The steward understood at last. He bowed before his lord with haughty grace and left the presence with a sweep of flowing robes. At the castle gate, upon the top step of the marble flight which drops from thence to the parade-ground, he paused a moment to survey the village he had ruled for years. It hung beneath the palace like a beard. He heard the groaning of a water-wheel, the clink of a hammer on iron – familiar sound which in a second had become outlandish. Then, passing down the steps to where his horse was tethered, he mounted and rode home by stony ways.

His wife and daughter, struck with wonder at his quick return, were loud in question. He only answered with one word, "Deposed," and, ere the horror could distil in speech, withdrew into a room apart and shut the door.

There, sitting cross-legged, with eyes fixed upon the ground, he reviewed his whole career with perfect clearness. The feat of evocation was a light one for the knowing Druze whose mind had never been obscured by any fumes, whose will was iron from a life's resistance. He was once more a young man, newly married, and wore the turban with a sense of pride. The day was that on which his lord and foster-brother[38], a mere boy newly come to his inheritance, had cried out in the hall of audience, "Ali is my steward," and forthwith embraced him. Once more he felt the tumult of the heart, the upward rush of tears, the strange emotion which those words and that caress had roused in him. He had sworn then, to his conscience, by his father's grave, to prove a faithful servant to that dear one, and there was no doubt but that, in the sequel, he had kept his oath. Never once in all the thirty years of his stewardship, had he robbed his lord of one para, or wittingly allowed another creature to defraud him. Only – and this it must be which had come to the chief's ears – filling so high a post, which all men deemed remunerative, he had been forced to put on airs of fraud for self-protection. At first, when they beheld in him an honest man – that is, for all men's minds, a simple fool – he had been assailed on every side by clever rascals. By the sole expedient of assuming looks of guile, of giving signs of greater wealth than could be come by honestly, had he at last succeeded in shaking off such pests. When once convinced that he was as rapacious as themselves, they thought him cleverest where all were clever, since no one could divine the manner of his fraud. Thus he enjoyed high honour on the mountain-side and came in time to prize that honour for its own sake, as his best possession, apart from any thought of its foundation. It was the loss of all respect, the fall to ignominy, when men came to realize that he was poor, after thirty years' manipulation of a princely fortune, which appalled him in this moment of his fall. For he had no savings. He had even borrowed money in his need to entertain the notion of ill-gotten wealth in neighbours' minds. His son had received the costly education of a doctor because it was the mode for well-born youths to study medicine; while two of his daughters, thanks entirely to his reputation, were married to young men of rank and property. The youngest, still remaining in the house, was in a

[38] Meaning they had shared the same wet-nurse as infants, thereby forging a close relationship.

week to have espoused a wealthy chieftain of the second rank. That honourable match would now be broken off. His girl would be with scorn rejected by the bridegroom's house when they beheld him poor after such opportunities – a pitiful, deluded fool in all men's sight. Grief for his darling goaded him to think: "There is still hope. Could I but see my lord alone, one minute, all would be explained."

"Return not hither till I send for thee."

The stern command was like an iron hand upon his breast. His active brain sought how he might evade it favourably. His child was much beloved of the chief's wife and daughter. There was a way to reach the hearing of his lord.

Opening the door of the room, he called his wife, who came lamenting, asking details of the great calamity. When he had told her all, she cried: "Alas, our honour! Alas, the glory of this house, our honour! Thou art poor. Without the money of thy office, we are dirt for all men."

"In sh'Allah, there is yet a chance," he told her. "Let Sa'adeh hasten to the presence of the ladies; let her kiss their feet and say that I am innocent of all offence; whatever has been told my lord I can explain. The ladies love our house; they will make prayer for me to be admitted to a private audience of my lord. That only let her ask – a minute's private audience."

"She goes at once," his wife replied, with zeal.

The day wore on, and friends and neighbours poured in to console with him. Their tone was very reverential, for they thought him rich as ever. Many of the Knowing[39] expressed indignation because the person chosen to succeed their friend was of the Ignorant, a town-bred oaf, a smoker and a winebibber, whose elevation to the post of steward was of bad example. They endeavoured to bring comfort to Sheykh Ali, saying: "As for thee, it is no matter, but a mere affront. Thou hast enjoyed the place so many years, and thou art skilled, none like thee, in the way of business. It is simply to withdraw a crutch from one long healed of lameness."

The old man bit his lip at such remarks, but smiled and gave due praise to Allah for his boundless mercy. His mind was not with them, but with his daughter at the castle.

At length the servant brought the longed-for summons.

"Praise be to God," cried the Sheykh Ali, rising. "My friends, I must leave you for an hour. Budge not, I beg of you. Be seated. Take your ease. My house is yours."

---

[39] A section of the Druze who have been given access to the mysteries of the religion, in contrast to the Ignorant.

His horse – a fiery black stallion – was at the door already saddled. His friends, as from the archway of the house they watched him mount and ride away, could not consider him a ruined man, beholding him astride of such a charger, attended by a well-dressed servant, also mounted. Above dim olive-groves and shadowy orchards, where white-washed dwellings shone out blue amid the twilight, the upper windows of the palace flashed the sun-set, which reddened the bare mountain side above. The chief came seldom to his mountain home. He loved the life of cities where men learn distrust and lose remembrance of the strength of old affection. He had forgotten that his steward here at home was still his foster-brother; the same Ali who had held him in the saddle when he learnt to ride, who had tried to keep him from debauch as he grew up; a man more strongly bound to him by love than interest. This, if once made plain to his intelligence, would change his Honour's views, thought the old servant as he rode up to the old castle, through the village.

The chief received him in an upper chamber. He did not rise to greet him from the divan where he sat, nor manifest the least emotion on his entrance, beyond a little movement of impatience when his hand was kissed.

"Well," he observed. "What is it that thou hast to tell me, of such moment? My daughter lay open the ground and clasped my feet, in tears, till I consented to receive thee from the simple need to move. Be brief, I beg, for I return to-morrow to the city, and have much to see to ere I go. The people here are like a plague of flies. From the moment I arrive they never leave me."

"To-morrow!" gasped Sheykh Ali in dismay, the purpose of his visit clean forgotten in a twinkling. "O my dear lord, it is a sin for thee to haste away. Here all men love thee for the sake of thy father and thy father's father – all thy noble race! They guard thee as the banner of their pride. Yonder in the city, canst thou find such loyalty? There men cringe and flatter thee for selfish ends."

"Wonderful!" exclaimed the chief satirically. "Thou art here upon thy trial, and still scoldest me! Will nothing teach thee policy, friend Ali? Thy business, I beseech thee, for I have no time to waste."

Casting himself upon the ground, the aged steward then poured out his story in heart-broken tones. He told his lord the truth, how he had never robbed him, how he had but assumed the mask of guile in self-defence.

The chieftain scoffed: "A pretty tale, but little to the purpose, O Beloved, because my grievance is not that thou hast defrauded – Allah forbid that one with wealth like mine should grudge his servants and his folk their gleanings – but that thou dost make boast of peculation, real or feigned; that, while so boasting, thou dost treat me like a naughty child, presuming even to refuse me my own money – thou knowest, that has happened more than once – when the purpose for which I happened to require it failed to satisfy thy high morality. I do not ask for restitution of one small para; I seek for no account of thy past dealings. I simply take another steward, who will be my servant, not my tutor. Come, Ali, we are brothers by the bond of milk, and I have always had a love for thee. I did wrong – I now confess it heartily – to speak to thee in wrath this morning as I did. I have no quarrel with thee, O my dear one. Go in peace!"

"Alas, my honour! O my lord, consider! Behold me henceforth dung in all men's sight."

"Thy honour!" laughed his lord. "Pray, what is that? Honour, thou sayest! Is not mine of some account? Was it pleasant for me, think you, to hear people saying: 'Behold him. He is but the sheep of the Sheykh Ali. See how our wise Sheykh Ali feeds and shears him?' No, go thy way, old friend, without more words. I have another steward, but I do not hate thee. God grant in spite of all thy protestations that thou hast filched a fortune from me to make glad thine age."

Stupefied by this revelation of an attitude of mind, which had never in his life before occurred to him as possible for man to take, Sheykh Ali left the presence, groping, as one blind. When he reached his house again, it was already night. His wife and daughter, hearing that his errand had been fruitless, wailed aloud. The former clung to him, imploring:–

"Publish not the truth – at least to-night. Let us preserve our honour for a few hours longer. Some way out from this pit of woe may yet be opened. Say nothing at the meeting, I entreat thee. It is nearly time to start."

In his trouble the Sheykh Ali had forgotten that a meeting of the Knowing Ones was to take place that night at the old stone Khalweh[40] in the pine-wood on the mountain-side above the village. Doing his best to banish worldly cares, he made haste with his ablutions, and set forth beside his wife (who also was of Those Who Know) on foot and wrapped in silent meditation.

The Khalweh in the pine-wood, a cube-shaped building on the pattern of a tomb in that it had no windows and so low a doorway that people had to crouch to enter, was furnished inside like a common room except that on one wall was scrawled a rough presentment of a calf, the emblem of false guidance and of wrong belief linked intimately with the secret history of their race. It was depicted there for malediction at appointed seasons. Four goodly candles set in brazen sconces gave what light there was, and alone in all the building smacked

[40] A building set apart for meetings of Druze elders, the Knowing.

of luxury. When all the Knowing – fifty persons of both sexes – had arrived, the door was shut by one who stood in readiness.

"The door is shut," an aged man intoned. Another answered: "Of a truth the door is shut, from centuries behind us to the end. The number is complete and changes not. May God have pity on the Ignorant who, born upon the threshold, may not enter. The curse of God rest ever upon those without."

Then the Sheykh who had first spoken took in his hand an ancient manuscript, and proceeded to expound a chapter of those wondrous Scriptures which seem as nonsense to the uninitiated. In that assembly, rich and lettered men were mixed with ragged labourers and simple women; for wealth and poverty, learning and its opposite, are only products of some chance, are outward things. Here all were equal, having passed the crucial tests enjoined by a religion glorifying force of character even at the expense of what the devotees of outward faiths call righteousness; all were proud, the pride of an exclusive race enforced in every case by stern asceticism.

While the Sheykh Ali sat and listened to the words of meaning, his mind found rest, intent on inward things. But when the talk came round to tidings of the day, his anguish was renewed. They spoke of him with praise as a true Unitarian[41], a credit to the circle of the Knowing, one who had carved an independence out of honourable service without scandal, as behoved a man; of his successor as a lewd fellow and a winebibber, a fool to boot, who had not sense enough to hide his triumph with a mask of care. They spoke of the approaching marriage of his daughter as of a festival to which they all looked forward.

"All is from God," he murmured, for the congregation, fending off their curiosity with pious phrases and misleading smiles. At that moment he beheld himself as nothing, the splendour of the name which he had made as all.

It was then, as he sat there, acutely suffering, painfully conscious of his wife's imploring gaze, that a plan which seemed miraculous occurred to him and with it a sensation of intense relief. He brightened then, and played his part without an effort.

Once more in his own house he showed his wife the project he had formed. It was to go next morning to the city, to their son the doctor, and confide in him. With his help it should be possible to raise a sum of money sufficient to give Sa'adeh a splendid wedding such as would be talked of on the mountain-side for years. That done, his wife and he would simply vanish.

"Our Lord reward thee!" was the woman's comment. "To die in one place and be reborn in new surroundings is but the course of every one beneath the

[41] In this context, a believer in the One-ness of God.

sun. It is no hardship, and we save our honour. I could not bear the pity of former friends."

The story they would tell the neighbours was that, tired of innovations and the spread of Frankish manners, Sheykh Ali, having seen his daughter married, would emigrate to that more distant mountain[42] where the customs of the race survived in all their vigour. Their daughter would of course cry out to share their exile. She must be told some portion of the truth, and bidden to keep silence for their house's honour.

The couple sat up talking till the dawn appeared, and a bird chirruped in the shadows of the garden. Next morning, when the chieftain left the castle in his carriage with outriders, attendants, and a lively company, the Sheykh Ali, riding his black stallion, saluted and begged leave to join his train.

"Praise be to Allah, thou no longer frownest!" came the laughing answer; and the sheykh was bidden ride beside the carriage at his lord's right hand.

Arriving in the city, the Sheykh Ali stabled his horse at a khan and thence went straight to his son's lodgings. The young man was within. They spoke with heads together for an hour, the phrase "the honour of our house" recurring often in their conversation. Then the son rushed out to borrow money where he could; the father strolled into the markets to procure rich stuff for gifts, and delicacies for his daughter's wedding feast. That night they reckoned up the sum available. It was enough to leave Sheykh Ali's name a byword for profuse expenditure. Both took a childish pleasure in the thought.

Returning on the morrow to the mountain village the Sheykh announced a sale of all his property; which, he said, should be delivered to the purchasers on the day succeeding that on which his girl departed for the bridegroom's house. His wife had noised abroad his wish to emigrate, and, none suspecting his real need for money, he obtained good prices.

"It is natural," said the neighbours, "he should wish to go. It stabs his soul to see another in his place. He is rich and independent. It is sure he desires some place where he can enjoy without a pang the dignity to which his wealth entitles him; where none will call him the discarded steward."

To show their sympathy the neighbours made good bidding for his goods, and with the money thus received he paid all debts to his own race, and added something to the splendour of the wedding feasts.

Those feasts began, upon a scale unheard of in the mountains. From the evening when the bridegroom's cavalcade arrived to claim the bride and were entreated to remain a week, a year; when the first guns were fired and strains

---

[42] Jebel Druze, in what today is southern Syria. The area is also called Hauran.

of music heard; until the end, old friends and neighbours held their breath and almost worshipped, awed by the vision of Sheykh Ali's wealth. They would have given him their souls to keep, for honour. They praised his name like courtiers round a king. Gold flowed from him; he scattered presents broadcast as housewives fling out grain to fowls, yet without arrogance. The courteous word and modest mien were his. Each costly gift was made more precious by the compliment which told of friendly thought for the receiver.

As for his wife, her pride in this display was feverish and so acute as to resemble pain. She moaned at thought of the approaching end, which seemed like death itself, yet when Sheykh Ali murmured weakly of abandoning their plan of flight through tenderness for her, she stormed at him. How could she face the neighbours when they knew her poor? This final triumph made it quite impossible. Having put her foot upon their necks this once for all, she could endure the scorn of strangers; of these, never! She told him conversations she had overheard: how one old friend was thankful he was going; another called his wealth his only virtue, bereft of which he would have been a thievish dog. Moreover, she informed him how the bridegroom's father, who paid him such distinguished honour now, had two days since made strict inquiries of his fortune.

It was upon these revelations that Sheykh Ali cried:–

"The Hauran is too near! I will discard them utterly. Let us journey to some place remote from all our tribe; to some great city where a man is lost in multitude as a single grain of sand on the seashore; where our own children shall not know our hiding-place, lest from that knowledge shame adhere to them."

His wife, for prudence, murmured: "Is that wise? Thou hast good introductions to the great ones of the Hauran, sufficient to secure thee honour, even though destitute."

"The tidings of our plight would travel thence to wound our daughter in her honoured home," answered the Sheykh. "Her husband and his people would revile her. No, by Allah! We will hide us in the city of the Muslims."

After some argument his wife agreed. Even death itself appeared to her less dreadful than to face the pity of those neighbours who had graced her triumph.

The rejoicings lasted for three days; upon the morning of the fourth, the bride, in tears, was carried from her father's house, the bridegroom's cavalcade escorting her. The people of the village sped them on their way, men firing guns into the air, and women giving forth their joy-cry. And then great silence fell upon Sheykh Ali's house. The old man and his wife sat still, and thought together, until the neighbours came requiring farewell ceremonies, when they nerved themselves to undergo the final ordeal.

All was done correctly. When questioned why he took so little luggage, the Sheykh replied that much would be a needless burden, since he could purchase all things needful at his journey's end. His fortune, he informed his hearers gravely, had been confided to a banker of Damascus, who secured him credit until such time as he could place it out anew. He answered every question proffered with such candour, that none suspected any secret in his going.

When they left the place next morning in a hired carriage, with no more luggage than a bundle on the seat before them, the couple were escorted by a noisy crowd, which, after running by their side and after them for quite a mile, at last stood and screamed farewell to them with waving arms. Then they were driven, jolting, for two hours until they came to the Sultan's high road[43], high up upon the mountain-side, commanding miles of fertile plain and coast and sea. There the driver got down off his box and helped them to alight.

"Good time!" he told them. "It wants an hour before the coach will pass." They urged him not to wait. He wept a little and kissed their hands repeatedly before he climbed back to his box; and as he drove away, he returned repeatedly to shout some farewell blessing. When he had passed from sight Sheykh Ali and his wife sat down in the shade of a tree by the wayside; and taking articles of clothing from the bundle, altered their appearance into that of humble Muslims. Then they rose and turned their faces towards the inland city[44], poor people, on the mercy of the Most High.

The woman wept a little at the start, yet walked erect, with a firm, approving hand on the man's shoulder. They were of the Knowing, so had perfect vision of the vanity of all they weakly mourned.

"It is but as reincarnation, a new birth," the woman said, when she had grieved awhile. "The gloom and pangs of death, and then fresh light and youth."

"Aye," said Sheykh Ali, "and so life turns for ever like an endless wheel. We die to-day, but we are reborn instantly, although no memory remains of what we were. To be able to relinquish all things without sorrow is but to show obedience to the will of our Exalted Lord."

After two days of patient travel, they came into the city of the Muslims, the city of warm hearts and courtly manners; where men blessed them as at setting out from home, but for another reason. There it had been their wealth that called forth kindness, here their apparent poverty moved every heart. A man, the first to whom they made appeal, showed them a ruinous old house where they could live for nothing, and helped the Sheykh to find some light employment.

---

[43] The Beirut to Damascus highway.

[44] Damascus.

They lived a life devoid of actual hardship, received by all around them as true Muslims, observing every practice of a religion which they scorned, in obedience to the injunctions of their higher faith; for all religions are but painted cloaks, the Knowing say, which those who bear the truth in mind may don and throw aside as seems expedient. They were not discontented, although too old to find enjoyment in new habits. They longed sometimes for the communion of the Knowing, for the talk and ways of thought of their own folk. The Sheykh believed that there were other Druzes in the city. His eyes were ever watchful of the passing crowd and, if he saw a man's face of a certain type, he put this question casually to some passer-by: –

"Do they sow the seed of Halîlaj in your country?"

"The seed of what?" was the amazed reply; at which the old man sighed and turned away to try his question at some other point of concourse, till Halîlaj became his nickname in the markets. But his piety found favour with the Muslims; his probity in every work he undertook, as well as a certain air of grandeur, won him respect. He was appointed door-keeper of the great mosque, and remained in that employment till he died, having survived his wife by just two years. By that time, by his great devotion and austerity, he had earned the reputation of a saint. The Muslims built a shrine above his grave, which people visit who are plagued with evil spirits, for his intercession. His wife is buried in another place among the gardens.

Their worn-out shapes repose in Muslim graves in a strange city; but they themselves in new attire, as children, now feel the sun elsewhere among the chosen of their race.

FATHER SABA

This story first appeared in Tales from Five Chimneys, published in June 1915.

It is a melodramatic tale about lawlessness and intense confessional conflict in Lebanon. Pickthall knew the area well and in the 1890s stayed in a Druze village, fifteen miles south east of Beirut, with a former chaplain to the Anglican Bishop of Jerusalem.

The story, although entitled after the priest turned brigand leader, Father Saba, revolves mainly round his discarded lover, Miriam. She is a spirited and self-willed lady, who determines her own life. Her force of character is indirectly portrayed. She told her husband what to do; he was "accustomed to obedience".

"Open, O my brother! I am the bearer of grave news for thee. The Sheykh Abdullah from the village has come to talk to the Superior. He vows to make an end of thee, for thy misconduct with his wife. Open the door, I say! Why dost thou bolt it? Hast thou a girl inside there?" said a plaintive voice outside the cell.

There followed an eclipse of the light which came through a round hole in the lower part of the door as the visitor knelt down and put his eye to it.

The inmate of the cell threw down the knout he had been wielding, and hastened to conceal his bleeding back beneath his cassock. Unbolting the door, he let in the afternoon sunlight and, haloed in the midst of it, a fellow-monk, a little roundabout man, whose plump form and roguish countenance appeared misplaced beneath the towerlike head-dress, above the severe black raiment, of a religious of the Orthodox Eastern Church. At present he was severe enough, and seemed much frightened on his friend's account.

"May Allah help thee, Saba!" he continued, pushing back the long hair off his ears. "Abdullah swears thou hast been making love to his young wife. Think not I blame thee, O my soul's delight, except for keeping thy good fortune hidden from thy loving comrade. Even now I can hardly believe it; thou hast such a solemn air. I thought thee hardly human. Is it true?"

"By the Cross of our Redemption, by the life of Allah, it is a lie – a filthy lie!" cried Saba with so terrifying a suffusion of his swarthy face, with such a bound of his gigantic frame, that the little monk retreated and began to whine:–

"Be not angry with me, O my dear. Allah witness, I did not believe it. Do I not know thee for a very saint? I only came to give thee warning. Guiltless though thou art, it may go ill with thee; for our father, being a Hellene[45], loves to find fault with us children of the Arabs. It is likely thou wilt be imprisoned for long months with penance. In thy place, O my sweet one, I would fly at once. Thou art not like the rest of us, of no account; thou art the son of a good house. Fly to some of thy relations and abide with them till they can make good terms for thy return. The courtyard is now empty and the gate unguarded; all the brethren are assembled in the prior's anteroom, straining their ears to overhear Abdullah's charge against thee."

"Thy advice is good. I will walk forth and think. Said this Abdullah anything about the girl his wife?" said Saba pensively.

"Ha, ha, dear brother! I do after all suspect thee!" chuckled the little monk, as one eased of a sad load. But one glance from the other's eyes subdued him.

Paying no further heed to his well-wisher, the monk Saba strode out through the vacant courtyard.

His fellows in the convent on the mountain-top had assumed the monastic habit for a lazy life or from a clear vocation; not one of them could see into this man of passion. Profoundly religious and impressionable, tormented by desires, Saba had sought in the cloister a refuge from the violent temptations which assailed him in the world. He stood six foot two in his sandals, and was broadly built; his long black hair grew thick and curly; and his eyes, habitually downcast, showed such fire when raised as secured for him a reverence not all religious.

As he strode now down the mule-path winding in and out of sun-baked rocks, he cursed his shadow leaping there beside him. The road declined so rapidly that the convent was in a minute lost to sight. Nothing but a mass of boulders, stone on stone, was seen above; while below, the rocks sloped steeply to a gorge of depth invisible, beyond which rose another stony height.

Suddenly at a turn, the village came in view; its gardens as a smudge of green upon the mountain-side. The red-tiled roof of the Sheykh Abdullah's house shone forth down there like a carbuncle. To escape the stare of it, which hurt his

[45] Until the beginning of the twentieth century the leadership positions – bishops, priors of monasteries – in the Orthodox church in Greater Syria tended to be held by Greeks, Hellenes.

brain, Saba here left the road and, clambering from stone to stone, attained the shadow of a monstrous rock which hid the village.

The Sheykh Abdullah's young and pretty wife had always smiled to Saba when he passed her door; once, when her husband was away from home, she had invited him up on to the terrace, in the shade of the vine arbour, and there regaled him with choice fruit and sherbet. And he had taken pleasure in her talk, had flushed beneath her gaze of admiration. That was all that had ever passed between them; and for that the monk had flogged himself three times a day until the blood flowed from his shoulders to the ground. To-day he had believed his flesh at last subdued, when the tidings of Abdullah's blundering lie revived the evil. The girl must have said something to arouse her husband's jealousy, something to inform her husband that she loved him (Saba); that was the thought which rose up close before him, like a fire, or like a woman's form with arms outstretched; and when he turned from it and looked back to his cell in thought, it was to see the same temptation waiting there. For if the Superior imposed long penance, as he surely would, that penance would commemorate the sin forgone, and fan the fire within him till it passed endurance.

It seemed as if the fiend had been vouchsafed this hour in which to let loose all seductions and all terrors against the weakest and most tempted of God's servants. The desolate and stony place was full of sensual allurements for the monk. He hid his face in his hands and prayed distractedly; both hands and face were dry and burning hot. For all this agony he had to thank the fool Abdullah – the vulgar, base old man who whined to the Superior of an injury which, if received, could only be washed out in blood. May God destroy him!

Possessed by rage against the man, he sprang up suddenly. After all the best thing he could do – assuredly the last thing that Abdullah would expect or wish – was to go back to the convent instantly, and face his enemy. The righteous anger seething in his brain, if once expressed, would shrivel up the lying charge and him who laid it.

Fired by the prospect of a personal encounter, Saba regained the mule-path, and was proceeding to climb up it towards the convent with great strides, when he heard the voice of some one singing from the rocks above and, looking up, espied a white umbrella moving, then a tarbush and grey turban, a brown face with white moustache – the head and shoulders of his enemy, the Sheykh Abdullah. The old miscreant was trotting homewards, croaking a facetious song and laughing "Ho, ho ho," between the snatches – the laughter of a man who has well trussed his enemy.

The tall monk stood concealed behind a rock, with fingers busy at his neck as if he suffocated. The Sheykh came close upon him suddenly round a bend of the road and started back aghast, all thought of singing as of laughter clean knocked out of his old body.

"May thy day be blest," he murmured lamely, scorched by Saba's blazing eyes. He seemed to shrink in bulk.

"Thou comest from the convent?" questioned Saba huskily. "Did thy errand perchance concern me? If so, here I stand: fulfil it."

The Sheykh Abdullah hesitated for the moment necessary to reflect that the monk was returning from the village, so could not possibly know anything about the scandal of the monastery, before replying:-

"No, by Allah. My errand was to the Superior." Emboldened by the other's presumed ignorance of what had passed, he added slily: "As for thee, thou comest from the village. Did thy errand perchance concern me?"

"Explain thy meaning!" answered Saba very softly.

"Is it not clear to thy intelligence? – Ha! ha! Thou art a handsome youth, none like thee; and a priest too, pledged to discretion. Thou hast thus two passports to a woman's favour. And I am an old man with a young wife. I would not have thee call when I am absent. Do not blame me! – He, he, he!"

The knowing laugh of the old fox drove Saba mad. He felt a cruel taunt in this low jest – he, a religious, bound to sigh in vain and sinfully for all that such a man as this enjoyed in honour. He gave one sob, then sprang.

"Ha, ha! I do but jest!" his foe cried out. But Saba had him off the ground. "Be careful! O my soul! Be gentle with me! I am not a wrestler. Bethink thee, I am very old. I did but jest! Allah knows thou art most welcome any time; my house is thy house, my honour is thy honour, O best, O most benign of men! Help! Help! O Christian people! O good God!"

Saba, having shifted his hold suddenly down to the old man's knees, swung him once in the air, then brought his head down crash upon the nearest rock. He stood for some time, silent, looking down upon his work, shuddering, yet glad the die was cast. He could never now go back to the convent; he could never henceforth hope to rank among the saints; the strife was over.

"Our Lord have mercy on me. He was not a man," he said, as he once more bestirred himself.

Having concealed the body in a crevice of the rocks, the monk walked down the mountain-side till he came near the village, when he turned aside and hid himself in a garden until after dark. At the second hour of the night he stole towards the house of his victim, which stood apart from other houses of the village. There was a light in the wide central archway, he observed, as he approached it by a terrace under olive-trees. He listened for some sound of conversation, but none came. The woman was alone. As he came up the steps into the sphere of lamplight, she rose astonished, laying down some needlework.

"Go! Go, O rash one!" she exclaimed in terror. "What ails thee to come here at such an hour – and on this day of all the days that God has ordered? My husband has gone up to the convent to complain against thee wrongfully. God knows I tried to stop him. He is mad with jealousy. All the neighbours took my part against him yesterday: what will they say to-morrow should he find thee here? He may return this minute. He will kill me. Have I not suffered enough on thy account? – for nothing!"

"That man will not return. I killed him," answered Saba coolly; and after a long pause he added: "Come!"

"What is that thou sayest? Killed him? Thou hast killed him? He is dead? Our Lord have mercy on him!"

Miriam staggered back against the wall. For a long while she said nothing, seeming at the point of death. Then, suddenly, she flung herself on Saba, pleading: "Let me fly with thee! If I remain here they will say thou killedst him on my account, that all he spoke against me was the truth. My brother or my father will destroy me, for the honour of the house. At first sight I desired thee, O my dear; thy soul must know it! Now thou hast killed that teasing devil for me, I am thine till death."

"Come!" said Saba simply. "We cannot stay here."

"Go, conceal thyself until the whole world sleeps; then I will join thee at the cairn beside the road towards Ain Jurâdah. Go, I will not fail."

The time of waiting was not long for Saba. He spent it in pacing slowly up and down a terrace of old fig-trees near the trysting-place, forgetful of his vows, his awful crime, of everything except the woman's love. A sound of hoof-beats drawing near, of stones displaced, made him crouch down for hiding.

"Where art thou, Saba?" he heard Miriam whisper. One minute and he held her in his arms.

"O Saba, I was terrified alone. I know not how I found the courage to set out," she whispered. "See, I have taken thought for both of us! Here is the mule, and all the money I could find is in a leathern bag between my breasts. But, Saba, think: if we should meet with robbers?"

"Fear nothing. Am I not a murderer?"

He lifted her up on the mule and, taking the bridle in his hand, set forward, feeling well content. It meant relief for one who from his birth had fought with devils to yield at last and feel their power behind him. He trudged on through the night without fatigue, the woman speaking to him drowsily from time to time. When daybreak came they were already far from the village and the monastery, following a rough road on the edge of a great chasm, above which woods and fields and villages and towering peaks were seen as a cloud landscape high in air. An hour after sunrise they sat down beneath a group of walnut-trees and partook of the food which Miriam had brought with her; then they went on again along the heights of Kesserawân[46], where in the villages the children, being Maronites, spat at sight of the Orthodox monk, and called out "Heretic!" Soon after noon they found a wayside khan and being very tired, spent the night there.

Thus they journeyed for some days, without direction, living in a kind of dream. The woman was the first to speak the question "Whither?" But Saba had already given thought to it, for he replied: –

"I am not yet quite certain, O my soul; but I think of going to the land of Shûf[47], the Mountain of the Druzes. There dwell many outlaws of our faith, with whom I could associate."

"Outlaws! They dwell in caves, and are hunted like the bears and leopards," pouted Miriam; whereas we have enough to live at ease. Let us rather repair to the town where life is merry. Thou hast but to change thy dress and cut thy hair, and who would ever know thee in a crowd?"

"No, that I will not!" replied Saba flatly.

"Why?" she inquired.

He could not then have told her; the reason being still far from clear in his mind; but already he had begun to feel remorse for his wickedness. His life there in the monastery, his self-chastisement, his anguished prayers, seemed now, as he looked back, desirable. He had an inkling that with men repressed and passionate, the object of desire is so transfigured in imagination that actual contact and possession cannot but bring disappointment. With this great thorn of disillusion in his flesh he could not face the prospect of a life of ease. The twinges of remorse, too, urged him to some course involving risk, excitement and forgetfulness. In hardships and in perils he might expiate his crime, if Allah willed.

He said: "The vows of priesthood are irrevocable. Allah knows I am a priest, and it is useless to hide myself from His gaze. As for the sons of Adam, no one who regards God cares a jot for their opinion."

---

[46] The mountainous area north and north-east of Beirut.

[47] The area to the south of the Damascus-Beirut highway.

"All very fine, no doubt. But what of me?" rejoined the woman. "Could I live happy among savage outlaws?" She protested, however, only in the way of pretty pouting, feeling certain of her sway over the heart of Saba. The man who had committed murder for her sake would not refuse a small boon, if she prayed in earnest. She was therefore in no real anxiety; and when she saw him frown, preoccupied, estranged from her a moment, forbore to harass him with questions or reproaches. It seemed natural that the father of such deeds should have his hours of brooding and remorse at first.

After six days they reached a village in the land of Shûf, where a rich peasant of their own religion made them welcome. Knowing nothing of their history, and taking Saba for a priest allowed to marry, their host felt proud to entertain a holy man. He kept them in his house, where Miriam helped the women, while Saba ranged the mountain on his mule, seeking, as she supposed, some place to dwell in. That recollection preyed upon his mind she guessed, for she had heard him weeping in the night, and knew for certain that he scourged himself in secret. But he did not shun embraces, so she felt secure, believing that in course of time remorse would cease. She was altogether unprepared for the announcement, which he made to her one night, in level tones:-

"Soon I must leave thee, O my soul, though Allah knows how sad the thought of parting makes me. There is a band of outlaws dwelling near this place. I have spoken with their chief; he bids me welcome. My call is to these outcast men, who are as I am; perchance I may do good among them, may even shape them to a weapon Allah's hand will not disdain. It is the one way of atonement. Do thou pray for me, O Miriam, as I shall pray for thee each hour while life endures. God knows how greatly I have wronged thee. To-day I told our story to the master of this house. He has compassion on us, and consents to keep thee in this house so long as thou desirest to remain here. In thy place I would go into a nunnery. They would receive thee. And it is the guarded way. That way is barred henceforth, alas! to me, a sinner."

"May thy father perish!" shrieked Miriam when she could find her voice for rage. "What is this thou sayest, O unnatural malefactor! Leave me thou wouldst, forsooth, and make atonement? As if this crime of leaving me were not the worst! Do what thou wilt, scourge all the flesh from off thy bones, eat dirt, pray day and night with fasting, thou canst never, though thou live a hundred years, atone for that; it is unforgivable by Allah, after what has passed! The money, mind, is mine; thou shalt not have one small piastre of it; and the mule – that too – is mine. Behold thee beggared!"

"Allah knows that I seek nothing from thee save thy prayers!"

"Prayers! Thou shalt have my curses; hear me swear it. May the curse of God be on thee both in this world and the next, O destitute of all compassion. Thou didst kill my husband, thou didst bid me fly with thee: I judged from these things thou didst love me truly; I gave myself to thee, I followed thee to a strange land, and after that thou canst forsake me. Burn eternally! Thou wouldst leave me here alone to bear thy child, with no more hesitation than one has in shaking dust from off one's feet. By the Cross, it is the worst of all thy deeds. Thy fine atonement, thy compunction, shall be vain, I tell thee. Thou shalt suffer the great punishment hereafter, O thou devil!"

Screaming, she flung herself upon the floor, pulling out her hair by the roots and tearing her bosom with her finger-nails. The master of the house, his wife and daughters, came and tried to comfort her, but she repelled them.

"As well now as in the morning," she heard Saba tell them; and then: "May our Lord bless the poor one, and grant us both forgiveness."

Lying half-demented, she did not realize that he had said farewell for ever and gone forth alone into the night. When that knowledge came to her it brought despair. She bit the dust with cries to Allah to restore him. Then, when at length she recognized the vanity of such petitions, a great and righteous hatred of him saved her brain from madness. She resolved to remain where she was, one place being as good as another in which to pray for his destruction. She asked Allah to let her kill him with her own hand – this murderer and seducer, who now played the hypocrite. From an acknowledged saint, a man of holy life, she would have taken her dismissal meekly, she believed; but from that evil-liver – that young monk with passionate eyes, and lovely as the night – it was unpardonable. She hated him as she had loved him, for her own.

In course of time she gave birth to a boy, the care of whom became the object of her lonely life. She sent no word to Saba of the birth, though the master of the house implored her to do so. She never spoke of Saba, letting the world suppose she never thought of him. When a man of substance in the village who had often taken notice of her child, sheepishly asked her to marry him, she consented, as it seemed with pleasure; and she made him a good wife. Yet looking at him sometimes she would think of Saba, as, looking at a monkey, one recalls a man; and never a day passed but she asked Allah to destroy her former lover.

So years passed; till Saba's fame waxed great in all the mountain. He had become the chief of a great company of outlaws, whom he had transformed from vagabonds and petty thieves into an army, for the protection of poor Christians, good or bad, and the punishment of their opponents. He surprised a guard of Turkish troops on the Damascus road and set free twenty convicts who were

Christians. He raided the palace of a Druze Emîr and rescued a young girl, a Christian, whom the infidel had meant to ravish. He even entered cities with his men, in support of Christians, whether innocent or guilty. The whole country rang with his praises. All poor people who were not Mohammedans, looked to him as their deliverer. "Our Father Saba," they would say with reverence. His followers were called "Companions," as of a Saint. Marvels were related of his prowess and his sanctity. It was said that he had healed sick persons with a touch. Although a price was set upon his head he moved secure.

In the midst of this excitement, hearing Saba's name at every turn, Miriam kept her lips tight closed and prayed to Allah inwardly.

How long could this blasphemy, this insult to high Heaven, endure? This brigand chief, who had seduced her, still wore the habit of a monk of the Orthodox Church, though excommunicate. Up there, in his mountain hold, he had administered the Blessed Sacraments, and given absolution, to unbelievers, so she heard. He was reported to have said that angels talked with him. There were no bounds to his wickedness and his presumption. And yet our Lord in Heaven held His hand, and did not strike down the blasphemer. By day and night she plotted to betray Saba to the Muslims, or else kill him with her own hand. But his band numbered more than a hundred fighting men, and the countryside was solid for him. She could descry no helper.

At length one evening, as she sat on the roof of her house, hearing one of her younger sons repeat his catechism, there came a noise of people running in the narrow way between the houses. Looking down, she cried a question to those passing.

A young Druze stopped and told her: "It is our Father Saba. A report has reached him from the city that El Islâm will slaughter Nazarenes this night. Our father and his men are on their way to slay the slayers. They have stopped at the house of the Sheykh for a little refreshment. I, too, go with them. All our youths are volunteering."

"But what has it to do with thee? Thou art a Durzi[48]."

"Nazarene and Durzi are alike to Father Saba!"

"A true word," thought Miriam to herself. "Saba is indeed become the worst of infidels."

Suddenly she felt desire to see him once again, and, if it might be, throw misfortune on him with her eyes. Tense with resolution, she went down into the house and veiled her head, then sallied forth alone. Before the house of the Sheykh of the village there was a noisy crowd. She had to fight her way with

[48] The correct singular for Druze; the word Druze is a collective plural.

strength to gain the door, which was guarded by two brigands armed to the teeth. Of these she craved admittance, but it was denied. Resigned, she stood and waited till the chief came out. His long hair and his beard were nearly white; in his eyes burned the fire of madness, she remarked with glee; but his step was still elastic, and his form erect. He wore the black gown and tower-like head-dress of a priest; a belt supporting pistols and a sword confined his cassock at the waist. And a long, burnished gun was slung across his shoulders.

He would have passed her by, unrecognizing, had she not called to him by name.

He looked at her inquiringly; then murmured:-

"Is it thou, O Miriam? How is thy health? I pray for thee daily, hourly. Have no fear for thy salvation! Have I not atoned for both of us? I have assurance that our Lord has pardoned me. He sends his angel graciously to guide my hand, and inform my mind of things that are to come. The Church will triumph one day in this land. As for me I shall be worsted at the last, but my foes will not take me alive."

"Thou art blessed indeed," said Miriam sneeringly. He spoke as if God were with him. Some supernatural power he had assuredly, but she knew well it was the devil's.

"Farewell, O beloved! Have no fear, I tell thee! I am praying for thee; and my works, too, intercede. We have kindled a fire in the land, which shall spread until all evil is consumed!"

He was certainly possessed. As she watched him mount his horse and ride off towards the coastal plain, Miriam cursed him in the name of Allah through clenched teeth. She willed it that he should not see another day.

That night she asked her husband, of his goodness, to have the donkey saddled at an hour before daybreak as she wished to go into the city on the morrow. The man, accustomed to obedience, wished to bear her company, but she denied him, saying that her eldest boy must be her escort. The son of Saba was by then a man full grown.

"But there is fighting in the city!"

"Have no fear! I shall avoid the scene of fighting."

In the middle of the night a cry went up: "Alas! Our Father Saba." Miriam sent her husband to learn the matter. He returned and told her: "A calamity! One has come up from the city with an errand to our father to inform him that the rumour of a massacre was false, nothing more than a trap set for him by the Government. He sped up by the shortest way, so missed our father and his companions in the darkness. Pray God they be not slain even now!"

Miriam announced her will to start at once for the city. Her son was roused from sleep. The donkey saddled; and she set forth in the starlight.

At daybreak, on the footslopes of the mountain – slopes still veiled in darkness though the sea was white already – a man's voice cried for help in Allah's name. It proceeded from some brushwood just below the road. Miriam made her son go down and see. He called out presently: "It is a dying man, one of the companions of our Father Saba – may God bless him!" Miriam dismounted instantly and went to look, bidding her son return and hold the donkey.

A young man lay there, groaning, in a pool of blood. She took his head upon her lap and soothed him as a mother might, while deftly questioning. His answers were articulate but very faint. In the outskirts of the town, as they stole forward gleefully, Saba's men had suddenly found themselves surrounded by the Turkish troops. Not more than twenty, and those sorely wounded, had forced their way out of the death-trap. The speaker himself had staggered to the mountain-side to die in peace.

"And what of our father himself? How fared he?" questioned Miriam.

"We hid him in a hut in the garden of Yuhanna, the scribe, outside the town. He is wounded. The least injured guard him. His enemies shall not take him alive; he himself foretold it – O lady, for the love of Allah, give me water!"

Miriam straightway left the sufferer and resumed her journey. Her son beside her cursed the wicked Muslims, and wished he could have fought and died with Father Saba.

When they came among the orange groves which extend far out from the town, she made inquiry for the garden of Yuhanna, the scribe. At length they found it. Tying up the donkey to the pillar of the gate, Miriam and her son went in and saw the hut.

A man with bandaged head, who had been squatting by the door, sprang up and bade them halt.

"Does our father still live?" said the woman sorrowfully. "Do but tell him here is Miriam come to say farewell!"

The man then let them enter, with a shrug.

Within the wretched hut, upon a bed of cloaks, lay the monk, his clothing soaked with blood, his face so distorted with pain as to be hardly recognizable. Beyond him sat four more of his adherents, their eyes never quitting his face, moaning from time to time, like faithful hounds. All four were badly wounded, yet they thought not of themselves.

"May our Lord bless thee!" exclaimed Saba hoarsely, when he knew whose form it was that came between him and the sunlight. "I wronged thee, O beloved;

I did all things wrong at first. Please God I may have done things right of late, so made atonement. Yet I cannot tell. O Miriam, in mercy fetch a priest, that he may ease me of the burden I have borne so long alone. A secular priest will not refuse to come to me, for am I not the champion of God's poor? The hour of my death is near. My enemies, the infidels, are fast approaching, and Allah has promised that they shall not find me living. Make haste. A priest, I beg of thee!"

"Move not, O my mother! I will run like lightning."

Miriam smiled grimly as the son of Saba fled from her side upon his father's last behest. One of the attendant outlaws whispered: "O my lady, if thou wouldst serve our father, go and call a doctor. His case may not be hopeless; if only we could move him to the mountain! No one of us dare show his face in the town. As thou desirest Heaven hereafter, do this kindness!"

"Upon my head be it. I go," said Miriam.

With their praises in her ears, she went back to the donkey and mounting made haste to the Government Offices. There, obtaining audience of a high official of police, she laid her information as to Saba's hiding-place. That done, she left the donkey at the nearest khan, and wandered aimlessly about the trees. Her work was done. When all was over, she would seek her son, and they would return together to the mountain village and its brute inhabitants. At present she was feeling angry with the boy for his readiness to leave her at a word from Saba. When choosing him for her companion on this journey, it had been her thought that he might kill his father.

She had wandered for a long time in a kind of dream, when all at once loud shouting smote her ears. A crowd came surging round a corner, swept her back against the wall.

The people were escorting with loud acclamation a small company of soldiers who bore by way of ensign a man's head upon a pole. The head had long white hair and a long white beard. To add to the mockery they had put on its accustomed covering, the tall cylindrical cap of an Orthodox priest. The eyes were closed; the mouth hung open.

Miriam gazed upon the horrid object without fear or loathing. She now no longer hated Saba. He was hers once more.

A man, pushed close to her by the crowd, kept crying shame on the procession. She turned and studied his appearance. It was one of the brigands who had been with Saba at the last. He recognized her also, and cried out, as if in terror:-

"Our Lord console and comfort thee, O lady. Thy son, he too, was killed by those wild beasts of soldiers. He died a martyr for the Faith. Our Lord exalt him! Thy son brought in a priest who shrove our Father Saba and gave him the viaticum[49] as he was dying. Then, after he had breathed his last, the soldiers came. We told them: 'He is dead! Respect our grief!'; but they rushed in and hacked the head from off the body. May God repay them! Bûtrus, our comrade, fell upon his sword, for rage, and died immediately. Thy son – God bless him! – snatched a pistol from my belt, and with it shot the mutilator. Then they killed thy son, and we that were left alive ran forth demented. They cut that head which they are carrying from off a corpse, let all men know it! Allah is witness! May the curse of Allah be upon their seed for ever!"

Something gave way within the brain of Miriam, and with it vanished all the years of hatred. Saba had gone away; he had taken his son up with him into Heaven; and she was left alone, whose only happiness had been to be with Saba.

[49] The eucharist, last rites, given by a priest to someone believed to be dying.

COUNT ABDULLAH

This story first appeared in Tales from Five Chimneys, published in June 1915. The story is told exclusively from the point of a young British lady who is by herself for a few days in a Levantine city – presumably Beirut. Just as Pickthall was able to empathise and identify with Egyptian brigands, Syrian rogues and Suffolk farm labourers, so he can see with kindly and charitable understanding the world and unhappy experiences of a naïve young lady outside her comfort zone.

Dorothy Lee had made the voyage from Alexandria to the Levant seaport expecting to be met there by her great friends, Jane and Henry Leggitt, whose intention it had been to make that place the starting-point of their tour in Asia Minor. But as she stood by her luggage on the deck of the Khedivial steamer, waiting to disembark, a young Syrian in Cook's uniform came up and, lifting his peaked cap, pronounced her name inquiringly. He brought a letter which, when read, informed her that Jane Leggitt had been taken ill at Athens, so that she and her husband could not hope to join her for another week at least.

It meant a week alone in a strange country, where she knew not a soul. But Dorothy was undismayed. She was thirty years of age, her own mistress, and, with the fashionable craving for the unconventional, was really capable and self-reliant. Besides, as seen from the sea, with its bright-roofed houses interspersed with foliage, and great, coloured mountains in the background, the seaport town[50] seemed an earthly paradise.

Going onshore in Cook's boat, she lost that pleasing vision. She was driven through the filthiest streets in a dilapidated fly to the best hotel the city boasted,

[50] Probably Beirut, albeit an unlikely place to embark on a tour of Asia Minor. It could be Alexandretta (Iskenderun) though the mountains are further back from the coast. But Count Abdullah reads an Arabic newspaper. And few would have called Alexandretta, charming though it is, the Paris of the East.

which was far from splendid. There she was assigned a fairly decent bedroom, with a view over the sea. Having seen her luggage brought in by a procession of porters, she procured hot water, and a pot of tea, and spent the hours till dinner happily, arranging matters in her bedroom.

In a quiet dress not too low-necked, she went down to the dining-room. Her appearance seemed to paralyse a group of loungers in the hotel entrance; and when she had been shown her place by an obsequious waiter, she met the stare of the said loungers, who had followed to the doorway. Her seat was at a little table, by herself. A fezzed[51] and frock-coated Turk, with a long white beard and spectacles, sat near her, at another little table. There was nobody else at that end of the huge room; but at the other, given over to a kind of ordinary, sat and dined about a score of men – Syrians. Greeks and Italians to judge from their appearance – who conversed together loudly in bad French. Dorothy was the only woman diner.

The dinner was well cooked and promptly served; but the waiters, native Christians, dressed in European clothes, looked mean to one accustomed to the grandeur of Egyptian servants. Their brown hands, peeping out of linen cuffs, looked dirty; and they had forfeited the dignity of Orientals by leaving off the fez and showing narrow foreheads. The constant coming and going of chance people during dinner annoyed her rather, though she feigned serenity.

A bare-footed urchin, with no other clothing than a skull-cap and a long shirt, ran in from the street and gave a newspaper to one of the diners at the long table, then, being paid, saluted and ran out again.

The recipient unfolded the paper and, at the request of those near him, read from it aloud, translating as he went. Dorothy had already noticed this individual, on account of the refinement of his clear-cut face compared with those around him. Though older than the others, he looked more alive. Alone of all those present, the old Turk excepted, he impressed her as a creature of some breeding. She had judged him at a glance Italian; but now, seeing that he read with ease an Arabic journal, she supposed he must be, after all, a native of the country. He gave the news in French. She caught what he was saying, and grew interested. He, in the distance, saw that she was listening, and read towards her. Their eyes met once or twice; and she was conscious that he felt attracted. Foreseeing some relief from dullness, she rejoiced. He was the only man in the hotel she would have wished to speak to her.

It was no surprise to her when, after dinner, he came into the lounge upstairs, where she sat reading, and addressed her. His English was as fluent as his French.

[51] Pickthall spells this word in this story mostly with one z.

He asked if she was staying long, and when she said, "A week, perforce!" seemed glad to hear it.

"You shall not regret it!" he exclaimed. "Our city is the most beautiful city of the Orient. Its high society is so elegant and highly civilized that it is called the Paris of the East."

Dorothy did not see how the elegance of the society was going to enliven her week's sojourn, and she said so. The city, she confessed, had looked divine when she beheld it from the steamer's deck; but on landing, she had been chiefly struck by the squalor of the place, the savage rudeness of the people. To compare the place to Paris, for a minute, she considered, on the face of things, preposterous.

"You speak the truth!" he laughed, and eyed her sharply. "The fact is, all is ruined by bad government. The city here would be in truth divine, if governed properly. The municipality, for instance, has much wealth, but the members eat it all; and so the streets remain as you behold them."

He was a native of the place, he told her, but no longer lived here. Twenty years ago, he had migrated to Constantinople, where he had married a Greek lady of the best society. He showed her photographs of his wife and children, which he had in the breast-pocket of his well-cut coat; and gave her his card, on which she read –

Le Comte Abdullah Salaman.

The countship, as he hastened to explain, was something of a joke. It had been bestowed upon his father, a rich banker, by the Pope of Rome to reward his conversion to Roman Catholicism from the Nestorian heresy[52]. His talk was like the peepshow of an unknown world to her; and she was really sorry when he rose to go, which he did a thought abruptly, in the manner of a man who has forgotten duties for a moment in unwonted pleasure. When she held out his hand, he raised it to his lips and then withdrew.

Dorothy thought herself extremely fortunate to have met so civilized a being in this uncouth place. She had not known a type existed among Orientals so different from the unwieldy, gross-lipped native magnate she had seen in Egypt. Count Salaman had an ascetic, intellectual face; his hands were manicured; his clothes would have done credit to a Bond Street tailor.

The next morning Dorothy spent in writing up her diary; at lunch the Count did not appear. So, rather than have no one to speak to, she succumbed to the blandishments of an English-speaking dragoman, and went out in a carriage to inspect the sights of the town. The streets presented hillocks three feet high and corresponding depressions; the driving was so wild and brutal as to keep

52 He would have been a member of the Assyrian Church of the East.

her nerves on edge and prevent her from listening to the guide's account of public buildings which all were new and ugly and yet squalid-looking. She saw two fights and a dead donkey in the open street; and returned to her hotel with feelings of nausea, anything but refreshed by the short outing. Secure in her own room, she even cried a little. Why was such a place, why were such people, allowed to exist in the world? She would have subscribed then and there to any practicable scheme for their destruction; and naïvely wondered that no such scheme had ever been proposed by the civilized nations of the world in the interests of humanity. She felt so miserable that it was only by an effort at the last minute that she summoned courage to go down to dinner.

Count Salaman, in his place at the long table, bowed to her as she entered, and, when dessert was going, came across to where she sat.

"I grieve," he said with a most courtly bow, "that business has this day prevented me from placing myself at your service as I should have wished to do. Well, how do you find our city on acquaintance?"

"I hate it," said the Englishwoman vehemently, tears in her voice. "I have seen nothing good in it."

"You look very nice when you are angry," said the Count paternally. "But in truth I feel for you most heartily. It is terrible to be alone in a strange, foreign place. What you require is a little – I seek the English word – a little *divertissement* this evening. Now will you permit me to offer you a *loge* at the theatre, and to accompany you? I too am alone like you are; it will be great kindness. There is a cinema – it will seem poor, perhaps, to you who come from London; but for us it is very good indeed."

Before she could consent in words or thank him he had called a hotel-servant, and given a command in Arabic.

"The name of the theatre," he told her," is Zahret-esh-Shark, which means Flower of the East. It is the most beautiful theatre in all this country. There is no need to make a grand toilette. Will you be prepared in half an hour? Good! Then I will meet you in the hall upstairs."

She found him there, when she emerged from her bedroom, a quarter of an hour later, having put on gloves and draped a black mantilla, Eastern-fashion, on her golden hair. The Count, on his side, had assumed a trim light overcoat, and carried in his hand a bowler hat.

Bare-headed, he conducted her downstairs and through the entrance hall to a carriage which he had there waiting and handed her in; then, putting on his hat, he took his seat beside her, crying –

"Yallah[53]!"

The coachman thrashed his horses cruelly. "Oh, tell him not to do that!" she cried out in anguish; and the Count obeyed her.

"They are beasts, these drivers; they know nothing!" he said soothingly.

Through narrow, crowded streets, where they seemed always on the point of colliding with some other vehicle or knocking down some group of footfarers; with jolts and bumps that jarred their teeth, and ceaseless shouting; they came at last into a crowded square and stopped before a big shed lighted tawdrily. The Count helped Dorothy to get out, then paid the driver. He led her through a door into a squalid café packed with men, and thence by steep stairs up to a wooden gallery, where a slipshod serving-man unlocked a crazy door and let them into a private box assigned to them. This was bare and very dirty, containing but one chair which the Count placed for her, standing himself till the attendant brought another.

The boxes were all occupied; in some of these she noticed well-dressed women. The floor below was packed with men in fezes. Hardly was the Count well seated ere a fight broke out, which threatened for a moment to become general, but was somehow pacified. Three similar fights occurred before the curtain rose, revealing a white sheet, and the clicking of the apparatus made itself heard and felt. Then a hush fell. Individual coughings and expectorations, the striking of a match, the moving of a chair became distinctly audible.

The moving pictures were quite good. Dorothy was able to share the Count's enthusiasm. She forgot her hatred of the city till the interval when, the lamps being re-lighted, she was annoyed by the persistent staring of some men below. The offenders were a little group of would-be exquisites, wearing decent European clothes beneath the red tarbush. One of them left his place and disappeared; a minute later came a knock at the door of the box, and the same youth entered, staring at her from the threshold.

"A friend of mine," the Count presented him. She failed to catch his name, and generally strove to emphasize her lack of interest in his appearance. He stared the more for that – it seemed, contemptuously. The imagined insult made her cheeks like fire. It spoilt the rest of the performance for her. What was her anger, going out at length behind Count Salaman, to find the same youth and his friends drawn up in line along the exit, to have to run the gauntlet of their smiles and whispers!

She complained of their behaviour to the Count as they were driven back to the hotel. He ridiculed her indignation gently, as a father might.

---

53 Off we go!

"Do you really wonder," he inquired, "that young men line your way and smile to you? My friend assured me he had never seen so fair a lady."

"That's nonsense!" answered Dorothy impatiently, rejecting the flattery with a shake of the shoulders. "I disliked that place intensely. I will never go there again.'

"I am sorry," said the Count in so forlorn a tone that, remembering his kind intention to amuse her, she could have bitten her ungracious tongue out.

"Till to-morrow!" he suspired gallantly as he kissed her hand in the entrance-hall, in the presence of the night-porter and another native servant. "To-morrow, if you permit it, I will take you for a drive in the afternoon."

In spite of his politeness Dorothy felt wretched. Those young men had detected something wrong in her appearance. She had been treated by them to the bold stare of the connoisseur which, in Europe, is reserved for shameless hussies. Her colour was her own, her hair was natural, her dress as quiet as could be imagined. She lay awake a long while in a vain attempt to solve the riddle.

In the morning, after breakfast, she went out to do some shopping. The hotel people had advised her where to go, and she had no difficulty in finding all the places, which were close at hand. In her going and her coming back, she was much stared at by young men; so much so that she now accepted the Count's theory. Yellow hair and blue eyes, a pink and white complexion, common in England, were unusual here. The discovery was animating, and she was unusually vivacious when she set out with the Count that afternoon. It was the fashionable hour for driving. They encountered many carriages containing people whom the Count knew well, and named to her. The men all gave her that peculiar stare, which she now regarded as the tribute of these demi-savages to dazzling beauty. All the carriages, even that of the Turkish Pasha, looking shabby, and the majority of their inmates underbred. Still she enjoyed the outing; and the view, as they returned, of splendid mountains flushed with the sunset, behind the city roofs and palm-trees, and across the bay, was simply heavenly.

But at dinner that evening, a number of young men in fezes joined the company at the long table, and she recognized among them one or two of her admirers of the theatre. They all seemed to be friends of the Count, and all kept looking round in her direction. The Count alone stood up and bowed to her as she passed out.

He came afterwards to the lounge upstairs where she sat reading, bringing two of his young friends for introduction. These, though formally polite, observed her knowingly. If admiration moved them, it was quite untempered by respect. Even in their farewell bows she felt a point of irony.

Greatly annoyed, she spoke of their behaviour after they were gone, when the Count, seeing tears in her eyes, became infuriated.

"They are beasts," he said, "uneducated savage beasts. They were my friends, I knew their fathers, but I will reject them. It is enough, if they have made you sad. They are ill-mannered, having never travelled out of this unhappy country. To-morrow I will beat them soundly. I will nearly kill them. They shall ask your forgiveness, weeping. It is finished."

"Please, don't do anything! They're nothing to me!" exclaimed Dorothy, with so much vehemence that Count Abdullah looked at her, and, looking, took her hand in great compassion.

"Please do not be unhappy, dear Miss Lee. I grieve so much to see you sad. Our city, our people, our manners, our young men – all do not please you, for which I am so very sorry. I would do anything; but what can I propose to make you happy? There is nothing but the cinematograph, and that also does not please you, does it? In two days I leave this place; I return to Constantinople; I may never see you any more. And I would give myself the pleasure, while I may. Say, will you come to-night again to the theatre. No one shall harm you, or insult you, while I live."

"Yes!" said Dorothy with sudden resolution, feeling penitent. Count Salaman had been so kind, she so ungrateful, in their short acquaintance.

She went accordingly, and was stared at as before, and again at coming forth passed between two rows of grinning men, some of whom smacked their lips to suggest kissing. She felt furious; but, for the Count's sake, made no comment at the time.

At luncheon the next day at the hotel there were more young men in European suits and fezes, whose sole aim seemed to be to make her life unbearable. Some of them came up afterwards to the lounge and ogled her, till she fled into her room and locked the door. At four o' clock she took tea with the Count, and afterwards went for a drive with him, which soothed her. To dinner also her rude admirers came in force. She beckoned the Count over to her table.

"If you have any power over those brutes," she said, "tell them to go away and not come near me."

"I obey," he replied, bowing; and returned to his own place.

He sat alone with her that evening till she went to bed, telling her curious stories of the country, which she found more entertaining than the cinematograph theatre.

"It is good-bye," he murmured, when at last he rose to go; "I go on board the steamer early to-morrow morning. May God bless you and keep you always, dear young lady!"

Really touched by his emotion, she gave him both her hands. He pressed them hard with his lips, then tore himself away. In all their *tête-à-tête*, unconventional intercourse, he had never made the slightest movement towards flirtation, though so evidently enamoured. Now that he was going, she felt half in love with him; protesting in her heart that she had never met a truer gentleman.

When he was gone the place seemed desolate. At luncheon the next morning she sat down without defence against her shameless persecutors, whose numbers seemed to have increased. Passing the end of the long table, as she was obliged to do, on her way out, she heard a whisper: "Chérie!" and again "Je t'aime!" and then a burst of laughter. Her cheeks flamed. What had she ever done to earn such treatment?

Then, as she sat by the great window in the lounge, some one came and breathed on the back of her neck, whispering words of love. She sprang up, furious. It was a youth whose face she knew – the same who had come up into the box that night . . . . She struck his face, then ran into the room and locked the door. As soon as she could think, she rang her bell and called for the hotel manager.

That worthy came, appearing much embarrassed. She told her grievance; he looked merely sheepish, and said he had been wanting to speak to her for two days past.

"I wish to ask, lady, if you mind goin' to another hotel."

"Why? You have plenty of room."

"Yes; but it's best you go!" The man looked miserable. It was plain that he spoke thus only from a sense of duty. "I not the proprietor. The proprietor he come to-morrow back from Egypt. I try to do the best I can, but fery difficult."

"But why? You must give some reason."

He would not give one. The proprietor was away, he repeated, in Egypt, and he did not like to take strong action on his own responsibility. He, therefore, begged, instead of ordering, her to leave the house.

"But I know of no other place, I am a stranger here."

"Oh, we will find you a nice place, neffer fear." He seemed tremendously relieved.

"Well, I'll leave to-morrow, if you insist on it; but I shall complain to the British Consul."

"You do what you blease, lady. It is my duty."

Soon after he had quitted her, there arose a noise of shouting, at first in the hotel, and then in the street without. She leaned out of her window but could see nothing. Another knock at her door! It was again the manager, who entered boldly this time, with eyes frankly reproachful.

"You hear that noise, lady? That was a fight because of you. Yesterday there come only Christians, that was bad enough. To-day three Muslims heard of you and came to look. They make fight with the others, bring the mob to our hotel. You go to-morrow certain; and, blease, this efenin', take your subber here."

"But what have I done?" shrieked Dorothy, beside herself. "Are you all mad? Why should men come to look at me?"

"Ah, that you know, lady. I only know that they come and make bad business."

"Please call a carriage for me. I shall go straight to the Consulate."

"As you please, lady!"

If only the Count, her friend, had still been there! Alone, she felt so helpless and so miserable that it was all that she could do to speak and move consecutively.

Presently a servant came to tell her that a carriage was in waiting. In her descent to it she was as closely guarded as a state prisoner; only when the horses broke into a gallop did the posse of hotel-servants fall away. It being too late to find the Consul at his office, she was driven to his private house. In her relief at sight of a real Englishman she wept a little in his presence ere she told her griefs.

"I can't make it out," he said. "You are sure you have told me everything? It is the best hotel we have, and entirely respectable. I never had the least complaint from there before. Please tell me all that you've been doing since you arrived."

She did so, to the best of her ability.

"Well, all that seems fairly harmless; though I ought to tell you that it is not usual here for a lady to go out in the evening with a chance acquaintance. Abdullah Salaman bears the reputation of a rogue financially; the fortune of the whole family was made by shady means; but the same might be said of any wealthy Levantine."

"Count Salaman was kindness itself to me."

"I can make neither head nor tail of the affair," the Consul sighed. "I can't think that they would have requested an English lady to leave the hotel unless they believed that they had some very good excuse for taking so extreme a step. If you'll allow me, I'll send one of my Cawwâses[54] back with you. He will be at your service, and at the same time can make inquiries."

"I shall be most thankful!"

[54] A messenger or minor official of the Consulate.

The sight of the gold-laced back of the Cawwâs up on the box beside the driver was of comfort to Dorothy as she returned in the carriage through the vile, half-savage city. And that, or something, changed the manner of the hotel servants. These were now obsequious. At the top of the steps, up which she hurried, leaving the Cawwâs to follow at his leisure, friendly hands caught hers; she gazed, delighted, on the faces of her friends, the Leggitts. They had come at last.

"We found a steamer sooner than we thought. How are you, dear? Have you been very lonely?"

Dorothy dropped her head on Jane Leggitt's breast, and there wept comfortably.

That same evening, having heard her story, Henry Leggitt called up the manager, and questioned him. The man confessed that there had been a great mistake, for which he offered most profound apologies; he could not be induced to say how that mistake had in the first place arisen. If the gentleman would only wait, he said, until to-morrow, when the proprietor was expected back from Egypt, all should be explained. He was only the manager, and that temporarily, and had done what he believed to be his duty in circumstances which he now saw he had utterly misjudged. The matter, he now saw, was much too high for him.

"I suspect your friend Count Salaman is in it somehow," Jane remarked to Dorothy.

"You wouldn't say that if you knew him!" was the warm retort.

But the Cawwâs from the Consulate had, it soon appeared, deduced the same suspicion from his shrewd inquiries.

"But how, and why?" asked Dorothy, incredulous.

The Cawwâs would not explain; the hotel servants, fearing to be blamed, were still more guarded. It was not until the owner of the house arrived, that they spoke out freely and the truth was known. Henry Leggitt had a long talk with the landlord after dinner before he joined the ladies in the lounge upstairs.

"Well, what is it?" inquired both the women feverishly, when at last he came to them.

"It is that you, Dorothy, don't distinguish your right hand from your left."

"Don't talk nonsense, Henry; it's very serious to me."

"I mean that every Oriental deems his right hand honourable; his left hand vile. And out of this the native Christians have evolved a kind of masonic code for placing women. Your gentleman-like friend Count Salaman put you always on his left hand, in the carriage, at the theatre, and when he sat with you here;

thus giving all his friends to understand that you were . . . well . . . in short, his mistress. Those young men who pursued you he had told plainly, at first by gestures only, but afterwards in plain words, that you were that, and he was tired of you, and meant to leave you behind when he returned to Constantinople. They were simply competing for the succession."

"But it's impossible. It is too mean, too devilish! If you saw the man!"

"I am only quoting my informant. I have only to call him up, and you will hear the truth at first hand."

"Yes, do ask him to come up."

The hotel proprietor, when he appeared, was circumstantial. Abullah Salaman, he said, had always, from his youth up, borne the worst of characters where women were concerned. He gloried in this reputation, which he had well earned in his young days, and now that he was getting elderly would still live up to it. He confirmed what Henry Leggitt had already told her, and subjoined:–

"The young men who annoyed this lady are well-known to me. Directly I got home and heard the story, I went and questioned them. He who insulted you here is much ashamed; and swears that he will go to Constantinople straight, and kill Abdullah. He says he paid Abdullah twenty pounds, to speak to you for him; he admired you so; and that Abdullah told him you wished to see him."

"But what made Abdullah do all this? There seems no sense in it," cried Dorothy.

"First, no doubt, madam, he wished to seem a great man with the ladies just as formerly. Second, he wished to tell a funny story to his friends in Constantinople. He got about a hundred pounds from different beeble for something that did not belong to him, and left us all in false bositions. Many beeble think that clever, and extremely funny. As for me, I only say that, if I had been here, it would neffer have happened. I know Abdullah well, and should have warned this lady. Also I should have seen at once it was not as they thought." He bowed to Miss Lee. "My men, sir and ladies, are a little stubid; and do not often see a young and bretty English lady travellin' quite alone like that. Do blease forgif them; they believed all he said – the wicked liar. Ah, he shall never come in here again."

Miss Lee's dismay was such on these disclosures that she desired to fly at once from such a nightmare of a country. But her friends detained her, and, after six weeks' travel with them in the wilds, she saw the funny side of her adventure, and valued it as an addition in her store of anecdotes.

JENÂB UL AMÎR

This story first appeared in Tales from Five Chimneys, published in June 1915. The mountainous areas of Lebanon between 1860 and the First World War were governed by a Mutesarrif, an official appointed by the Ottoman authorities in Istanbul. Britain and France took a close interest in the administration of the region and its appointments since the conflicts of 1860, when Christians and Muslims (with Druze as allies) had been at war.

Below the Mutesarrif was the Qaimmacam (qa'im maqam), district official, a man selected from one of the local prominent families.

Pickthall defines the characteristic of people by their dress. The Emîr wears the official Istanbul dress, symbolic rather than convenient in the Lebanese mountains. The story is melodramatic, with the guns being shot just as the Emîr is about to ravish the maiden. There are no half measures in his fall from grace.

I

The Emîr Ali Muhammad reclined upon the cushioned couch in his presence-chamber, smoking his narghileh. Around the walls of the room, upon the bare stone benches, sat some thirty of his vassals and dependents, their eyes obsequiously watchful of the great man's face.

The dark green leaves of a pomegranate tree, interspersed with scarlet blossoms, brushed the lattice, through which a fresh breeze stole into the vaulted chamber. The coolness and shadow within formed a pleasant contrast to the heat outside, which veiled the slope of Lebanon in a quivering white haze, and hung – a liquid mist – upon the green plain, the yellow sand-belt, and the blue sea beyond. Below the terrace of the Emîr's palace silver olive-groves dipped in terraces to the verge of a wild ravine. To the right was the village, its flat-roofed houses seeming a natural growth of the mountain side.

The Emîr was clad in a long morning-robe of striped silk, pale blue and yellow. Later in the day he would array himself in the official frock-coat and Frankish trousers, with only the fez to mark his nationality. But now, in the early morning, with only his retainers about him, he found ease and coolness in the garb of his country.

He was an enormously fat man, about forty years of age, with a flabby sallow face, from whose folds a pair of bright brown eyes looked shiftily. He lay among his cushions in silence, puffing away at his narghileh, and blowing from time to time a cloud of smoke into the faces of those who sat nearest.

Of the thirty men in the room, not one but had his eyes intent upon the face of the Emîr, but watched every puff of smoke, every wink of an eye, as it had been a matter of life and death. Some of those present had come from distant villages to pay their respects to the great man, and sit for half an hour in the same room with him, simply to keep their names alive in his memory.

To have spoken aloud in such a presence would have been little less than sacrilege. The splash of the fountain in the courtyard made itself heard through the arched doorway, enhancing by suggestion the coolness of the presence-chamber.

"Amîn!" grunted the Emîr at length, without raising his head. "Bring coffee for these people!" The Emîr's use of his native language was almost entirely restricted to the imperative mood. He was wont to converse with his equals in Turkish or French.

There was a general movement throughout the room. Heads were bowed, hands held on hearts, and a murmur arose, half-grateful, half-deprecating. An old man with a long white beard, and yet whiter turban, who had till then been squatting in the doorway, rose hastily, and shuffled off to do his master's bidding.

"Is there any greatness to compare with his?" whispered a reverend Sheykh in his neighbour's ear. "See! He puffs his smoke into the face of Hamid Bek! You and I, Hasan ibn Mustafa, are as dirt before the face of our lord the Bek. What are we compared with his grace the Emîr[55]?"

Hasan ibn Mustafa shrugged his shoulders, and spread out his hands, seeming to say: "What would you?" He was a young man, tall and well proportioned, whose eyes of deep blue contrasted strongly with his black hair and swarthy skin. He wore a striped cloak of camel's hair, black and white, which allowed a glimpse of a crimson plush waistcoat, braided with black, and trousers of the Turkish

---

[55] His Grace, the translation of the title of the story, Jenâb el Emîr.

pattern. Like most of the other men in the room, he wore a spotless white turban wound round his tarbush.

"No doubt but that he is great, O Sheykh!" he whispered, "Yet why should he treat us like dogs? He is not greater than the Emîr Selîm of Ain Warda, yet the Emîr Selîm is accessible to all who wish to speak with him."

"Be silent, thou fool!" whispered the Sheykh. "Wouldst speak of Selîm and our Emîr in the same breath? Wouldst exalt the wolf with praises when thou liest between the very paws of the lion? Our Emîr is to his Excellency Abdullah Basha as the light of his eyes. One word of his mouth has more power than all the speeches of Selîm."

"But the Emîr Selîm is head of our race," insisted Hasan. "It was his father, as I have heard our old men tell, who was leader in the great war of the year Sixty[56], when the blood of our enemies flowed like water, when every village of the Mowarni[57] was as a slaughter-house. But this Emîr loves the Turks more than the Drûz. He only divided our strength, leading many of our best men, as thee, O Sheykh, to become the slaves of the Muslim; whereas the Emîr Selim –"

"Silence!" interrupted the Sheykh in an angry whisper. "Speak not of Selîm in the house of his enemy save to curse him! Since thou hast come to dwell in the village of our Emîr, and art about to wed the daughter of one of his men, it were well for thee to give thyself wholly to the service of his Grace, the Emîr Ali Muhammad."

Hasan was about to reply when Amîn returned with the coffee.

The Emîr withdrew the amber mouth-piece of his narghileh from his lips, and blowing another puff of smoke into the face of Hamad Bey, who sat next him, murmured, "Peace be upon you all," with eyes staring listlessly at the vaulted ceiling.

The company rose as one man, and, with hands upon their hearts, exclaimed: "Upon thee be peace and the mercy of Allah and his blessings."[58]

Then the coffee was handed to the Emîr, who gulped down the contents of his tiny cup, dregs and all, and replaced it upon the salver, before his guests were thought of.

"See how great he is," whispered the Sheykh in Hasan's ear.

"I warrant thee, Selîm would have offered it to his guests first."

"That is true," agreed the other rather sullenly.

---

56 1860, the year of armed conflict between Druze and Muslims on one side, and Christians on the other. The conflict is the background of Pickthall's 1903 novel, *Saïd the Fisherman.*

57 Maronites.

58 A literal translation of the response to the greeting, Peace be upon you, *al-salam alikum.*

The coffee being disposed of, and the servant having retired with the tray, the Emîr, without moving his head, murmured: "Let those speak who have anything to say."

Again the whole company rose as one man, bowed low, and exclaimed: "If Allah will, may your Excellency be ever happy."

"And you also," grunted the Emîr Ali Muhammad.

The company resumed their seats, and there was some whispering between a Sheykh of patriarchal aspect and Hamad Bey, in the course of which both looked across to where Hasan was sitting. The Emîr smoked on carelessly as ever.

At length Hamad Bey, the Cadi of the district, arose and bowed himself before the great man. He asked his Excellency's leave to state that his Excellency's most devoted servant, the Sheykh Fâris Shemdân, was about to give his daughter in marriage to a young man, whom he (the Sheykh Fâris) had brought thither that morning for his Excellency's approval. His Excellency's word was law to all his people; therefore, should he not approve of this youth, Sheykh Fâris would seek some other husband for his daughter.

The Cadi would have gone on to say much more to the same effect – he had been an advocate before the interest of his patron made him a judge, and he gloried in the sound of his own voice – had not an impatient movement of the great man's hand warned him that his eloquence was ill-timed. Hamad Bey faltered, bit his lip, cast a reproachful glance at Hasan, the cause – as he considered – of his confusion, and at length said: "Sheykh Fâris earnestly desires your Excellency's approval, without which no man who has ever gazed upon your face can live!"

"What is his name?" grunted the Emîr.

"With your Excellency's permission, it is Sheykh Fâris."

The Emîr raised his head and looked angrily upon the face of the Cadi out of the corners of his eyes. "May thy house be destroyed, dog!" he said, sinking back to his former listless position. "I ask thee the name of the young man, and thou tellest me Sheykh Fâris. Stand aside, madman, and let the Sheykh speak for himself!"

With something like a moan, Hamad Bey resumed his seat. Sheykh Fâris came forward, bowed over the Emîr's hand, and waited to be questioned.

Ali Muhammad smoked on in silence for some seconds, his eyes fixed upon a scarlet blossom of the pomegranate tree without the lattice.

"Speak," he said at length, puffing smoke upon the flower. "What is the name of the young man?"

Sheykh Fâris glanced meaningfully first at Hamad Bey, then at Hasan. Then, with eyes cast down and trembling voice, he murmured: "With your Excellency's permission it is Hasan Artali, son of the Sheykh Mustafa."

"What sayest thou?" exclaimed the Emîr suddenly, turning upon the trembling man.

The Sheykh repeated his statement.

"I forbid it," said Ali Muhammad fiercely. "No dog belonging to Selîm shall marry into a household of mine." He lay back among his cushions with closed eyes.

The Sheykh glanced sidelong at Hamad Bey, as much as to say: "I told you so!"

"But with your Excellency's permission," he pleaded, "Hasan is willing to swear allegiance to your grace. He has promised to dwell in this village, to be one of us."

"Bring the man here!" said the Emîr with an impatient frown.

Hasan came forward and bowed before the great man, who never so much as deigned to look at him.

"Tell him he may take the daughter of Sheykh Fâris to his house if he will be my man and fight my battles. Let him have his horse, and his gun, and his tongue – all things that are his – ever at my service," said the Emîr, without opening his eyes.

"To hear is to obey," faltered Hasan.

"Let him kiss my hand."

Hasan touched the flabby hand with his lips, and was returning to his seat, when the Emîr spoke again: "Tell him that if he be not faithful to me, there is no man who can punish as I can. Now go, all of you! I am tired!"

The men rose, and, one by one, stepped forward to kiss the hand of their chief, who submitted to this salute, lying motionless, with closed eyes. Then they trooped out into the sunshine of the courtyard, and the Emîr was left alone in the cool shadow of the presence-chamber.

II

Upon the lowest step of the flight which led from the raised courtyard of the Emîr's palace down to the meydân, sat Ibrahîm, the giant doorkeeper. His bushy white beard proclaimed him an old man, but age had robbed him of none of his strength. A pair of green eyes, like a cat's, gave a strange, almost weird expression to his brown wrinkled face. Like a cat, also, he sat blinking in the full glare of the noontide sun, as if it were his native element.

As Hasan and Sheykh Fâris passed him on their way to seek their horses, he rose, with a yawn, stretched himself, and went with them.

"What said the Emîr?" he asked, laying his huge hand on Hasan's shoulder, and grinning down upon the young man as a cat might grin at the mouse he worries.

"It is well, Ibrahîm," Sheykh Fâris answered for his son-in-law. "The Emîr has accepted him.

Ibrahîm's grin became wider. "Thou hast changed sides for the sake of a girl's bright eyes?" he purred. "Is it worth the trouble? Truly young men are possessed with a devil. I also was a son of folly at thine age. I took a slim girl to my house for the sake of her eyes, that looked upon me as two stars out of heaven. Then I thought them stars, now I know them for two lumps of fat, set somewhat crooked in the face of a hag. Then I loved to kiss her lips, now I take pleasure in beating her upon the back with my staff. A woman soon grows old, and when she has borne children it is hard upon a poor man to be rid of her. Thou, Hasan, wilt learn wisdom when it is too late."

"Be silent, O Ibrahîm," said Sheykh Fâris. "Let Hasan learn wisdom from his own experience. Thou wilt honour my house with thy presence to-morrow, at the hour of sunset – not so? At the wedding feast of my daughter Nesîbeh there will be meat enough to fill even thee, O Ibrahîm."

"May my head be struck off if I come not," purred the giant. "As to the meat – I have eaten a whole sheep in my youth. But that was in the year Sixty, when men grew hungry from much killing. But now that I am old, and there is no killing to be done, my appetite grows less. The Emîr goes down to the court this afternoon to make sure that Ahmed Effendi, whose children threw stones at his Grace's carriage as he drove up from Beyrût last month, be duly punished. Hamad Bek[59] had better drown himself than be lenient with the rascal."

"I know Ahmed Effendi, that he is a good man and a peaceable," exclaimed Hasan indignantly. "Surely the Emîr will not ruin him for what his children have done!"

The giant grinned, and his green eyes had a peculiar expression as they looked down upon the young man.

"In thy grace I depart," said Sheykh Fâris, vaulting into his saddle.

---

59 A variant of Bey, a courtesy title.

"With my peace," purred Ibrahîm. And he stood grinning after the horsemen until they were lost to sight in the shade of the olive-groves that lay between the palace and the village.

"This Hasan has turned traitor to the Emîr Selîm," he thought, "even as I did years ago. He changes for love, I changed for gain – that is the difference. Yet Selîm was a better master than this fat pig, Ali Muhammad. But for this man's influence with the Mutesarrif, I had gone back years ago. But Bashas fall like other men, Selîm's turn may come – and then Ibrahîm will know how to take advantage of the change."

III

Early in the afternoon, the Emîr Ali Muhammad, arrayed in frock-coat, black waistcoat, and dark trousers – all very much too tight for him – mounted his horse at the steps of the palace, and rode at a foot's pace down the stony path, through the olive-grove, and into the village. Beside him walked Ibrahîm, the giant, holding a white parasol to shade the great man's head. Before a long flat-roofed house the Emîr reined in his horse. Two soldiers, dozing by the door, sprang to their feet, and, laying aside their carbines, ran forward to aid his Grace to dismount. A hum of voices came from within. Puffing and panting, his face streaming with perspiration, the Emîr alighted, and waddled into the house, leaving Ibrahîm in charge of the horse.

On a raised dais, at one end of a long room, sat, or rather squatted, Hamad Bey. Before him, in posture of cringing entreaty, stood a man resplendent in zouave jacket and silk trousers, the advocate for the prisoner. In the remotest corner of the room, almost hidden by a motley and unsavoury crowd of witnesses, stood the prisoner himself – a soldier at each elbow. The frown of importance and authority into which the brows of the Cadi were wont to be knitted vanished suddenly upon the entrance of the Emîr. Hamad Bey rose and bowed himself nearly to the ground. Coming down from the dais, he conveyed to his patron by a series of expressive shrugs and gestures that he, Hamad Bey, was but as the dust upon the boots of his Excellency, that his jurisdiction was at an end as soon as his Excellency set foot within the court, that the seat of judgment and honour was at his Excellency's disposal.

Bestowing a casual nod upon his servant, the Emîr waddled up to the dais and took his seat upon the cushion which the Cadi had just vacated. Then he took a cigarette from his pocket, allowed the prisoner's advocate to light it for him, and lay back, his head against the wall, the soles of his patent leather boots presented to the inspection of the court. "Let the trial proceed," he grunted.

"With your Excellency's permission," faltered Hamad Bey, "the prisoner has all but established his innocence. There remain but two witnesses to be questioned."

"What say'st thou?" said the Emîr, beside himself. He sprang up, flung himself upon the judge and with his riding-whip struck him about the head and shoulders before all men present. Then out of breath he once again subsided in his place against the wall.

"Come hither, thou dog!"

Hamad Bey in tears drew near, expecting to be whipped again.

"Show no mercy to this man!" hissed Ali Muhammad. "He is the dog of mine enemy, Selîm – dost hear, ass? Now do thy duty," he concluded aloud. "Let not thine ancient friendship for the Emîr Selîm prejudice thee in favour of the evil-doer. Pronounce sentence!"

A thrill of amazement and horror ran through the court.

"With your Excellency's permission," sobbed the Cadi, "there still remain two witnesses to be examined,"

"Two witnesses – two liars!" said the Emîr fiercely. "Pronounce sentence, dog!"

"To hear is to obey," murmured the Cadi; and never did judge look more like a criminal.

"In the name of Allah, Merciful, Compassionate, it is my solemn duty as friend and master of justice to say and to pronounce that this man, Ahmed ebn Mahmûd, is guilty of a great crime; on account of which crime, and in expiation thereof, he shall be confined in prison for five years, subject to the will and pleasure of his Excellency, the most illustrious Abdullah Basha, Mutesarrif of the Mountain, who, having ever shown himself a true friend to justice, and to our lord the Emîr Ali Muhammad, will surely ratify this sentence.

A murmur of protest arose from the witnesses, who, coming for the most part from the prisoner's village, were disposed to take his part. Then the court broke up, and the Emîr, with the assistance of Hamad Bey, waddled to the door and mounted his horse, regardless of the fierce eyes and sullen faces of the bystanders.

While Hamad Bey was taking somewhat voluble leave of his patron, one of the loungers took occasion to draw Ibrahîm aside. "Two hours since, as I was upon the high road, riding upon mine ass," he said, in a mysterious whisper, "there passed me two horsemen, soldiers, galloping furiously. A little behind them came one that seemed a great one, riding furiously also, as it were for his life."

"What is this that thou tellest me?" said the giant disdainfully. "Is it some new thing that thou shouldst meet his Excellency the Basha upon the Sultan's highroad?"

"A little after," the man continued, "I met one who told me that a new Mutesarrif has been sent suddenly from Istanbûl, and that Abdullah Basha is no longer our ruler. Thou, O Ibrahîm, art the first to whom I have told this thing. It is worth money, this news, – not so?"

"Thou hast done well," purred Ibrahîm, stroking his beard, – "very well. And thou shalt have thy reward. Tell no man of this that thou hast seen and heard, and it shall be well with thee."

With that, Ibrahîm put up the white parasol, and, taking his place beside the Emîr's horse, they set out on their return to the palace.

IV

Nesîbeh, daughter of Sheykh Fâris, was returning from the spring in the cool of the afternoon, a pitcher of water upon her head. She glided lightly down the stony path through the olive-grove – a mosaic work of golden light and grey-blue shade at that hour – crooning a love-song softly as she went.

The Emîr reined in his horse at the sight of her coming towards him. In a peremptory whisper he bad Ibrahîm stand and be silent. The faces of master and man were strangely alike at that moment. Both had the hungry look of a cat at a mouse; but the Emîr was looking at Nesîbeh, Ibrahîm at the Emîr.

Catching sight of them, the girl drew her veil hastily across her face. She hesitated a moment whether to advance or retreat, and finally stood a little aside from the path to allow them free passage.

The Emîr urged his horse forward. "Whose daughter is this?" he asked Ibrahîm in a whisper.

"What know I of girls?" purred Ibrahîm, with his widespread grin. "They are alike to me. Every girl of the village wears a white veil. Allah alone can distinguish one from the other."

The Emîr's face was very red, seeming fatter than ever. There was a strange gleam in his little eyes. "Ibrahîm!" he whispered hoarsely, "bring her to the palace, and secretly. Place her in the little chamber above the gate. Lock the door, and bring the key to me. Take heed that no man know of it. Canst thou arrange it?"

"To hear is to obey," purred the giant, with a grin even more catlike than usual. "She will keep her veil about the place, so that none but Allah shall know who she is; and Allah is merciful – He tells nobody. Who shall gainsay your grace? It is an honour that the greatest would seek for his daughter."

"Then stay thou here with the girl while I ride on," whispered the Emîr hastily. "Bring her with all secrecy to the palace. When thou hast her in the chamber give her food, and – wine. If she refuse the wine, force it upon her. See that none other have access to her until I come." With that he took the parasol from the hand of his servant and rode on up the path.

Ibrahîm drew near to the girl. "May thine evening be happy, O Nesîbeh," he said, patting her shoulder with his huge hand. "To-morrow is the day of thy wedding, – not so? The Emîr has heard of it, and he wishes to give thee a present and his blessing. Wilt come with me to the palace?"

Nesîbeh trembled, she knew not why. She glanced eagerly up and down the path, but no one was in sight. "My mother awaits my return," she murmured. "She has need of this water which I carry. If the Grace of the Emîr desires to honour me, let my father bring me to the palace."

"What dost thou fear?" purred Ibrahîm. "Am I not an old man and a friend of thy worthy father? As for thy pitcher, bring it with thee. His Grace the Emîr will not detain thee long, and fresh water does not spoil in half an hour. Why dost thou tremble, foolish one? Come with me!"

He clasped her shoulder as he spoke. And the weight of his hand convinced the girl that it was useless to resist. So she turned back and walked with him to the palace, her colour coming and going beneath her veil. A group of men squatting round the fountain in the courtyard, eyed them curiously as they went. But Ibrahîm explained matters by a knowing look, and they passed unquestioned, without other comment than a burst of laughter. Having mounted a flight of stone steps within the house, Ibrahîm unlocked a door and bade her go in.

"I will not enter," she exclaimed, with a sudden firmness. "I will await the coming of the Emîr in the courtyard."

"What is this?" purred the giant. "Thou wilt not? Thou art mad!"

He thrust her forcibly into the room, and locked the door upon her. "I will not give her wine," he thought: "it will make her too much the slave of that fatted pig. And now to tell Sheykh Fâris how the Emîr has rewarded his fidelity. I advise him to send a messenger to the Mutesarrif with all speed. A man new in office has a ready ear and a strong arm. Besides, there is discontent in Ain Warda about the matter of Ahmed Effendi. This Hasan is a fiery youth. He has many relations and friends among Selîm's men. If I mistake not, we shall have fighting before half the night is spent." And Ibrahîm, remembering the slaughter of the year Sixty, smacked his lips in anticipation.

V

The Emîr Ali Muhammad lay by an open window of his palace, looking out upon the village. The twilight was fast fading into night, and shadows were deepening westward, as the light of the moon grew stronger in the east. The Emîr closed his eyes, and his lips parted in a complacent smile. He grunted, as very fat, self-indulgent men will, like pigs, for no assignable reason.

The quavering voice of Amîn, the old major-domo, roused him from his lethargy. His Excellency's evening meal was prepared, the old man said, with a profound salaam.

"Bring hither a bottle of wine," grunted the Emîr. "I will eat later, at an hour of mine own choosing. Stay!" he added, with a chuckle, noticing the look of horror upon the face of the old Druze. "I had forgotten that thou art a true believer, and hatest wine. Speak to Ibrahîm that he bring it to me. Thy glance at the bottle would change my drink to vinegar."

"But with your Excellency's permission, here is his honour the Cadi, who wishes to speak to your Excellency. He has news of importance to lay before your Grace."

"May Hamad Bek's house be destroyed, and all that is in it! If he has anything to say, let him come to my presence at the wonted hour. Go, madman, and send Ibrahîm hither!"

The Emîr picked up a rose that lay upon his couch, and held it to his nose. It was his frequent habit to carry a flower about with him – not that he prized its beauty, but that its perfume might defend his nostrils from less pleasant smells. As he was fingering the stem carelessly, a thorn chanced to prick his thumb. With an oath he dropped the rose, and then, picking it up, proceeded deliberately to destroy it, petal by petal.

"So perish all enemies of your Excellency!" said a purring voice from the gloom of the doorway. "Here is the wine which your Excellency has commanded. May your Grace have the health of two men in drinking it."

The Emîr brushed the litter of rose-leaves from his lap. To complete his revenge he broke the stem in two and flung it from him. Then he turned to Ibrahîm, and bade him pour out a glass of wine. "Hast found out to whom this girl belongs?" he asked, glancing sidelong at the giant.

“I have obeyed your Excellency’s commands in all respects. She awaits your pleasure even now in the chamber above the gate. Of her father she has told me nothing. But what is that to our master, the Emîr? Small men and great, rich and poor, all are alike his servants.”

“Thou hast spoken to no man of this business?” The Emîr never looked straight at any one, but his eyes were piercing upon his servant’s face as he spoke.

“What am I, that I should disobey the commands of the Emîr?” purred the giant, with a cringing movement of his body. “My life is between his two hands. How should such as I dare to disobey him? Who would dare to uncover that which the Emîr has hidden?”

Ali Muhammad grunted his satisfaction. He was apt to be blinded by the fumes of his own greatness.

“What is this that Amîn has told me of Hamad Bek, that he has news to tell? If thou knowest anything of it, speak.”

“My lord the Bek is a good man and a just,” purred Ibrahîm reflectively. “But he is timid – with the permission of your Grace – a little too timid. He has not perfect confidence in the power and majesty of your Excellency. He reads misfortune in the frown of an enemy, and ruin in a poor man’s curse. There were many who cursed this afternoon, when justice was done upon the evil-doer, Ahmed Effendi. There were some who vowed revenge. Hamad Bek forgets that such people are as dirt beneath the feet of our master the Emîr, whatever they may be to the wicked Selîm of Ain Warda. He has doubtless come hither to warn your Grace of the threats that have been spoken. My lord the Bek is very timid.”

“I think so too,” grunted the Emîr, He shall be punished – downgraded! He to doubt my power! Cannot I, the Caimmacam, who set him up to be judge also drag him down? I shall speak a word in the ear of the Mutesarrif. Now follow me! I go to visit this girl.”

“With your Excellency’s permission,” whispered Ibrahîm, as he followed his master from the room, “as I, bearing the wine to your Excellency, passed by the door, I heard her weeping.”

The Emîr’s fat sides quakes with merriment. “It is a rosebud – a rosebud with the dew fresh upon it,” he chuckled.

And Ibrahîm, as in duty bound, laughed consumedly at the great man’s wit, but without noise, for fear of calling attention to their proceedings.

“Stay thou here and keep watch!” whispered the Emîr, pausing at the door of the girl’s prison-chamber. “Let no man pass this way. If she scream do thou sing aloud. Thy singing disturbed me once when I wished to sleep – then I had a mind to kill thee for it. But now sing on, and afterwards I will raise thee to great honour."

So saying, the Emîr turned the key, and, slipping off his shoes, entered the chamber stealthily, locking the door behind him.

Nesîbeh lay stretched upon the floor, her face buried in her arm, her slender form convulsed with every sob.

The Emîr stood smiling at her for a few seconds; then he went to a couch at the end of the room, squatted down, and proceeded to light a cigarette. "O light of my eyes!" he murmured, in a hoarse whisper.

The girl raised her head. "Who art thou?" she sobbed. "Oh, whoever thou art, let me go from this place. My mother awaits me since the ninth hour of the day, and now it is night. Let me go to my father's house with the pitcher of water that I was ordered to bring!"

She pointed to her pitcher, which stood in a corner of the room, beside it a dish of meat and rice untouched.

"My beloved!" grunted the Emîr. "Wilt come here and sit beside me on the couch, my soul?"

"No, no, no!" sobbed the girl. "If thou art the Emîr – whoever thou art, let me go!"

For answer the Emîr laid aside his cigarette, rose and went to her. He stooped down and strove to raise her in his arms. A piercing scream rang through the palace – another, and yet another. But all save the first were drowned in the inhuman din of an Arab love-song, which Ibrahîm, sitting on the stairs, chanted at the pitch of his voice.

The girl was on her feet, struggling with the Emîr, who, his face streaming with perspiration, his little eyes red and fierce as a rat's, was mastering her slowly but surely. All at once a sound made itself heard above the chanting of Ibrahîm, above the screaming of Nesîbeh – the report of a gun.

As if at a known signal, the love-song came to an abrupt end. The Emîr, still keeping firm hold of his victim, paused to listen. The sound of firing was continuous from the direction of the village.

"Open, O my master!" shouted Ibrahîm, thundering on the door. "The enemies are upon us! It is the men of Ain Warda, who have come to avenge Ahmed Effendi. Save thyself ere it be too late!"

The face of the Emîr changed colour slowly from red to ashy grey. The sweat upon his forehead was frozen to beads. Nesîbeh had no further need to struggle. With faltering steps he went to the door and turned the key.

The giant burst in. "Fly, fat pig!" he shouted, seizing the Emîr by the shoulder and shaking him. "Fly, offspring of a thousand swine!"

"Thou shalt be punished for this, dog that thou art!" muttered the Emîr, with shaking knees. So terrified was he, that he did not notice Nesîbeh as she slipped past him. "But say, whither shall I fly? I am an old man and weak: there is no strength left in me!"

"Then hide thyself, fool!" shouted Ibrahîm. "Go to the roof – to the stables – there are places enough. But stay not here, or I will let the air into thee with this," – he brandished a long, murderous-looking knife in the Emîr's face – "I, Ibrahîm, thy servant! Shall I not have revenge as well as another? Run, little pig! Bah! I spit upon thee!" Suiting the action to the words, the giant grasped the Emîr roughly by both ears, stooped down and spat in his face. "Now run, fat pig – run! Or thou shalt feel this goad of mine, that it is sharp."

"Thou shalt be killed for this," stuttered the Emîr. "But say, whither shall I go? They will take my jewels and my money. I will make thee Cadi in Hamad Bek's place. Son of a dog. If thou wilt but save my treasure."

"Run, old pig! Run if thou lovest life!" Ibrahîm grinned, and stuck the knife into the Emîr's flesh. "Hark! They are already at the gate. There will be none found to resist them. None love thee, pig – not one of all thy house. Run!"

The Emîr stumbled along the passage to the steps that led to the roof, cursing and praying by turns. Ibrahîm, the old massacrer, rushed with knife drawn down the steps and into the women's quarters, where his master's treasure was.

Ten minutes later he emerged upon the meydân[60], clasping a strong box with one arm. There he met a disorderly rabble running like madmen to the gate of the palace, firing shots at the windows as they went. Among the foremost, his face set and pale, his eyes ablaze with hatred, was Hasan ibn Mustafa.

"Y'Allah!" shouted Ibrahîm. "The fat pig, Ali Muhammad, hides upon the roof. Kill him! Kill all and spare not! The Drûz are the best of killers. Y'Allah!"

When they had passed, he set off at a run down the path to the village. A great pulse throbbed in his brain, so that he did not hear the tramp and jangle of a cavalcade approaching, until he was in their midst.

"Stand!" cried a voice.

"Who art thou that bidst me stand?" panted Ibrahîm.

"Madman, I speak in the name of the Mutesarrif!"

But Ibrahîm heeded not the answer. His knife was already plunged to the hilt in the body of the soldier; the warm blood was upon his hand. The victim swerved in his saddle, and fell without a cry.

---

60 The square of the village.

Ibrahîm made a spring for the shelter of the olive trees. There was a flash, and the report of a gun. The giant let fall the box, threw up his arms, and fell forward upon his face.

"Thou hast done well," said the Mutesarrif to the soldier who rode before him. "That shot of thine shall bring thee to honour. But go, one of you, and bring hither the box. Doubtless it contains plunder from the palace yonder. The Emîr Selîm will take command of my men as well as his own . . . . I shall be exceedingly obliged to you, my dear prince," he added, relapsing into French, his favourite language, "if you will ride on and quell the disturbance. For myself, I must stay behind and examine the box. It is a matter that must be looked into."

"What an unfortunate business!" said the Mutesarrif, an hour later, as he sat with the Emîr Selîm in the frenchified *salon* of Ali Muhammad's palace. "A dozen men shall die for this."

Loud wailing of women came from a neighbouring room, where the body of the Emîr was being laid out for burial.

"An unfortunate business – most unfortunate!" he repeated. "But at least it will assure the Powers of Europe[61], by whose favour I hold my appointment, that I have more energy than my predecessor. This Ali Muhammad had a bad name among the Franks. It is an excellent thing – as you well know, my dear prince – for a public man to establish a reputation for zeal and energy at the beginning of his career. He can rest upon his laurels afterwards. After all, I am not sorry that I have had occasion to distinguish myself on my first day of office. I had no time to rest from the fatigue of my ride from Beyrût before news came of the abduction of this girl. And then you came with your tiding of a riot to rescue this Ahmed Effendi – very amiable of you, my dear prince – and I rode off at once at the head of my men. If that does not convince the Powers of my fitness for the post, nothing will. I name you Caimmacam in the room of Ali Muhammad deceased. But the best of all is that box which we took from the giant with the white beard. On the whole, my dear prince" – the Mutesarrif rubbed his hands together and chuckled softly – "this is a most fortunate business for all of us, except – ha, ha, ha! – except the fat Emîr and the white-bearded giant. Most fortunate!"

---

[61] The administrative arrangements of Lebanon were introduced at the bidding of the European Powers, chiefly Britain and France, who were guarantors of the settlement.

THE BATTLE OF THE TREES

This story first appeared in As Others See Us, published by Collins in October 1922.

It is a story of conflicting perceptions in a changing world. The drivers of the construction of the telegraph wires were remote urban sophisticates who had nothing in common with the people through whose lands the telegraph wires passed. In the Arab lands of the Ottoman Empire older rivalries persisted leading inexorably to conflict.

Several of Pickthall's young characters are vainglorious young men, uneducated but full of dreams of fighting and "respect". As a contrast the wooed young lady in this story has a firmer grip on reality.

Down in the wady there were streaks of verdure, with here and there the pink of oleander-flowers. On the mountain-sides grew thistles blue and yellow, and a thorny scrub. In all the landscape there was nothing to be called a tree except, high up beneath a towering sun-bleached crag, one solitary terebinth, of which the shadow made a spot as black as ink upon the burnished heights. That was a sacred tree, and of its goodness served as sundial to the people of two villages, ten miles apart, which lay concealed amid the wilderness of tumbled rocks.

Abdullah and Mahmûd, reclining in a nest between two boulders on a jutting crag six hundred feet above the glen, were forced to crick their necks in order to consult it. Having ascertained that it was past the middle of the afternoon, their eyes returned to keep close watch upon the valley, becoming as the eyes of hunters, sly and eager.

Through the glen from end to end, there wound a new white carriage road; beside which, at a point immediately beneath their eyrie, was a camp of workmen, just now as busy as a hive of bees. The navvies were preparing to move on. The finishing touch which they had given to their work was seen in a line of telegraph poles, which ran as far as eye could see in both directions, crowding in perspective.

"Praise be to Allah! They are going," whispered Abdullah son of Hasan, to Mahmûd his brother. "This night, in sh' Allah, we shall reap the harvest without danger, as a child might pluck wild berries. It is wealth for both of us. Never in my life have I beheld so many trees! How many are there, think you?"

"A lot of tens," returned his brother sagely. He could not count beyond the sum of ten.

Abdullah hugged himself. "Fine trees," he murmured, "tall, straight, thick, solid, all that man could wish! They must be worth two Turkish pounds apiece, whether for firewood or for carpentry. If we succeed in gathering but ten to-night, behold us both rich men!"

"We can get more than ten," replied Mahmûd. "Our father will be with us and our mother and the girls."

"Remember that we have two axes only!"

"Bring pick and spade as well and dig them up. The camel and the ass between them can bear more than ten, supposing that they make three journeys to and fro."

"With my share of the riches I shall buy a gun. The one I have at present is old-fashioned. Then I shall go and try my fortune with the brigands."

"That would grieve me, O my dear one, for our father needs us. Stay in the village and buy sheep and goats."

"Nay, but my soul desires to see some fighting."

"Have patience. We will fight together. We will form a band!"

While they thus talked the tents below them had been packed and placed upon two trolleys drawn by mules. The workmen piled their baggage on another trolley, and took seat. The train went off with merry din of bells.

The watchers rose and went back to their work in what was called a field, a kind of pocket in the rocks which held good soil. Abdullah guided the light plough, whose pointed share but scratched the surface of the ground; while Mahmûd drew it, stopped often to pick up loose stones and throw them on a cairn hard by.

"They must be mad to leave that wood unguarded," mused the latter, wondering.

"They could not guard it all," replied Abdullah. "There are tens upon tens of trees – uncountable."

"Our father will rejoice when we inform him."

"Our mother also. What a stroke of luck!"

The shadow of the heights across the wady was drawing near them up the mountain-side when they set out for home. Mahmûd the serviceable carrying the little plough. The village where they lived was hidden like the field among the rocks and boulders. In olden times, the march of conquering armies through the glen had taught the fellâhîn to hide their cornfields and their dwellings as cunningly as small birds hide their nests from depredators; even in these days warlike Drûz and raiding Arabs[62] would ride by with hawklike gaze upon the heights for plunder. To a first glance the village, even when in sight, seemed part of the surrounding rocks.

As the young men drew near to it they saw an elder with white turban and a black and white striped cloak leading a donkey half concealed by brushwood, a blue-veiled woman following with a second load of brushwood on her head.

"Wait, O my father," cried Abdullah, girding up his loins to run. "O lucky day! The infidels have gone. The trees are ours – a forest – for the felling!"

His parents sat down on a rock and waited while he ran to them and told his tale. Mahmûd came up more slowly, with the plough. The old man, as he listened, scratched his ear. He said: –

"Your plan is good to take the trees, my children; but bad to keep the treasure to ourselves. The trees are many. Labour as we might, we could not hope to gather more than one kirât[63] of them. And tidings of our exploit would be sure to get abroad, provoking envy. The sheykh of the village would denounce us to the father of the road. Whereas if I reveal our project to the sheykh, the village will be with us. With two hundred of us working as one man, with tens of axes swinging, in one night we shall have garnered all the poles – ten times ten tens and more; and thus our share, upon a fair division, will come to more than we could hope to gather by ourselves."

The youths, though disappointed, bowed to his decision; and the four moved on into the village where, having stabled the donkey, they went out on the threshing-floors – the only level place above the wady. Out there upon a ring of green beside the village spring, which gushed beneath a ruined arch well-lined with maidenhair, a number of the elders sat discoursing while blue or white-veiled women filled their pitchers at the fountain. The father of Mahmûd

---

[62] Bedu.

[63] Kirât (cf. *carat*), the twenty-fourth of anything. (Pickthall's note.)

approached this group with confidence, smiling and rubbing his two hands together. He was drawn at once into their conversation, which grew animated. The two boys at a little distance watched and waited. Presently the headman of the village beckoned to them to draw near, and said: "You are good lads, and lords of high intelligence. Be sure that we will not forget you when we portion out the spoil."

The sheykh then rose and all the elders with him, crying: "Yallah! Set to work. The night is near."

Within two hours the village was in motion, streaming down into the valley under cover of the night. A crowd of children led the way on the rough track. Then came the sheykh and his five sons on horseback, a servant with a lantern throwing light for them; then all the able-bodied men the village boasted, armed to the teeth and carrying axes, leading with them beasts of burden of all sorts and sizes; and lastly a long train of women and young girls, some of them balancing pitchers full of water on their heads, clapping their hands in rhythm to a joyful chant.

"It is like a night of Ramadan," exclaimed Abdullah, speaking to Mahmûd, his shadow. "This is no labour, but a feast with lights and music. My heart beats proud within me. I desire to fight. O Allah, grant that some one may oppose us!"

The scene upon the road, when they came down to it, was gay and busy. Those who had spades and axes set to work at once upon the nearest poles. These, when hacked down or rooted up, were carried by the crowd of helpers to where the little herd of camels, mules and donkeys waited. The hewers then passed on to other poles, the women and the swarm of children moving with them, until they were some distance from the point where they had first come down.

The women doled out water, slabs of bread and salted melon seeds to every one who craved refreshment; and work went on beneath a running fire of jokes, accompanied by songs and merry laughter. Suddenly, no one knew exactly whence, awe fell upon the throng. Voices were hushed instinctively, and in the silence the sound of other axes could be heard distinctly, together with a murmur of a crowd no great way off.

Some boys, sent running to spy out the land, returned with news: –

"It is the folk of Kefr Hamad. They steal trees from us."

"The thing is filthy!" cried the sheykh with anger. "It cannot be borne. Come, O my children, let us shame these robbers!"

"Praise be to God, we fight, we fight at last!" whispered Abdullah fiercely in his brother's ear. Drawing an ancient sword, his father's gift to him, and waving it aloft with yells, he started running.

The sheykh and his attendant horsemen galloped off, the whole crowd following as best it could.

Abdullah was not far behind the horsemen, but, already, when he came upon the enemy, a heated altercation had begun.

"These trees are ours of right," the sheykh of Kefr Hamad was contending vehemently. "This is our territory. Your land does not extend beyond that rock."

"All on this side of the torrent bed is ours, as well thou knowest," cried the sheykh of Deyr el Hûr, with indignation. "Therefore the road is ours, with all that grows by it as far as eye can see from hence by daylight."

"Thou liest, O devoid of manners as of principle! The road is the Sultan's and free to all. As for these trees, they are outside the law, being the work of infidels."

"The land is ours, I tell thee, the trees too."

"The land is the Sultan's, the trees are for all comers."

"Son of a dog!"

"Degraded pimp!"

"I know thy mother!"

"O thou clot of dung!"

The speakers could not see each other in the darkness. Other voices then took up the quarrel. The men began to push each other forward, while the women in the rear of each party shrieked offence. All at once a gun went off; a child's cry followed; there was panic. Every one who had a gun or pistol let it off amid a storm of execration, screams and yells. And then the fight began in earnest, the two armies closing in without the room to swing an axe or lift a scimitar. They kicked, scratched, tore and even bit each other. Abdullah, fighting with his wits about him, full of joy, soon found his strength prevail amid that terror-blinded throng. He tried to keep Mahmûd in sight, but lost him and, supposing him to have been killed, smote with redoubled fury. Managing to free his axe he brought it slantwise down upon the turbaned head of an opponent, and laughed to find it sticking in the skull.

The men on either side were drawing off by that time, their thirst for murder slaked. And then the moon came up; they saw each other; and sudden shame came on them, with the fear of God.

"It is your fault, God knows," cried out the sheykh of Kefr Hamad, very bitterly. "O sons of greed, O tyrants and oppressors, to claim our trees as well as those you have of right."

"In all this wady every tree is ours by law," returned the sheykh of Deyr el Hûr, sobbing loudly. "The fault is yours for daring to oppose us. Behold the fruit of your contumacy! Are there not corpses on the ground between us?

Henceforth, unless the balance is adjusted, there must be war between us till the Day of Judgment. Go, take the trees! We give them to you, out of pity, O you poor doomed wretches! For every man of ours that you have killed or wounded here to-night, be sure that we will kill ten men of yours!"

"Men, say you? You have killed a woman – cowards that you are!"

The glen was filled with noise of lamentation. Abdullah had espied Mahmûd and run to help him. They stood together, stained with blood from head to foot, holding each other's hand, and waiting for some new event.

The folk of Kefr Hamad moved away, carrying off with them poles which had been lashed already to their beasts of burden; while those of Deyr el Hûr began, with tears, to load their animals with those which they had felled. That done they also streamed away towards the village, bearing their dead with them.

Abdullah saw with wonder that the people were departing homeward though many of the trees in sight were still erect. His heart beat faster. The sheykh of the village had acclaimed him as a hero publicly, and now he saw a hope of winning private fortune. He and his brother both had axes, with which much execution might be done before the morning. Calling his mother and his sisters, he commanded them to lead the camel and the donkey home, unburden them, and bring them back at once to fetch another load. That done, he bent himself to work, as did Mahmûd, his shadow. Before the dawn they had sent two loads home, and in addition had amassed a heap of poles too big to carry. Five of these they managed to accommodate upon the camel. A sixth they chopped in lengths and stacked upon the donkey's back. The rest, with the assistance of the women, they dragged and carried to the torrent bed, and there concealed beneath a scatter of loose stones.

Then, weary but content, they climbed up to the village, which they reached as day was breaking.

They slept all day. When they awoke, it was to find that they were persons of importance, who had till then been treated as mere senseless boys; and Abdullah, the imaginative, dreamed of sovereignty. He charged his mother to demand for him Nesîbeh, the daughter of the Sheykh Rashid – a girl who by her beauty and arrogance had ensnared his soul – and went his daily round as if the world belonged to him, attended always by a group of courtiers, weak-minded, servile youths who thought it bliss to be with him. He hungered for more fighting, and the times were favourable. Warfare was in the air. The men of Kefr Hamad raved of vengeance. One day, when he was passing near their village a bullet grazed his ear. Another man from Deyr el Hûr was set upon among the rocks by ruffians armed with scimitars, and done to death. A girl from Deyr el Hûr was violated. Shots had been fired at persons from the village while at work in the outlying "fields". Abdullah organised a band of desperadoes to avenge these insults. One night he even raided Kefr Hamad, killed a man or two and carried off the daughter of the headman of the place, whose house he entered. This girl he handed over to the sheykh of Deyr el Hûr, who sent a messenger to say that he would have her killed in the most shameless manner known in history unless the Hamdis at once paid over fifty Turkish pounds or their equivalent, and swore thenceforth to be subservient to Deyr el Hûr.

On that the father of the girl, with other notables of Kefr Hamad, invoked the overlord of all that region, Ali Bey Terâwi, who rode one morning from his castle of Judeydeh, twenty miles away, accompanied by many cavaliers, his sycophants, to the lone terebinth upon the heights of Deyr el Hûr, where deputations from both villages awaited him. The lower branches of the sacred tree were hung with strips of clothing, new and old, the votive offerings of generations of the mountain people. The great man sat down in the shade beneath those rags, upon a carpet he had brought with him. One of his servants held a parasol over his head for dignity; another kept off flies and other insects with a silken swish. His courtiers squatting round him on the carpet, applauded all he said. He questioned the contending parties patiently for half an hour, and then informed them that their quarrel was all nonsense. The poles belonged of right to neither village. They belonged to him. He commanded them to make peace instantly on pain of his extreme displeasure. The captive girl must be restored to Kefr Hamad, which village in return must pay ten pounds to Deyr el Hûr as indemnity for damage done to life and limb, and each village must pay twenty pounds to him in compensation for the trees. The sentence was at once accepted. The sheykhs of the two villages ran forward and embraced each other; the girl was handed over to her father, and an instalment of the money paid. The great man rode away contented with his morning's work. He had not noticed the small gesture – it was hardly noticeable – which in every instance had accompanied the vows exchanged for his delight – a jerk of the left thumb over the left shoulder, signifying "Backwards", which rendered all those vows of no effect. More potent than that scenic reconciliation in the cause of peace, was the fear, which shortly came upon both villages, of vengeance from the fathers of the road.

On the very day of peace-making, two unbelievers in a carriage drawn by horses had been seen examining the places where the trees had stood. And two days later more of them appeared, examining and measuring and taking notes.

A man of Deyr el Hûr, espied by them among the rocks, was asked by their interpreter if he knew anything about the disappearance of the poles. He said that he did not, but thought it was the work of gypsies or of Bedû – wandering, wild people who had no respect for anything.

The trees had been chopped up and hidden with great care, yet fear lest something should transpire to show their guilt was lively both in Deyr el Hûr and in Kefr Hamad. It grew to horror when some soldiers came and camped beside the road, protecting a new gang of Frankish workmen. The business of the latter gave much food for speculation till it was seen that they were putting up more trees. Then there was laughter and thanksgiving that such fools should live.

"Praise be to Allah!" cried Abdullah rapturously. "By their folly I shall soon be able to obtain my bride."

The parents of his heart's desire had sworn that they would not take less than fifty Turkish pounds for her, or the equivalent of that amount in trees or other property. The store which he had buried in the wady might be estimated at thirty pounds at most, and was not all his own, belonging partly to Mahmûd. It was therefore necessary to procure more wealth immediately before some richer man should come and buy Nesîbeh. The conduct of the girl herself excited him. When she met him, going to the fountain, or saw him pass her father's doorway, she would taunt him, saying she was not for him; or throw him a bewitching glance of her great eyes and, when his eyes responded, burst out laughing. He would get her, or else kill her and himself, he swore it.

"By Allah, I will fight and conquer, slay and rob for her," he told Mahmûd. "I will bring the wealth of all the country to her father's feet. And when I get her I will tame her finely, little serpent that she is!"

In truth, he was prepared for any rashness.

The workmen would not this time leave the poles unguarded, he considered. They or the Turkish soldiers would stay near them for a year at least. Whatever guard they left, he would attack and overcome it with his little band.

"I will pounce down on the soldiers while they sleep," he told his brother. "I will kill a dozen of them ere they find their whereabouts. With twice ten lads like thee behind me I am sure to win."

"You cannot find so many," sighed Mahmûd, whose mind was literal. "But I and those thou knowest will be with thee."

The brothers were prepared to fight against tremendous odds, and only waited till the work was finished to attack the trees. These seemed from what a man could gather from the heights – for none ventured down into the valley since the troops arrived – even taller and more solid than the former crop. The fathers of the road would guard them strongly, the villagers surmised with deep regret. What was their amazement, then, when they went out one morning to see the glen quite empty, the soldiers and the workmen all clean gone, the long procession of fine trees quite unprotected in appearance.

No doubt it was some stratagem, they thought. The soldiers would return at night and lie in ambush. But when upon the next day and the next the glen remained deserted, the men of Deyr el Hûr were minded to go down and reap the crop. Abdullah had convoked a council of the village notables, who hung their hopes on his valour and his gift for strategy, when a messenger arrived from Kefr Hamad with these words: –

"In the name of Allah, Merciful, Compassionate, the word of the sheykh and notables of Kefr Hamad to those of Deyr el Hûr. To-night let us go down to reap the trees. Let there be fair apportionment beforehand. Give us half, and peace shall be between us evermore."

The sheykh of Deyr el Hûr cried: "What is this? The trees are ours by law and ancient right. Since the men of Kefr Hamad beg of us, we grant them five, in pity of their indigence."

To these high words the messenger replied: "Then have I yet another errand to your honours. My lords of Kefr Hamad challenge you to fight a battle, your braves against our braves, in presence of the people, with swords and axes, this evening in the wady. The side which wins shall gather all the trees, and shall be lord over the other till the Day of Judgment."

The headman and the elders hesitated, something scared; but Abdullah urged them to accept the challenge, pledging his life that they should be victorious; and in the end their answer was: "It is agreed." Abdullah then assembled the young men of valour, looked to their weapons, and instructed them. Two hours before the sun set all was ready, the villagers began to go down towards the glen. As Abdullah came out of his doorway fully armed, the headman happened to be riding down the narrow way between the hovels, and his cruel mistress to be standing at her door hard by.

"Thou art our lion, our one hope," the sheykh called out to him. "Spare no effort, I adjure thee, to secure our victory. By Allah, I will pay thee gold for every wound thou takest."

The youth, with head erect and flashing eyes, looked proudly at Nesîbeh, who laughed jeeringly, and said: "Our lion seems to me much like an ass!" He ground his teeth. His heart beat in his head. He swore to win the day, and make her his.

The scene of combat was a level space beside the road, but hidden from it by some intervening rocks. The women, children and old men of either party sat up upon the stones. The able men stood ranked in the arena, the champions in the forefront of each host.

When all was ready, a huge brawny man of Kefr Hamad stood forth and with a yawn proclaimed that he was thirsty and desired much blood to drink. He was a butcher and saw many sheep before him. Why did they tremble? It would soon be over. He would undertake to finish any of these bleating milklings in less time than it takes to draw a tooth. He brandished an enormous antique scimitar.

A man of Deyr el Hûr strode to meet him, with fierce insults. The shouts of the two armies, each seeking to intimidate the other, were blood-curdling, while the champions danced defiance in the usual way. It was some time before they closed, but when that happened the Kefr Hamad man was instantly victorious. His opponent lay upon the field with head half severed. There were howls of triumph on the one hand, bitter wailing on the other.

"My thirst is not yet quenched. Here stand I! Lambkins, come!" called out the victor.

Mahmûd, the brother of Abdullah, ran out and attacked the boaster furiously, without the prelusory dance and insults, being mad with rage. The giant appeared shaken for a moment by the sudden nature of the onslaught, but he soon recovered. The battle had not raged five minutes when his adversary was disarmed and forced to kneel. The monster then bent back the young man's head upon his knee, drew a long knife from his girdle and, with a grin at the dejected host of Deyr el Hûr, he cut his throat. That done, he flung the body on the ground, and kicking it, crying: "Another! Bring another! for my thirst is great. Ha! These struggling weaklings grudged us half the trees. The right was with them. We will take them all!"

For a minute the scene swam before Abdullah's eyes, he seemed about to swoon. The brother whom he loved above all else on earth lay slain before his eyes, as fowls are slain. He heard his mother and his sisters wailing; his own heart was dead; but suddenly his wits grew more acute than he had ever known them. He saw the way to kill the monster – saw it quite distinctly, and without emotion. The trees – to win the trees – was his one painful thought, and incidentally his brother's death should be avenged. He had noticed that the Hamadi was heavy, that he fought in one position and did not turn quickly.

As swift as thought, Abdullah darted out and ran straight towards the challenger till almost within reach, then gave a sudden swerve and circled round his adversary. Round and round he ran, now drawing in to try a blow at the bewildered giant, now darting far beyond his reach, for ever circling till he saw the monster was half-blind with rage and growing giddy. Watching his opportunity he darted in and, stooping, hamstrung his opponent neatly with his axe. Then, springing clear as the big man swung round upon him, lurching forward, with a yell of pain, he darted in again and with a lightning flourish of his axe, smote down with all his strength. The blow fell on the bare nape of the giant's neck, and it was final.

Deyr el Hûr sent up a shout of joy, and before the conqueror had time to wipe his forehead he was assailed by all the host of Kefr Hamad. His own people rushed in to the rescue. His father, though an old man, stood beside him, fighting bravely with an ancient sword. Abdullah's one thought was to kill and kill again. Even when his father fell, he felt no grief, but smote the man who killed him and pressed on. Remembrance of the trees and of the girl he loved was in the background of his mind, as something which might still be saved amid the wreck of happiness. He was wounded in a dozen places; blood streamed from him. It seemed to him that all his veins were open, yet he fought on with undiminished zest.

The sun had set before he slew the giant. Before it grew quite dark the foe was in retreat, the field was won; the trees were theirs, and Kefr Hamad would for evermore be subject to the men of Deyr el Hûr. Abdullah, to his own amazement, felt elated. He had seen his brother and his father die, but he yet lived; the sequel of their life on earth was in his hands; no end of trees were his, with which to buy the girl Nesîbeh and make his name respected far and wide. Most of the villagers were gathered round the dead and dying. Beneath a crescent moon already near its setting, the keening of the women filled the glen. Some dauntless spirits cried: –

"The trees! The trees are ours. On to the trees and cut them, to assert our right. Thou, O Abdullah, art our chief, the bravest in the land. It is for thee to strike the happy blow!"

They led Abdullah to the nearest tree. The hero was beginning to feel faint from loss of blood, his brain was sometimes reeling, sometimes ominously still. Yet he was proud to strike the first blow at the trees, the cause of all the fighting which had brought him so much honour and such bitter woe – the trees which were to win for him Nesîbeh, the one pleasure left. Nerving himself with a tremendous effort, he threw up his axe, swung it over his head, the brought it down upon the tree.

A shock went through his frame from head to foot. The pole gave forth a dull, metallic sound. The axe glanced off, he heard a murmur of astonishment with disconcerted laughs from his companions, before he fell upon the ground insensible. These trees were hollow iron painted over.

KNIGHTS ERRANT

This story first appeared in As Others See Us, first published in October 1922.

Pickthall had travelled around Palestine in the 1894 and 1895, living with villagers and would have been familiar with the class and ethnic tensions of the country at the time. He was mindful of the divergent attitudes of Bedu, villagers and cultivators, townsmen who were satellites of the Ottoman administration, merchants (and usurers) and Ottoman soldiers who may well have been recruited soldiers. He also collected legends and folktales some of which were heroic tales of brigands. In this story he alludes to the heroics but presents us with the grimmer reality.

It is not known when the story was written. But it was published decades after he had been closely involved with rural Palestine. During the First World War, at a time of personal crisis – he declared his Islam in November 1917 – he also wrote up the relaxed happy times of his youthful wanderings in Oriental Encounters, published in 1918.

The great Sheykh Hamadan, chief of a whole nation of the desert Arabs, sat in his tent towards evening with the leaders of his host. At the tent-mouth appeared a throng of shrouded heads, with black tents on a sun-red slope behind. With face in shadow from his flowing head-shawl, he frowned and held his beard in a firm grip of anger. His eyes blazed. On a dead silence he let fall the words: –

"Bring hither Rih and Rihân."

After some scuffling in the entry, two young men of gallant bearing were pushed forward.

"Where is the saddle of the tax-farmer?" the chief inquired.

The young men looked at one another and then shrugged, as who should say: "So small a thing!"

"The saddle of the tax-farmer," observed Rihân, in the sly tone of one who would try fortune with a joke, "is interposed between the fattest region of his person and his horse's back."

But no one laughed. Rih and Rihân exchanged another glance. Their proud demeanour vanished all at once. The evening sunlight and free air appeared a great way off.

"By Allah, we know nothing of it," whined Rihân; "but we will seek it if it is Your Honour's will."

"Aye, by my courage," whimpered Rih in servile ecstasy, "Rihân and I will find it though it be beneath the sea, or held by giants, at the roots of mountains."

"Speak but the word, O King of Kings!" pleaded Rihân, as burning to set off.

But even as he spoke a saddle, highly padded and hung about with silken tassels and much gold embroidery, was brought into the tent on a man's head and shoulders; and the bearer cried: –

"Behold the stolen, O our Sovereign Lord!"

"Where found?"

"In the tent of Rih and Rihân."

The chief's gaze scorched the culprits!

"Sons of a dog," he cried; "you knew that we had given a safe-conduct to that townsman."

"Nay, that, by God, we knew not!" cried the young men eagerly; and many persons in the tent supported them in this contention, declaring that it was unlikely that they could have known.

"However that may be, you lied in answer to my question. Do that a second time and you shall die a painful death. Is my justice to be set at naught by dogs like you? Out of my sight!"

The youths slunk off dejectedly, threading their way as in a dream among the tethered horses and the tent-ropes till they reached their own abode, a low, black tent of camel's hair. Creeping inside, they wept together in a tight embrace. Then Rihân fell and ground his face into the dust, while Rih cried out to Allah for redress.

They were cousins, of the sub-tribe of the Billi. It was but two months since they left the pastures of their people, to join the armies of the sovereign chief, hoping to gain renown. Already they had won distinction in the warlike pastimes of the camp, and in a battle with the Bani Sakhâr they had unhorsed two champions, and gained two noble steeds of Kheylân breed. At tilt and tourney there was none to beat them, nor yet at shooting at a mark from horseback. But the prize on which they built their hope of lasting fame had been the saddle of the tithe-farmer.

When riding out one day in search of exploits, they met a man on horseback, armed to the teeth with every kind of weapon that could by any means be stuck or slung about his person, seated upon that monstrous saddle which in the sunlight could be seen from afar. This person was attended by a troop of Turkish soldiers; but these, being ill-mounted, were a mile behind when Rih and Rihân accosted him, inquiring in a friendly way how much that saddle cost, who made it, and why he was condemned to ride on such a cumbrous thing.

For all reply, the horseman called them sons of dogs, and bade them haste away or they would get a beating from his armed attendants. Such language from a townsman being insupportable, Rih and Rihân seized the boaster, one on either hand, and swung him clear out of the saddle to the ground. Rihân leapt down and sat upon him, while Rih removed the gorgeous object from the horse's back. Then they re-set him on his naked steed, and were themselves remounting when the soldiers, summoned by the great one's cries came within range. Then, for a moment, there was fear from bullets, and the cousins crouched along beside their horses' necks; but soon their thoroughbreds had borne them out of danger; and up before Rihân was set the saddle of the tax-farmer.

It was for this bold deed that they had been insulted and disgraced. The chief had played a dirty trick on them in sending men to search the tent, while they were absent. They had been ready to give up the prize at his command. He should have let them do so, to preserve their pride.

Some of their comrades came with words to comfort them, but such commiseration made them wail the more. When the last visitor had gone and night enveloped the great camp, Rih and Rihân, still sobbing, faced the question: what to do?

Their fame was ruined in the tribal chivalry. The head of all their race had proved a churl. It might be, as the visitors had claimed but now, that Hamadan had raised their nation by his discipline. "But that is not our object," blubbered Rih. "The nation's power is no man's glory. We might as well be in the Turkish service, moving together at a shout, like silly sheep."

"There is but one way to regain our honour," said his cousin. "We must invade the settled country and there do great deeds till all the world re-echoes with our fame; till the Turks entreat us to desist and make alliance with them. Sheykh Hamadan himself shall send an embassy to beg us to return."

"Yallah!" said Rih. "Let us depart at one. My soul is dead until we quit this place of shame."

They crept to the tent-mouth and listened. Jackals were howling on the hills around, but in the circle of the camp there was a silence broken only by the coughing of a horse, the snarling of a dog occasionally. The cousins stowed their few belongings into saddle-bags, then stole out and prepared their horses for the start; loosed them and led them cautiously to open ground beyond the tent-ropes. That done, they left the chargers lightly tethered and stole back through the camp with bated breath.

By the pavilion of the mighty chief, against the wall of camel's hair, they stood and breathed defiance with an inward speech.

"This day thou hast dishonoured men of worth, O proud Emir," said Rih within his soul. "The day will come when thou shalt go upon thy face to those heroic men and lick their feet."

"The scorn that thou didst heap upon us, O man devoid of manners as of sense," Rihân soliloquised, "is not a tithe of that which men of honour feel for one like thee. I spit between their eyes: I pluck thy beard and, as an earnest of my high contempt. I cut thy tent-rope."

He had pulled a knife out from his girdle to perform this threat when, a slight noise within the tent alarming them, the cousins fled, proceeding snake-like on their bellies till they reached the horses. They knew the standpoints of the watchers and avoided them, retreating northward on soft ground till out of earshot of the camp, when they climbed up into the hills in a direction south by west.

At dawn they saw before them a great lake with towns and villages upon its further shore, and rode down to the water's edge, where it was easy going. Near the lake's southern end they found a camp of half-bred Arabs, who received them with due honour as superiors. The adulation of those mongrels, the relief of boasting, restored their spirits and their self-conceit. Again they rode into a mountain till they gained a ridge from which they saw the mighty sea[64] rising from far below them to the eye-line like a great blue wall. Along that ridge a road meandered, and upon the road were Turkish soldiers marching northward in close bands. Having no wish to answer questions, Rih and Rihân rode down into a wady and there rested till the foes of chivalry had quite gone by. Returning to the road, they came to a large village, where they were horrified to find more soldiers halted.

An officer approached, asking to know by what authority they rode, thus armed for war, along the Sultan's highway.

---

[64] The Mediterranean Sea.

Rih and Rihân looked and perceived they were surrounded, save at one point only, where a laden donkey stood across the road, its owner talking to a white-veiled woman in a doorway.

"Thou wouldst see our permit for these weapons?" asked Rihân, assuming an appearance of extreme stupidity.

"Aye, by Allah!" said the officer, the soldiers and the fellâhîn in one derisive roar. Rih whispered to Rihân, then shouted: –

"Yallah! Read it! It is written on my horse's rear hind-hoof." He cleared the donkey and its panniers in a leap, Rihân beside him. Before the soldiers could recover their surprise and fly to arms, the two knights errant were but specks upon the road.

Thereafter, having had their lesson, they avoided villages and gave up their first intention, which had been to go into the Holy City[65] and make vows for their success, and also challenge the polite inhabitants to single combat on the town meydân. The government had no regard for chivalry and, if they fell into its hands, they might be made to drill or work like slavish townsmen or low fellâhîn. They made their vows one morning at a lonely shrine upon a mountain-top from where they saw the Holy City afar off. The guardian told them that it was the tomb of Prophet Samuel. Neither Rih nor Rihân had heard of him; but since he was a prophet, he was good enough. Though both were Muslims by profession, they knew nothing of the form of prayer, their practice of the faith consisting only of swearing by Allah and the Prophet upon all occasions and reciting the belief when challenged by the guard at night. On this occasion they prayed simply: –

"O Allah, grant us victory and great renown!" standing before the mosque of Prophet Samuel and looking towards the city which they feared to enter. That done, they rode again towards the south.

At length, descending on the fertile plain which lies between the mountains and the sea, they found a pleasant village amid olive-groves, to which the people, terrified by their appearance, made them welcome. Here were no marplot soldiers, no base-minded governors. The foes of chivalry lurked afar off at Jaffa and Gaza. It would take time for news of any feat of arms to reach them and arouse their ire. The nature of the country too was favourable for campaigning; for the plain was not dead flat, but well diversified with hill and valley, marsh and woodland, and miles of sand-hills all along beside the sea. The mountain gorges were at hand for hiding. And the land was rich. The soap and oil merchants of Jaffa, Gaza, Lydda, Ramleh were always going to and fro among the villages,

---

[65] Jerusalem.

from which they got their wealth, with bags of money; so were the Christian usurers who supplied seed to the fellâhîn in autumn, and claimed a large share of the harvest in return when summer came. Rih and Rihân decided to redeem this pleasant land from dull prosperity and render it illustrious by warlike deeds.

They pitched their tent in a secluded dell below the village, disdaining here as everywhere to sleep in houses, and made the fellâhîn bring food and fodder. Men, women and children gathered round and listened to their boasting, half amused, half awed. The cousins questioned of the country and of its wealth. At length Rih said: –

"O sons of water-melons, which grow fat exceedingly and yet remain attached for life to one small stalk, hear what I say! I am the great Sheykh Rih and here is Rihân, my cousin. Our presence brings renown to this your land. Your village and your conversation please us. We shall stay among you, returning always hither always from our valiant exploits. Become our helpers and grow rich beyond all dreams. Betray our secrets by a breath and we destroy you utterly. The choice is there. What say you, O devoid of spirit?"

The people hesitated for a minute. One exclaimed: –

"Bear witness, that we may be sure that you are Muslims and will not make us partners in some hateful crime."

Rih and Rihân bore witness loudly, and Rih added: "By the Koran, we are the best of Muslims – we pure-blooded Arabs. The Prophet – may God bless and keep him! – came of us."

The village preacher muttered in his beard: "And that, by Allah, is the greatest miracle!" but few of the assembly heard him; and none heeded. So the pact was made. Rih and Rihân became as lords in all that country, for no one of the fellâhîn dared stand against them; and the friends of order were far off in Gaza. At first there was much secret murmuring against their lordship, because of the supplies of food and fodder which they claimed of right. But after they despoiled a certain usurer, who was returning on the road to Jaffa with a train of camels, of all that he had taken from three villages in return for seed provided in the autumn; when they repaid both corn and money to the fellâhîn, the two knights errant were acknowledged to be lords of goodness deserving of the best that could be set before them.

The scene of their first triumphs was the tract of sand-hills between Ramleh and the sea. There they charged down on peaceful wayfarers, and trains of mules or camels, with appalling cries. They waved their lances in the air, or fired their guns, till their opponents, scared to death, fell prostrate on the sand, begging them for the love of Allah to take all they had. Having gone over all the goods and taken what seemed best to them, Rih and Rihân would condescend to spare the people's lives and, as they rode away, would say, exulting,: "Praise be to Allah, who has given us the victory!"

After a season of such prowess without one reverse Rihân assumed the title of the Conqueror, while Rih informed his sycophants among the fellâhîn that they might thenceforth call him the Redoubted Monarch.

Rih had a weakness which Rihân deplored. He loved the daughter of a poor fellâh of Yebna, a girl with roguish eyes and a small tree tattooed beneath her underlip. Rih left her in her father's house and only visited her there occasionally. Rihân would certainly have washed his hands of him had he become a house-dweller.

"What have we to do with women?" he would cry impatiently when Rih went off to visit his beloved. "Till we have earned eternal flame we should abjure their pleasures, save only in the way of vengeance on some hostile house. When we have gained our object we will marry two princesses" – meaning the daughters of some Bedawi of long descent – "and raise up seed of honour. Are there not sufficient half-breeds in this land already that we, the noblest of the noble, should increase their multitude?"

The half-breeds of his condemnation were the broken Arab tribes which wander in the settled country for protection with their flocks and herds.

Rih gloried in his weakness. On their warlike expeditions he would sing interminable songs in praise of Leylah – "for all the world," observed Rihân disgustedly, "as if she had been some princess of lofty birth." His love demanded bracelets of blue beads, also a silken robe for his delight, also a head-veil and a pair of yellow slippers; and Rih, who knew no comfort when she frowned, ventured into Gaza, though he feared the government, for, people said, a price was on his head. He dismounted before coming to the town at a friend's garden, and there hid his horse, which far more than himself attracted notice in a land where every beggar is a judge of horseflesh. Then he passed the gate, sauntering through the perfumed markets where the merchants called to him, spreading their choicest wares to tempt him, upon either hand. The many colours in the shade were pleasant to his eyes, his nostrils opened to the scent of musk and incense. He felt in no great hurry to complete his purchases, and when at length he had bought everything that Leylah wanted, it was growing late. Then he remembered an injunction of Rihân that he should try to find out if the government was moving; so he went into a tavern full of people, dropping his head-shawl so as to conceal quite half his face. He sat down in the darkest corner and drank coffee.

Rih and Rihân were then in every mouth, for they had cut the road along the coast to Jaffa; and Rih was shocked at the ill names those townsfolk called them.

"You will see," said one. "The end of such men is already written. A party of shadirmas[66] will set out from Jaffa and another from our city simultaneously. They will sweep the road. Those sons of dogs will either be destroyed in battle, or else be taken captive and securely hanged. Such miscreants deserve to be unburied. They are food for fire hereafter. Curse their father!"

The applause which followed this insulting speech struck Rih like blasphemy. These townsmen were indeed devoid of honour. They lacked the fibre which responds to valiant deeds. The vileness of their talk so fascinated him that when he left the tavern it was night.

He hastened to the city gate, to find it shut. He prayed the guards to open for him; but they only laughed and, knowing from his accent that he was a Bedawi, declared that it would do him good to spend a night enclosed. He told a woeful tale of how his wife lay sick and he had come into the town to purchase medicine. One of the soldiers then held up a lantern and took note of his appearance.

"By Allah," he exclaimed, "this is the greatest villain – Rih and Rihân in one! And we shall gain much glory by his capture!"

"Rih and Rihân are malefactors!" shouted Rih, though even in his terror the word hurt his throat. "I am a poor peaceful herdsman from the tribe of Malaha." He named one of the broken clans which haunt the villages.

"Malaha wear the shawl upon the other shoulder," laughed the corporal of the guard.

They pounced on Rih and carried him into their den. "Methinks thou comest of a tribe which for a while has sent no soldiers to the army," remarked the ombashi[67] when they had set him down.

Then Rih forgot his noble origin and all his fame; remembered only that he was the prey of soldiers in a kind of dungeon, and in immediate danger of three years of drudgery. The vision of his bride awaiting him in breezy Yebna, of his horse tethered in his garden near at hand, came to increase the horror of his plight. He fell upon the ground, he shrieked and blubbered; he embraced the feet of those base Turkish soldiers, hailing them lords of kindness, kings of men. They roared with laughter. And in the end they let him go for two mejidis[68]. That was the harshest part of it. His agony of terror, his despair, had been uncalled-for.

---

[66] Turkish troops.

[67] Corporal. Literally, in Turkish, a man in charge of ten.

[68] Turkish coins.

The soldiers only wanted a small fee, receiving which they opened the town gate for him, wishing him a pleasant journey and a happy night.

Humiliated to the dust, he found his horse and rode towards Yebna, cursing the day that ever he was born.

But as he journeyed in cool air beneath great throbbing stars, his soul revived and in his mind there grew a story of appalling danger and triumphant cunning, to redeem his shame.

Rihân was deeply interested in the news, which Rih had gathered in the Gaza coffee-house, that slaves of power were soon to march against them. For many days they were in great anxiety, watching the distant outlines of the country when they rode abroad.

One morning, after a successful foray, they went down to the gardens of Wadi Elmeyn to feast on oranges and sugar-cane by invitation of the fellâhîn; hiding their horses, as their custom was. They were sitting in the shade beside the bridle-path, devouring oranges, when four shadirmas (Turkish troopers) came in sight moving in their direction. The servants of the government were mounted on kadîsh, the common horses of the town, mere beasts of toil. The heroes and their entertainers quickly disappeared into a patch of sugar-cane. Only the gardener remained, sitting in the shade beside the water-tank. The soldiers, coming up, asked leave to enter and pluck oranges.

"Do me the kindness!" cried the gardener politely. "All is yours."

The soldiers got down off their horses and went in, leaving their guns and other weapons on the saddles. They asked for tidings of Rih and Rihân, and the gardener in confidential tones assured them that the brigands were resting in a village not far off. "Then we shall catch them before night, exclaimed the four shadirmas; and thereupon they ate till they could eat no more and lay down in the shade, made sleepy by the hum of bees. Hearing their snores, Rih and Rihân with their familiars came stealing from the patch of sugar-cane. The soldiers were fast bound when they awoke, exclaiming: "I seek refuge in Allah!" like people who suppose themselves bewitched.

Rihân addressed them with imperial mien: –

"O poor, manged dogs," he said; "does the Caîmmacâm, your master, think that Rih and Rihân, the greatest heroes of the age, are creatures like to you, that he lets you out of his protection in so small a number? Does he think that mules like those" – he pointed to their common horses – "are worth the half or quarter of a thoroughbred? Come, O my cousin, let us place the saddles on these men who are but asses, that they may bear them to the governor with our defiance.

We dare His Excellency to rise forth like a man and meet us in the field with lance and gun."

The saddles were then taken off the horses and fixed upon the backs of the dejected soldiers, who were driven, thus accoutred, to within sight of the Jaffa gardens. There Rih and Rihân unbound their arms and left them with barbed words of scornful pity. The common steeds, the swords and guns, thus captured from the government, they sold by auction to the fellâhîn.

That victory increased their honour, and their boldness grew; though for a while, through prudence, they forsook the sand-hills and shed their glory on the inland roads.

Then came the time of pilgrimage to the Prophet Reuben, when the road along the coast was more frequented than at other seasons of the year. A fellâh of Shahmeh, coming from the Gaza market, told Rihân that several parties of importance were about to start for Jaffa from that city, hearing that the sand-hills were now clear of brigands, and relying on the crowds of pilgrims for protection if they should appear. Among these would-be travellers was the son of the Cadi of Gaza, who had said, when people begged him not to risk his life, that his father's reputation as a righteous judge secured him like charm in that country.

Rihân was in Wadi Sarrâr when he received this news. He galloped off to Yebna, where Rih dallied with his low-born bride.

"Oho! Is that the case?" cried Rih, affronted. "Do they think we should be daunted by a thousand of their chanting pilgrims? Do they think we care a doit for their old doting Cadi, or esteem him just who has condemned so many lights of chivalry to common work? Well, they shall learn!"

His wife besought him to be cautious, for she knew his rashness, and knew also the prestige attaching to the Cadi's name. She was a pious girl, and feared the judgment of the Lord if Rih should interfere with pilgrims on the Prophet's road. But he made light of all her scruples and remonstrances. He and Rihân replied to all who would dissuade them, that they had been insulted and defied, challenged to show their prowess by ignoble townsmen.

The sanctuary of Nebi Rûbin (the Prophet Reuben) is a noble mosque uprising on the edge of marshes by the sea. It boasts a harbour, a small village, and some cultivated lands, but the mosque alone is to be seen from the main road, which runs to landward of the marsh, beneath the fields of Yebna, which rise up to meet the flat-roofed village on its hill. The day had been intensely hot. The Cadi's son and his attendants rested in the shade at Ashdod, intending to pursue their way by night. Rih and Rihân, in Yebna, had wind of this through their informers; and did not go to watch the road till after dark.

It was full night; the crickets in the stubble of the cornfields were silent save for a short note occasionally; hundreds of jackals over all the countryside were howling, answering one another from hill to hill, when Rih heard human voices drawing near the rocks on which he stood. He fired his pistol in the dark and was himself astonished, rushing forward, to see a man fall off a donkey close before him.

"Bâtil!" (a bad shot), he cried. "God knows I did not mean as much as that."

At the noise of the pistol-shot, the travellers dispersed in all directions. The son of the Cadi was left quite alone, huddled upon the ground beside his ass, which had not moved a step. Rihân rode up, dismounted, struck a match and lit the lantern which he carried with him. They searched the dying man, who groaned and prayed incessantly, and found a sum of twenty Turkish pounds.

"Tfû, aleyk" (contempt upon thee), muttered Rih, spitting towards his victim with intense disgust. "Thou, an effendi, a person of consideration, to start upon a journey furnished with so small a sum! . . . What of the donkey?" he subjoined reflectively.

"It is a poor one. Better leave it!" said Rihân. "Already they are howling there in Yebna. Their noise outshrills the barking of the jackals. And such is their respect for their accursed Cadi, that Allah knows but, in their consternation, the low-born curs may turn on us, their benefactors. Up and away!"

The cousins mounted and rode off.

The folk of Yebna howled through all that night, but no man of them dared go down on to the road till day-break; and then, when they beheld the dead man lying huddled and the donkey standing by him with dejected head, they looked at one another and declared: –

"This true believer is the victim of an accident. His ass was frightened by some jackal or hyena appearing from behind those rocks; and he fell off and died. If a robber had attacked him, he would certainly have taken this strong donkey, which is worth four pounds at least – and he had all the night in which to drive him – if not this robe of silk which clothes the body."

They raised the corpse and bore it up into their village where it was washed and shrouded, and then buried reverently to the chant of the Khatib[69] and wailing of believers.

The place where this crime was committed being midway between the towns of Jaffa and of Gaza, there was a dispute between the Caîmmacâms[70] of those two cities as to jurisdiction; the magnitude of the occurrence making both averse

[69] Preacher.

[70] The ascending hierarchy of Ottoman local government was Caîmmacâm, Mutesarrif, Wali.

to taking the blame. But the Cadi, father of the murdered youth, a man of influence, telegraphed to the Mutersarrif of Jerusalem and the Wali of Syria, superiors of both the Caîmmacâms, for help and protection. The Wali sent a squadron of cavalry with orders to bring Rih and Rihân to Damascus, dead or alive.

Then did our heroes lead the life of hunted beasts. The horsemen were distributed among the villages and never rode about the country save in force. The cousins were obliged to shun the haunts of men. Their friends among the fellâhîn provided them with food and fodder secretly; but most of the villages, whose sole desire was for protection, were now their open enemies, conspiring with the Turkish soldiers to entrap them. Warned by their spies they fled from place to place, too proud to leave the country tamely after all their boasting, yet anxious not to be surrounded and cut off from flight. Even their allies among the people urged them to depart. If they remained the end was written; they would forfeit life.

"We will challenge them to single combat, one after another, and prove that we are their superiors in feats of arms and horsemanship. These riders are no better than those asses whom we saddled and sent back to Jaffa with our challenge to the governor. By Allah, we will spit upon them," the two heroes boasted, with heads still full of tales of Antar and of Khâlid. But the fellâhîn, with pity and contempt, rebuked their folly. The villagers had lost their old respect, and dared advise them now as equals. This change was very bitter to the cousins, more especially to Rih, who had been wont to plume himself on the devotion of those people. But a dose more bitter was in store for him. He ventured into Yebna to embrace his wife, who, far from showing pleasure at the sight of him, flew in a rage and called him ugly names. He beat her soundly, till her father and her brothers came and held his hand. His wife, dishevelled, weeping, cried that she had always loathed him, declaring that the meanest peasant was his master in the arts of love. He was a boaster, selfish and vindictive, and a coward. "Coward! Coward!" she kept harping on the hateful word.

"Better divorce her," said her people, "since the case is so." And Rih pronounced the sentence of divorcement under their dictation.

At once, to his surprise, their aspect changed. They drove him from the place with blows and insults. He wept with fear lest they should call the soldiers; and as he slunk away he heard the voice of Leylah crying: "Praise be to Allah, I am rescued from that stinking Bedawi."

With teeth still chattering with fright, tears streaming down his cheeks, Rih rode by secret paths until he found Rihân, who told him that he had received a warning from the petty tribes to flee the country on pain of death. That was another insult hard to bear. The cousins wept upon each other's neck. It was as if the creeping things of earth had risen up against them and become redoubtable. Fear chilled the very marrow in their bones. By race they were afraid when people ceased to fear them.

The soldiers lived upon the country, and it was known that they would not depart until the heroes had been caught or driven out; so now all mankind was opposed to chivalry. Yet still the cousins lingered, fleeing on from lair to lair, not knowing in the morning where to lie at night. At length the Turkish captain, weary of scouting, gave command to sweep the plain. The game was up.

"We must do something to secure our fame!" the cousins moaned.

They then implored some fellâhîn of Shahmeh, who undertook to help them once again upon condition that they straightway left the country. The captain received information that the brigands were in hiding at a certain place. He went there with his men and learnt from one who stood there that the cousins had that minute galloped over an adjacent hill. The squadron rode off in pursuit. As they drew near to Wadi's-Samt in fine array, they saw Rih and Rihân to all appearance dying of fatigue, though the fact was they had but that moment started, having spent the night in Wadi's-Samt. As soon as the pursuers came within earshot, Rih called out: –

"O lord of kindness, halt your men a moment. We would parley. Our horses are outdone. We cry your mercy."

Thankful to see the end of his long task, the yuzbashi[71] agreed good-naturedly, and gave the order; when Rihân, rising in his stirrups, cried: –

"We dare you to a match on the meydân before us." He waved his hand towards a stretch of level ground. "Gallop, O sons of dogs, and you shall learn whether Arabian horses ever know fatigue."

The horses darted off. Their steeds were fresh, while those of the pursuers were already tired. The Turkish yuzbashi soon had the chagrin of seeing the two rogues pass out of sight.

"Another victory!" exclaimed Rihân. "Thanks be to Allah!"

"The crown of all – a deed whose fame will live for ever!" blubbered Rihân.

And heart in mouth, with frequent tears, they galloped southward towards the desert, afraid of every speck on the horizon.

[71] Major. Literally, a man in charge of one hundred.

EGYPT

KARÀKTER

A SYMPTOM OF YOUNG EGYPT

'Karàkter' first appeared in the Cornhill Magazine in early 1910 and was reprinted in Littell's Living Age in May that year. It was reprinted in Pot au Feu, published in February 1911.

The story is about a wealthy Egyptian farmer who is ambitious for his son, Ahmad, whom he sends to England for his education, in particular to obtain karàkter, character, seen as the quality that has given public school educated Englishmen their authority in the imperial control of Egypt.

The story is remarkable on several levels. In some ways Pickthall could be seen as writing about Egyptians with haughty condescension. The clothes and manner of speech are apparently mocked. We see Ahmad through the eyes of official British Egypt but much else is perceived through Ahmad's eyes. The house of a prosperous Egyptian with its glass windows and Frankish furniture, but above all his first impressions of England – "a land cloud-coloured, wrapped in cloud, the sea that lapped its cliffs seeming colourless as foggy air".

Ahmad returnes to Egypt after an English public school and a year at Cambridge, is found a job in the Public Works Department and gets along for a while with a British colleague, who then suddenly turns on him with racial abuse. Ahmad quits the job and joins the nationalists. The theme is repeated in a slightly different way in the last Egyptian story in this collection, "Between Ourselves".

In An Arab Tells His Story (John Murray, London, 1946, pp 137-38), Edward Atiyah (a Christian from Lebanon) tells a similar story. In the 1920s he worked for the British in Anglo-Egyptian Sudan working at the Gordon Memorial College and for the Intelligence Department. It was made clear that, in spite of his Oxford education, he was not "one of us". His Arab consciousness was sharpened by this encounter. He went on to be a founding official of the League of Arab States.

This story is discussed by Claire Chambers in Britain through Muslim Eyes (Palgrave Macmillan, London, 2015), 116-20.

"Karàkter – karàkter – karàkter!" The barbarous words kept recurring in the speech of the white-bearded fellâh, as he sat, with hands reverently folded in his hanging sleeves and eyes downcast, on the outmost edge of the chair proposed to him by the English official to whom he came as a suppliant.

"Karàkter! I want the boy to learn karàkter, that by its virtue he may become a power in the land. In the English schools they tell me that karàkter is placed first among the subjects which the pupils study. I came to hear of it by chance – O happy chance! – when the champions of Tanta[72] came to play our boys at football. They of Tanta called on Sayyid el Bedawi to give them victory, and we invoked our lord Ibrahîm ed-Dessûqi. But the Sayyid Ahmed was the stronger, or else our saint was asleep; for they won. Efendim[73], I was watching the battle, all eyes for my son's prowess, when, marvelling at the energy of the combatants, I cried: 'Wallahi[74], excellent. They surpass their instructors. Our sons outstrip the English, our good lords!' But one at my side said: 'No, for they lack karàkter; and without it there is no superiority.' At once I asked him what karàkter was; and he told me that the English, alone of all mankind, possess the secret of it, but it can be acquired in their schools for money. Efendim, we have money nowadays. Formerly one dared not hint at the possession, least of all in the hearing of a ruler like your Excellency; but to-day all that is changed – the praise to Allah and our English lords. And because I love our English lords, and admire their qualities, I would have my son instructed in karàkter, by the knowledge of which they are above all else distinguished. Efendim, do but name to me the best school in your country for that science, and my son goes there to-morrow."

The old man bowed his head and waited patiently for an answer; while his son, the same who was to learn karàkter, stood, silent and apparently indifferent, beside his chair. The boy, about fourteen years of age, wore a European suit of the cheapest sort – pale yellow patterned with a large black check – which might have fitted him two years before; but he had now so far outgrown its capacity that two inches of white sock showed between the trousers and his yellow boots – the hue of duck's feet – and the sleeves of the jacket could by no means be pulled

---

72 Tanta is a city in the Nile Delta, built around the shrine of Sheykh Ahmad Badawi, who was seen as the patron saint of the town. Ibrahim al-Disuqi was another Delta holy man.

73 Turkish term of address, Originally a Byzantine Greek word.

74 By God.

down to hide his strong brown wrists. He wore his fez well forward, at his father's bidding, in honour of the English inspector.[75]

The latter sat at his desk, with face half turned towards the visitors. He arranged some papers with one hand, while the other stroked his hair, and seemed to be struggling with a wish to laugh.

"You want me to recommend a school in England for your son here present?"

"Efendim, yes; that he may learn karàkter. The English schools are first in all the world for instruction in that science."

"But, O sheykh, karàkter is not a science. It is strength and durability of purpose; it is power of judgment. Some have it in them, some have not. It is not a thing which can be taught like mathematics!"

"No matter, efendim. It is found in England. Ma sh'Allah[76]! My son is intelligent, and has been well taught. He speaks English like an angel from Allah. Speak a little, O Ahmed, O my son! Let his honour judge of thy accomplishment. Compliment his honour prettily in English, as they taught thee in the school."

Thus adjured, the boy, with a sudden smile that seemed spasmodic, enunciated in high level tones:

"Great sir, may God bless you and all which are near to you. I luf to stand before your noble face. True, sir, this is the hab-yes day of all my life."

"You see!" exclaimed the father proudly, "he speaks the English like his mother tongue, after studying it for only half a year; he is so quick to learn. If I send him to school in England for three or four years he will acquire a knowledge of karàkter too, in sh'Allah[77]."

"But schools with us, O sheykh, are not for nothing. Here in Egypt rich men grumble if asked to pay a pound a month towards their children's education. In England twenty pounds a month for learning, food, and lodging is paid without a murmur."

The old fellâh, so humble in dress and appearance, made no demur. He said: "We have enough, the praise to Allah. Twenty pounds a month is not too dear for sound instruction in karàkter, which makes men like your Excellency. Of your charity, efendim, make inquiry for me; and when you have found the school, deign to write me a line – a single line with the hand of kindness. Just the name of the master and the address of the institution. My son reads English

[75] The inspector was the British official in charge of a district under the British occupation of Egypt.

[76] Literally, Whatever God wills. Here Sheykh Abdul Câder is emphasising the veracity of what he is about to say.

[77] If God wills.

writing. Ennoble my name: it is Abdul Câder Shazli. My izbah[78] is called Tût, belonging to the village of Mît Karam. And the name of my son? Is Ahmed, efendim – Ahmed Abdul Câder[79]. May thy good increase!"

Father and son then retired from the presence, the former calling blessings on his noble Excellency, the latter staring vaguely straight before him. Outside the government rest-house a mule and an ass were waiting in the charge of a ragged servant. The pair mounted, and jogged along the Nile-bank to their own place, marked in the distance by a grove of trees. Ahmed gazed at the familiar outline of those trees, and was glad. The outlines of the government rest-house, both without and within, being strange, had seemed hostile, carrying a chill to his heart. His mind was easily foiled by externals, playing with them, puzzled, like a drowsy kitten, supposing them good or bad, but vaguely and without vehemence. Set upon a dust-heap in his father's yard, he would stare for minutes at a time at the brown sheep or the poultry, and, roused at last, would as likely as not move peculiarly, in unconscious imitation of a strutting rooster. At school, too, whither he, with other sons of wealthy farmers, went with alacrity, regarding it as a place of games, where strange puzzles were propounded to amuse the sight and hearing – at school he would sit staring at the page before him till he knew the position of every vowel-point and lurking hamzeh[80], and could recall the whole at will, with each inflection of the master's voice when he read aloud for an example. It was the same with the English text-books of history and geography. Having once learnt to connect the shape and sound of words, he could remember their relative position on the printed page, and reel off the whole book by rote. This facility of learning won the praise of his instructors; he came to regard himself as of the cleverest where all were clever; and it was with a shock that, when an English inspector came to examine his class, he found that he could not understand the question put to him. Its significance was explained: "By what places would you pass in going from Cairo to London?"

Still regarding the question as bearing upon what he had learnt, Ahmed answered from the book, observing:

"London is the capital of England; it is the largest city of the world. It contains more than fife million inhabitants, or about half the bobulation of the whole of Egypt."

---

[78] Hamlet or country estate.

[79] One's name consisted of the personal name, followed by the name of the father.

[80] Short vowels in Arabic script are represented by accents or a single apostrophe above or below the preceding consonant. This is vowelling. The hamzeh is a voiceless letter, like a glottal stop.

The inspector stopped him in a voice of anger. He repeated the question: "How would you go there?"

"How should I know?" muttered Ahmed in Arabic. "I have never been, to find out. The khawâjah[81] is mad; he is cheating. It is not in the book."

And when the Englishman was gone, the Egyptian masters also said that he had cheated.

From that incident Ahmed had derived a bad opinion of the Franks as people ever ready to take mean advantage. To-day, in presence of the high official at the rest-house, he had felt the same as at that examination, and had expected to be asked some unfair question. If he desired to learn karàkter, it was only because his father told him it was the thing which made the Franks unanswerable. Knowing it, he would be their equal, if not master.

At the farm, consorting with the children who herded buffaloes, or playing a game with pebbles on a dust-heap, eating well, sleeping soundly, happy to sit in the sun and watch a dungbeetle, he awaited the promised message. After two weeks it came. A shawîsh[82] on horseback rose up to the doorstep of the grand new house with glass windows, which the Sheykh Abdul Câder had built for show, not habitation, and had filled with Frankish furniture. The soldier, as emissary of the great, was allowed to enter its closed rooms, and there regaled with coffee and a variety of sweetstuff, while young Ahmed in the foul old-fashioned homestead, close behind it, deciphered and translated the Englishman's note. A school and a master were named; there followed a list of clothes and other requisites.

Ahmed was taken by the train to Cairo, to grand foreign shops where both father and son were dismayed by the fixity of price, to the governorate and to the English consul's office. Then, with his new luggage, he was conveyed to Alexandria; basking in the atmosphere of importance without forethought, till he found himself alone on board the steamer, which began strange movements, when he crept into his bunk, and gnashed his teeth, for eighteen hours.

Awaking in a dark and stuffy place, he heard curious noises, and stole out to seek the cause. Along a dim corridor and up a staircase, he burst forth into sunlight, and felt sudden joy. Sailors were washing the decks; they smiled to him; the sky and sea were smiling. He sat down on a coil of ropes and watched the dance of sun-flakes on the waves, for ever rushing past, yet always there beside him. An Englishman on board had promised to take care of him. The man was kind; he often talked to Ahmed, and he looked after him in the landing at Marseilles and throughout the long train journey till they reached another sea,

---

[81] A term, related to Turkish, hoja, meaning teacher, but applied to Europeans.

[82] Junior military, like a watchman or a messenger.

and taking ship, saw England. Ahmed beheld a land cloud-coloured, wrapped in cloud, the sea that lapped its cliffs seeming colourless as foggy air. The crowding of strange sights, the cold, the lack of brightness reduced the young Egyptian to a state of sullen torpor. He arrived at the school and, after a brief inspection by the master, a most awful figure, was left to face the stare of other boys.

These fell upon him, dragged him this way and that, jabbering meaningless sounds to signify his native tongue, called him by evil names such as "nigger" and "slave"; but the native sociableness of the Egyptian soon disarmed them. Ahmed took everything in good part, even their laughter at his way of speaking. He accepted their point of view, laughed with them at his own ridiculousness, for was not their star manifestly in the ascendant? It was the season of football, and he was an excellent player; the goal in front, the flying ball, exciting all his faculties with the sense of an immediate aim. Cricket, when the time came, proved too slow, the object too remote, to please him greatly; yet he played it slavishly to please his comrades, and won praise. The elder boys took notice of him, and the younger sought his friendship. The whisper ran that he was a prince, and Ahmed smiled assentingly. He was whatever they liked, their servant to command, provided only that they did not bully him.

The holidays he spent at first in a household recommended by the man who had escorted him to England; but afterwards, when his popularity was established, at the homes of schoolfellows; upon whose sisters he cast longing eyes made shy by fear of vengeance did he dare assail them.

At his studies he was very diligent, and quite as happy as at play. He was quick at languages, and great at every science that depends on formulas. As his mental power increased, he could deduce from what he learnt corollaries, which, however, never passed the mental sphere, or bore the slightest application to the facts of life. Learning was, for him, a game of the wits, worth playing chiefly since it won applause. He became as popular with the masters as among the boys. "I am not only equal with the English," he was able to write to his father, "but I am on my way to become the chief among them. I am praised daily by my instructors; all my comrades love me."

In the same letter he asked his father's permission to proceed to the university, as that was the chief place for the formation of character, no Englishman being regarded as complete who had not been there. In conclusion, he assured his father that the cost of living at the university would not exceed the sum which was being paid annually for his schooling. His father consented, in a letter full of moral reflections, urging him to seek and secure for himself karàkter as the talisman of all success in life.

Therefore, in course of time, he went to Cambridge, changed his friends and learnt new formulas, was initiated into the mysteries of love and fashion, and shone in coloured shirts, in ties, in waistcoats. He bought a little dog and tried to like it, but every time the creature licked his hand he shuddered, conscious of extreme uncleanness. He was in his second year, at home and popular, with the prospect of distinction in the Mathematical Tripos, when a letter from his father shattered everything.

"Seeing thou art a man full grown," wrote the Sheykh Abdul Câder, "and must by now have learnt karàkter and all the other wiles of the English, tarry there no longer, for my heart yearns after thee. Besides, a certain great one with a kindness for me promises to exert his influence on my behalf, to obtain for thee a good position in the government. So return to us at once without delay, and may Allah strengthen and preserve thee ever."

When Ahmed opened and perused this letter, he was not alone. A man named Barnes, a mild and weak-eyed youth, was seated with him, smoking a briar pipe, in Ahmed's cosy rooms, whose walls were hung with photographs of grinning women.

"What a nuisance!" said Ahmed, frowning in the approved manner, though his heart was glad. "Dash it all, my dear ole man, I'm to go back to Egypt at once; the gufnor says so. Must gif up thought of my degree. The dear ole gufnor. He doesn't know how much it means to me."

"Can't you write and explain to him?" said Barnes feelingly.

"No, no, my dear ole chab! Impossible. He would neffer understand." Here Ahmed sighed profoundly. "We are still awf'ly primitive at home in Egypt – quite behind the times. . . . I must leaf at the end of term; there's no helb for it. I shall be deflish sorry to leaf all you good fellows."

"I shall be sorry too," said Barnes heartily.

This Barnes was of the order of amateur missionaries to be found in every generation of undergraduates, for whom the Mohammedanism of Ahmed Abdul Câder was an irresistible attraction. The gentleness and urbanity of Barnes pleased Ahmed greatly; they had become inseparables, and, without any promise of conversion, it was understood between them that Ahmed was to be the apostle of a new era in his native land. Barnes made his friend a parting gift: the Bible, which Ahmed accepted with a profusion of thanks, even with tears, hardly restraining the impulse to embrace the donor. But in the confusion of packing he forgot the present, which thus, being left behind, became the perquisite of his bedmaker.

Ahmed was extremely glad to go. He looked forward with a natural longing to his father's house, to the sight of camels raising dust upon the Nile-bank, of buffaloes wallowing and grunting in a reedy pool. To see the crowd of fellahîn assembled at the wayside station, to hear the familiar greetings as his father kissed him, was like waking from a dream to blest reality.

"Look at him, how he walks! Behold his modishness!" cried the Sheykh Abdul Câder, quite beside himself with exultation. "It is well seen that he has learnt karàkter thoroughly. We, too, are become more modish since thy going, O my son. By Allah Most High, we have a treat in store for thee."

The treat turned out to be a great gramophone, installed in the best room of the grand new house, thrown open to the world that day in honour of his home-coming. It was kept going incessantly by the efforts of two bare-legged helpers. Ahmed was annoyed at the sight of it, having learnt in England to despise such noisy instruments; but when he found the records were of Arab music, reproducing the chant of the best singers, male and female, and splendid versions of the Call to Prayer, he smiled at the trumpet-mouth as at a friend.

"Thou hast learnt karàkter, is it not so, O my son?" inquired the Sheykh Abdul Câder, speaking loud against the music.

"By Allah, that have I, O my father. It is a matter hard to catch as is a lizard; yet I have caught it, knowing thy desire."

His boast was, in truth, no vain one. He had acquired the English character superficially just as he had learnt by heart whole text-books in old days at school. He could assume it instead of his own, at any minute. He could even constrain himself to think like an Englishman for hours at a stretch.

"Praise be to Allah!" said the old man fervently. "To-morrow I will present thee to the notable of whom I wrote thee word that he has promised to take care of thy career – one set high in wealth and station, who sees the need of more karàkter here in Egypt. It is not simple now as it was formerly; thou wilt have to undergo examination. But that, I doubt not, will be passed with honour; no other competitor can have had thy advantages. In sh'Allah, by force of karàkter, thou wilt soon rise to greatness.

"In sh'Allah!" echoed Ahmed cordially; for the prospect of an easy rise to power seemed good to him. He was not without ambition of a supple kind.

The preliminaries were soon over. His father's friend approved of his demeanour; he passed the examination easily; and soon afterwards obtained, by influence, his first appointment as secretary to an English official in the Public Works Department. The post entitled his taking rooms in Cairo, whereas he had hoped for employment within a riding distance of his father's izbah. He had married in the weeks since his return, and his father would not let his bride go up to Cairo; better one than two in the city, he declared, where food is costly; on the farm an extra mouth made no great difference.

Ahmed, however, put regrets behind him, and repaired to the office with a will to please his chief. That chief was young, not five years older than Ahmed, and his mind was set on the acquirement of Arabic, of which he knew already many vulgar and obscene expressions. Finding his English speech not well received, Ahmed was quick to divine the other's foible, and flattered it by addressing him in flowery Arabic, and praising his excellence in that tongue.

"I haven't mastered it yet, though," said the Englishman, relapsing into English, "I should be obliged if you'd help me a bit."

"Most willingly," responded Ahmed with his ready smile. It was all he wished – to be of service, to win the regard of his chief, so that their work together might go forward comfortably.

The Englishman showed him copy-books and brought him exercises written in a hand like print, and Ahmed gave advice and made corrections – this in the intervals of office-work, which, being a routine requiring memory, seemed easy for the Egyptian. After a little while, the pair grew intimate; the Englishman forgot his first desire to air his Arabic, and conversed with his secretary freely on all kinds of topics. His character was of the simple English type, well-known to Ahmed, who had therefore no difficulty in anticipating his views and wishes. The Egyptian sometimes forgot their relative positions, and talked to his chief as he had talked to Barnes and other men at Cambridge. And his chief made no objection till a certain day, the blackest of all days, a day to weep on – which became the turning point of Ahmed's life.

They were sitting together in their room as usual when a clerk of lower grade came in with a request about some trifle. Seeing his chief get up and look unduly worried, Ahmed, with no other thought than to save a good friend trouble, exclaimed:

"Don't be a fool, old man! Sit down. It's nothing, really."

He had been sitting back in his chair, with legs crossed nobly, in the English manner; next minute he was on his feet, his face livid, his body shaken from head to foot by shame and grief. For his friend flashed round on him, ejaculating:

"Damn your insolence! What the hell do you mean by speaking to me like that?"

The clerk of lower grade was grinning from ear to ear.

"Why, whateffer did I say?" questioned Ahmed, his voice trembling with rage.

A flood of oaths was the answer. Ahmed drew himself up.

"I haf you know, sir. I haf been to Cambridge."

"Go to hell!"

And when the clerk had retired, the still angry Englishman quoted, as he sat down again at his desk, a vile Arabic proverb, an invention of the Turks, to the effect that if you encourage Ali, he will presently defile your carpet. It was an offence unthinkable.

How he got through the rest of that day's work Ahmed never knew! It was performed in anger, dimmed by acrid tears of shame. He hardly heard his chief's repeated adjurations to him not to be an ass; and answered all his orders with a simple "Yes, sir."

"There now, I'm sorry if I hurt your feelings. But you mustn't really use that tone to me, least of all in the presence of subordinates. Come, don't sulk any longer. Make it up, old man."

Ahmed heard the words and felt the hand on his shoulder, but made no response. When at last he left the office, he went not to his lodging but to the Nasrîyeh railway station.

At dusk he entered the yard of his father's izbah. The people greeted him with shouts of joy. The welcome loosed the fountain of his grief, till then restrained by pride. He ran to the threshold, and there fell down and wept, and moaned convulsively. The Sheykh Abdul Câder, leaning over him, attentive to the broken words his woe flung forth, piecing them together patiently, at last obtained some notion of the matter.

"Is it of thy khawâjah that thou speakest? Did he beat thee, O my son?"

At the question Ahmed roused himself, and spoke intelligibly.

"No, O my father! Would to Allah he had done so, that I could have prosecuted him for the assault, and made his name a byword for tyranny! He cursed me, O my father; he blackened my face with foul and grievous insults; and all because I addressed him in the usual English manner as a friend. I will no longer endure such treatment, I will be a nationalist. I was a friend of greater men than him at Cambridge. My best friend, Barnes, is the son of an English lord, whereas this dog is but the offspring of a base merchant – he himself confessed it! I will write to Barnes and have this dog degraded!"

The women and the neighbours wailed in concert, without any clear conception of the call for grief. But the old man raised his hands and eyes to heaven, crying:

"Praise be to Allah! Behold me justly punished for my proud ambition. I asked karàkter for my son, and see, he has it – more than I can bear. What Son of the Nile before him ever resented the curses of one in authority? Are not our backs and the soles of our feet still sore from the Turkish whips? Yet see, my son resents this cursing which to me is nothing. He must join the malcontents, the wastrels of the land, because of it. He is becoming even worse than an Englishman; he is all karàkter!"

A CASE OF OPPRESSION

This story was first published in the collection, Pot au Feu, in February 1911.

It tells a tale of contrasting views of law, rights and custom. Pickthall's sympathies were broad. He applauded the intentions of the British occupation of Egypt under Cromer and his successors, but was able to empathise with individuals under the occupation. Cromer himself was a fan of Pickthall's writings.

In this story there is an implicit acknowledgement of the solidarity of Muslims, believers, in contrast to the unbelievers. Pickthall, throughout his work, both in his fiction and in his religious writings, refers to the quiet people who accept with resignation oppression by the mighty, with the confident faith that God will put things right in the eternal afterlife. As the old man, the central character in the story, never given a name, says, "The great were ever thus, grasping, insatiable, eager to defraud the poor. . . Allah is above us both, and in the end He will redress the balance."

Across the wide green plain the sun was setting, and the town sent up its cries of glad relief. In the suburb of white-washed, red-roofed buildings round the railway station, as incongruous with the mud-built native town as a gramophone on a camel's back – which may also be seen to-day in the Egyptian delta – some masons, who for three months past had been engaged in the erection of a fine two-storeyed house, knocked off work for the last time. The job was finished, they gave praise to Allah; and were in the act of removing tools and hods and barrows from a temporary wooden shed put up to shelter them, when an old man came and wished them a happy evening. They returned his greeting casually, and were resuming songs and private jests, when the stranger added:

"Whose is this house? I wish to buy it."

Then they stopped their work and looked more closely at him. Their stare revealed a soiled white skull-cap, own brother to that which sheathed the crown of everyone of them, except their sheykh, who wore a turban also; two pointed ears which stuck out much above it, seeming handles to a wrinkled face of childlike gravity; a robe that had once been blue, open at the chest, and leaving bare two gnarled brown legs with feet encased in the cheapest of slippers – a poor man, if ever there was one, one no richer than themselves.

"Whose house is it?" the object of their gaze repeated, unperturbed.

The sheykh of the builders stepped close up to him, and laughed in his face.

"May Allah keep thee, O thou blessed one! Art an afrît[83] or what? The house is a fine one as thou sayest, and convenient; and I would let thee have it were it mine to sell. But know, O lord of wealth, that it belongs to the Government, and will shortly be occupied by one of their grand officials. It is worth ten thousand pounds; hast thou that much in thy hand at present?"

The old man gaped at first at this announcement, but presently he smiled, as seeing light, and said:

"I mean not that great stone house, but this small wooden one. Behold I am a pilgrim of three years ago. Three years have I taken to return from the City of Light[84]; and I am weary and would settle down. I find this city pleasant for repose, and when a minute since, I spied this little house and you, its inhabitants, in the act of moving, I said in my soul: 'O soul, behold the very place for thee and me to dwell in till the end.'"

The masons turned and glanced at one another with furtive smiles and winks, as who should say: "A fool! A Godsend!" They conferred in whispers; then their sheykh stood forth:

"That is another matter, O my uncle. I understood thy words to refer to that great palace, and, of course, derided them. This little house is mine, its price a low one. Step inside, I entreat thee, see how nicely built it is, all of the choicest wood and nails of iron – the nails alone are worth the price I ask, which is five pounds Egyptian. Only! It is a gift I make thee!"

The buyer shook his head, while cunning crept into his childlike smile.

[83] Afreet; a powerful jinn or spirit.

[84] A literal translation of the Arabic, *al-Madina al-Munawwar*, epithet for the city of Madina in the Hijaz, where the Prophet Muhammad is buried and one of the two cities visited by Muslim pilgrims.

"It was a fancy of mine to ask the price," he told them, "but I am not a lord of wealth as thou didst, jokingly, name me. I cannot afford to gratify each passing whim. Now, hadst thou said two napoleons[85] –"

"I seek refuge in Allah! O old man, it is well seen thou art a devil! Why, look around thee, see the excellent workmanship, the strong materials. This solid wooden post alone is worth thy two napoleons."

"Or three – ?"

"I call Allah to witness! . . . . Hear my last word: Thou shalt have the property – land, wood, and nails – for four napoleons paid into my hand this minute. It is to give the place away, I know that well; and I would ask any other than thyself three times as much. But because thou art here before me, the money with thee, and because we have to catch the train which waits for no man, I will take that price. What! dost thou still shake thy head, old madman? That, for a freehold which has not its like in all the town, adjoining palaces!"

"Hadst thou said three napoleons and a half – ?"

"Then let it be so, though Allah knows I thus defraud myself; for the love of thy old beard! Call it my present to thee. Tell down the money now, and all is said."

Two or three soldiers from the police-station up the road, a beggar woman, and some children had drawn near to watch the bargaining. The sun had set; the white road and the scattered, white-washed houses wore a ghostly pallor, the many windows of the latter staring like dead eyes.

"First," said the old man slyly, "I must have the paper."

"Paper! In the name of Allah, what paper? Hast thou the face to ask for papers, when I make a gift to thee? It were a shame for me to record the print on paper," quoth the seller angrily. "My enemies would make sport of my good nature. No, no, my promise is enough security; and all these grown-up men, my sons, are here as witnesses to the contract."

"Merciful Allah! Are all these thy sons?" murmured the buyer, staring round upon the grinning builders. "Ten of them! Thou art blest indeed!"

"May Our Lord bless thee! . . . . Come, what sayest thou?"

"The security is good, no doubt, as between man and man; but the law requires that I must show a paper, which is called my title to the house and land. No need, my dear, to name the price in it; write any sum that pleases thee, to save thy name."

"O Allah, hear him! He instructs us all. He knows the law, this dotard, and must have a paper. It is enough. We will not sell to him. We must be going!"

---

[85] A napoleon was a French coin equivalent to 20 French francs.

"Nay, go not!" the old man pleaded. "Is it so much to ask – a piece of paper?"

"The demand is just," put in a soldier, looking on. "Moreover, Hasan, thou must go with him before the cadi."

"Be silent, O Rashîd, O wicked joker!" snapped the sheykh of the masons crossly. "Meddle not in business that does not concern thee. The cadi, forsooth! The cadi means more money than the price itself. The buyer would be mad to ask it; since he must pay the fees, I will not pay them."

"I ask the paper only."

"Who has paper?"

"I have!" cried one of the confederates, and produced a fragment.

"A pen? Hast thou a pen?"

"Catch – a lead pencil!"

"Well, let us see. Bismillah[86] – canst thou read, old man?"

"Never a word, O my brother."

"Capital!"

The sheykh of the builders laid the bit of paper flat on his left hand, and wrote with the pencil on it hastily. Rashîd, the soldier who had once before interrupted, drew near and read aloud over the rascal's shoulder.

"'Praise be to Allah, who made some men asses.' That is all he has written, O my lord the buyer. Reflect, I advise thee: is it worth thy money?"

The sheykh of the masons sprang up in a fury and assailed the marplot, who retreated laughing. But the old man waited patiently upon his heels, smiling as one inured to cruel banter.

"Here is thy paper, O my soul. Now give the money."

"It is seemly that we recite the Fatiha[87] hand in hand –"

"Of course, but afterwards; I know the order. The money first, in my hand here present."

The sheykh of the masons thrust the hand beneath his nose. Cautiously, with hesitations, that old man took a purse out of the bosom of his robe – a leathern bag it was, suspended by a cord around his neck – and, holding it so that no one could observe its contents, picked out coins to the amount stipulated, and dealt them one by one into the seller's hand. No sooner was the tale complete than, with a cry of "Yallah[88]!" the masons snatched up their tools and ran like

86 In the name of God.

87 The Fatiha is the first section of the Holy Qur'an, recited by parties together on the conclusion of an agreement.

88 Literally, "By God!", but meaning, "Let's be off!"

madmen. In the twinkling of an eye, it seemed, they had vanished in the rising bloom of night; the buyer sat alone, amazed, but smiling.

"They stayed not to recite the Fat'ha!" he observed to the group of soldiers and street-urchins who still watched him, "neither had they the politeness to offer me a cup of coffee."

"Perceivest thou not that they have robbed thee, O my dear!" said Rashîd, with compassion for his guilelessness. "That Hasan is a son of sin, none like him! He has got thy money."

"And I have this little house. How, therefore, am I robbed, efendim? Is not this nice house mine to live and die in?"

"May Allah bless thee, for thou art a good old man and simple – much too good for this low world. Think not that I covet the house. It is thine so far as I and all men are concerned, till the English judge comes to live in that fine building. Then he may order it and thee to be removed. The land is his; to hear is to obey."

"Allah is greatest! He is my Protector. The great in every place torment and tease the poor. Nevertheless, I am a Muslim, I resign my name to God. I and my house are small, we my escape his notice."

"In sh'Allah!" said the soldier with a shrug, as he departed with his comrades. The old man said his prayers, then went into his little house and shut the door. The beggar woman and the children went away.

In the morning the new householder was out betimes in the market, buying requisites. Rashîd and another from the police-station, passing the shed at noon, beheld him on the ground before the door, making his meal of bread and onions.

"Do me a kindness, O my father!" called Rashîd. "Show my comrade here the paper which that rascal gave thee for a deed of sale."

"It is not with me," said the old man quickly; as if he suspected the soldier of intent to destroy it and claim the house for himself.

"Remember, it is true what I told thee: 'Praise be to Allah, who made some men asses'; that and nothing else is written."

"So thou sayest."

Rashîd then tried to shake the dotard's faith in the validity of the sale by argument, by heated demonstration, but in vain. His listener still smiled incredulous. The soldiers surveyed him as a holy marvel.

"Our Lord preserve him!" laughed Rashîd as they went their way. "He is a good, harmless man, and I feel just as if he was my father. In sh'Allah, the judge will spare him and his little house!"

On the following day he went again to the shed, and found its tenant employed in fitting up an awning for the door. A cat moved round him, purring, rubbing her arched back against his calves, his shins.

"She came last night to supper," he told the visitor with childish glee. "She ate with me[89] and slept indoors beside me. The house is happy with her music."

He stooped to stroke the cat, which rose to butt his hand. Rashîd stayed and helped him with the awning.

The dweller in the shed was soon well known in all the town. Despite his mean appearance, he paid for what he bought in ready money, thus gaining the respect of one who has a hidden store, none knows how plenteous. Yet his only extravagance was the purchase of six petroleum tins, four of which he placed at the four corners of his house, while the two remaining were employed indoors as receptacles, the one for oil, the other for water. His intention, so he told Rashîd, was some day to plant creepers in the outside tins and make his house a bower. As he moved about his small estate, planning and disposing, the cat was always with him, rubbing up against his legs.

One day the judge arrived. Rashîd had warned the old man of his coming, trying to arouse in him a proper fear of dispossession; but had got no more than: "Allah is greatest; He repays the tyrant!" Still the owner of the little house was standing at his door when the judge drove up to his palace, and made obeisance to his Highness from afar. Rashîd, who had met his Highness at the station and brought on his luggage, as soon as duty permitted, sped to the wooden house.

"I have told him thou art the watchman, the ghafîr[90] belonging to him. Thou art in luck, O my uncle, for now, in sh'Allah, thou wilt keep thy house and he will pay thee wages into the bargain. . . .Walk up and down with thy staff, keep folks from walking on this ground. It is a small thing for thee, and the pay is great."

"By Allah, no, I will not! I am no ghafîr. Allah knows I have toiled enough in life. Now, praise to Him, I have a little money and would live easy till my dying day. Let his Honour employ some needy man to guard his property; I have enough to think of in my own salvation."

"Well, Allah help thee! I have done my best."

The dotard pursued his own way as if the great house had been still unoccupied. When the judge, in passing, wished him a happy day, he returned the salutation kindly but without servility. One morning the great one reined in

89 But cats do not usually eat bread or onions.

90 Guard of a house.

his horse before the shed door and spoke peremptorily in baby Arabic[91], ordering that the petroleum tins should be removed, calling them ugly, bad, and sinful. The old man, regarding the command as gross impertinence, made no reply, but, stooping, stroked his cat.

"Dost hear me, O ghafîr?"

"I hear thee, O khawâjah!"

The judge rode on, appearing satisfied. But next day he stopped again and, pointing angrily at the petroleum tins, asked why they were still there. His voice, raised high in indignation, carried as far as the police-station. Rashîd came running to protect his aged friend.

"Efendim!" he exclaimed before the judge, bringing his heels together with a click and throwing his hand up to his brow, "the ghafîr is deaf. His intelligence is like walled up. An upright man, none better in the town. What is your Excellency's will concerning him?"

"He must remove those tins."

"Upon my head[92], efendim. It is quickly done."

Rashîd in a trice had put the tins indoors and piled them one upon another in the farthest corner. Their owner offered no resistance, but sat still in the sun before his door, stroking the cat in his lap, and repeating over and over again the statement that he was a Muslim and looked to God for redress.

"Of thy kindness, efendim, look upon me as thy servant with respect to him," said Rashîd as he again saluted previous to withdrawal. "If thou hast any will concerning this ghafîr, do but send and call me; I will make him understand. He is a good old man. I love him like my father."

The Englishman thanked him kindly, and accepted the proffered service.

It was not long before Rashîd was summoned on more serious business. He found the judge in the verandah of his house, frowning at shells of nuts, at crumbs of bread, and rags and bits of paper which defiled its floor. A number of people had been sleeping there the night before. Footprints ran all over the unplanted garden.

"What good is thy friend as a ghafîr?" the judge said crossly. "I shall have to dismiss him unless he shows more vigilance. His place is here at my door, not shut up in that shed. That shed must be pulled down, it is ugly. The builders should have moved it when they left. And another thing about the ghafîr, my cook tells me that he has set up a kind of tavern in that shed, sells coffee, and

---

91 The first indication that the man is a foreigner.

92 A literal translation of colloquial Arabic, meaning "I take responsibility."

food, and sherbet to the people. It must not be upon my property. Come with me now and talk to the old fool!"

"Hâdir[93], efendim!" Rashîd was quite aghast at his friend's madness. To set up a tavern, after the incident of the petroleum tins, after all his warnings, was the crown of indiscretion. He felt annoyance, and at the same time a sort of admiration for such saint-like obstinacy. Trusting in Allah to preserve the aged maniac, he accompanied the judge to the shed. There, to be sure, was the fool bringing out a tray with coffee to two men who sat on little stools before his door, playing the taverner. So it was true; the Berberi[94] cook had not lied in his report to the judge.

"What is this, O ghafîr?" shouted his Highness without other salutation. "Why didst thou let those people sleep in my balcony?" He pointed to the crowded footprints on the newly dried-up ground. "Art thou my ghafîr? If so, what mean these marks right past thy door? Dost thou understand me?"

"I can hear; no need to roar at me," rejoined the old man quietly. The customers on stools had turned their heads at the first outcry, but after that paid not the slightest heed to what was said, sipping their coffee tranquilly. "I am not a ghafîr, though thou hast called me so. Praise to Allah, I am granted independence; I serve no master in my old age."

"Hearest thou that, O Rashîd? He is no ghafîr; he is not my servant, and he is not deaf."

"O Excellency of the Judge[95], it is a miracle!" the soldier gasped.

"Listen, O sheykh!" pursued the Englishman. "What right hast thou to keep a coffee-shop without permission? I will not have strange people on my land. I will have this shed pulled down."

"Efendim, let me speak to him; I can make him understand," Rashîd thrust in, forgetting manners in his agitation. Clutching the breast of the old man's robe, he cried:

"Hear, O my uncle! Thou art in luck's way. His Highness intends nothing but kindness and great honour for thee. He appoints thee guardian of thy splendid mansion, and will pay thee monthly wages more than thou didst earn in all thy life before. Thou wilt dwell at his door day and night, and take thy toll of all who call upon him."

---

93 Literally, "Present, ready", meaning, "I am ready to do it."

94 Berbers, from the hills of Libya, Tunisia, Algeria and Morooco (along with Nubians from Upper Egypt) often provided the household staff for large houses in Egypt.

95 A literal translation of the Arabic address.

The old man calmly replied, "I do not wish it. I seek neither gain nor honour, but tranquillity. This is my house, and I will keep to it. Have I troubled his Highness with intrusions? Let him, on his side, cease from vexing me. These honest men are witness how he comes and worries me."

The honest men referred to gave no sign of hearing. Observing that they had finished their coffee, the old man took up the tray and carried it back into the shed.

"What was that he said?" exclaimed the judge in great astonishment. "His house! The house is mine, and I will have him know it. Hi! O ghafîr, O sheykh, come here and listen! Tell me, whose is this little house of wood in which thou dwellest?"

"Wallahi, it is my own!"

"By what right?"

"By the best of rights, the right of purchase."

"Hast thou the title-deeds?"

"I have."

"Then kindly show them."

"Nay, that I will not, here and now; it is not seemly. But come with me to-morrow to the Mehkemeh[96], before the judge, then I will show my paper."

"Show it at once, O ass!" whispered Rashîd fiercely. "Is not he who asks for it the judge in person?"

The old man showed his paper with extreme reluctance.

Slowly the judge spelt it out: "'Praise be to Allah who made some men asses!' This is no title-deed nor record of a sale, O sheykh, but simply a joke some wicked man has played on thee."

"Your Highness is pleased to say so," rejoined the claimant with a smile of much longsuffering. "Rashîd here present has made known to thee his jest at my expense, and thou hast deigned to share it. Thou art great and powerful, I am nothing; thou hast much, I little. It is a shame for thee to covet my small house of wood of little value, when thou hast that magnificent palace close at hand. But the great were ever thus, grasping, insatiable, eager to defraud the poor. Despoil me if thou wilt; thou hast the power; but seek not to cast doubt upon my title-deed nor to make any show of legality. Such wiles are beneath thee, surely, being rank hypocrisy. And remember Allah is above us both, and in the end He will redress the balance."

"But it is as I tell thee. 'Praise be to Allah, who made some men asses.' That and nothing else is written on this paper. Is it not true, O Rashîd?"

[96] Court of justice.

"By Allah, by the Prophet, it is true."

"You make a mock of me; these righteous men are witness! I am a Muslim, and resign my cause to God."

"Efendim, I will tell thee how it is!" cried Rashîd as though enlightened by a sudden guess. "This poor old man – may Allah heal his intelligence! – must have seen the builders moving their implements out of this little shed, and, thinking it would make a house for him, have asked the price. They sold it to him for a joke."

"Shame on them! Tell me where to find those builders."

"Efendim, they have gone their way; who knows their present whereabouts? For myself I know no more than that their foreman was named Hasan. It is in truth a shame, for this is a simple, pious man. I beg, efendim, be not hard on him."

The judge then turned to the offender, friendly-wise, and asked:

"O old man. Come and be in truth my ghafîr, and guard my big house yonder. Thou shalt eat in my kitchen, and in addition I will pay thee two napoleons every month."

The offer was a handsome one; Rashîd extolled it; but the old man shook his head and answered doggedly:

"No, I will not! I will dwell at peace in my own house."

"But this wooden house, I tell thee, is not thine. It is my property, and in a day or two it will be pulled down. What wilt thou do then?"

"I shall go my way, giving praise to Allah, as is due, and asking Him to destroy all tyrants who oppress the poor."

"To-morrow, I tell thee, this small house will be destroyed. See, I give thee money, more than it is worth. Come and be my ghafîr!"

The other refused the money without glancing at it.

"Nay, O my lord, it is no sale but robbery. O Muslimîn[97], behold me here, oppressed, despoiled. These two believers can bear witness how the tyrant tried to bribe me, to procure my silence. Had the house been really his, would he have acted thus? Would he not have haled me forth without parley or politeness? He has robbed me. My paper – O my paper!"

The judge, convinced of its worthlessness as a legal document, had not bothered to return the scrap of paper. With it crushed in his hand, he was striding back towards the great house. The two customers, who, in his presence, had seemed deaf and blind, directly he was gone, gave tongue to indignation, cursing his cruel tyranny, and asking Allah to have mercy on a much-wronged

---

97 Muslims.

man. They stayed with the old man all day and told his story to the passers-by, so that others stopped and tried to console him, murmuring curses on the tyrant. In the three weeks since his coming, he had made himself familiar in the town; greeting every man with childlike friendliness, and boasting the convenience of the little house, which thus became his by common knowledge and repute, the best of titles. When Rashîd next morning came to introduce the workman charged to demolish and pull down the little house, he found his aged protégé the centre of a considerable crowd of angry sympathisers. Seeing a chance of disturbance, he sent for two armed comrades from the police-station. With this support, he set to work to help the old man move his few belongings.

"Where is the cat?" he asked.

"She forsook me yesterday. She has gone to the kitchen over yonder." He pointed to the white-faced, red-roofed palace. "When she knew I was despoiled, she went over to the tyrant like a child of Adam. Allah is greatest[98]."

The judge came again and offered money to the old man, and also the appointment of ghafîr, but to no purpose; and Rashîd begged him earnestly to withdraw, for the murmurs of the crowd were waxing louder, they were anathematising the oppressor. Rashîd, for conscience, bought the six petroleum tins at a fair price; and at last the dotard, having wrapped his pots and pans up in his bed things, took the bundle on his shoulder, and trudged off down the road, the crowd escorting him with loud compassion.

A few days later, Rashîd read in a news-sheet from the capital two columns of denunciation of an English judge, who had evicted a poor man from his humble freehold and annexed it wrongfully. Knowing the rights of the story, he laughed loud with his comrades.

"But it is the fault of the English," he felt bound to admit. "They act like common men, not rulers, seeming doubtful of their right; so others doubt it also. A ruler has one word, with force behind it."

---

[98] Literal translation of *Allahu akbar*.

THE MURDERER

This story was first published in Pot au Feu in February 1911.

The dialogue is archaic. Pickthall was creating a distinctive style to transport his readers away from twentieth century Britain to another world. The language is comprehensible but deliberately contrived. He used the style in Saïd the Fisherman and in other Middle Eastern novels and short stories.

Pickthall had wandered around the villages and small towns of Lower Egypt and was familiar with the details of life among the villagers and the relationships with the British occupiers. But this is not his best Nile Delta story. The characters are too stereotyped and the story is not as convincing as others. Was the writing rushed? But the murderer's wife is an example of the forceful lower class Egyptian woman, not at all a stereotype.

A full moon shining through the palm-leaves made strange play of light and darkness on the flat-roofed houses, growing one out of another, which made the village seem as a fungus-growth within the grove, as Idrîs, the hired assassin, stole softly to the dwelling of Sheykh Ferîd. An owl kept hooting near at hand. No owl but hoots if she beholds a murderer. Idrîs was used to her harsh cries of disapproval; but, being religious, would have deemed himself accursed had he omitted the proper formula to avert their omen. He repeated it now.

At the Sheykh Ferîd's door he coughed, and then exclaimed, "O Great Protector!"

By this pious injunction of the Most High, his presence was made known to those within. The door was opened by the Sheykh Ferîd in person, saying:

"Is it thou, O Idrîs? Do us the kindness! Enter! Honour us!"

Idrîs was too experienced in his profession to presume on the advantage which the shameful nature of his business gave him with superiors. A novice would have taken liberties; Idrîs refused a seat on the divan, and remained standing reverently before the conspirators, who were the Sheykh Ferîd and his two brothers, all old men. Idrîs was not yet thirty. He was what is called in lower Egypt a "shûshâni", that is to say, half negro, half Egyptian. His broad, thick-lipped face would have had the negro's childish friendliness had it not been for an angry scar upon his forehead. That wound he had inflicted with his own hand and with prayer, to impart the ferocity needed for success in business. With eyes downcast, he waited for his lords to speak.

His reverence appeared to irk the Sheykh Ferîd, who moved the Frankish lamp upon a stool or low table, which was the only movable the room contained, and cleared his throat repeatedly before beginning:

"Listen, O Idrîs. Thou art like a son of my house, and I speak freely to thee. This is why I sent for thee: there dwells in this village a vile malefactor, whose presence is a poisoned wind in all our faces. He grows in pride with every day. He despises my authority as omdeh[99], and yesterday refused me salutation. I require of thee no crime, but a good deed. What sayest thou?"

Idrîs made a gesture of deprecation. "What is his name?" he inquired.

Again the Sheykh Ferîd moved the lamp, looking down upon the floor, then glancing at his brothers interrogatively. The greybeards nodded; seeing which, he said:

"His name is Muhammad abû Hassan."

"I seek refuge in Allah!"

"I will pay thee thirty pounds."

"Nay, O my lord, it is too dangerous. To kill a man of the village where one lives is dangerous; and it is never done. Moreover, the faction of the Sheykh Muhammad is a strong one, and I fear their vengeance."

"Son of a dog!" cried out the Sheykh Ferîd. "Art thou also of that faction, that thou refusest a good offer? By Allah Most High and His Apostle, thou shalt hang. I know how thou didst kill that man at Kafr Adas, and can find witnesses. Am I not here the omdeh, and to be obeyed?"

"Am I not thy slave?" replied Idrîs. "Nevertheless my case is hard, at your Honour's mercy."

"Well, then, I will give thee forty pounds, of which ten now in advance."

"Efendim, it is the custom to pay half beforehand."

"His demand is reasonable. Let him have the half," said one of the old men, brothers of the Sheykh Ferîd, producing as he spoke a purse.

Idrîs, having received his fee, withdrew politely. He responded not at all to the jokes and caresses of his employers. Putting on his slippers at the door, he sighed:

---

99 Village headman.

"O Giver of Victory, O All-knowing, O Beneficent, O Merciful[100], O Allah and my parents, approve!" – the common prayer of men embarking upon serious business.

Back in his own house, he found his wife awake and on her feet, carrying to and fro the baby, which was crying. When Idrîs took the child from her, its wail at once subsided. The woman, with a sigh of thankfulness, lay down again.

"What fortune?" she inquired.

"As black as pitch!" replied her husband sadly. "I am ordered to slay a righteous man – our neighbour in this village. Just when I had bought some land, and settled nicely. My employer is a devil, and he knows my history. He has sworn to have me hanged if I should fail him. O Allah, show me some way out of it! My wit is dead to-night."

"Is the money much?"

"Not much, for such a deed."

"And the cause of hatred?"

"Envy – always envy! No sooner has a man grown rich than he perceives one richer with the eye of rivalry, which leads to hate. May Allah Most High destroy the house of Envy, for it is the cause of all wickedness in Masr[101]. I seek refuge in Allah from Satan the Stoned[102]."

He laid the baby, now asleep, beside the woman, and, squatting down upon his heels, sighed desperately.

"Listen, O Idrîs!" his wife said presently. "Canst thou not go to the victim and put fear on him – thou, who has the trick of making men afraid – and persuade him to fly to hiding for a time? Thus thou may obtain the credit for his death, and time wherein to sell thy piece of land."

"Praise be to Allah!" cried Idrîs. "It is good counsel. I must work at once."

He passed out again and crept in the shadow of mud walls till he came to a space clear of palm-trees as of houses, which divided the village into two unequal parts. Beyond it, in the grove, the dwellings of the Sheykh Muhammad abû Hasan and his adherents looked like large anthills. In the middle of this glade, upon the dustheaps, were gathered the village watchmen, twelve of them, nursing their staves and talking in low tones.

"Attest the Unity[103]!" they cried in concert, springing to their feet, as Idrîs appeared before them suddenly.

[100] These four titles are all names of God.

[101] Egypt.

[102] A customary invocation by pious Muslims.

[103] That is, declare that you are a Muslim, acknowledging the oneness of God.

"There is no god save God, and Muhammad is the Apostle of God! Have no fear, O my brothers! It is I, Idrîs."

"We have no fear of thee, old devil. In other places thou art feared enough," their leader answered. "Eblîs[104] himself is kindly to his own. Whither away?"

"To the house of a comrade over yonder."

"Thou must be brave to walk alone at night."

They sat down once more among the dustheaps, while Idrîs went on to the dwelling of the Sheykh Muhammad. There, leaning to the crack of the door, he called upon the sheykh by name, at first softly, then with fierce impatience, so loudly that the dogs began to bark.

"Who cries out there?" exclaimed a voice at length.

"By Allah a friend, charged with an errand which concerns thy life. Art thou alone, O sheykh? For none must hear us."

"Thy name is what?"

"Idrîs the murderer, saving thy presence. But have no fear, I come in kindness. I am unarmed. By the Prophet, if thou hear me not, thy fate is sealed."

"Swear by thy salvation not to harm me or my house."

"By my life, I swear it."

The door was opened by the Sheykh Muhammad, a small grey-bearded man, with shrewd black eyes, holding in his hand a lighted candle. He had doffed his fez and turban for the night, and wore in their stead a close, white skull-cap.

Having ascertained that no one else could hear – for the house was a grand one, boasting four good rooms – Idrîs explained his errand to the sheykh, who, as he listened, had a fit of ague."So I must kill thee – I could kill thee now, left-handed, armed as thou art" – Idrîs glanced scornfully at the pistol in the sheykh's belt, – "unless thou come to terms at once with me." As it were distractedly, he made a clutching gesture, which brought his fingers within reach of his companion's throat. The trick was done; the fear was put on him. The Sheykh Muhammad shrank in abject terror.

"I give thee fifty pounds to spare my life."

Idrîs extended his mud-coloured left hand – he kept the right for honourable dealing – and, tapping its palm, said bluntly:

"Put!"

"I will go and fetch the money. Have no fear!"

"Fear!" scoffed the murderer, and remained chuckling all the while his host was gone.

The money in his pouch, he changed his tone for one of deference.

---

[104] Demon, devil, Satan, derived from the Greek *diabolos*, whence diabolical.

"Now deign to listen, O my lord, while I, thy slave, instruct thee what to do. There is but one way for thee to escape death; it is by flight immediately. If thou remain in the village, I must kill thee; or thy enemy will have me hanged. You, who art a lover of the poor, consider me, a poor man, in this sore dilemma. A month's retirement will not hurt your honour, while it will save my life, and give me time to sell my land and leave the district."

"Agreed, I will take leave of my dear ones, and fly with the first light."

"May thy house be destroyed! Wouldst thou secure my ruin?" Idrîs became once more savage. "Thou wouldst tell thy wives, thy sons, and have the story known to the whole world? Fly at once, this minute, or, by the Lord, I kill thee!"

That was enough. The murderer himself procured a mule and, mounting the sheykh upon it, led him forth, walking for many miles across the plain. At dawn, in a region where he was not known, Idrîs, with pious blessings, turned and left him.

Relieved of awe by his departure, the Sheykh Muhammad recovered the use of his wits, and rode for the chief town of the province, intending to lay his case before an English inspector.

Idrîs returned to his house about the fourth hour of the morning, and slept until the third hour after noon. He then arose and broke his fast, before repairing to the omdeh's house.

The Sheykh Ferîd was busy when Idrîs entered. The latter took a low seat and abode his turn. When everyone was gone except the two old brothers –

"It is finished," he exclaimed dramatically, drawing his left hand sharp across his throat.

"Good," observed the Sheykh Ferîd, so carelessly that Idrîs, alarmed, was moved to state his claim.

"Where are the twenty pounds, in kindness, O my lord?"

The Sheykh Ferîd surveyed him very haughtily. "What mean these words, O insolent? Come not here with thy demands, O lacking in manners[105]! I know nothing of thee or thy deeds."

"But thou didst swear before two witnesses here present."

"Thy speech is strange to us," replied the brothers.

The omdeh added angrily: "Begone immediately and mend thy manners, or, by the Prophet, I will have thee hanged."

Such bad faith was a new thing to Idrîs, who, up to now, had always met with liberality from his employers. Horror getting the better of his habitual

[105] A literal translation of *adabsiz*, the Ottoman Turkish word.

servility, and disgust at such treatment maddening, he called the three sheykhs atheists and pledge-breakers, and with a talent of malediction turned his back.

A few steps from the door he saw what he had done, and burst out weeping. He had offended the small tyrant of the village, who had power to make his daily life a hell. Yet his cause was just; the omdeh had behaved iniquitously. Where was justice, where was conscience here in Egypt? Surely nowhere but in the credulous imagination of the poor murderer! Stumbling along the narrow paths between the hovels, blind with grief and indignation, he cried to One Above for succour, and asked all true believers to attest his wrongs.

"O Muslimîn!" he howled. "Oppressed! Oppressed! I, a Muslim, am oppressed most sorely. May Allah make an end of tyrants, contract-breakers! The omdeh has sworn to persecute me, only because I claimed my just due. He is great, I little. What help for me, my masters, under Allah? See me ruined!"

At these cries the hovels poured forth their inhabitants. Idrîs was caught and held by friendly questioners and, when it was clearly known that he had right on his side, was led out to the dustheaps where was space for gathering. There the mob resolved itself into a council – a process not unheard of in Egyptian villages – in which the poorest and most insignificant, even small boys and women, had the right to speak – a council whose decisions, wise or foolish, are redoubtable. It was agreed on all hands that the omdeh had behaved abominably. The hottest lovers of the Sheykh Ferîd cried shame on him. A deputation was appointed to rebuke him, saying:

"This true believer had a contract with thee, to rid thee of thy enemy for a certain sum. He did rid thee of thy enemy, yet thou withholdest half the wage. He is a simpleton, a truth-teller, by no means clever like your honour. The whole village is incensed at such conduct. Thy face is blackened[106], with the faces of us, thy adherents. Pay him the money quickly, that men may praise thy name as heretofore."

But the business of the deputation was forestalled by the omdeh, who had heard of the formation of the court, and feared its judgment, appearing on the scene of conclave with his two old brothers. A woman shouted, "Shame on thee, O sheykh!" and the cry was taken up on all the hillocks. "He did what he was hired to do – he slew the enemy. Pay him the twenty pounds which thou still owest!"

"What means this talk? The man has lied to you. My quarrel with him is a trifle not worth mentioning. He demanded rudely, and with insult, a sum which

[106] That is, shamed.

I had promised him in bounty. See, I am come to pay it – it is nought to me – to put a stop to this commotion in the village."

Someone near enough to hear this raised the shout: "He pays!" whereat a roar of satisfaction rose.

The Sheykh Ferîd went up to Idrîs and told the gold into his hand ostentatiously, whispering:

"Thou art cleverer than I am. But remember, I know nothing of this talk of killing. I promised the money in pure kindness.

But the murderer, beyond the reach of hints in his excitement, supposing that his right was called in question, cried:

"A gift, thou sayest? Canst thou deny that thou didst summon me last night –"

"Be silent, madman, liar, ass!" the old sheykh screamed; but Idrîs, infuriated by such epithets, spat at him, and called out:

"O Muslimîn, hear the whole truth. Last night he paid me money to assassinate the Sheykh Muhammad abû Hasan – "

At that name there arose a violent disturbance. Though Idrîs continued speaking, he was quite unheard.

"It is true. He is missing. He cannot be found. One came in the night and fetched him, it is said. God gave us vengeance on the men who slew him," cried the partisans of the Sheykh Muhammad; while lovers of the Sheykh Ferîd declared it was no matter.

The court of ready law was turned into a faction-fight.

The women alone were undivided; and these rushed with one accord upon Idrîs, who then knew fear. His great strength helped him not at all against them. Did he lift a hand they cried: "Aye, kill us, do! – weak women! O thou hero! – Thou shalt see, we will tear thee in pieces, O miscreant, who slew his neighbour, a good righteous man, for gold! May Allah blast thee for attacking friends and neighbours."

"Listen!" he wept at last, as some began to claw him. "Allah witness, I am most innocent of all men living. The Sheykh Muhammad is alive this minute. I am a poor pious man, no devil. I saved his life by a stratagem – at great peril to myself; for the omdeh hates me, and had sworn to hang me if I failed."

"Then thou hast not earned the money which we made him pay."

"Yes, yes, by Allah – yes, as far as he knew! He believes that I have killed the Sheykh Muhammad. It was, therefore, wicked of him to refuse to pay me."

"True; the right is with thee."

Idrîs had come to this point in his contest with the women, and began to see that he must forthwith change his place of residence; the rival factions of

Muhammad and Ferîd were joining battle close at hand among the dustheaps, when a ghafîr came running out from the village with loud cries of "News." He sped to the omdeh and conferred with him. The tidings spread like fire; a great one of the government was close at hand; and the villagers had not recovered from their consternation at this rumour ere the said great one appeared – an Englishman on horseback, clad in a white suit and a broad white hat, followed by ten mounted policemen. Idrîs, forgotten in this new excitement, mingled with the crowd, bent nearly double to disguise his stature. He heard men say the omdeh was arrested.

"So it is certain that he did assassinate the Sheykh Muhammad."

"No; he still denies it vigorously, calling Our Lord to witness."

Idrîs pressed onward, eager to learn for himself. At length he was so close to the Englishman that he could hear the jingle of his horse's bit above the clamour. He was sidling nearer yet, in hopes to overhear the conversation with the Sheykh Ferîd, when a shout of praise to Allah rent the air. Springing upright for a moment, he beheld the Sheykh Muhammad emerging from the village on his mule.

"It is himself," was cried on all hands. "He is alive – Muhammad abû Hasan."

The Sheykh Ferîd forgot discretion in astonishment. In a terrible voice, he shouted: "O Idrîs, O clever devil, where art thou? Come hither; give me back my forty pounds!"

The cry was heard afar. The Englishman laughed loudly, and remarking, "Out of thy own mouth, O sheykh," had him arrested. The amusement of the crowd of villagers dawned slowly, after the manner of appreciations which will last for ever; but in five minutes men were helpless on the ground with laughter, girls were dancing madly, giving forth their joy-cries.

"Hear, O people!" said the Englishman in intelligible Arabic, when the uproar had in some degree subsided, "Are you not ashamed of your most wretched state? It is this day seen how the hired assassin is the king among you, extorting gold from whom he will; sparing, killing at his royal pleasure. And why? Because he is the best among you, the one brave and resolute amid a host of cowards, little children. . ."

Idrîs stayed to hear no more. With a sob of thanksgiving, he fled to his own house, and told his wife the government had done him justice and exalted the poor murderer. He bade her prepare at once for departure, and helped her make their few effects into a bundle.

When the Englishman rode forth from the village an hour later, a little behind his escort, having stayed to light a pipe, Idrîs was waiting for him by the nearest sakieh[107]. His wife, the bundle on her head, the baby in her arms, was there behind him. The murderer ran out and kissed the horseman's boot.

"What is thy errand to me?"

"Efendim, I am thy slave till death, for the sake of those kind words thou spakest but now concerning me. Let me but follow thee, and be thy servant. By Allah, I will guard thee like a lion."

"I do not understand. I do not know thee. Say, who art thou?"

"Efendim, may it please thee. I am that poor murderer whom, of thy kindness, thou didst call the best of men. May Our Lord reward your Excellency for praising me thus nobly in the ears of all – me, who am of the race of the poor despised, whose good deeds, whose piety, men are wont to overlook. I have done ill deeds, efendim, but always by compulsion and never without the proper prayers to God for pardon. I never neglected my religious duties, as many who cry shame on me do daily. Efendim, I implore thee, let me go with thee. I am a good man, to be trusted. I am ruined here. These people do not understand things like your Honour."

"What canst thou do?" the horseman asked good-humouredly. "Canst thou groom a horse, or cook, or wait at table?"

"Efendim, no; but I can put thy fear on people. That is my business: to make people afraid."

"And thou knowest all the rascals, all the malcontents, and, if occasion rose, could lay your hand on them."

"Efendim, yes! And I will serve thee truly."

The inspector thought a moment.

"Well, be it so!" he said at length with a laugh. "That is a great gift – to put fear on people. Come, and we will see what we can make of thee."

Idrîs stooped down and kissed the rider's stirrup, giving praise to Allah for this high preferment. Calling to his wife, he started on the dusty tramp along the dyke-path. He wept tears of pride. Thenceforth he was a member of the government.

[107] Water-wheel used to extract water from a canal for irrigation.

THE COOK AND THE SOLDIER

This story first appeared in Tales from Five Chimneys, published by Mills and Boon in June 1915.

It tells of a dispute between two Egyptians, both called Ahmed, one a soldier, the other a cook. The story is based on the world of Egyptians that were usually invisible to Pickthall's probable British or American readers. The British occupation is remote and the two British who are in the story, both nameless, appear almost as intruding outsiders. The two Ahmeds have plenty of personality, the British are shadowy caricatures, the reverse of contemporary literary practice.

It all arose out of a handful of lentils, as Arabs say. Ahmed the cook kept a little eating-house at Bûlâc[108], in a narrow street, within sound of the hammering from the shady boat-builders yards, and not far from the point where one takes the ferry to Gezîreh[109]. Ahmed the soldier, being in barracks at Abdîn, found his day one day to the said eating-house, and, meeting kindness from the professor, returned there often.

Now Ahmed the cook – in Egypt styled "professor" – was a one-eyed man; which means he saw more with his mind than is the way with two-eyed men, who stare all round them. He was also a wicked wag. As he became acquainted with the character of Ahmed the soldier, he discerned in him a heaven-sent subject and played upon him to the joy of other customers, who held their sides to see an upright man abused and mystified.

The soldier was childlike; his mind possessed no fold of guile or subtlety. This world was for him a place of peril to the soul, whose chance of safety lay in

[108] A suburb of Cairo, on the east bank of the Nile, north of the centre.

[109] The island, *jazira* or *gazira*, in the Nile in central Cairo.

strict adherence to the divine rules; observing which he felt secure as for himself, and had no time to spare to look at others.

It was long before he perceived that Ahmed the cook made fun of him; and then he took no notice, philosophically, since in return he got well treated in respect of food. When, one day, his host beguiled him into handling with great reverence a donkey's hair, under the persuasion that it had been plucked from the tail of the Prophet's mule, he did indeed curse loudly when the fraud was shown to him. But he still returned to the eating-house; and, Ahmed the cook going gently for a time, he soon lost the suspicions to which the touch of blasphemy had given birth. For months things went on amicably, till a certain afternoon when Ahmed the soldier came to the shop fatigued and irritable.

The usual guests sat out beneath the awning upon stools, and along the edge of the platform where the professor had his brazier. Across the street there glowed a stall of fruit and vegetables, diffusing pleasant odours in the shade. Ahmed the cook embraced his soldier namesake, and made him sit up in the shop itself, a place of honour. He gave to him a mess of rice and meat, winking aside to his cronies, who looked on with secret smiles. When Ahmed the soldier made an end of eating, Ahmed the cook paid him the usual compliments, and, pouring out a cup of coffee, added: –

"Thou art indeed most blessed, O my brother. Thou art become, indeed, a marvel and a gazing-stock, seeing there is that this minute in thy belly which no one of the sons of Adam ever ate before thee."

"What is thy meaning?" asked the soldier, spilling the coffee handed to him in his great concern.

"That meat I gave thee was the flesh of jackals."

"O son of a dog! It is understood thou liest."

"By my beard, I tell thee! Ask all these here present."

"The curse of Allah on thy faith, O atheist, O evil-doer. May Allah cut short thy life for this foul crime!"

Springing to his feet, Ahmed the soldier spat at the professor, then fled the place, gesticulating like a madman.

The audience remained, convulsed with laughter.

"Saw the man ever the like for simplicity of understanding?" gasped out Ahmed the cook in the intervals of his amusement. "Now he will curse his belly and go vomiting for days, for the sake of a little mutton mingled nicely with a mess of rice. To-morrow I must tell him."

"By Allah, if thou do not, he will know no cleanness till the Day of Judgment!" laughed his friends.

Meantime the soldier wandered in the neighbouring streets, bemoaning his disgusting plight, adjuring Allah and all true believers to behold and succour him. At the cry "Ya Muslimîn!" men came out of their doorways. A crowd soon gathered round the wretch, and questioned him. Ahmed the soldier told his story, weeping sorely, solemnly cursing Ahmed the cook, the joker, who, by a trick, had robbed him of salvation. Every listener expressed his horror at such wickedness.

"That professor is a hellish joker. Fools laugh, and egg him on from deed to deed. But now he has passed all bounds of decency. He has sinned against the religion of Muhammad. . . . To serve the meat of jackals to a true believer, an honest customer at his shop! Heard one ever the like? It seems that there is no security. No one can tell what filth is set before him. To the shop, O Muslimîn! We must teach this pig, this atheist, a lesson."

So it came to pass that, while Ahmed the cook still chuckled with his friends, the street grew full of noise. They saw their consternation mirrored in the countenance of the vendor of fruit and vegetables across the way, who saw, before they could, the crowd approaching. In a trice their council was dispersed by furious men, who used religious war-cries as against the heathen; the stools, snatched up, were used as weapons; the brazier was upset into the street; the cups, the pitchers, and the shishehs[110] smashed to atoms; Ahmed the cook, thrown down upon his back, was being beaten, before one present had time to cry for mercy, or so much as guess the cause of the assault.

"Take that, and that, O atheist, O filthy dog!" cried one man, striking the professor with a wooden stool. It was who could get near enough to spit in the face of so obscene a wretch. Learning at length from the cries of the assailants what the matter was, Ahmed the cook began to scream that he was innocent, that Ahmed the soldier was a credulous ass, a madman, a born idiot. But he would none the less have very been bashed to death, had not one of his adherents, making off up the street, with intent to jump into a tram and fly to Cairo, met two policemen striding to the scene of riot. Pouring into their ears the true story of the disturbance, he went back with them to the shop, now wholly wrecked, as likewise was the fruitseller's across the street. The policeman forced a way through the press. They rescued Ahmed the cook from twelve assailants, and heard his explanations, which, when known, appeased the crowd – some of its members being moved to merriment, while others still cried out it was a shame. The ringleaders gave money to the police, so did Ahmed the cook, rather than be put in prison. Then people moved away.

[110] The water bottles of nargilehs, hubble-bubbles.

Alone at last among his smashed utensils, the professor gnawed his lip and glared straight downward with his only eye.

"Would to Allah," said he viciously, "That I had fed that devil jackal's meat in very truth; for see what he has brought me to – the dolt! – the madman! By the Prophet, I will give him viler food when next we meet. I will give him his own flesh, and see him eat it. The worst is, now he knows it was a joke. I could enjoy my ruin, did he feel himself defiled eternally."

Ahmed the cook was wrong in this surmise. Ahmed the soldier had not lost his sad delusion. When the indignant Muslims, his avengers, went to wreck the cookshop, he had turned away, still weeping bitterly. What they were after was an act of retribution, of religious justice; but it could not purify him. He went back to the barracks, and there told a comrade under bonds of secrecy.

His friend suggested an emetic; they went together and bought one in a pharmacy, and Ahmed used the stuff not once nor twice, yet he could not feel clean. As the days wore on, he grew inured to his predicament, to the fear that at the Last Day he might arise together with an unclean beast; and only brooded on his woe when downcast. But if ever there was talk of wicked men, deserving slaughter, he said that he had known one such, and hoped to kill him.

His good conduct and alacrity commended him to all his officers, though his extreme simplicity seemed an obstacle to much advancement. Whatever could be done to help on such a blockhead was done by the authorities. He was appointed shawîsh to an English chief inspector in the provinces – a post which even Ahmed, it was thought, could not fail to make lucrative.

Ahmed satisfied his English master, and came to cherish a respect for him, while lamenting his indifference towards religion; and the Englishman, on his side, swore by Ahmed as regards integrity, while sometimes irritated by his slow perceptions. Five years had passed since the little riot at Bûlâc, when the chief inspector had occasion to engage a new cook, the old one having waxed too bold in peculation. Ahmed was seated on a stool beside the garden-gate, beneath a bright blue flowering tree, in conversation with the negro door-keeper, when the professor appeared – a one-eyed man, exceeding fat and of malicious countenance. At a glance he recognized with horror his defiler, Ahmed the cook. The surprise was great, for he had always thought of the atheist as a part of Cairo, and now here he was in Minieh, hundreds of miles from the capital.

The professor, however, passed him by without a look, repaired to the kitchen and went straight about his business, incurious concerning the personality of the tall shawîsh, whom he supposed to be, like others of his kind, a strutting peacock, all conceit and plumage. Ahmed the soldier, who had followed, stiff with horror, watched him shifting pots and pans and peeping into drawers, and heard him sing a chant of innocence; till, unable to bear the sight a minute longer, he went close up to the wretch, and sternly bade him look upon his face. The cook obeyed.

"It is not a very nice face," he observed compassionately; "but we will make it do, since now it is too late for thee to get another."

It was plain he did not recognize it in the least.

"Dost thou not know me, O accursed malefactor? I am he whom thou didst foully wrong!"

The professor stared at him again, and stood remembering.

"Ha! Thou art that foul hog who wrecked my shop and ruined me," he snarled at length with lowered brows. "By Allah, I did never harm thee, well thou knowest. But for that ill return for all my kindness, the wrecking of my shop, I yet will pay thee!"

He was going on with his work, when the soldier screamed: –

"Say that again, O atheist, unblushing perjurer! How! Thou didst never harm me – when thou didst feed me jackal's meat?"

At those words the cook's face brightened suddenly, and his whole frame was contorted with unhallowed glee.

"Ha, ha! Thou recallest that? Oho! The merry jest – well worth the wrecking of my shop . . . ."

"Cease, devil, pig, blasphemer! Leave this place! Dare not to stay where I am. I shall surely kill thee."

"Go? And wherefore, pray? Have I not as good a right as thou hast to be here? Go and mind thy business, lest our master beat thee."

"Thou shalt depart this day, I swear. My lord shall scourge thee forth."

"And for what cause?"

"By Allah, I go straight to tell him that thou art an atheist."

"That will be to say I am his brother. He will love me."

"I will tell him thou didst feed me jackal's meat."

"The Franks eat all uncleanness with avidity."

"Then I will kill thee."

"Only try, I pray."

The professor snatched up a great knife and tried its edge upon his sleeve, keeping watch upon the soldier out of the corner of his one eye.

The latter, for his part, knew not how to act. He thought it sin, on public and religious grounds, that so obscene a creature should be left alive; yet feared to kill him. He procured an audience of the chief inspector that same day, and told him what was known of the new cook; how he was a thief, a liar, and a famous poisoner employed, it might be, by the Nationalist party, his lordship's enemies. The chief inspector yawned and shrugged his shoulders, saying that he could not be bothered to change again so soon. And the professor cut the ground from underneath the soldier's feet by turning out a first-rate cook and economical. Ahmed the soldier bore his burden, with much prayer to Allah, contenting himself with personal abstention from every scrap of food his foe had handled. He fed now in the market at his own expense.

He wished for peace, but Ahmed the professor would not let him be. At every chance encounter, he would whisper "Jackal," or "How is thy belly?" with malicious glee; and when the soldier sat out in the garden amid the palm-trees and sweet-flowering shrubs, the cook would steal forth from the kitchen, cough to catch his eye, and then put out his tongue and rub his stomach. Moreover, he had told the story to the gardeners, base negroes who had no religious delicacy, and Ahmed the soldier felt them grin behind his back.

Things came to such a pass that one day in his master's presence, the soldier wept and pleaded for the cook's dismissal.

"Why?" was naturally asked.

"Because he mocks me always and makes game of me."

"I will tell him not to do so any more."

Ahmed the cook was summoned from the kitchen. He heard the charge against him with entire dismay. Then, when the chief inspector finished speaking, he smiled deprecatingly.

"Efendim," he submitted, "this soldier is a very foolish man. I am afflicted with a dryness of the lips which necessitates my thrusting forth my tongue to lick them frequently; also I suffer much from indigestion, which obliges me to rub my belly for relief. He thinks – the silly fellow! – that I do these things at him, by way of insult. Judge now of his unreason, O my lord!"

"Well, let me hear no more from either of you."

"Thou seest all thy malice is in vain," sneered the professor when they left the presence. He put his tongue out, rubbed his belly, and then strode off towards his kitchen with a swaggering gait.

Two days later, when the chief inspector was enjoying his midday sleep, Ahmed the cook came out into the garden, and discovered Ahmed the soldier reposing on his back in the shade of a hybiscus hedge, snoring loudly, with his mouth open. The professor, stooping, picked a lump of dirt up off the ground, popped it in the soldier's mouth, and while the sleeper woke, alarmed and spluttering, escaped as quickly as his fat would let him.

Ahmed the soldier followed to the kitchen, crying: –

"Now will I kill thee, O thou wicked devil! Thou didst feed me jackal's meat, as doubtless thou hadst done to others. It will be a blessing to mankind, a deed pleasing to Allah, to rid this world of thee and thy iniquities."

The cook snatched up a carving-knife and faced him valorously, snarling:

"Jackal's meat, sayest thou? By Allah, I will feed thee pig's meat, dog's meat, rats and mice, vultures, dung-beetles! I make thee eat thy own foul flesh; and justly too!"

The shawîsh, strong and active, closed with him and flung him down. Finding the knife snatched from him, seeing death at hand, Ahmed the cook fastened his teeth upon the soldier's wrist, and, thrusting a hand into his assailant's mouth, strove hard to tear it where it joins the cheek. Both gave forth gasping cries like men half-murdered. All at once the door burst open. They gave no heed, absorbed in their death-grapple, till blow on blow came down on both impartially. The cook first loosed his hold. He was lying on his back, so saw the new assailant. The soldier saw the look on the cook's face, when he too slackened hold and turned his head.

There was the chief inspector, in his sleeping-suit, flourishing a chair out the dining-room by one leg.

"Go out, O shawîsh!" he thundered, "And thou, O professor, stir not from this kitchen. I will settle up this business in an hour."

In less than the time mentioned, the two men called on to appear before his Excellency, who sat upon the divan in the entrance-hall, by his side another Englishman of the high officials of the province. He caressed in his hands a formidable whip of rhinoceros hide.

No sooner did the culprits spy each other than, forgetful of the presence, they began again to quarrel, screaming foul abuse, gesticulating insults.

The chief inspector rose and cracked his whip.

"Efendim, this man fed me jackal's meat – he truly did. Five years have I lived defiled! . . . . O offspring of Eblîs, confess the awful crime!"

Even at that moment, when his place depended on it, Ahmed the cook would not relinquish the advantage he so much enjoyed. To deny the reality of the jackal's meat was to leave Ahmed the soldier victor, having wrecked his shop. For answer, he grinned teasingly, then put his tongue out slowly. The chief inspector used his whip in earnest.

After conferring with his friend a moment, he turned to the culprits, who stood trembling with their mutual rage, and said urbanely: –

"Listen! You have a grievance against one another, is it not so? – and you wish to fight. Capital! Most excellent! Nothing could be better! We English, as a race, are fond of fighting. But a fight like yours – a combat such as never was! – should not be done in secret in a dirty kitchen, but openly, upon the meydân[111], for the joy of all. Moreover, you must fight like heroes, not like wild beasts. You must fight with quarter-staves, your country's weapon, and that with every compliment and form of war.

"Now hear what I shall do. I write at once to the mudîr[112], and all the notables, and also to the leading foreign residents, inviting them to witness your great fight, which will take place on the open shore beside the river, this evening, an hour before sunset. It will be as in old days – a single combat making sport for multitudes. He who dies will die most gloriously, and he who wins will hear the shouts of thousands. The people will enjoy a splendid show for nothing, and you two heroes will settle your difference in a creditable and becoming manner.

"Be ready at the hour appointed. Now depart."

But neither of the champions showed desire to move. Both looked profoundly downcast. They exchanged shy glances, now no longer furious.

"Efendim, Allah knows I have no wish to kill this man, nor any ground of quarrel with him save his foolishness," muttered Ahmed the cook sullenly.

"I would not hurt him if he would leave me alone," murmured Ahmed the soldier, his voice choked with tears, "though Allah knows he well deserves to die. He fed me jackal's meat – a dreadful crime!"

"It is as I have said. You fight this evening."

"Efendim, by the noble Corân, I never fed him jackal's meat," Ahmed the cook cried out despairingly, his point of vanity at last lowered. "I fed him mutton; and he was fool enough to think it jackal's meat, because I said, to tease him, it was jackal's meat."

"Say that again!" screamed Ahmed the soldier, starting forward with intent to hug the sly professor. He checked himself and asked: "Canst thou bring witnesses?"

"I can – five excellent witnesses, none like them for veracity and honour, all of them men thou knowest in Bûlâc. I will take thee back to Masr[113] and confront thee with them."

Ahmed the soldier flung his arms around the fat cook's neck.

---

[111] Public square.

[112] (British) provincial governor.

[113] In this context, Cairo.

"Then there will be no fight?" inquired the chief inspector in tones made mournful by great disappointment. "A shame to rob the city of so fine a spectacle! Make but a show of fighting, I entreat you; give but a little cudgel-play that the mudîr and the notables may not be baulked of all enjormant."

"Efendim, mercy! I am a peaceful man, fit and most unwarlike," pleaded Ahmed the cook; while Ahmed the soldier kept vociferating: –

"Praise be to Allah! Praise to the best of Creators! Praise to the Healer, to the Purifier! Praise to the Most Merciful of those who show mercy!" in an ecstasy of thanksgiving for his sudden cleanness.

HASHÎSH

This story first appeared in the collection Tales from Five Chimneys, published in June 1915.

The addiction to hashish was seen as a major social problem before the First World War. Pickthall tells the story of an addiction, with neither sentimentality nor censure. It is a matter-of-fact tale. As in many tales, the main theme is focussed on the male world, but the women are not just cyphers or perceived only through male eyes. Mustafa's wife gives advice with such authority that her husband follows it.

A merchant of Mansûrah[114] left two sons, of whom the elder, Mustafa, succeeded to his father's business, while the younger, Muhammad, gave his share of the inheritance over to his brother, content to live upon the latter's bounty. The two had always been attached to one another. The generous trust of Muhammad affected Mustafa to tears.

"Allah witness, thou shalt have thy part of everything – whatsoever I succeed in gaining by my efforts," he cried out ecstatically. "The business is sure of a blessing owing to this deed of thine." With that he fell upon his brother's neck and blubbered; while Muhammad held him in his arms and wept, he, also, protesting that the money was a gift.

But, though accepting the impeachment of nobility of soul with such emotion, Muhammad had been animated by mere laziness. He could not be bothered to employ the money on his own account, and, having to fear his brother's censure of his idleness, thought it pleasant to disarm it in this childlike way. It were a sin to harass by a word of blame one who had thus thrown himself on the mercy of God. Mustafa thought so; and thenceforth he worked for both, happy to know that one of Allah's simple ones, who bring good luck, was

[114] City in the northern parts of the Nile Delta.

interested in the profits of the business. Muhammad heard the story-tellers in the taverns or sat out with his cronies in the fields where there was shade. The rascal's gift of improvising a facetious couplet upon any subject endeared him to the strolling minstrels and low dervishes; and one of these it was who first induced him to make trial of the drug hashîsh. The stuff was set before him in the form of jam; he ate three mouthfuls by his friend's direction. At that time he was sitting in a squalid hut outside the town, in the company of three men, partakers like himself, and of the landlord of the place, one Ali. A little later, though he had not moved, he was seated on a cloud which floated high in the air, not far from three companions, also sitting upon clouds, and shining gloriously. Their conversation had acquired a heavenly brilliance. They said the wisest, quaintest things, and laughed uproariously; now close to one another, now a good way off. Stories were told of wonders each had seen and done, of men changed into birds, of magic journeys through the sky.

Then all at once a senseless earthly voice, proceeding from the tavern-keeper, of whose presence Muhammad had preserved a dim perception, intruded: –

"O my masters, all that happened long ago. Since strangers came and built the iron road[115], all the devils have fled to the Mountain. May our Lord have mercy on them!"

The hashshâshîn[116] sat up, astounded. That voice was as a bee that buzzed around their heavenly wits. It stung at length, and then their wrath descended. With eyes dilated, with appalling cries, they sprang towards the hound who dared address them – a figure only half-discerned.

"The curse of God on the religion of the English! Defiled be he who built the iron road!"

They rushed upon the tavern-keeper with intent to kill; but somehow ran right through him – there was nothing there. They stood and gaped a moment, puzzled, till one cried: –

"Run! May Allah help us! Run, for life!" Then they sped between the palm-trunks, with a sob and chuckle, skimming the ground like swallows in low flight. Entering the town, they saw the traffic of the streets as silly shadows, and pushed men aside.

"Oàh! Oàh! Curse thy father, son of a dog! Thou didst all but overturn his Excellency, the English inspector."

Muhammad was seized by a policeman with strong hand, and the strokes of a cane resounded on his loose black cloak. Escaping from that grasp he turned

---

115 Railway, a literal translation of the Arabic.

116 Arabic plural of hashshâsh, one addicted to hashîsh (as Pickthall spells it).

and ran again with fears renewed. Alone, in a quiet spot, he cast himself upon the ground, and wept and railed against the evil influence which had somehow fought with and destroyed unheard-of bliss.

"The English! May the English perish utterly! The curse of God on the religion of the English," his lips kept muttering without his will. As his normal wits returned the utter cheerlessness of life appeared to him, and he was seized with shudders.

Seeing he could take no food when he came home that night, his mother and Mustafa supposed he had a touch of fever, and wished him to remain indoors next day; but, after noon, he stole out unperceived, and bent his steps towards the tavern of the hashshâshîn.

As he acquired the habit of the drug it ceased to treat him magically as at first; but, in revenge, it never quite released him. He became half-witted; only, after each fresh dose, his half-wit flashed with preternatural brilliance. The reasoned likes and dislikes of his sane existence were now confused with prejudices found in dreams. Thus, the love he bore his brother Mustafa became a frenzy equally with the aversion for the English he had never seen. To mention the latter in his presence was to call forth endless cursing and expectoration.

When he sat out in the doorway of a morning, people passing on the Nile bank would throw questions to him, taking omens for their business from his random answers. At weddings and at circumcisions he was in request for merry-making. He loved good cheer and songs and girls and laughter. The giver of a feast which he attended was a king, the guests all princes; as such he referred to them afterwards in the tavern of the hashshâshîn. When his brother Mustafa espoused the daughter of a rich fellâh[117] his joy was boundless; he went from house to house, sobbing for happiness, informing all men that the bride was the pearl of her time, and that his brother had paid a thousand pounds, red gold, for her; he danced and sang in person before the procession of the bridegroom to the bath, and at the feast itself recited a species of epithalamium in which the facetious, the poetical, and the obscene were blent so deftly that all who heard it were delighted.

Mustafa, on his marriage, left the mud-built house beside the Nile for a new building in the heart of the town, where, as in Cairo, each floor held a separate household. Muhammad saw this building as a palace. Each day he went and sat upon its doorstep, hugging himself as he remembered that his brother dwelt within. He carried a provision of hashîsh about with him in these days; only repairing to the tavern for congenial company, as an angel, weary of his work

[117] Farmer, peasant, cultivator.

on earth, might fly to Heaven. There his talk was all of the grand marriage of the prince, his brother, of the charms of the princess, the bride; which latter he extolled so knowingly that the hashshâshîn sighed gustily as men enamoured.

"Bid the emîr, thy brother, have a care," one counselled. "Many are sure to covet such a pearl!"

This admonition, oft repeated, supported by a thousand stories of the craft of women, put Muhammad in a tremble for his brother's honour. He passed the warning on to Mustafa, bidding him beware especially of the English as accomplished ravishers; and his brother, while he laughed about the English, felt troubled, being but a homely man, with no pretensions to good looks or bravery.

"Keep her close, I tell thee!" hissed Muhammad, "for the whole town is watchful of her lattice. They name her in the markets. Men have sworn to reach her."

His drugged brain having power to visualize its own imaginings, he spoke as of the thing that he had seen and heard.

"The guile of dervishes is great; the guile of the devil is greater; but the guile of women equals both together!" was another of those earnest warnings, which gradually terrified the bridegroom.

About this time it happened that Mustafa was obliged to go to Cairo for the day. This of itself was an alarming prospect, since he had been there once before, in boyhood; it meant, moreover, leaving his young wife alone for hours. Who was to protect her from the lust of wicked suitors, as well as from the promptings of her woman's nature? There was no one he could trust implicitly except Muhammad. The hashshâsh, having no business of his own, could keep a watch upon the door till his return.

"Trust me!" exclaimed Muhammad, when the task was laid on him. "I swear by the Prophet (may God bless and save him) the dogs shall enter only over my dead body. Our mother must also stay with her in the house lest one of them should bring a ladder and invade the window."

At earliest dawn upon the day in question Muhammad took his station on the landing just outside his brother's door, a pitcher of water and two slabs of bread upon the floor beside him, a provision of hashîsh within the bosom of his robe.

"Have no fear, my son! She will be safe with me," his mother told him, as she entered. "The girl is good and docile. Thou canst go thy way."

Muhammad shook his head and chuckled knowingly, the guile of old women being worse than young ones to his certain knowledge. His mother also had the woman's nature. A bribe from any suitor would secure her favour. When

Mustafa departed for the railway station, Muhammad bade him have no fear, the house was guarded.

Then he sat down again, and waited. He thought what he would do when they began to come. By Allah! He would grip their throats and strangle them; then fling the corpses down on to the floor below, on to a certain flag which he could see illumined by a ray of sunshine from the doorway. By Allah! He would take his pocket-knife and stab their eyes! At the outset he felt strong enough to cope with thousands. But as the day wore on his courage waned. He imagined a man fully armed – a big, strong suitor – coming up against him, and conceived grave doubts.

He had neither sword nor battleaxe: he was defenceless: he could offer no resistance to men armed and resolute. Realizing his own weakness, he began to cry. These suitors were strong and powerful. They kicked him aside. What could he do, save weep and wring his hands?

Another dose of hashîsh, and he beheld them, all the great ones of the city, the Mufti[118], all the ulema[119] – fie! Fie! Such holy ones – all the rich merchants, all the English in the world. They had gone into his brother's rooms, where, did he follow, they would mock him, perhaps kill. He sobbed forth imprecations, as he sat and rocked his woe.

Someone descending from the floor above stopped to inquire the cause of his great grief. He imparted the whole story, hiding nothing. They were all in there – the great ones, the oppressors – in there, together with the lovely bride. Mustafa – poor man! – had gone a journey. Alas! The guile of women! Woe the day!

"Allah protect us!" gasped the listener, and fetched the neighbours out to hear the marvel.

"Come, stop that noise! Be silent! Come inside!" Muhammad's mother looked out at the door and spoke severely. "There is no need to sit and weep out there. She is thy brother's wife: thou art admissible."

"No, no! By Allah, no! I will not enter while these men remain. Go back, O wicked, O abandoned woman!"

The bride herself came out with wish to soothe him, but at his look retreated hastily and barred the door.

He made so fearful and prolonged a din that the neighbours in the end lost patience and ejected him.

---

[118] Principal interpreter of Islamic law.

[119] Men learned in religion.

Hurled forth into the road, thoughtful of nothing save his brother's honour, he ran in the direction of the railway station, shaking his fist back towards that house of sin. It was the hour of sunset, and the train had just come in. As Mustafa emerged from the gateway, Muhammad ran and knelt to him and kissed his robe.

"Have mercy! Oh, have mercy, O my brother! Allah witness, I was powerless to withstand them. What was I, poor and unarmed, against those great ones? No sooner wast thou gone than they began to come – the Câdi[120], all the English – the whole world! They bribed our mother, poor old woman, with red gold and jewels. They kicked me aside, laughed at me, spat on me – all the ulema – I do assure thee! And when I cried aloud for help they beat me grievously and flung me out upon the road for dead,"

The speaker's grief was unmistakably genuine. Making allowance for his brother's known insanity, which garbled everything, it still seemed clear to Mustafa that more than one strange man had seen his wife that day. The news confirmed his fears. He also wept. A group of his acquaintance gathered round him.

"Be witness, all of you!" he cried aloud. "I divorce Bedr-ez-zamân, the daughter of Hâfiz. In the name of Allah, and according to the Law, I divorce her, I divorce her. Three times. Without recall. Amîn[121]. Now be so good as to attend me to the scene of crime, that none may say I had no ground for furious action.

They went, a goodly crowd, the hashshâsh with them. When they came into the street where the house stood, people lounging in their doorways inquired their business, and, on being told of it, laughed loud.

"It is a lie, O Mustafa. By Allah! Nothing of the sort has happened. It is all in the imagination of this mad hashshâsh."

"A lie you say?" called out Muhammad wildly. "Was not I cast out from this house and beaten by defiled adulterers? Be ashamed of such false testimony, sons of shame!"

"Come up with me and judge, all you, my witnesses!" cried Mustafa, who still attached some credit to the story. "If strange men have been in the chamber we shall spy some trace of them."

They all went up together, and soon heard the truth. Mustafa's wife complained with anger of Muhammad's conduct, declaring that she would return at once to her own people rather than submit a second time to such indignity. Mustafa's mother bore out her report.

---

[120] Judge of a religious court.

[121] That is to say, Amen.

As he ushered out his friends the master of the house made moan: "O Lord, have pity on me! See what I have done in haste and blindness, on a false report! I have divorced my love three times, without recall. How can I tell her that she is not now my wife? O Lord, have mercy!"

"Say nothing about it," counselled one old man. "All we, thy witnesses, will keep the secret."

"But I divorced her before Allah. It is sacred law. She is not, cannot be, my lawful wife."

Go to the Câdi's court to-morrow early, with all who can by any means confirm thy tale. His honour can annul thy words, since they were spoken on false information. Else, as thou knowest, there is no return save through her marriage and divorce by some one else."

Muhammad was by this time in the tavern of the hashshâshîn, where he told his story with feeling to those sympathizers that they wept with him, making loud outcry as if thrones had fallen.

Next morning a crowd of more than two hundred witnesses accompanied the luckless bridegroom to the Câdi's court. Muhammad joined them, unobserved, in exultation.

"Now their guilt will be established – all those great ones!" thought he to himself, supposing that the witnesses were on his side.

There was not room for all of them in court; but Muhammad fought his way as if men's lives depended on it. Feeling a tickle in his head at the moment of entrance, he removed his skull-cap for convenience of scratching, and so appeared before the judge bareheaded[122].

"Cover thyself, this instant, O devoid of manners!" cried an usher, enforcing obedience.

"State your cause, O people!" cried the judge; and Mustafa had begun to speak in humble tones, when Muhammad interrupted, crying out in a frenzy: –

"Hear, O monarch of the age! I denounce the Mufti, and the Câdi, the great notables, and the ulema, with all the English – curse their religion! – for misconduct with the wife of this my brother. I was set to guard the door, but they pushed by me. What could I do, alone and unarmed as I was, excepting weep and cry to Allah for redress."

There ensued great uproar. "Out of my sight, O rogues!" the judge screamed out. "May Allah destroy your dwelling-place for this impertinence."

---

[122] In contrast to the custom in Britain, in Egypt a century ago it was a mark of coutesy to keep the head covered.

Mustafa and all his witnesses were driven forth with beatings. Out in the street they swarmed like hornets round the madman, striking him, tweaking his nose, his chin, spitting between his eyes, and heaping curses on his parentage.

"I am as vexed as you are!" roared Muhammad. "There is no justice since the English order everything. Saw one ever such a mockery of trial? His Honour did not even stay to count the witnesses."

"Approach his Honour privately, O Mustafa," a friend advised. "Whatever happens leave behind this marplot."

The bridegroom, acting on this counsel, secretly obtained the judgment he required before the evening. His wife, however, was unpleasant with him, vowing to sue for a divorce herself unless he sent away his hateful brother. That, he explained to her, was hard to do, since Muhammad had confided to him his whole fortune.

"Return to him his money, with the interest," the girl insisted, "or I leave thee. To force me to consort with him is gross ill-usage, and a crime in law."

Thus threatened, Mustafa at length consented. He reckoned up his just debt to Muhammad, and managed to procure the sun in ready money. This he paid to his brother in the presence of witnesses, on the understanding that Muhammad would depart to a far distant village where they had relations. The hashshâsh wept profusely, lamenting that his brother's love to him was turned to sternness; he swore, however, to obey his will in all things. Mustafa embraced him tenderly, and all seemed done.

But next morning when the elder brother set out for his shop, there was Muhammad on the doorstep just as usual.

"Thou art not gone then?"

"No, my mind is changed."

"Merciful Allah! And the money?"

"I threw that away."

In point of fact he had taken the money, seven hundred pounds in gold – "red gold," as he expressed it gloatingly – to the tavern of the hashshâshîn, where, in an orgy such as poor men never knew, the visionaries had thrown it in the air and stood and bathed in it as in a fountain; had kissed and fondled it, and played sly games, as with a bride. Two of them swallowed some of it. Then, in the end, forgetting all about it, they had returned each to his own dwelling. In the small hours of the morning, Muhammad, suddenly remembering the heap of gold, had sped back to the place, to find it empty. The tavern-keeper had decamped with all the money. Realizing this, he had returned quite simply to sit upon his brother's doorstep as before.

"Allah's will!" he shrugged.

Mustafa also saw the hand of Allah in this strange occurrence. Nothing thenceforth could persuade him to discard Muhammad. His wife, enraged, returned to her own people, and obtained divorce on the ground of his unreason in compelling her to bear the pranks of a malignant madman. When, a year later, Muhammad was sent to an asylum after an attempt to kill an English tourist in the open street, it was too late for Mustafa to regain his pearl of women. He wedded an inferior bride, whom he chastised severely by way of satisfaction for his ruined life.

HIS HONOUR'S PLEASURE: A STUDY IN PURE NERVES

The story was published in Tales from Five Chimneys, published in June 1915.

It is a darkly humeruous story of the contrast between the life of the village, with its feuds and informal modes of managing differences, and the efforts to introduce an alien law and order by the officials of the British occupation. The perspective is very much from the point of view of the villagers. The British individuals are never given names and are described only by the people of the village and in accordance with their experiences of alien authority.

Pickthall had wandered around alone in the Delta and was acutely observant of the physical features of the village.

The little daughter of the Sheykh Selîm, who had run out into the fields to guard the buffaloes, was brought home in the evening lifeless, made unrecognizable, beaten ruthlessly to death with sticks as men destroy a noisome reptile, and the house was filled with fearful lamentation. The Sheykh Selîm himself went mad with grief, tearing his flesh with teeth and nails, grinding his face into the dust, then springing up and rushing towards the door, intending with his bare hands to assail the murderers. A host of kindly neighbours, his adherents, wrestled with him. In the end they dragged him violently from the death-room, and bore him up on to the house-top; where, seated round him in a hedging circle as he howled and bit the mud, they called on Allah to console him, and waited the return of reason with sad eyes.

After an hour or two, the stricken man sat up, assuming a more decent garb of grief. He cast away his cap and turban, and threw dust upon his forehead, sobbing: "O Allah, pity! O kind Lord, avenge me!"

His comforters gave praise to the Most High.

"Half of the village sorrows with thee," they assured him soothingly; "and the other half has equal cause for grief, seeing that the first-born of the Sheykh Mahmûd was slain this evening, and the grandson of his brother received serious wounds."

"What is all that to me?" the Sheykh replied. "My dove, my pretty one is slain! The fiends! Our Lord reward them![123]"

He wept and gnashed his teeth, gazing blindly out across the flat roofs interspersed with palm-trees, across the veiled plain, to the range of desert hills whose jagged outline was cut clear against the sky. The stars, pulsating with their cold essential life, seemed conscious of his woe and yet indifferent.

"Now Allah witness my decision!" he exclaimed at length. "Those children of Eblîs have slain my brother and my brother's son, the foster-father of my younger wife and other relatives, not to speak of friends and servants. But now they have done worse – the work of devils! I will make an end. If they have hired assassins, so will I. I will send this minute for the mighty Bâsim, acknowledged sheykh of all the murderers in Egypt."

Upon that resolution, which was much applauded, he went into the house to find a messenger.

In the dwelling of his enemy, the Sheykh Mahmûd, meanwhile, a scene precisely similar had been enacted. The aged notable, distraught with grief and fear, likewise resolved to have recourse to hired assassins. He sent a runner to the town of Kafr Tînah, to a rogue named Câsim, already bound by ties of service to his family.

The origin of this relentless feud was so obscure that all involved ascribed it to the spite of devils. The village had been peaceful till a month ago; although the faction of Mahmûd had long been jealous of the Sheykh Selîm, who, owing to his natural talents and his readiness to trust new-fangled institutions such as banks and companies, had risen till his grandeur rivalled theirs. Selîm, on his side, had endured a jaundiced life through envy and resentment of their claimed supremacy. Each party, crediting the other with the deadliest hate, had walked in daily apprehension of some outrage; but courtesy had marked their intercourse until a certain day, when a quarrel of two children in the fields, no rare occurrence, was followed by four cruel and mysterious murders. Since then there had been slaughter every evening, performed so secretly and with such inhumanity that many deemed it not the work of men. A scream, a shot, was heard; the watchmen ran in the direction of the sounds, to find some fellow-

[123] The Arabic verb, *jâzâ*, means both to reward or to punish. It would appear that Pickthall is thinking in Arabic as he writes the dialogue.

creature – a woman or a child, it might be – dead or dying, but not a vestige of the slayer came to light. The inhabitants of Mit Surûr were nervous in the daytime, which was rendered sinister by wailings and the chant of funerals; but when night fell their fears became a frenzy. Each clutched a weapon, ready to shoot or strike at anything that moved, to beat its life out savagely, and flee in terror. The leader of the village watchmen, Kheyr-ud-dîn, was in despair, and vowed with tears that these unheard-of crimes were due to witchcraft. Everybody spoke of summoning the prefect of police, but feared to do so, conscious of some share of guilt.

All this and more was known to the redoubted Bâsim from the conversation of his guide, by the time he reached the village at the fourth hour after noon. The hardly less redoubted Câsim had arrived before him.

This prince of rascals was big-limbed and burly, of a cheerful countenance. As he rode his donkey through the narrow ways of Mit Surûr, clad in a cheap blue gown and a white skull-cap, nothing spoke of hurry or concern. He rode into the courtyard of the Sheykh Selîm, and there, dismounting with all customary blessings, accepted some refreshment, then talked business with his host. The Sheykh poured out his grief, concluding: –

"Now thou knowest. Allah witness I have had enough to bear. The whole of that accursed brood must be exterminated. Deal with them as thou wilt, bring in a hundred helpers. I will pay."

"Ah!" nodded Bâsim with his pleasant smile, "there be many who talk thus before the deed, yet when the deed is done belittle it and grudge the price."

For answer his host rose and fetched a bag of money. Bâsim weighed it in his hand, then loosed the neck and peered in at the contents.

"Good!" he murmured. "With thy permission I will set to work at once."

"Thou hast the list of names I wrote for thee?"

"By Allah! Have no fear! Trust Bâsim!"

After pausing in the yard to light a cigarette, the murderer proceeded leisurely down paths so narrow that he brushed a wall with either elbow, stepping over sleeping dogs, winking at women who looked out from door-ways, smiling always like a man at peace with all the world, till he came before the gateway of the Sheykh Mahmûd. It chanced that Câsim was emerging from it at that moment.

"Is it thou, O Bâsim? Lucky day!" the other answered. "What brings thee here? Some good, in sh'Allah."

"Wallahi. I am the right hand of Selîm. And thou?"

"The right hand of Mahmûd! Then we are enemies! I will not have it so. I will retire."

"Do nothing, O beloved! Come and talk!"

Bâsim therewith took hold of Câsim's hand and led him to a pleasant spot outside the village, where a tall mimosa hedge kept off the sun's rays. Here they sat down and eyed each other lovingly. Both, being half-bred Soudanese, possessed the negro's grin and flash of teeth."

"What thinkest thou of our affair?" asked Bâsim.

"Black as pitch," was the rejoinder.

"How many have been given thee to slaughter?"

"Twenty-five."

"And me, nearly forty. O Divine Protector! Am I a pestilence to kill so many? The deed were madness, but the money is good money."

"Wallahi! But the deed is madness, as thou sayest. What is to be done?"

"Listen! Instead of slaying half the world, we will preserve them. Bring me hither the chief watchman."

"God forbid! He is a fool, a bribe-refuser. He would sit upon a cactus hedge to please the Government."

"Bring him," said Bâsim, in a certain tone, and Câsim ran.

After about five minutes he returned escorting a lean athletic man of eager profile. The captain of the watch was in his uniform, a brown robe and a high cylindrical felt cap, alike in hue, a few shades lighter than his anxious hawk-like face. He carried in his hand a quarter-staff.

Bâsim rose up and blessed his coming with choice compliments, which Kheyr-ud-dîn returned with watchful glance on both the strangers, well known to him by him as vile miscreants.

"A grievous trouble, this we hear of in your village," began Bâsim amicably. "May Allah comfort thee, for well I know how it must vex thy soul. My surprise is great that any son of Adam should dare disturb a village guarded by a man like thee."

At that the watchman's circumspection vanished; he cried out in anguish:

"Allah witness! It is not by men the place is troubled. None but devils – our Lord knows it – could escape my vigilance. And the proof is that the cry comes always in the dark when fiends have power, and never in the light of day."

"None the less," laughed Bâsim condescendingly, "the criminals are sons of Adam, men thou knowest. Bend down and listen. I will name them to thee."

Kheyr-ud-dîn inclined his ear. A minute later he sprang back, incensed, protesting: –

"Cut thy life! What words are these? Those men are high in honour. Come with me and repeat thy charge before the omdeh!"

"God forbid! Thy omdeh is among the chief offenders, being brother to Mahmûd. Câsim here is just come from from his presence with orders to exterminate the faction of Selîm. And I have orders from Selîm to massacre the whole house of the omdeh."

Kheyr-ud-dîn collapsed upon the ground, defiled his face and wept aloud, a strange sight in that pleasant spot at that sweet hour.

"But we," concluded Bâsim, "have religious principles. We seek refuge in Allah from killing madmen. We tell all to thee, entreating thee to go at once and warn the prefect!"

At that request, the watchman's first distrust returned upon him. He sneered: "Extremely nice! And while I am away, you slay and ravish."

"Nay, we bear thee company."

"In that case, I must take two others with me."

"Take twenty, if it please thee!"

"Good. I go."

The deputation came to Kafr Tînah at the sunset, when clouds of dust went up from all the roads, enveloping the town and palm-trees in a golden haze. The title of the Captain of the Watch, his great excitement and the plea of urgent business, oft reiterated, procured them audience of the prefect at his private residence – a whitewashed house which gleamed in the blue twilight. The dignitary gnawed his thick moustache and mopped his forehead, as he heard their story.

"This is a case for the English inspector," he declared with awe. "O Abdul Halîm!" – he summoned a young clerk – "at once dispatch this telegram to the respected Mister." Beneath his breath he added: "God forbid that I should put my own hand in a nest of hornets."

The deputation then returned to Mit Surûr. A new moon setting plunged the village in double shadow. They were standing in a group about to separate, when some one, issuing from an alley which crossed theirs, received the clamour of their voices suddenly, screamed, fired a shot and ran. Kheyr-ud-dîn made a bound to follow, but the hired assassins held him back, reminding him: "We have resigned things to the Government."

"The right is with you[124]," the chief watchman shrugged and sighed. "Well. I have learnt one curious fact from this encounter; which is, that it is the killer not the killed who gives the death shriek."

---

[124] Another expression, awkward in English, but a literal translation of the Arabic.

"That is known," laughed Bâsim. "May thy night be happy!" And he went his way, with many an uneasy glance behind him. The hooting of an owl deprived him of existence for a moment as he set foot in the courtyard of the Sheykh Selîm. In the guest-room, which was crowded, his employer hailed him with an eager question: "Has the work begun?"

"Trust Bâsim!" was the answer. "But I have grave news for thee. At sunset as I walked outside the village, a fellow passing on the dyke cried out to me: 'A happy night, O thou who wilt be hanged to-morrow!' I ran and seized his throat and asked his meaning. He told me that the English, hearing of the crimes at Mit Surûr, are coming to take vengeance on the criminals. Considering thy welfare, O my lord, I then made haste to Kafr Tînah where I ascertained that the great Krûmer[125] will arrive to-morrow with his executioners!"

"Praise be to Allah, my two hands are clean. I will place myself in his protection," said the Sheykh Selîm.

"Pretty!" laughed Bâsim. "But the English are a curious race. If a son of the Arabs or a Turk were the Inquisitor, he would search for men like me and see us hanged. But with Krûmer it is altogether different. Show him a man like me, he cries in anger: 'This is but the hand. Bring me the heart, the head, that I may eat it!'"

"Merciful Allah!" gasped the Sheykh Selîm. "Then I must hide."

"All fugitives are guilty in their sight. The adversary will remain and they will hear him."

"O Protector[126]!" wailed the Sheykh, completely terrorized. "Is there no help? Are all roads closed against me?"

"Trust Bâsim!" said the murderer with kindly emphasis. "Bâsim knows all their ways even as he knows his own old donkey's tricks, and can frustrate them. A gift to Bâsim is not money wasted."

"Thou hast much already."

"More is needed. Is not the tremendous Krûmer more redoubtable than a host of wretched frightened fellâhîn?"

"The right is with him," cried all those who listened. "Do all he asks of thee to save our lives."

Câsim, meanwhile, had played the same tune on the heart-strings of the Sheykh Mahmûd and with the same result. The plan had been devised by Bâsim on the road from Kafr Tînah. Both sheykhs were scared out of their wits, and

---

[125] Lord Cromer, British Consul-General of Egypt, but through advisers to Ministries, effective ruler of the country.

[126] One of the names of God,

terror spread like wildfire through the village. A wholesome fear of men for their own skins it broke the foul, inhuman spell which had bewitched the place. Although it was a dark night, the hour of dread, men went from house to house as if by day, their panics hushed like strife of sparrows where the falcon hovers, made brethren by the whisper: "Krûmer comes!" Mahmûdi and Selîmi[127] spoke together, and both sought counsel of the hired assassins, as frightened children have recourse to grown-up persons. Before day came again, the Sheykh Selîm and all his following were seated in the guest-room of the Sheykh Mahmûd debating how to meet the common peril.

"But when he sees us friendly," moaned the Sheykh Selîm, "surely he will know they lied who told him there was blood between us."

"Not so," said Bâsim, "for your crimes are known. Are there not thirty murders, well authenticated, not to speak of lesser woundings, rape and robbery?"

"True! True! O Allah, pity!" wailed the audience.

"A gift of money, all contributing," suggested one.

"The English count that worse than murder!" groaned another.

"Perhaps His Majesty loves feasting," said Mahmûd, "or women. There are sweet girls in the village."

"Fear nothing; only wait! Trust Bâsim!" grinned the murderer, who in truth knew nothing of the English or their habits, beyond what people said, that they were easy to deceive and so made better masters than the Turks.

"By Allah, we must truly save our men or flee the country," he remarked to Câsim, when at length they left the house. "It is important for me to see the Inquisitor and fathom all his nature before these brainless ones flock round and spoil the view."

Accordingly, he took the road betimes that morning. It was certain that His Honour would arrive by train at Kafr Tînah, there take a horse and escort from the station, and ride out on the dyke to Mit Surûr. Bâsim and Câsim strolled to an inviting group of trees, and there sat down, observant of the morning stir upon the fertile plain, the changing colour on the desert hills. Here they were joined by Kheyr-ud-dîn and fifteen watchmen, come out to pay due honour to a great one of the Government.

At length a troop of horsemen came in sight, preceded by a single rider – the Inquisitor. At his approach the waiting group sprang up. The watchmen ran before, brandishing their staves and bellowing to clear a way which none obstructed. Bâsim and Câsim made profound obeisance, and then presumed to walk beside His Honour, who was riding slowly. The arbiter of life and death was

---

[127] That is, partisans of Mahmûd and Selîm.

tall and stiff and had a reddish beard. He wore spectacles, as they believed, on purpose to make his rigid face the more inscrutable.

"Command me, O my lord!" said Bâsim humbly. I am he who first gave warning of the evil doings. I can tell thee."

"Await the time and place," replied the great one.

Bâsim smiled obedience.

"It is a nice place – Mit Surûr," he hazarded. "All good things abound there. A delicious feast will be prepared for thee at noon."

The great one took no notice. He was not a glutton. Bâsim tried once more: –

"And girls, efendim! Ah, the girls are sugar. A sight to make the heart ache and the mouth run water."

Again the Englishman was quite unmoved. Had he no feeling?

"Efendim," pursued Bâsim, "am I not thy servant? I will tell thee, what they need, these fellâhîn. They are good, harmless people when oppressed, but in prosperity grow jealous and cause fear in one another. Oppress them, O my lord. Apparently –"

His speech was interrupted by the one word— "Go," pronounced emphatically. The rogues fell back in horror. Bâsim sank down beside the way and tore his raiment.

"Now Allah teach me what to do," he moaned. "For that he is in killing mood is very evident. When our sheykhs are brought before him, he will string them up like onions. Woe the day!"

"Fly! Let us fly at once," urged Câsim warmly.

"An easy thing to say for one like thee, who has no property. But I own house and land; and the report against me will fill all the country if my sheykh is hanged . . . . Praise be to Allah I still see a way! He wishes our men dead, so they shall die. Up, run like lightning to thy man and make him dead!"

"Merciful Allah! Must I kill him?" spluttered Câsim, horrified.

"O ass, I said not 'Kill thy man!' Make him seem dead; and I will do the same with mine. The Inquisitor seeks nothing but their death. Hearing that Allah has forestalled his vengeance he will go away again, and ours the glory. Run, make haste."

Câsim required no further bidding, he outran his chief, and rushed into his patron's house wild-eyed and breathless, with brows dripping sweat. His terrible appearance winged his errand. The Sheykh Mahmûd, who, being deaf, had no conception of the matter, was flung down on a bed, while one son rubbed his face with flour, another stripped him, and the women brought out grave-clothes and began to wail. Câsim dashed out again, and bent his steps towards the omdeh's house, approach to which was choked by a great crowd through which he fought his way. Declaring stoutly that he was a witness, he gained access to the presence. Bâsim arrived a minute later, having done his business, in like manner, with the Sheykh Selîm.

They were only just in time, for hardly had they mopped their brows and glanced around them ere the Englishman commanded: –

"Call the Sheykh Selîm."

"Efendim, he is dead. Our Lord have mercy on him!" said Bâsim in heart-broken tones, then wept aloud. "Our Lord have mercy upon him," gasped the whole assembly.

"When did he die?"

"An hour – two hours ago. What do I know?" sobbed Bâsim, mad with grief.

"Then call the Sheykh Mahmûd."

At that word, Câsim uttered shriek on shriek, as if reminded of a grief that stung like bees. "Dead too! All of them dead!" he bellowed. "O despair! O Allah!"

"Mahmûd – my brother – dead? It cannot be!" exclaimed the omdeh at the great man's side.

"Where is his corpse?" asked the Inspector dryly.

"Efendim, it is in his house prepared for burial."

"And the Sheykh Selîm is dead too?"

"Very dead," sobbed Bâsim.

"I must see the bodies."

"Honour them!" was cried on all hands.

The Inquisitor bestrode his horse once more; the watchmen ran before to clear the way. The great one found two households mad with grief, and saw two stiff recumbent forms attired in grave-clothes. He was puzzled.

"Of what illness did they die?" he questioned Bâsim, who held his stirrup in the courtyard of the second house.

"Of plague, Efendim," said the rascal promptly.

The foreigner started and blanched visibly, but only for a moment, then his face resumed its wonted cast of incredulity.

"And the burial is when?"

"The third hour after noon."

"I shall be present."

As soon as he could slip away unnoticed, Bâsim sought his colleague, burdened with this fresh anxiety. They looked at one another, shrugged and sighed profoundly, then set to work with the fervour of inspired fanatics. It was as much as they could do in the short time available to overcome the strong reluctance of the sheykhs to being coffined.

"It is impossible!" Selîm kept groaning.

"Then come to life and let him hang thee," thundered Bâsim in a rage. "Have I not told thee, the Inspector attends the funeral? He is sure to look into the coffins; and what will happen when he finds no corpses? – Have no fear! He will not wait to see you in the grave. When he departs, you rise up, cleared of blame for ever."

At last persuasion triumphed, and the funerals set forth. Loud chanting and the wail of women filled the sunlight. The two trains met and moved united towards the cemetery. At every turning Bâsim looked for the Inquisitor, but descried no vestige of him till they reached the place of graves – a brown patch rough with mounds amid green fields. There the tyrant was discovered with his escort, waiting in the shadow of a ruined dome, the shrine of some forgotten saint, which stood between the graveyard and a field of maize. As the funerals approached, the soldiers met them, speaking softly to the bearers. The foremost mourners heard the words, "By order of the Government," and passed them on. The soldiers claimed the coffins and their occupants, because, they said, their lord the Mister had a shrewd suspicion that the two recipients of Allah's mercy had been poisoned. He therefore claimed the bodies for examination, as was right, that wickedness might not be hid nor crime unpunished. They would rest beneath the old saint's tomb until the morning, when a doctor from the city, a good Muslim, would pronounce upon them.

Bâsim, beside himself with apprehension, approached each coffin secretly, and whispered: "Hush! They put you in the cubbah[128]. It is open. You walk out."

Having seen the coffin carried to the ruined shrine, the crowd returned towards the village with much exclamation, regarding Krûmer as the cleverest of clever devils, who had trapped the two sheykhs nicely, to torment them at his leisure.

Bâsim and Câsim awaited afar off, meaning to release their clients when the coast was clear. But, walking round the ruined shrine a half-hour later, with that end in view, they found to their dismay a solid door new fitted; which door was locked, and sentries placed to guard it.

"I seek refuge!" grunted Bâsim. "He has won. He buries them alive – a fearsome death! It is time for me to travel. I bequeath my donkey to the village."

"And I my mule!" said Câsim. "Yallah! Let us walk, and quickly." And they set out for the open country with great strides.

---

[128] The "rined dome, the shrine of some forgotten saint".

The two sheykhs, thus imprisoned, lay quite still till after dark. They feared to move so long as they heard voices, and the sentries talked till late. When all was still, the Sheykh Selîm sat up and shouted to the Sheykh Mahmûd, who sat up likewise. Both wished to stretch their limbs.

"Wallahi, I am very hungry," sighed Mahmûd.

"And I would give a guinea[129] for a drink of water," groaned Selîm.

"Where is Câsim?"

"Where is Bâsim?"

"Patience, doubtless they will come when all is safe."

Through a rift in the dome they could behold great peaceful stars, a strip of jewelled blue let into darkness. They held each other's hand and wept a little in pure wretchedness. Then Selîm heard the grumble of a sentry turning over in his sleep, and told Mahmûd, who was a deaf old creature, "I hear some one. Doubtless it is Bâsim come to let us out."

"Praise to Allah! It is Câsim, a good faithful lad."

"Ya Bâsim! Ya Bâsim!" howled Selîm with all his might.

"Ya Câsim! Ya Câsim!" piped Mahmûd, whose voice was weaker.

And when their cries brought no release, they yelled the louder, weeping, driven mad with fear. But there was no longer anyone at hand to hear them, for the guards had fled, believing that the heavenly examiners were at their work on the deceased, whose awful howls denoted sins past thinking.

The captives wept and wailed through the night, pressing one another's hand, made one by misery. When the eye of day looked down upon them, they were quite worn out, and slept a little in their own despite. Selîm was awakened by a noise of some one fumbling with the door. He roused his comrade. Expecting the deliverers, they both sat up, but at a foreign voice of stern command, fell back again as stiff as corpses, sure of death by torture. Selîm was conscious of some son of Adam bending over him, then of a startled cry: "This person lives!" and of the sound of many feet retiring hurriedly. Conceiving all hope lost, he sat up slowly and began to say upon himself the prayers of death.

"And is the other man alive?" asked the Inquisitor.

"Alive, Efendim," groaned the Sheykh Mahmûd.

"What does this mean?" exclaimed the great one in a voice of wonder. "I am weary of this village full of lies and riddles. In the name of Allah for what reason did you two feign death?"

"They said it was your Honour's pleasure," whined Selîm.

---

[129] The Egyptian pound was called gineh, guinea.

“Merciful Allah! What is this I hear? I come here with no other purpose than to see you reconciled.”

“The praise to Allah! Then they lied to us. The Sheykh Mahmûd is dearer to me than my eyes!” cried Selîm wildly.

“I swear by Allah and His Apostle (May God bless and save him) that the Sheykh Selîm here present is my soul and liver!” shrieked Mahmûd.

The pair would have embraced each other had their shrouds permitted. The transports of their love found vent in tears.

The Englishman, with shoulders shaking, gave command: –

“Release them! The feast of reconciliation will take place at noon.”

By that time Bâsim and Câsim were quite forty miles from Mit Surûr; and still they fled.

THE STORY OF HÂFIZ

This story first appeared in Tales from Five Chimneys, published in June 1915. It is another story about village life and popular attitudes towards the alien authority of the British occupation.

The girl, Selîmah, is an example of one of the strong female personalities in Pickthall's fiction. She is not seen from the perspective of the men of the village, but in a few words is described, without adornment or judgment. The story, and Selîmah's role is discussed by Professor Afra Shiban in Marmaduke Pickthall Reinstated edited by Ebtisam Ali Sadiq (Partridge Press, Singapore, 2016), pp 158-60.

This tale is of a man devout and upright, who, believing in his neighbours, kept no watch upon himself, any more than one looks to the charging of his pistol in a friend's house: and so, when disillusion came at last, it snatched away his reason, delivering him over to the fiend which lurks in every man beneath a scorching sun like that of Egypt.

The iron road, which runs so close to El Fakhârah that the smoke from passing trains blows in at doorways of the village and defiles its palm-trees, brought one advantage unsuspected of its founders. It banished the whole swarm of jinn, ghîlân[130] and afârît[131], with which the place had been infested from of old. Such creatures shrink from the approach of iron, as savage beasts dread fire. At the clank of the first rails they left the village and lurked in the adjacent palm-grove, watching anxiously; at sight and noise of the first locomotive – tons of iron – they fled with wailings to the desert hills.

[130] Plural of ghûl, ghoul.

[131] Plural of afrît, demon.

But there is another kind of fear which walks in darkness, and this the presence of the iron road did not dispel. Bad men have more temerity than devils; as was proved one sultry night when shots rang out, and all the inhabitants of El Fakhârah sprang awake immediately, though the thunder of the night express had failed to rouse them. The women screamed; the dogs were barking furiously. Every one ran out, snatching up things of value, and fled in the direction opposite to that from which the fear proceeded.

The brigands fired a second volley, then a third, and then sat down and waited, listening; until they judged the village empty of inhabitants, when they advanced to pillage at leisure, never troubling to reload. But they had not reckoned with the valour of the village watchmen, who, encouraged by their leader Hâfiz, a brave man, waylaid the rascals in a dark and narrow place, and brought their staves down hard. The watchmen being ten in number, while the robbers were but five, with guns unloaded, as already stated, the latter were compelled to take to flight. They had left donkeys tethered in the palm-grove. Three reached the place and, mounting, rode away, belabouring their little steeds with fury. The donkeys broke into a plunging gallop. One fell and threw its rider, who was taken prisoner.

Clear of the palm-trees on a bank above the open plain, the two survivors slacked speed and rendered thanks to Allah, deeming themselves safe; till, glancing back, they saw men running steadily with loins girt up, prepared for a long chase.

"Separate! Let us separate at the first chance," panted the robber chief to his companion, as the pair resumed their panic flight. Accordingly, at the first branching of the dyke they parted company, the chief rogue choosing for himself the shortest cut to safety, an embanked path running straight up to the desert hills. Not until he reached the beach of sand at the foot of those hills did he pause to look behind him once again. Then, at the sight of only one man following, he chuckled to himself and chose his ground. He urged his donkey up a little gully, not more than twelve feet deep, but strewn with boulders, affording plenty of cover from which to take cool aim at the pursuit.

By then the dawn was breaking. The desert range, upstanding, caught mysterious light. Hâfiz, the watchman, shuddered as he reached the sand, for it was to this wilderness that all the devils of the plain had fled for refuge at the coming of the rail road. But his heart was set upon the capture of the brigand chief, so, commending his cause to Allah, he strode on, undaunted. Though densely stupid in the market or the guest-room, as is the way with men endowed with bravery above the common, in his own business he was not devoid of guile.

On entering the small ravine he used precaution, having nothing but his quarter-staff for attack, whereas his enemy possessed a gun and pistols, and moreover occupied a strong position. He ran, exposing his whole form with seeming recklessness, then ducked behind a rock, then ran again obliquely to his former course. In this way he had gained the shelter of a little cave without eliciting the shot he needed to locate his adversary, when a movement of the donkey caught his ears.

It sounded close at hand. With a shout he sprang out and exposed his body for two seconds, flung up his hands and fell. The shot rang out, arousing awful echoes in that lonely place. Hâfiz the watchman lay quite still upon his face, with arms drawn in as if to ward a blow. He heard his foe give fervent praise to Allah, and knew that he was coming forward to inspect his work.

The rogue drew near and gloated on his fallen foe. He kicked the corpse and was addressing it facetiously, when both his feet were plucked from underneath him.

Then Hâfiz rose and chuckled in his turn, for the robber chief lay senseless. His head in falling had come down upon a rock, a stunning blow. The watchman tore off strips from his brown robe and bound the wretch; then, bringing up the donkey, lifted his captive, still insensible, upon its back; picked up his staff and made the ass move forward, himself supporting its limp burden tenderly. In truth this captive was as dear as life to Hâfiz, being his claim to honour in the eyes of all mankind, a heritage of glory for the son on whom he doted, and of his children's children to the end of time. As he issued with the donkey and its burden from the shadow of the little gorge, the sun appeared and laughed into his face, strewing the sand with rose-leaves for his triumph.

When he reached the village at the third hour of the day, the women raised their joy-cries and the men cried blessings on him, pressing forward to spit upon and smite the helpless robber; and an enraptured crowd beset his progress to the omdeh's house, where fresh honour was in store for Hâfiz, for the omdeh, the official headman of the village, fell straight upon his neck and kissed him tenderly. The prisoner was at once dispatched with a strong escort to the chief town of the district; and, that done, the headman offered food and drink to Hâfiz with his own hands. Nor was that all. When he had heard the watchman's story, he caused it to be written down and forwarded, along with the official report of the incident, to the local governor. Thus Hâfiz reached the pinnacle of glory.

He remained a simple soul, devout and docile. The blast of popularity but fanned his zeal to fresh exertions. He and his men became fanatical about their work. They never strolled or walked; they ran like madmen. But, when off duty, Hâfiz was the same as ever, afraid of his old mother's scolding tongue, a slave to every caprice of his little son. His wife had died a year before, but he had not yet manifested any longing to replace her, absorbed in his devotion to his boy, contented with his mother's way of housekeeping.

If he ever showed a sinful pleasure in his fame, it was upon his child's account, who would inherit honour. They say in El Fakhâreh he assured the child that he need never feel ashamed to name his father, without the "In sh'Allah!" prescribed for boastful phrases. For this, some folks maintain, misfortune fell on him. However that may be, misfortune came; nay, even in the heyday of his reputation, it was gathering.

The omdeh had made mention of his servant's prowess to the local governor, thinking only to gain credit for himself thereby; and the local governor, in reporting the brave exploit to an English inspector who watched three provinces with a paternal eye, had no other object than his own aggrandizement. What happened was as unexpected as it was disgusting to these functionaries. Hâfiz himself was summoned to the capital and there, in presence of a group of foreigners, received a silver medal for his daring. From that day forth the omdeh hated Hâfiz, now a personage, though he judged it wisdom to caress him while his vogue endured; and the local governor was much put out over the incident. Were not the village headman and provincial governors held responsible for all the evil-doing in their districts; ought they not therefore to obtain the praise accruing from any good which might be done by anyone from time to time? How was discipline to be preserved in Egypt, if the English rulers slighted chiefs and honoured menials? Thus they reasoned, grumbling. But the omdeh, accustomed as he was to cringe to every caprice of authority, accepted the position for the nonce; fearing that, if he acted as his feelings prompted. Hâfiz would run whining to the English, and procure his downfall.

The watchman wore his medal proudly on the bosom of his long brown robe. The omdeh could not bear the sight of it. The watchman's fervour of devotion to the Government was wearisome, and tacitly reproached the omdeh's sloth. From the speech which had been made to him when he received the medal, Hâfiz had gathered something of the wishes of the English with regard to village government, along with an unbounded admiration for their wisdom and their generosity. In his eagerness to further their desires, he sometimes gave advice unasked, forgot his station; for he credited all servants of the Government, however lofty, with a devotion equal to his own. His mistakes and the exasperation of the headman were observed by many in the course of time; but no one cared to warn him;

it was no one's business, and to interfere with such potentates seemed ticklish work. At length, a girl, the village beauty, one Selîmah, took him to task one evening as he sprawled upon the dustheaps in a leisure moment, playing with his little son.

This maiden, by her coquetry and her good looks, joined to great physical strength and utter fearlessness, had risen to a kind of sovereignty occasionally reached by women in Egyptian villages. The men deferred to her in their disputes; the women recognized her as their champion; and her voice was heeded in all village councils. Betrothed in early childhood to a neighbour's son who grew up imbecile, she pleaded her betrothal jokingly with other suitors, and thus had reached her eighteenth year unmarried, with all the men of El Fakhâreh at her heels. Nor were the women jealous, for she kept no secrets from them; if she had to box the omdeh's ears, she told his wives; and it was known that her desires were fixed on Hâfiz, who was no one's property. For men in general – those who thought themselves intelligent – she cherished a robust contempt; for him, the upright fool, she felt both kindness and respect. As she stood upon the dustheaps, looking down on him, her headveil loose, a pitcher on her head, her form transfigured in the evening light, Hâfiz, who was lying on his back, the child bestriding him, could only gasp in admiration: –

"O delight!"

"Am I so dear to thee? Then heed my words!" she answered smiling. "Thou art become a busybody and a nuisance. The omdeh is offended with thee, all men see it. He only waits an opportunity to work thy ruin. Mend thy ways, I pray thee; fall behind him; go his pace! Thy restless fervour is a plague that turns him yellow."

"What words are these, O sweet one?" Hâfiz laughed, incredulous. "They have deceived thee, for the omdeh is my loving patron. This very day he praised my zeal and energy. Say now, who told thee? Let me know the liar!"

"I know; that is enough. Accept the warning." Selîmah whispered, seeing people coming. She did not care to tell him that the omdeh himself had told her of his aim to ruin the chief watchman, swearing to renounce that purpose only in return for favours she would not accord him.

Hâfiz thought her fears preposterous, but it fretted him to think that anybody could conceive his services to be unwelcome. He kissed the omdeh's hand upon the first occasion, and asked point-blank if his kind lord had aught against him. The headman, in alarm at this home-thrust from one whom he believed to have the English up his sleeve, declared by Allah and the Prophet it was not so, that he loved this best of watchmen as the apple of his eye, and prized his service above earthly joy.

"I knew they lied!" quoth Hâfiz in exultant tones. "It is done from guile, my lord, for thou and I together, head and hand, are much too strong for evil-doers in the place. They think, if they could sever me, the hand, from thee, the head, authority would die in El Fakhâreh and they could work their will, the malefactors!" Having thus said and made obeisance, he went his way, light-hearted as of yore.

"O fool!" Selîmah murmured, when they met again. "To go and ask the fox himself: 'Art thou a rogue?' and to believe his answer!" She spoke without contempt, in utter sadness.

"How knowest thee of that?" said Hâfiz warmly. "Did he tell thee?"

"No matter how I know! Thou art a fool in this world, though altogether worthy of the other."

The watchman, scornful, bade her have no fear on his account. But the strangeness of her manner had impressed him; he became uneasy, doubtful of the headman's favour, very eager to secure it by correct attendance, by a brisk obsequiousness which, in the state of feeling of his chief, was wood to fire.

At last, one day, when irritated beyond bearing, the Sheykh cried: –

"I ask pardon of Allah! Who am I to be thus honoured by thy countenance, and conversation? For the love of Allah, do what pleaseth thee! Leave me in peace!"

At this rebuke the watchman louted[132] and withdrew, his face distorted, the blood in all his body turned to poison by that smart rebuke. It made the medal on his breast a mockery. Arrived in his own house he tore it off and sat down in the darkest corner by the wall, pushing his little child away with fury, repelling his old mother's consolations; gnashing his teeth and moaning, till the evening, when, his grief abating, he went out to join his men, and set the watch as usual.

"What did I tell thee?" called Selîmah from her father's doorway. "And if thou art so downcast at the first rebuke, what will thy plight be in the face of cruel wrong? I know thee. Thou canst think no evil. When evil thrusts itself upon thy notice, it will drive thee mad. Thou wilt slay thyself and all those dear to thee for grief that such things can be done in God's creation. Take my advice, sell all thou hast, and go!"

"No, that I will not!" answered Hâfiz proudly. "I have done no wrong!"

"Our Lord protect thee, then! At least perform thy duties quietly in future, and avoid his presence. In time he may, perhaps, forget his enmity."

---

[132] Bowed down.

“Allah reward thee!” murmured Hâfiz. “I had thought of that. Henceforth he has no cause to blame my forwardness.”

But if from that day onward Hâfiz shunned the omdeh’s sight, he did so in a manner which proclaimed his sense of wrong. He could not bear to look upon a fellow-creature who disliked him. This sullenness increased the omdeh’s loathing which was kept concealed through a terror of the English, till a certain day, when, visiting the chief town of the district, he waited humbly on the local governor. In the course of conversation, the visitor from El Fakhârah chanced to mention Hâfiz delicately, as a personage enjoying high protection.

“What!” exclaimed the great one. “That base watchman? And the English? Pshaw! Having given him that medal, to affront me, they have forgotten his existence as completely as the sea forgets the ship when it is past.”

The omdeh, once assured that this was so, laughed soft and long and rubbed his hands together. He was now free to show his feelings towards the watchman, while waiting opportunity to wreak full vengeance. A good excuse was needed lest Hâfiz should set up an outcry which might reach the English and arouse their memory. In the meanwhile it was in his power each day to make the watchman’s life unpleasant in small ways.

Hâfiz, grown used to slights, no longer raged; but went about his work with patience, saying, whenever any friend condoled with him: “I am a Muslim, and resign my cause to God.”

When his mother shrieked her indignation at his evil treatment, he rebuked her sadly, and he sometimes wept when gazing on his little son. Selîmah often urged him to forsake the village, but he would not hear of such a course, repeating: “I am a Muslim, and the fault is his. What have I done?”

The omdeh had professed his readiness to spare the watchman if Selîmah would but gratify his passion. He thought to catch her through her love for Hâfiz. She refused with scorn. She was herself, and Hâfiz was another. God has said: “The fate of every man is bound about his neck, nor shall any laden bear another’s burden.” Moreover, there was no concern of love between them, the watchman being by this time too profoundly occupied with his misfortunes to be other than an object of commiseration. She tried to make him see his danger; tried to raise the indignation of the village, but in vain. The people, sympathizing with him, grumbled, but they feared to brave the omdeh. Having done her best to put a stop to it, she watched his persecution with the thrill of interest one has in listening to a tragic story; sure that in the end – the next world – all would be repaid.

The dignity inherent in all innocence kept Hâfiz from succumbing to a host of petty tyrannies, designed to rouse him to commit some breach of discipline. He wore his medal proudly, as a protest, a reminder to beholders of his service in the past. He could now do nothing right, to that he grew resigned; but when the tyrant passed from simple fault-finding to lying statements, sneers and gross abuse, his brain throbbed painfully and he had much ado to keep his fingers from the old man's throat. Still he endured it, crying, "Lord, how long?" and praying that the trial next to come might not break through his strength of self-control. This posture of long-suffering still more incensed the omdeh, who took counsel with his sons how to destroy the hated creature in some manner gratifying to the English, whom alone he feared.

It was then that he bethought him of the iron road, running so close to the village, that the watchman might be blamed if aught went wrong with it; beloved of the English, who made laws for its protection such as guard the state of kings.

One night, two hours before the great express was wont to pass, a goods train came up slowly, whistling as the driver's compliment to El Fakhârah. All at once the noise ceased with a bumping sound, and the whistle sounded of alarm. Hâfiz and his men, seated not far off among the dustheaps, sprang up and hurried to the spot. The engine had gone off the line. The lanterns showed large bits of wood upon the metals and bundles of thick dhurra stalks – a barricade. Hâfiz despatched a runner to the nearest signal-box, himself with the remaining watchmen offering to lift the engine bodily upon the rails. They were trying to persuade the driver that this plan was feasible, when the omdeh came upon the scene with two of his sons.

"What is this, O Hâfiz?" he cried out in anger. "Curse thy religion! Is not this thy doing? Whoever laid all this upon the road must have been seen by thee. The deed has not been done an hour, and thou wast near. Thou hast dishonoured the whole village, thou hast brought my house to shame. The curse of God upon thee, O thou hog!"

The omdeh's fury was unfeigned; he was beside himself. As he uttered the last words he rushed on Hâfiz, seized him by both ears and spat in his face deliberately; then flung him off. The watchman reeled and staggered like a drunken man. Recovering his strength, he gave one gasping cry and ran off sobbing towards his house, a madman.

At the door, his little son, who had been wakeful, met him with a shout of joy. It seemed the worst of insults to his frenzied mind. He seized the child and dashed his brains out on the doorpost, then rushed indoors, and sank down, making hideous moan. At that time he felt no compunction for his awful deed. His thought was: "Now the omdeh will be sorry."

His aged mother, witness of the crime, ran out, as mad as Hâfiz, and aroused the neighbours. A minute, and the little room was full of mourners, who prayed for Hâfiz ceaselessly throughout the night; while wailing women took the body of the child into another house and laid it out for burial.

As Selîmah glided towards the fields betimes next morning, a tray of basketwork upon her head, she met the omdeh. Accompanied by two policemen from the mudîrîyeh, he was strolling towards the house of Hâfiz with complacent looks.

"My dear, may Allah comfort thee!" he cried to her. "A sad calamity! I share thy grief. Did I not always tell thee that the man was bad? O rashness to put things upon the iron road! O wickedness to try to wreck the honoured train!" With head held loftily and curling lip, she dropped one scathing glance on him from out the corner of her eyes as she swept by. "And now he has defiled the village by a crime unheard of," was called after her. "Our worthy lords, the English, will be horrified. Thy poor lover will be hanged; our Lord have mercy upon him! Even now we go to take him to the prison."

Selîmah stood stock-still a moment ere she turned upon him.

"Hanged! Who says it? Art thou mad, O thing of dung, O stinking atheist? The blood is in his house, the sorrow his. No one save Allah has the right to judge him."

"It is the law. His crime is known. He will be hanged. The English will not suffer such a wretch to live."

Selîmah flung away her tray and ran about the village, screaming, "Ya Muslimin!" with all her might.

At that religious cry the houses poured forth their inhabitants. The omdeh, leaving the policemen to fulfil their task, fled back to his own house; but he was overtaken. A furious mob of men and women, even children, shouted death to him. Of a man respected and much feared, whose oppressions had been watched till now in frightened silence, the proof of irreligion made a dog, a noisome reptile. His cap and turban were plucked off and trodden under foot; men beat him solemnly with sticks, while women scratched his face and spat upon him; he was thrown down upon his back and kicked and trampled. He called for help upon the village watchmen, his own servants; but, as true believers, they declined to interfere. They did not beat him, but they smiled on those who did. In the end, when he was senseless and his death seemed sure, the crowd desisted and with smiles dispersed. His wives and children took his battered body to the house and there revived it. That night he fled with all his house from El Fakhârah.

In the meantime Hâfiz had been led away unnoticed; his old mother following him with tears to the gate of the prison, whence two days later he was carried to the public madhouse.

THE KEFR AMMEH INCIDENT

This tale first appeared in As Others See Us, published by Collins in October 1922, five years after Pickthall had openly declared his conversion to Islam. He was living in India at the time.

It is the longest of Pickthall's Middle Easteren short stories and is almost a novella, with the major theme of Anglo-Egyptian relations under the British occupation with a British official posted to a Delta village, with sub-themes of the Mûlid, the celebration of the birthday of a Delta village saint, rural power politics, the aspirations of a man to go on the pilgrimage to Mecca, and brigandage.

Unusually, part of the story is in the first person, the narration of a character like Pickthall himself; he has wandered round the Delta villages and is familiar with the customs of the region but, unlike Pickthall, appears to be unmarried.

The English official, George Sandeman, is seen as described from the perspective of the villagers. He speaks "baby Arabic" which they humour. He has blond hair and a red face, he sticks his elbows out as he struts, he laughs a lot aloud with open mouth; his "Ha ha!" sounds like "Wow! Wow!" He practises golf strokes and adores a small dog – cultural habits that are seen as very odd. When some old British school fellows visit him they sing their old school song enthusiastically. To the villagers this as the "roaring as of old wild beasts in a solemn cadence" and people fear it is the herald of an attack on the villagers. It justifies the inclusion of the story in the collection with the title, As Others See Us.

But the first person persective gives a more empathetic picture of Sandeman, as a not very bright Englishman, good-natured and humane, but culturally out of his depth. He stereotypes the Egyptians in racist terms and pines for marriage and life in rural rainy Devon – "I love the drip of trees after a shower".

This is the history of the Kefr Ammeh incident which greatly disconcerted some of the English governors of Egypt, though no notice of it found its way into the newspapers. A number of fellâhîn were tortured by the omdeh (headman) of a place of some importance out of sheer devotion, as it seemed, to Mr Sandeman, the English inspector for the district. To the authorities the case appeared inexplicable. To me, who had been able to observe affairs at Kefr Ammeh from the Egyptian no less than the English point of view, the "incident", however startling, appeared not unnatural seeing the strange popularity which Mr Sandeman enjoyed there and the almost mystical awe which he inspired in the inhabitants. He was, in fact, a kind of fetish for the population, and that for reasons for which he had no personal knowledge, reasons quite independent of his rank as an official. The key to understanding of the situation came into my profession quite by accident, three months before George Sandeman's appointment to the district, when I visited Kefr Ammeh for amusement at the season of the Mûlid[133] of the local saint. On the first night of the fair I chanced to stroll into a circus-tent, where I was privileged to witness a most strange phenomenon.

The ring was lighted by the flare of five tall cressets set at irregular intervals on its circumference. The large tent was crowded. Men and women of the poorer sort, with swarms of children, sat or sprawled on the ground around the ring. Behind them rose a mist of black robes, white turbans, and brown faces, tier on tier, from which there came the steadfast gleam of teeth and eyeballs. The audience was hushed, devouring with its thousand eyes the antics of some clever tumblers and a few conventional displays of horsemanship. Then came the clown, and there were murmurs of delight, since he was known to be the pearl of all his time for drollery. After mimicking an omdeh, a shawîsh and an Egyptian judge, oppressors of the poor, amid much laughter, he put his hand into the placket of his baggy trousers and fished up a wig of tow which he adjusted to his head. He then rubbed some red dust upon his face until it wore the colour of pomegranate-bloom, put on a Frankish collar and an old pith helmet brought to him by an attendant, took in his hand a cane and began to strut up and down stiffly with elbows raised, opening his mouth very wide and saying: "Wow! Wow!" at frequent intervals.

During his toilet you could have heard a pin drop in the tent; but now as he marched to and fro with that strange cry, a sigh arose; "What is he now? O Lord,

[133] Birthday, the day in the year when a local saint will be celebrated with pilgrimage and celebration. The most famous of the Egyptian mûlids is that of Sayyid Bedawi at Tanta, described in Pickthall's novel, *The Children of the Nile.*

inform us quickly: What is this?" and some one cried in accents of delight: "The name of God be round about us! He is become a ghoul – a sinful ghoul!"

A doll was thrown into the ring. With a shout: "It is my son!" the clown pounced on it and clasped it to his breast. He laid it upon one of two chairs which had been placed in readiness while he himself took seat upon the other, saying: "Rest thou there, my son, until they bring thee meat and milk and vegetables, all duly stale from having been enclosed in tins for many years!" And then the fun became so furious that those who witnessed the performance had no time to guess its meaning. Man after man came in, upon his feet, and the ghoul, with curses, made him go down on his hands and knees. "It is for your good," he cried. "We wish to see you all made equal under us. We teach you good behaviour. We are a just race."

At length three men came in at once. As fast as one of them went down obediently upon his hands and knees, his brothers rose up on their feet, until the ghoul grew so infuriated that his mind flew from him and he knew not where he stood. Retreating backwards to his seat wow-wowing loudly, he mistook the chair, sat down upon his child and squashed it flat.

"Wâh! Wâh! My son is dead!" he roared, holding up the doll for all to see. Then from the mighty crowd there came a shout of laughter with cries of "May our Lord have mercy on him, O thou foolish monster!"

"Bring water!" cried the ghoul beside himself. "Bring water, sprinkle and revive my son. No, no! It will do harm. It is not filtered. Hi, there, you doctors! Bring my son to life or I will cut your heads off!"

"O atheistic monster!" roared the crowd. "Canst thou not see that thy misfortune is from God?"

"Down on all fours, beasts that you are!" he cried. "Convey my son with honour to the hospital!"

They answered: "It is useless, O khawâjah! He is truly dead!"

The ghoul then seized a chair and killed the doctors with it, which done, he once more gave attention to his child. His brick-red face became convulsed with grief; he opened his great mouth and howled "Wow! Wow!" He stamped his feet and tore his wig of tow. Then the men who had been killed rose up and fetched an open coffin such as Muslims use. "No, no!" he bellowed on beholding it. "Go fetch a tin. All meat must be preserved in tins or it goes bad."

They changed the coffin for a kerosene tin into which they thrust the doll, then ran away with it, the ghoul pursuing them with shouts: "The lid! Where is the lid? My son will spoil!" Just as they were leaving the arena they flung away the tin, the doll fell out, the ghoul, with "Wow! Wow!" seized his child in one hand, the tin in the other, and ran out after them; the play was ended.

The audience drew a deep sigh of regret. There followed argument in whispers as to its significance. Some one said: "It was an Englishman." "No," came the answer, "it was nothing of the seed of Adam, but a cursed ghoul with some resemblance to an Englishman." A third exponent cried: "It was an atheist, and all the evil which befell him comically, was from God."

Kefr Ammeh, as I learnt, had no acquaintance with the English, though but a stone's throw from the town there stood a government rest-house where Englishmen occasionally came and spent a night. The sole exceptions were the omdeh, who had met with their inspectors, and the custodian of the rest-house aforesaid, a pious sheykh devoid of curiosity, who told his beads and gave scant heed to men who came and went. The watchman had not seen the clown's performance, but the omdeh had; and when the crowd emerged at length into the street of tents, alight and noisy underneath the stars, the latter was beset with eager questions. Was the tow-haired, red-faced creature with the curious voice an Englishman, as some were saying, or a ghoul?

A ghoul, most certainly, the omdeh said, the English being men of regal bearing, remarkable above all things for self-restraint. Yet some of the visitors to the fair from distant places vowed that the clown had played the English to the life. The men of Kefr Ammeh took the omdeh's word for it. What they had seen had been a ghoul most certainly; and the inadvertent squashing of his offspring, the derision which he met with in the end, had been the due reward of tyranny and atheism. It had been a moral tale unfolded comically, in the true Egyptian manner; and the fact that all points of its application were not absolutely clear made it the more attractive to the rustic audience, most of whom revisited the circus of the second evening of the fair, to see it and learn from it.

The clown portrayed the omdeh, the shawîsh, the judge, exactly as before; but when the people clamoured, some for the ghoul and others for the Englishman, he ran away with shaking of the head. The clamour went on vainly for some time. At length a juggler sprang into the ring playing with balls of light until their flying glitter attracted all those eyes, when murmurs ceased. Afterwards it was known that the Egyptian government official who had been sent to overlook the fair, informed of the performance of the previous night, had put a stop to it. This high-handed action fixed the clown's play permanently in the public memory. Men grieved for the suppression of a little drama which (as they said) combined amusement with religious teaching. They mourned their ghoul. And spoke much of him in the weeks which followed, laying stress upon the fact, as stated by the omdeh, that he had borne not the remotest likeness to an Englishman, to show the great injustice of suppressing him.

And then George Sandeman arrived at Kefr Ammeh.

Some children were at play one evening on the dust-heaps which extend between the government rest-house – a white one-storeyed building in the open fields – and the little mud-built town adorned with palm-trees, when a foreigner, emerging from the rest-house, came upon them suddenly, exclaiming: –

"Where is the house of the omdeh?"

The children all with one accord fell down upon their hands and knees.

"Security, O khawâjah! Guarantee but my security and I will show thee," cried one braver than the rest.

"Be not afraid!" the Frank replied; on which the guide ran off as one who flees from danger. The children's game was at an end. They followed awestruck.

A man who passed the stranger in a narrow place, stood staring after the tall, white-clad figure strutting along so stiff with elbows raised. He exclaimed: "I seek refuge in Allah from Satan the Stoned," and followed the weird apparition to the omdeh's house, which presently became a place of concourse. First one and then another of the village notables kept dropping in till the reception room was full; while at the doorway women, children and the poorer men gathered and stared intently at the foreigner. Was he, or was he not in truth their ghoul? He had removed his mushroom hat which had enforced the likeness, and laid it down on the divan beside him. His hair was not like tow in texture, but it was of a light colour, and ruffled as it was just then, recalled the wig of tow the clown had worn. His face was very red, though in repose the eagerly desired resemblance almost vanished. But when he opened his great mouth and showed his teeth and laughed their ghoul was present. The Englishman's "Ha! Ha!" which sent a shudder down the spine of every listener, was as near as could be to the mountebank's "Wow! Wow!" He bellowed every word as if his hearers had been deaf.

The omdeh used him with the greatest reverence, receiving with expressions of delight the information (conveyed in most peculiar Arabic) that he was English and had been commanded to reside at Kefr Ammeh for some months; but while making much of him as host to guest, he stole dismayed, inquiring glances at his face. Another laugh, "Wow! Wow!" rang forth, and meaning looks were interchanged all round the room. But it was when, in reply to a polite remark to the effect that English people were the lords of justice, he declared without the least demur that that was so, and added: "If we seem like tyrants sometimes it is for your good," that strong suspicion leapt to certainty and exultation reigned in every heart. A murmur of applause went up from the group of common people at the door, which group had now become a crowd which overflowed the little courtyard of the omdeh's house. On the hush which followed this betrayal of emotion came a child's cry: "O my mother, lift me up that I may see the ghoul!"

The Englishman at length took leave with loud expressions of goodwill, so loud as to seem menacing to all who heard them. A troop of little boys and girls adhered to him with no worse object than to gaze upon his wondrous face. He told them to begone, and beat those nearest to him, when, seeing they annoyed His Grace, a village watchman dispersed them with his quarter-staff. The watchman wished to guard His Honour to the rest-house, but the Englishman commanded him to go back whence he came and, when he tried remonstrance, used obscene expressions such as the worst of men in cities bandy, threatening, moreover, to chastise him to the point of death.

The town was thrilled and deeply interested, with the feeling one would have supposing some remembered dream come true in every detail. Inquiry of the cook at the rest-house, when he came to do his shopping in the sûk[134] next morning, elicited the fact that the khawâjah ate tinned foods and never drank a drop of water which had not been filtered. When this was known some women let their voices flutter forth in joy-cries, as is usual on occasions of festivity. The Englishman was certainly their ghoul. From that day forth he was assured of popularity. Though he was seen to be uncouth, devoid of manners as of understanding, and likely to prove dangerous at unawares, the people loved him and would crowd to gaze on him, hugging to their hearts the blest assurance that they saw his whole significance more truly than he did himself.

The Englishman was as strong as a camel and less sensitive, for he would ride like mad upon his business in the heat of noon, would exert himself sometimes with scarce a break from the third hour[135] until sunset; and when he had by chance an idle day did not repose, but rode his horse for pleasure for an hour or so, returning from which pastime he would change his clothes and presently come forth upon the dust-heaps to fatigue himself still more. Armed with some curious sticks, he would take stand with legs apart and unite with all his strength a small white ball, pursuing it from place to place until he lost it; when he would proceed to search for it for hours beneath the burning sun, assisted by the village youngsters, who were accustomed to observe his labours from some spot of shade, from which the offer of a coin alone could tempt them. Their

---

[134] Souk, market.

[135] The third hour of daylight – about 9am.

dreamy, serious eyes were always fixed upon his face, and in the earnestness of their attention they would mimic all unconsciously the strange grimaces which he made when bludgeoning the small white ball, which he seemed to look on as a sinful thing, his enemy.

He had a small white dog with black ears and a stumpy tail which attended him whenever he went out on foot, adhering to him like his shadow, walking when he walked, stopping when he stopped, always at his heel. This dog he loved above all other living creatures. When walking with it in the town, or out among the fields, he carried in his hand a monstrous whip, wherewith he was prepared to flay the pariah dogs if they attacked it. He spoke to it in gentle tones as to his soul's beloved, and once, when boys began to tease it and it gave a squeak, he beat and cursed the culprits so unmercifully that all the children who beheld the sight fell down before him.

"Whoso touches my dog," he roared, "I will hang him and his parents and defile their graves."

The children thought: "His dog is as his son. Please God, he will ere long sit down on it" – a contingency which seemed the less remote because the dog invariably kept so close behind him. All animals appeared to have his sympathy, except the pariah dogs aforesaid, which he persecuted. A boy had stuck a knife into a donkey to accelerate its pace: he flew in a great rage, chastised the boy and stole the knife. A man had lost his temper with a sullen mule: he lost his temper with the man, and threatened him with death and hell. Neither the mule nor the ass was his property, nor could the manner of their treatment, by any way of thinking, be esteemed his business. But it was apparent he could not help himself. At sight of beasts oppressed his mind flew from him, and in his madness he oppressed the sons of Adam. The men of Kefr Ammeh shrugged their shoulders, perceiving that the illness was upon him from the hand of God. The wise among them whispered that in regions where a beast is king one must expect dumb beasts to be preferred to men. The Berberine cook and butler at the rest-house told how the Englishman would take the small white dog upon his knees, and let it freely lick his face and hands; how it slept in the same room with him and shared his meals.

The ghoul, the small white dog and the small white ball had for the fellâhîn the charm of something magical, a mystery whose true significance was known to God alone. The children knew the ball, having all handled it, and they believed it to be made of human bones and skin pressed tight together. But a man, Selîm Ghandûr, who happened to encounter it upon the dust-heaps, declared with oaths that it was made of solid and essential fire. It had brought him near to death, but while he said the necessary prayers, writhing in awful anguish on the ground, the ghoul came to him with his mouth wide open, laughing "Wow! Wow!" and thrust a dollar on him. The ghoul was not a miser, very certainly. He rewarded all who did him service, and, having persecuted any one, would, when his wrath subsided, give him money. His intention, it was clearly seen, was not iniquitous. He often visited the omdeh's house, and honoured other houses when he was implored to do so. His awful voice and his blood-curdling laugh lost something of their terrors as they grew familiar. The omdeh, who had much to do with him as an official, pronounced him very simple, even brutal, in his methods, and very, very easy to deceive; though, while deceiving him, a man well knew that, did he but suspect a fraud, his vengeance would be terrible and all-destroying – a knowledge which imparted zest to the shy game. He was, upon the whole, extremely popular, and thanks to his discerned capacity for wholesale murder if enraged, respected. The fellâhîn were circumspect in their behaviour towards him, for none could tell beforehand what small thing would raise his fury, or whether he might not go mad spontaneously.

One evening there arrived two other Englishmen upon a visit to the rest-house. The loud wow-wowing of their welcome could be heard afar. Thereafter, at the third hour of the night, most frightful sounds alarmed the waking town. A roaring as of wild beasts, in a solemn cadence, lasted for several minutes at a time; then came a moment's hush, then a fresh outburst. The people thronged the roofs and listened, stiff with fright.

"Perhaps," the children whispered, "our ghoul has sat down on his son, the small white dog!" The sweet conjecture was passed on from roof to roof. The men said: "He could hardly make that noise alone – not even he! Two others of his kind arrived at sunset. The probability is that they have drunk strong drink until they have become intoxicated, and thus roar in madness."

"If they are drunk, then make fast every door; remove the women to a place of safety!" counselled one old man, a member of the omdeh's household, raising his hands in anguish to the stars. "They will presently break forth to slay and ravish. I remember, years ago when I was in the army, how the Circassian and Albanian officers would thus sit up and drink until their wits forsook them; then, rushing out, would chase us with their swords, calling us (save your presence) Nile mud and the accursed dung of Pharaoh. They would even run into the streets abusing all they met!"

"Merciful Allah!" cried the omdeh, who forthwith despatched a runner to the rest-house to inquire if there was any danger of a massacre. The two Berberines, the cook and butler of the Englishman, assailed with such a question, laughed contemptuously. In the manner of experienced stablemen explaining to some nincompoop the ways of horses, they told the messenger that Englishmen were most benevolent when thus elated. The dreadful roaring was the mode of singing in their country. They would roar till there was no more voice left in them, and then betake themselves like lambs to bed. This information, carried straightaway to the omdeh, somewhat relieved the apprehensions of the people; but few were they in Kefr Ammeh who deemed it safe to go to bed that night.

From the English point of view George Sandeman was not abnormal. He sported all the small inanities and irritating tricks of manner, varying with the mode from year to year, which mark the youthful Englishman of good society. A man with men, a gentleman with women, he dressed well without foppery, adorned his rather jerky conversation with the latest slang, and was in some demand for dances in the Cairo season.

He having failed in the initial step to various careers, one of his uncles, who was in the Cabinet, had forced him into the Egyptian Civil Service, much to the annoyance of the British lord of Egypt[136], who hated to submit to private influence. Sandeman was put into positions especially designed to prove his incapacity. But somehow he survived successive ordeals. He did not love his work; his whole delight was in field-sports and in the pleasures of the town; yet he did not do badly. It had become apparent that that the government would have to keep him after all, about the time when he was sent to Kefr Ammah. Once there, his unexpected popularity, reported in high quarters, was set down to tact as an administrator, and his name was made.

"It's a rummy thing," he told me when I spent an evening with him at the rest-house, "but I believe the beggars somehow take to me. And I like them too in a way. Can understand why a chap like you, who's read 'em up, can find them interesting, and all that. Do, myself, in a way. They're all right if you know how to handle 'em. I go in and call on 'em and have a talk – treat 'em like human beings; but they jolly well know I won't stand cheek or any nonsense from 'em. That's the way. They're tricky though; you can't see into them."

As an example of their trickiness or their opacity, I know not which, he told me how the omdeh had sent round one night, when he and two other Englishmen were singing school songs after dinner, to ask if there was any danger of a massacre.

"Now was that innocence or was it cheek? I ask you. What? When the cook came in and told us, splitting his sides with laughter, I felt pretty small. Didn't

[136] Lord Cromer, British Consul general of Egypt and effective ruler of the country.

sing much after that, I can assure you! We had, of course, been kicking up a most infernal row, enough to frighten people who had never heard that kind of thing. But I'm not so sure that message wasn't meant for cheek. D–d cheek, if it really was sarcastic. What? Yet he's a dear old thing, and quite a pal o' mine. They're rummy beggars."

He sat in silence for a minute, stroking the fox-terrier upon his lap, wrestling, it seemed, with some elusive thought.

"I tell you what, old man," he said at length. "I shall have to write a book about 'em some day. Started notes already. I come across some rummy things down here. I don't say I should ever print the stuff, but it'd be amusin' just to see what I could do. Keep me from going mad in this damned hole."

I praised the notion highly, being always eager to encourage the first shy movements of a mind in healthy flesh. He added: "I believe I've got upon the track of something – pretty big discovery, it seems to me – about the beggars."

He seemed desirous to be plied with questions. I, therefore, begged him, with effusion, to confide in me.

"You won't crib my notion? You've got to promise that before I tell you. Well. It may be nothing really – just an accident, or some other feller may have spotted it before – but I believe these beggars aren't quite men like we are – a bit nearer to the monkeys, Darwin and all that. What put me on the track was this – a rummy thing! If you talk to any of their youngsters a bit sharply, raise a stick to them or anything of that sort, it's ten to one they'll go down on all fours. As if" – he puffed at his cigar with zeal, manifestly struggling with a tough abstraction – "as if they felt safer, more at home, once they could get their hands on the ground. As if – some instinct, don't you know? – and all that! I never saw a man do it but once, and then he may have done it for a purpose, for he tried to lick my boots. But the little kiddies do it nearly always – nearer to nature. What? It's a queer thing."

He went on talking of the "beggars", as he called them, till we went to bed, which did not happen until after midnight. We met at breakfast the next morning, and then said good-bye, Sandeman going to his daily work, while I set off on my journey to another rest-house.

I did not meet George Sandeman again until the following winter, when he was much in Cairo, having some relatives and hosts of friends among the fashionable visitors. Then, as it happened, we met rather in attendance on a certain English family in which there was a very pretty girl. I may as well confess I offered marriage to the damsel, only to learn that she adored George Sandeman – a predilection which for my life I cannot explain except by the old adage about youth attracting youth. We remained good friends, however, and by her contrivance was wheedled into something more than toleration for my favoured rival. In English society I must say that the said George appeared to great advantage, being evidently in his element, which I was not. I felt much more at home in Kefr Ammeh.

"How is your book getting on?" I asked one afternoon, when I found him having tea alone at one of the little tables in the hall of the club.

"Oh, that!" was the reply. "I still jot down a note occasionally. But I may tell you that I've chucked the great discovery – all rot! I bet you knew that at the time, you secretive old beast – and wouldn't tell a feller!" He laughed without a trace of animosity.

"Their dropping down like that was simple cheek. I guessed you twigged that – eh? I caught them grinning once or twice. That was enough. I've put a stop to it for good and all. God knows what made 'em take to it. The only thing that I can think of's this: You know I'm devilish fond of my small dog. The children started teasing just once. I let 'em know that I'd jolly well hang, draw and quarter the whole lot of 'em, with their fathers and grandfathers – and so I would, by Jove – if anybody touched my dog again. Well, to rag me in return for that, the beggars made believe that I was only fond of beasts – a bit of a beast myself, no doubt – and so dropped down like that for mercy – kind of sarcastic business, don't you see? What first gave me a hint that they were not so simple as I used to think was the old omdeh sending round that night about our singing. Made me feel exceeding small, that did. So damned sarcastic! He's a dignified old boy. God knows what they think of us, or what they see us like with those queer eyes of theirs. I must say I should like to know for once."

I told him that he seemed to me to be developing, however tardily, the faculty of abstract thought – beginning to "take notice", as our nurses say. He flicked a crumb of toast at me, and then continued: –

"They really are quite decent in some ways. About my shooting, for instance. There's good sport around the place. They give me leave to go just where I like, and clear the ground of kids and cattle for me. I have one really ripping gun, and always make a point of cleaning it myself. You should see the beggars eye it! They've got a legend that it kills with every shot. I believe they think I worship that and my small dog. I have to row with them sometimes just to keep 'em in their place, but on the whole I find 'em jolly decent. Only don't go saying that to Joan or her mamma. They're always fishing for an invitation to come down and see me. No place for women, as you know. Do put them off! I shouldn't know what to do with 'em" – he blushed profusely – "should feel ashamed, an utter worm before the beggars. Can't explain. You might come down and look me up sometimes. Come the first week next month. Our Mûlid will be on, and if there's ever going to be fun in Kefr Ammeh, you'll behold it then."

I could not reply definitely to the invitation on the spur of the moment, but after a few days I wrote accepting it.

Alighting at Mastûrah station about ten o' clock one morning, I succeeded in procuring donkeys for my servant and myself and rode along the dykes to Kefr Ammeh. From afar I saw a line of tents much longer than the face the town presented, shining out against a palm-grove to the southward; discerned the flutter of innumerable small red flags and heard the hive-like murmur of the fair. Sandeman seemed pleased to see me. We had luncheon and then sat and talked till four o' clock, when we went out to pay a call upon the chief official of the fair. The crowd within the canvas town was dense, and Snap, the small white dog, was at his master's heels. He ought not to have been there, but we did not discover his attendance until it was too late to send him home. I noticed children calling out "Isnâb!" alluringly, and saw some of them stoop to pet the dog. They belonged to Kefr Ammeh. Strangers, who knew not Snap, were less considerate. Twice he received a kick which set him yelping, and Sandeman turned round and used atrocious language. Wherever the man learnt it I could never guess.

"That's one thing I do hate about the beggars, and one good reason why I can't have Joan down here. They're so damned cruel. It never seems to strike them that dumb beasts can feel," he told me as we shouldered through the press. Our goal was the marquee set up by the provincial government in honour of the Muslim saint who sleeps at Kefr Ammeh, who slept there as a Christian saint before the Muslim conquest, and as a god of ancient Egypt long before the birth of Christendom. One end of the marquee was open to the crowd; at the other, in the place of honour on a long divan, sat the representative of government, a black-bearded effendi[137], receiving the respectful compliments of divers notables. The atmosphere was reverent as in a church; till Sandeman with loud "Ha, ha!" strode in out of the sunlight, Snap at his heels, shook the official violently by the hand, nodded to all the company, which rose to greet him, and flopped down comfortably in the place of greatest honour, where Snap immediately jumped up beside him. The other visitors were mildly scandalised by the apparition of a dog on the divan above them; the representative of the provincial government betrayed alarm; until the omdeh of Kefr Ammeh, rising in his place, explained that Snap was not as other dogs which never wash but wander to and fro, eating

[137] A government official. A Turkish word, originally from Byzantine Greek.

all manner of abomination. This dog, he said, performed ablutions twice a day, lived in a house, slept in a bed, and fed on bread and milk and beans and onions. In all respects he was his master's soul.

The representative of the provincial government, thus reassured, and anxious to propitiate the soul of Sandeman, gave the dog a sweetmeat with his honourable hand, while all the notables showered praises on him. We drank a cup of coffee and ate sickly sweetstuff, while musicians squatting in the tent-mouth made a merry din; then Sandeman sprang up abruptly, wrung the great man's hand once more, touched his hat to all the others and marched out with Snap behind him.

I had overtaken him before I realised that half the men who had been sitting in the tent were coming with us, anxious, no doubt, to pay their court to one so arrogant. Those who were not fortunate enough to gain a place beside him attached themselves to me as we proceeded on our homeward way. Among these was the omdeh of the place, a fine old man in splendid silken raiment, who at once began to pour into my ear the praise of Sandeman.

The town, nay, all the country, were His Honour's servants. He was so strong and yet so generous, of such a brilliant and far-seeing mind and yet benevolent. Of a verity he was the marvel of his time for might and justice. A perfect Englishman, and all was said! All Kefr Ammeh loved him as men love the water-brooks. Would I be good enough to find out from His Excellency whether there was anything displeasing to him in the place; and afterwards let him (the omdeh) know, that he might have it altered. The population was, alas, uncivilised, however much devoted to His Grace, and might offend through ignorance of good behaviour. He (the omdeh) would far rather lose his right hand, he declared with vehemence, than that anything should happen to aggrieve that prince of Englishmen. There had been no disorder, praise to Allah, since his coming; but naturally there existed in the place a few bad characters, who might by some unhappy outbreak smirch its fame. One of the outlying hamlets, Mît Gâmûs, was a veritable hornet's nest of fearless brigands. He therefore begged me, as a personal favour, to persuade His Highness not to come into the fair again like this incognito, but with outrunners and attendants as became his state. Thus he would be guarded from the rude touch of the crowd, and the sweetest, most delightful of all little dogs would be secured from hurt.

I called to Sandeman to stop and listen, and bade the omdeh make his own request. He did so, but with evident reluctance, and in broken phrases which contrasted strongly with the eloquence of his discourse to me. While he frequently declared his love for Sandeman, I saw that he was very much afraid of him. All the bystanders supported his petition, talking baby Arabic intelligible to the perfect Englishman.

"Does Your Honour think of visiting the fair to-night? Let him but order, and we will provide a score of men happy and proud to be his personal guard of honour."

"Who told you that I thought of visiting the fair to-night?" snapped Sandeman. He murmured: "Beastly cheek!" beneath his breath. "Why should I come out when I am comfortable in the house? – They seem to think their beastly fair attractive," he remarked aside. I told him that I thought the omdeh had some fear of trouble with the crowd.

"Oh, that's another matter. Then we'll come, you bet! But don't you tell 'em that," said Sandeman with glee. I told the omdeh and the other notables that His Honour felt no great desire to see the fair again. They seemed relieved, and parted from us with a storm of blessings.

"Seems quiet enough," observed my friend some four hours later, as we moved once more amid the multitude, under the flare of torches, deafened by a thousand discords. "Let's turn in somewhere, see a show or two. This place looks promising. Come on, old man."

He put down money at a wicket and we passed into a crowded circus-tent. Our entrance was unheeded by the audience, all intent just then upon the antics of a clown who held the ring alone. I recognised the jester of my former visit, and tried desperately to get Sandeman out again under pretext of the foulness of the atmosphere. But in a trice he had become absorbed in the performance as completely as the fellâhîn around us.

"That's our omdeh to the life! Look, just below us in the third row, there's the man himself, and all his family enjoying it as much as any one!" he whispered, and then forgot me and the world together for a while.

Having finished his performance of the omdeh, the clown put on a wig of tow, an old pith helmet, and a Frankish collar, hung something like a pipe between his teeth, took in his hand a whip and swaggered up and down with elbows raised, now exclaiming, "Wow! Wow!" now looking back and whistling for a dog.

"That's me! That's devilish good! The cunning beggars!" came from Sandeman, entranced, and presently his laugh rang out above the others. That betrayed us. I caught the omdeh's gaze directed at us, and never have I seen such mortal terror in an old man's face. He sprang up on his seat and shrieked to the buffoon to stop, calling him evil names and cursing his religion. Not content with that, he scrambled down into the arena with remarkable agility for one so old, and flung himself upon the jester with intent to kill. Many of the audience followed his example, while others called out on Allah and the local saint. Sandeman wanted to go down into the *mêlée* and protect the clown. I deterred him by main force and dragged him from that pandemonium out into the street of tents, telling two soldiers who were standing by the door to stop the riot. We waited till the noise within had quite subsided, when the omdeh came rushing out like a madman, flung himself at Sandeman's feet and told him that the clown was captured and awaited judgment. Sandeman swore horribly and told him not to be a fool, which made the old man look more scared than ever as we moved away.

"What silly fools the beggars are!" sighed Sandeman, "spoiling the best part of the show like that! Whatever do they think I am – an ogre? What? Of course it was cheek of the feller, but I thought it damned amusin'. No need to half kill the joker, anyhow! Surprisin' beggars! Absolutely mad, of course. I sometimes feel as if I were bewitched, changed somehow, not myself at all, the way the beggars look at me! Can't grasp their point of view, you see. It's pretty maddening. Makes one downright homesick. I've had enough of this. Let's get indoors."

My friend was nearly crying with vexation. I told him that in my opinion the beggars, as he called them, were afraid of him, and suggested that the frightful language he employed habitually might peradventure have something to do with it.

"Oh, that! They're used to that. They like it!" he made light rejoinder, and went on to enlarge upon the subject of the homesickness which seized him sometimes when alone with them. He told me the whole history of his love for Joan, which dated from his sixteenth year, described his home, his earliest recollections, his first ride to hounds and other private matters in a sentimental tone. There dwelt in truth a very honest, simple soul beneath his self-assertive outer shell. After midnight, in his study in the rest-house, he described to me the height of his ambition: "Two thousand a year. You can't ask a girl to marry you on less, and a little country house – I know the very place I want in Devon – among trees, you know – I love the drip of trees after a shower – with decent shooting and a few good neighbours – and Joanie! I should be a king, by Jove! And here I am in this damned furnace of a country, acting nursery governess to a lot of bally monkeys. But there, the beggars are all right. I'm feeling down."

At this point he had paused with one hand on his brow, the other stroking Snap, who lay upon his knees as usual, when a droning, nasal chant, uplifted suddenly, assailed our ears. Coming from just outside the house, it startled me.

"My old Ghafir," said Sandeman. "He's at his prayers. Whenever I wake up at night I hear that noise. It's damned pathetic, the religion of these beggars.

Fine, I call it! – He's a rum old boy. God knows who pays him for his job. He's never had a sou[138] from me, I know. I've a jolly good mind to give him something now."

He went to the window and called the Ghafîr. The man came running. "O Ghafîr! A sovereign for you! Catch! Have you got it?"

"Praise be to God," replied a drowsy voice out of the darkness. That old night-watchman, who had kept the rest-house from its first foundation, was never seen again in Kefr Ammeh.

The Ghafîr had all his life been saving money, little by little, for the purpose of that pilgrimage to Mecca which, being pious, he accounted life's true aim. I gathered this, with other matters incidental to this story, afterwards from an Egyptian friend in Kefr Ammeh, who had been my host on more than one occasion of my visiting the place. The sovereign he received from Sandeman that night made up the sum which he put before him as the minimum required for his long journey. He had hoped to set forth in another year or two. This godsend made it possible to start at any time; and, as it wanted but a week of the departure of the yearly pilgrimage, he resolved at once to break the fetters of his worldly calling. By dawn he had made up a bundle of his few belongings, with which upon his back, and staff in hand, he set out for the railway station at peep of day. Wrapped in the praises of the Lord, he stepped out gladly, never turning to look back at the white house which he had guarded faithfully for fifteen years. About a mile from his own place, passing the hamlet known as Mît Gâmûs just as the sun was rising, he met some young men going forth to work. One of them, who was leading two white water-buffaloes, hailed him by name, inquiring: "Whither away?"

He answered with a phrase which told them that he was a pilgrim. The young men asked him who would guard the rest-house in his absence. He replied that Allah knew; the house was in His keeping; all was well. At that those young men exchanged lightning glances, and sped him on his way with hearty blessings.

Beside a sakieh they stood and watched him trudging on, a plume of dust uprising from his heels; then one of them remarked: "The praise to Allah. The gun which never misses is without a guardian. Meet in the palm-grove at the fall of night. We must devise a stratagem." Another cried: "The stratagem is found already. Lo, the watchmanship is vacant, and we alone have knowledge of the fact! Let one of us become the watchman till our end is gained."

"Dost thou consent to play the part, O Mustafa?"

---

[138] A former French coin of low denomination

"At thy pleasure," answered Mustafa, a swarthy youth, a kind of servant to the previous speaker, who was called the Sheykh Ridwân. "If thou desire it, I will go to-night and be Ghafîr."

"Capital!" exclaimed Ridwân. "Thou wilt make friends with the two servants and learn from them the habits of the Englishman. We shall await thee here to-morrow at this hour, for thy report."

The Sheykh Ridwân, aged seventeen, was a romantic dreamer. He had battened upon tales of strange adventure till the sober facts of life appeared unreal to him. He saw that quiet countryside as wonderland, and planned, while he performed his daily tasks, such exploits as had earned renown for brave and wily ones of old. Those exploits, being always well rewarded in the chap-books, he thought would lead perforce to high preferment and his recognition as the choicest spirit of the age. A mighty talker, of some eloquence upon his favourite subject, possessing, he alone of all his entourage, the power to read aloud from printed books; being, moreover, the son of a rich farmer, he had infected with his views a group of youths of his own age. They formed a band, united by most horrid vows. They pricked themselves with knives to get inured to pain; they prowled by night in order to get used to darkness. They thought of exploits which might make them famous, and if they heard of any treasure greatly guarded, would instantly devise some plan to get at it, with no idea of theft, but simply that mankind might recognise their dauntless guile. On the few occasions of their action hitherto they had succeeded; but when, as happened naturally, they bragged of their success, the men whom they had hoodwinked made complaint against them to the father of the Sheykh Ridwân, whose anger gave the youths a sense of failure through injustice.

"When Ali El Masri performed his clever rogueries at the court of Er-Rashîd," said young Ridwân with bitterness, "those whom he tricked sought only to outwit him in return and, when they failed, became his servants and admirers. But these low dogs come fawning to my father. They have neither heart nor liver. May they perish utterly!"

Therewith he swore to be revenged on them. Their names were entered in the black book of the band, and never mentioned without solemn execration. Any game at their expense was counted fair. It was this admixture of revengeful spite with their romance which made the band the growing terror of the neighbourhood. The father of Ridwân, although indulgent to his son, alluded sometimes to the English as relentless rulers, without indulgence to the sports of youth, who would not scruple to arrest the band in its entirety and cast it into prison if they came to know of it; and since the coming of the English ghoul to Kefr Ammeh, the omdeh, through the fear of him, had threatened action.

The band had seen the clown's performance in the circus; they had seen the Englishman, the small white ball and the small white dog at play upon the dust-heaps many times. Moreover, two of them had served the ghoul when he went out to shoot, and so beheld the wondrous gun which never missed. But while the other fellâhîn surveyed the prodigy with awestruck eyes, as a mystery whose inner meaning would never be revealed in this low world, Ridwân's small gang, intoxicated with romance, beheld him as a potent lord and possible magician – in fact, the only monster in the country. To overcome him by some stratagem would mean for them the moral lordship of the district. Ridwân's most cherished daydream was to picture the Englishman, outwitted by his skill, bestowing on him rank and honours as did monarchs of old days; and his disciples, taking fire from him as usual, saw in the English ghoul their road to glory.

At first their mind had been to carry off the small white dog, returning it after a while politely with a full description of the stratagem they had employed to gain it. But from the moment when they saw the gun which never missed, cupidity usurped the place of sportiveness. With such a gun the band would be invincible. And now, in the departure of the old Ghafîr, they saw their opportunity to get possession of it. Mustafa, after his first night as watchman at the rest-house, brought them hopeful news. He had been accepted as the new Ghafîr without a question. The Berberine cook, with whom alone he had held conversation, had asked him what had happened to the old Ghafîr, and, hearing he was gone upon the pilgrimage, had given praise to God. He had learnt from the said cook that the khawâjah was going to the capital to spend a night; Selîm the waiter would attend him thither, and the cook was thinking surreptitiously of going to Dumyâtt[139] to see some friends. He had asked Mustafa to give food and water to the small white dog at sunset for fear lest it should die and he (the cook) be blamed; had asked him, too, to see that it was kept indoors lest it should stray, when equal blame would be his portion.

"To-morrow, then, towards midnight!" cried Ridwân emotionally.

At the time appointed the band approached the rest-house, armed with pistols, quarter-staves and rusty scimitars. First they crawled about the dust-heaps on their bellies for an hour to make quite sure that no one of the village watchmen lurked in that direction. Then they stole up to the house.

Mustafa waited with the door-key in his hand. He opened for them and they entered, shuddering, in supernatural awe of their own daring. They closed

[139] Damietta, on a branch of the Nile as it enters the Mediterranean Sea.

the house door, lit a candle they had brought with them, and set out to explore the house. The small white dog, aroused from sleep, flew at them, barking, till in their terror they struck hard and made it dumb. For long they could not find the gun, search as they would. At last a queer-shaped case which they had passed repeatedly was made to open. It contained the treasure. With that in hand they went away again, creeping till they were out of earshot of the house, when they careered with horrid yells across the plain, in terror of themselves, such awful malefactors!

The Berberine cook returned next morning from Dumyâtt to find the small white dog a lifeless corpse and the gun stolen. He praised the Lord, then gashed his forehead with a knife, likewise his arm, and bandaged up the wounds. He then ran weeping to the omdeh's house, where in the courtyard he fell down and rubbed his visage in the mire, exclaiming: –

"Woe! Oh, woe! The house is broken open. The soul of the khawâjah, the beautiful, the priceless little snow-white dog, is foully slain. I fought with twenty. I was wounded, overcome. I am but now awakened from the swoon. O Allah! What to do? O Lord, relieve me!"

At that cry, the omdeh, the watchmen, and all the elders came together. They hurried out across the dust-heaps to the scene of the crime. The rest-house soon became the centre of a wailing crowd. When the omdeh, in tears, appeared in the doorway holding reverently in his arms the body of the small white dog, there were cries of mourning as upon the death of true believers. "Woe! Woe! O cruel day!" the people moaned. "Behold us ruined, shamed and made a dunghill. The good khawâjah will no longer smile on us. His goodness will be changed to fury. This priceless little dog was as his son, and innocent of all offences."

"Wallahi. I will have the lives of all concerned!" exclaimed the omdeh in a frenzy. "See that this corpse be buried with all honour, as one that was the soul of our good lord. I go to telegraph the dreadful tidings to the mudîrîyeh[140]. What can I do? My face is blackened till the Day of Judgment. I feel that I shall not recover from this great calamity. Nothing worse than a murder has been committed in my jurisdiction hitherto, and now some devils have assailed our lords the English. I must hasten to the telegraph. O High Protector!" In tears he ran away across the dust-heaps. In answer to the omdeh's telegram to the mudîr there came this message: "Inexpressibly horrified. Use all means to discover and arrest the miscreants. Am telegraphing to the noble victim of the wicked plot."

Immediately upon receipt of this command, the omdeh and the elders held a court of law and summoned witnesses. The Berberine cook, under

[140] Provincial headquarters.

interrogation, mentioned the new night-watchman and his likeness. The man described was recognised as Mustafa, a well-known member of the band of Sheykh Ridwân. Exalted by his wrath and fear above all ties of neighbourhood, the omdeh forthwith sent the village watchmen with orders to arrest not only the aforesaid Mustafa, but also Sheykh Ridwân and all his house. The gang which had intimidated a whole countryside was captured easily and brought to trial in an hour. The father of the Sheykh Ridwân strove hard to intercede for him, offering vast sums of money for his liberation; but the omdeh raised his arms to Heaven, crying: "Allah witness, I am helpless to befriend thee now. The crime is too excessive. All the land is moved with it. The Government will wipe out Kefr Ammeh and sow the ground thereof with salt as a memorial, if before sunset it is not avenged."

"But what proof have you that any of these lads are guilty?" roared the father of Ridwân.

"They shall confess their guilt before thee," said the omdeh grimly; and he ordered Mustafa to be brought forward.

Ridwân, that high-strung youth, was weeping bitterly, which made Mustafa, who loved him as his eyes, more resolute in keeping silence under question.

"What, O son of a dog?" thundered the omdeh. "Thou wilt not speak? Thou floutest me? Wait only! We will find a way to make thee speak. Here, watchmen, take those three dogs who are grinning there, and give them each ten stripes with the nailed whip."

"By Allah, we know nothing of the matter," howled the prisoners; all saving Mustafa, who in his obstinacy seemed of stone. On him the omdeh's wrath was concentrated. "Ha, I will make thee speak!" he cried once more.

"Put out his eyes!" roared the crowd. "Tear off his finger-nails. Pull out his tongue to make him speak and save our lives!"

The omdeh, though he paid no heed to their advice, still thought it an occasion on which modern dilatory methods might be put aside. Mustafa was slightly tortured. His frame went rigid and his eyes turned over in his head, but not a word escaped him. Such fortitude destroyed the patience of the crowd. They spat upon him where he lay upon the ground.

"Where is the gun which never missed? Inform me!" shrieked the omdeh.

"Who slew with felon hand the small white dog? Inform me straightaway!"

Mustafa compressed his lips and seemed to sneer.

"Then thou shalt forfeit thy right hand!" the omdeh cried. "My patience and my mercy are exhausted. The trial has already lasted for three hours. Here, make him kneel! Bring out the bucket of hot pitch. Now, O worst of malefactors, if thou confess not thou will lose thy hand of honour. Speak, I say!"

But Mustafa maintained a rigid silence.

The execution was just over when Sandeman thrust his way through the crowd, which had been too much absorbed in gazing at the horrid sight to any one who came behind it.

The surprise at his sudden reappearance, the cries of sorrow and condolence, the indescribable confusion which arose when they discovered that the anger in his face was for the justice done upon his foe, prevented any one from thinking of the unfortunate Mustafa, who had swooned away; till Sandeman himself commanded them to carry the poor creature gently to the rest-house, and to fetch a doctor.

"He is a wretch unworthy of Your Honour's notice!" wailed the crowd. "He murdered in cold blood Isnâb, our chief delight!"

At ten o' clock that night, Sandeman came into my flat at Cairo in a half-hysterical condition and told me the amazing story; how his own omdeh had flogged three men and cut off one man's hand, in presence of a crowd and with the popular approval, all for pure love, as it appeared, of him (George Sandeman) and horror at the death of poor dear Snap! What in the world was he to do?

"Rummy beggars! Unaccountable beggars!" he kept muttering. "I'm deadly sick about it, yet I want to laugh. It hurts, I tell you. This business does for my career out here. I lose the best part of my income and all hope of Joanie. . . . If you'd seen what I saw! I can't make out the beggars. God knows what kind of a beast they think I am. When I was doing what I could do for the poor devil, a chap came up to me, as pleased as Punch because he'd found a golf ball. Seemed to expect me to rejoice exceedingly! What does go on in their confounded heads?"

Late as it was, I called a cab and took him off to see the chief of his department who, by good fortune, was at home and able to receive us. I was the spokesman. Having heard the story to an end, he ordered Sandeman a glass of brandy, ere pronouncing:–

"I cannot see that you are in any way to blame for this occurrence, Mr. Sandeman. The only criticism of your conduct which I have to make is that you ought to be at Kefr Ammeh at this minute and not here. You ask me what you are to do? Use your own judgment. You seem to have unbounded influence in Kefr Ammeh. Strictly speaking, I suppose we ought to make what is called an 'example' of your omdeh, but the case is quite unusual, in no way exemplary. . . . . I should think that you might let the matter rest, if rest it will. But I will take advice upon the subject. Good-night."

I had to support Sandeman to the cab in waiting. He seemed dazed and did not speak till we had driven off.

"Well, thank the Lord!" he sighed at length. "I breathe again. It's jolly decent of him not to go for me. . . . Poor little Snap! I used to say I'd kill the man who teased him even; but when I saw that feller's hand chopped off . . . . Damned plucky feller! . . . He shall never want while I'm alive. . . . Don't tell Joanie anything about this business, mind . . . . I'll go down and frighten 'em a bit, and then proclaim a general amnesty. It was the thought of punishment for the affair that turned me sick. They're like dumb animals, at times; they aren't responsible. And, say what you like, old man, they are ingratiatin' beggars! What?"

CROSS-PURPOSES

A STORY OF EGYPT

This story first appeared in As Others See Us, published by Collins in October 1922. It is a story about the conflicting attitudes towards the authority of the British occupation.

Pickthall went to Egypt in 1907 as the guest of a British official of the British occupation. He travelled around the country, and clearly became familiar with the ways of life of Delta village life. In this story he is expressing non-judgmental empathy with all sides of the characters in the story – the brigands who had a set of values, the villagers, the Egyptian servants of the occupation, and (albeit most remotely) the British. The central tragic character is the omdeh of the village who is perplexed by the innovations of the "Frankish" occupation – the British, atheists, bring "haste and a greed of gain". But he is submissive to their authority on whom his own authority is dependent.

There is another example of a strong female character, the sister of Suleymân who exerts authority over her vainglorious blustering brother and his brigand comrades. They wish to complain to the governor of the district and she, with common sense, tells them to get their story straight.

Six youths were tramping in a wedge formation along a dyke which was stretched across the plain as far as eye could see in both directions between the fields of cotton and of sugar-cane, of corn and fodder-grass and bright green clover, with here a grove of palms upstanding like plumed lances and there a village like a cake of mud upon the landscape. The foremost was Suleymân Derwîsh; Mahrûs and Hamdi, sons of Yûsuf, walked behind him at each shoulder, the other three behind him in a row, keeping as close as might be to avoid their dust. The six had been released from prison that same morning; they had been walking since the fourth hour of the day now near its end; and lo! At last their village was in sight. Hamdi the son of Yûsuf improvised a song of gladness, which the others punctuated with a ready chorus.

"O abode of our delight! What save the thought of thee has been to us instead of water in the desert of our absence, cheering our hearts what time we did hard labour – we, the oppressed, pure innocents – with those who live in dungeons and in cells. There were others of God's creatures, swollen with pride, who ordered us about like dogs and carried guns to shoot us. We laughed 'Ha, ha!' at all their tyranny; the work seemed light to us, the food most excellent, because of thy sweet memory, O native place, gladdening our hearts like running water and the song of birds."

"Aye, by Allah! Say, O girls, have you forgotten the brave lads who gave you joy?"

"There is a smell of myrrh about thee, O dear native place, a smell of camphor also and of burning dung. I die of the remembrance which thy perfume wakens – the thought of the great deeds which we performed in thee. The miser and the foul oppressor knew and feared us. The love of us was in all joyful hearts. The heart of every maid went out to us. We were the gallants of our time, the brave adventurers! Say truth, O girls, have you not mourned for us?"

"Aye, by Allah! Say, O girls, have you forgotten the brave lads who gave you joy?"

"Alas, our enemies set snares for us. They bought with gold the tongue of one who knew our counsels. We were taken, spat upon, insulted and dragged before the judge, the foul oppressor, who cast us into prison for long months. The doves, the very palm-trees, mourned for us; but we were dauntless, thinking of the home-coming and of the vengeance we would wreak on our most wicked foes. And now we come! We come! O sweet-lipped girls, O straight-backed girls, behold us!"

"Aye, by Allah! Say, O girls, have you forgotten the brave lads who gave you joy?"

The last chorus was bawled loudly by all six. An answer came to it upon the evening breeze, so faint that they stood still to listen with lips parted. Hands shading eyes from the darts of the setting sun, they scanned the distance of the road before them.

A little crowd was waiting at the foot of the mound on which the village and its palm-trees stood uplifted. The joy-cries of the women could be heard, incessant, thrilling. The young men sobbed, then broke into a run; and in ten minutes every youth was in his mother's arms, with father, sisters, wife around him, shouting blessings. To celebrate the triumph of their safe return, a procession was then formed, marching to the quaver of reed pipes and soft, incessant beat of little drums, which led them three times round the village before going in.

The flat-roofed houses and the palm-trunks stood out black upon the sunset sky. The dogs all started barking, and the cooing of the doves took on an anxious sound. Their going was attended by a noisy swarm of children. At one point of the circuit, where the sunset light shone red on blind mud walls, the merry-makers came upon a group of the elders of the village set in circle on a dust-heap. Astonished by the sudden noise of concourse, some of the old men were about to scramble to their feet, but the omdeh, who was present, bade them pay no heed to the disturbance. He himself continued smoking his narghileh placidly and talking as if no one save his cronies were in sight, though the procession paused before him for a moment making louder noise. When the crowd came round a second time, the council of the elders showed the same unconsciousness – an attitude which so offended the proud spirit of Suleymân Darwîsh that, on the third occasion of their passing by the seated group, he stopped and shouted to the omdeh: –

"Say, O Sheykh, hast thou no blessing for poor, ill-used men released from servitude?"

The sheykh surveyed him coldly before answering: –

"I have this word for thee, O son of rashness! Thou hast beheld the consequence of brigandage. Receive the lesson wisely and with reverence, and in the future keep to honest work."

"What trade shall I pursue? Advise me, O my lord!" returned the rogue with mockery, for the reply enraged him. "Till thou, O Sheykh, didst throw me into prison, I was a gay, light-hearted youth, without malevolence. But now, by thy instruction, I am grown a man, and my intention henceforth is to work in earnest. What sayest thou to the business of a shroud-maker? And wilt thou be my customer, O Sheykh? All men must die – the praise to Allah! – so the trade is constant."

A burst of smothered laughter from the crowd acclaimed this sally. The procession thereupon resumed its way, passing in among the houses and dispersing. The music died, and night enwrapped the village.

Under cover of the night, a man with face well-hooded in a shawl stole from the shadow of the omdeh's house and, flitting through the alleys like a ghost, approached the dwelling of Suleymân Derwîsh. He fell down on the threshold of the room in which the brigand was at supper with his family, and lay there, writhing, while he murmured: –

"Forgiveness, for the love of Allah, and security! I had no wish to do that deed of shame. They bribed, they threatened, they corrupted me. Since thy betrayal by my tongue, my conscience has not known one hour of peace; at every meal my belly has afflicted me with awful pains; I have not had one wink of sleep on any night! Thou art and ever wast my soul's beloved! I wished to make atonement, but too late. Ask all thy house here present, if I speak not truth! Peradventure they may not have noticed it, but things were so!"

The suppliant was a short man past the prime of life and rather stout, with face much lined, and little anxious eyes. His robe of very good material proclaimed him of superior station to the youth whose pardon he so humbly sought. In point of fact, he was the omdeh's son-in-law, a man comparatively wealthy and of good position. Though he spoke in whispers, every word was clearly audible amid the hush which followed his appearance on the threshold.

"Is it indeed thyself, O Hasan, son of treason, O false friend?" exclaimed Suleymân Derwîsh with bitter scorn. "Thou who didst reveal our secrets for a bribe, and bear such spiteful witness against men who trusted thee? And comest thou to me with talk of pardon?"

"Now Allah witness, I have made atonement," whined the prostrate one. "Are my sufferings nothing? Are my tears, my inward torments nothing? And lack of sleep of nights? Wallahi, every word I say is the extreme of truth! – are these all nothing in thy thinking, O my soul?"

"Thou didst make me childless all this while!" exclaimed the mother of Suleymân. "For that may everlasting torments be thy portion!"

"Thou didst widow me for many weary months," exclaimed the brigand's wife. "For all that may all thy offspring perish horribly!"

"Nay, curse him not," put in the old man of the house. "He comes here as a suppliant, he clasps our threshold. He was the author of a deed of darkness, and while our soul was absent in the prison we slew him daily in our thoughts. But now our soul has been restored to us – the praise to Allah! – it behoves us to show mercy and not pride, lest the Most Merciful withdraw from us his favour!"

"For the love of Allah, hear him, hear thy father!" moaned the wretch.

"Well, before Allah, I forgive thee what is past, O Hasan!" Suleymân Derwîsh at length vouchsafed disdainfully. "That means we forgo our lawful vengeance in thy case. But look well to thy footsteps in the days to come."

"O lord of bounty! O most generous youth!" suspired the grateful Hasan. "Let me kiss thy feet!"

He was in the act of crawling forward to perform that duty when the noise of men approaching made him spring up suddenly and with a hurried blessing disappear into the night. Three of the village elders hailed the house. On being pressed to enter, they complied, filling the place of honour in the little room. They had come to offer an apology for their apparent coldness out there upon the dust-heaps, on the passage of the festal train. They had been restrained from manifesting their unbounded raptures by the presence of the omdeh, who, for his part, viewed the merry-making as a personal affront, since it was he who, in the course of duty, had caused Suleymân and his five friends to be arrested and sent up for trial.

"Allah witness, we all love thee as our eyes!" murmured the spokesman of the three with nods and coaxing smiles. "We desire thy welfare above all things. He arrested thee and cast thee into prison, so thou hast a grudge against him – it is natural. But, we ask thee, is it wise to flout him openly – the headman of the place in which thou hast to dwell? Thou puttest us, who are thy friends and his subordinates, in a position the reverse of comfortable. When we defer to him, as is our duty, thou wilt say. 'They wish me ill.' When we smile on thee, as our heart bids us, he, in his turn, will say, 'They are my enemies.' Think better of the matter, we beseech thee, for our sakes! His pride is deeply wounded. Go to him and ask his pardon. It is no shame for youth to ask forgiveness of old age."

These sentiments were much applauded by the people of the house, all save Suleymân himself, who answered sullenly: –

"I ask pardon of Allah. I will not ask the omdeh's pardon, to see him triumph in my self-abasement, thinking: 'The prison life has broken his proud spirit.' Never! I have now seen the world and talked with those who know the law, the new law of the English which is harder upon him than upon us. I know the limits of his power to harm me. He can cause me to be sent to prison once again. What matter? Prison life is not unpleasant. But if he overstep the bounds of his authority by but a hair's breadth, then I have power to drag him to the judgment and have him sent to prison in his turn. For me the prison is a merry jest; for him, disgrace. Now tell me, which is stronger, he or I?"

The elders plucked their beards and shrugged their shoulders.

"Well, may our Lord preserve thee!" were their spokesman's parting words. When out of earshot of the brigand he made haste to add: "May Allah quicken our intelligence to see where power resides at any moment and adhere to it."

Suleymân Derwîsh had many other visitors that night; some, like Sheykh Hasan, coming to implore his pardon for their past hostility; others, like the elders, to remonstrate with him lovingly upon his rudeness towards the lawful headman of the place. In the intervals of serious talk, the gossip of the village on the one hand, the prison on the other, was retailed; while Suleymân himself consumed much coffee which, following on great fatigue, excited him. He had come back as a monarch to his own; the whole world sought his favour. He condescended to his people, boasting of the justice he was going to do, the vengeance he was going to take upon his enemies. Successive visitors observed his bearing with despair, behind the mask of deference which they assumed through fear. They had all hoped for him to die in gaol. Yet here he had returned with his companions, more arrogant than ever and more ripe for mischief. Were prisons then no longer hells on earth? Were they made pleasant places as these rogues asserted? Then let the Government reserve them for the law-abiding and the timid, that these might have some refuge from the bullies, who henceforth, very certainly, would rule the world.

The omdeh too had many visitors that night. Men went from the one house to the other without shame, esteeming it the merest prudence to conciliate both parties to a feud, where both seemed powerful. In the omdeh's house at midnight one made moan: "O Lord have mercy on us! This tiger-cub was bound and caged and we were safe. What miscreants have now released the brute for our destruction? We deemed ourselves well rid of him. Who dreamt that he would presently return in health and spirits, brave as of old and thirsting for revenge! At once, on his arrival, he insulted our beloved chief. Yet if we frown on him he will destroy our houses. O God Most High, instruct us what to do!"

The omdeh, for all answer, shrugged and turned away. He hated time-servers – mere reptiles who have no conception of the law of God nor any vision of the Day of Judgment. Their consciences were those of lizards, not of men. He, the omdeh, had been insulted grossly in his own village, yet these men, his colleagues, sharing in his honour spoke of smiling on the rebel as a thing of course. Ah, had this incident but happened in old days, before the English theorists devised their code of laws for Egypt, he, the responsible, despotic omdeh, would have known what to do! But such a thing could not have happened in those days. For years he had beheld disorder on the increase, not in one village only, but in all the land.

When all the rest had gone his daughter came to him complaining of the conduct of her husband, the Sheykh Hasan.

"He is with those gaol-birds," she reported, "feasting and making merry. O Lord! That I should bear the shame of such a dog. I went and spied. One glance! It was enough. Suleymân Derwîsh was boasting – May God notice and degrade him! He said that thou art now as dirt before him, since he knows the law: that he will henceforth order matters as he chooses; and if thou or thy watchmen lay a finger on him he will summon thee before the judge and have thee punished. O my father, show thy strength upon him, or I die of shame!"

A little before noon upon the morrow, after one hour's travel and some three hours spent in waiting in a crowded ante-room, the omdeh was admitted to the presence of the chief official of the province, who sat enthroned at a great desk, with two assessors seated at a lower level.

"Thou art the Sheykh Fâris Abd-ur-Rahman[141], Omdeh of Mashrûtah, is it not so?" questioned one of these. "And thou bringest tidings of importance to His Excellency? State thy business!"

The sheykh with downcast eyes described the home-coming to his village of six brigands, who had spent eight months in prison with hard labour as the just reward of many crimes they had committed; the insult put upon him by their chief; the way the people drew away from him, the omdeh, and cringed in fear before those shameless boys.

"Of old, before the legal code came into force, my fear was on my people, and we lived in peace," he stated in conclusion. "If one did wrong I punished him in such a manner as to silence murmurs. The peace and order of the village were upon my head, and in return my jurisdiction was made absolute. The people knew that there was no appeal against my judgment. At first when the new code was introduced, the people knew it not and, bred up to obedience, still deferred to me; but now the rising generation becomes turbulent, having learnt that my authority is circumscribed by law. They know that it extends to this point and no further. They come up impudently to the boundary line, and mock me in the hope to make me overstep it. And therewithal, although effective power is now denied me, the Government still blames me for the misbehaviour of such rascals as much as formerly when I possessed that power. Is this justice, is it reason, O my lord? Since the code and not the omdeh has the power to-day, the code with its police, and not the omdeh with his watchmen, should keep order in the villages. Now I have laid my case before Your Excellency. What can I do to reassert my dignity, to save myself from further insult? I ask you, in the cause of all authority."

The old man stood with eyes downcast, hands hidden in his flowing sleeves, awaiting the reply of his superior.

"What can any of us do but trust in God? The code is on us all. We are quite helpless. Thy objections, being altogether vain, appear to me unworthy of a man of sense. They do but make us rage and beat our hands against a wall!" The voice of the mudîr was musical and friendly. The omdeh for the first time dared to look at him. He saw a portly personage with beard of iron-gray, whose face evinced good nature and good sense.

141 The original text has Fahman, which must surely be a typographical mistake.

The sheykh responded to the strain of humour in the great man's tone. "Allah forbid," he murmured with a smile, "that I should criticise the code itself, O my dear lord! It is no doubt perfect of its kind. I do but say of it as Caracûsh[142] remarked of the cat which Ali the Jester made of wool and showed it to him: 'It is a cat, a fine cat, yet there is something lacking.' Of the code I say it is a code, a fine code, but it does not work. It is – I crave forgiveness, O my lord, for speaking plainly in Your Excellency's presence – a thing imagined by ingenious men, and not at all the work of God, which is to say, a natural growth in this our land."

The great man laughed aloud, his two assistants echoing the mirthful noise, and, leaning over towards the omdeh, said: –

"Now, by thy beard, thou speakest truth, and neatly too! Thy thought is mine in private. Be sure I will remember thee and try to help thee."

The omdeh of Mashrûtah made his reverence. Scarcely had he left the presence when the English inspector of the province stalked into the room, the air of bustle common to his kind detracting somewhat from his dignity.

"Who was that who just went out?" he questioned sharply. He was always asking questions, and the mudîr, accustomed to his ways, replied: –

"The omdeh of Mashrûtah."

"What was his business with thee?"

"He came to make complaint of certain difficulties – the usual tale."

Therewith the governor recounted briefly, in a tone of ridicule, the omdeh's griefs, adding: "This omdeh is an ignorant, old-fashioned person. He cannot see the beauty of a legal code which robs him personally of so much prestige."

He used that tone to gratify the Englishman, whom he regarded as of course a lover of the code. He was amazed when the inspector answered: –

"He is right! The code is not entirely a success. Here, in the country districts, crime is on the increase. It is on that very business I have come to see you. There is a new decree. Henceforth we may deport our village brigands, whenever we catch them, without public trial. Only the charges need to be verified."

The mudîr and his assistants exchanged lightning glances, expressive of both rapture and dismay.

"But, O my lord," the mudîr murmured gently, "do you mean to say that we may kidnap malefactors?"

"Precisely," snapped the business-like inspector.

---

[142] A twelfth century Mamluk judge in Cairo, fabled as the deliverer of singular and sometimes tyrannical sentences.

"The praise to Allah! But are such measures legal? The Ministry has always laid such emphasis on strict adherence to the forms of law."

"It is efficiency before all things. When pure legality proves inefficient, we must supplement it. A law is to be passed immediately, and we have permission to anticipate that law when need arises."

The inspector, always in a hurry, then marched out, leaving the mudîr to stare hard at his two assistants, first one and then the other, with round eyes of glee. At length he let his mirth have way, exclaiming: "Praise be to God for this efficiency! The Lord preserve it to us all our days! For it has overcome the paralysing law, and made us government officials men again. But what a long way round they take to come to fact. In order to correct the code which was to banish tyranny, they institute a tyranny far greater than was ever known before the code existed. For what man living but prefers a flogging from the omdeh to banishment for life without a warning?"

Meanwhile the omdeh of Mashrûtah journeyed homeward. It in some degree allayed the perturbation of his mind to know that he possessed the sympathy of his superior. He had recovered something of his old serenity when, astride of his white donkey with its coloured trappings, he drew near his village. But in the palm-grove he beheld Suleymân Derwîsh sitting with several of his gang, much as the omdeh had been sitting with the elder son the previous evening when the procession formed in honour of those rogues annoyed him. For impudence, the young men remained seated even as the old had done, pretending not to see the omdeh as he passed. The habit of respect was strong upon them, adding a touch of awkwardness to their impertinence. They nudged one another when the old man wished them a good-evening, but returned no answer.

The omdeh's rage returned upon him at their rudeness. The bad manners, even more than the rebellion, jarred on one who was himself the very pink of courtesy. For the welfare of God's people here on earth, for the honour of Islâm, there must be chastisement. Were mere lads to grow up lawless and uncouth, the slaves of their own lusts, for lack of proper discipline, merely because it pleased the English to set up an unnatural law instead of order? No, a thousand times. He would rather earn the censure of the Government, had rather end his days in prison than have his conscience kill him for neglect of his plain duty. He would do right in spite of all the whims of all the English. At worst they could but punish his old body, while God, his Lord and theirs, would guard his soul.

Alighting at his house, he called the watchmen and ordered them at once to catch Suleymân Derwîsh and his companions, naming the spot where he had seen them sitting in the palm-grove. A chance mention of his visit to the mudîrîyeh gave them to suppose that he had orders from the governor. He then commanded his own servants to unearth the great kurbâg – a monstrous whip – which had not seen the light for many years. This whip was held before him by a serving-man when the rebellious youths were dragged into his presence, struggling and protesting violently with tremendous threats. He quietly commanded that they should be stripped and bound, and each receive five lashes. At that they shrieked for mercy, cursed and prayed, flinging themselves upon the ground and foaming at the mouth like madmen.

The gateway of the yard was full of frightened faces. When all was ready for the execution the omdeh made a little speech in mild, paternal tones. And then the whip, uplifted in a watchman's hands, descended on the bare back of Suleymân Derwîsh, then on the back of Hamdi, son of Yûsuf, then on the back of Mustafa, and so on, going up and down the line in measure, with "Heyli[143]! Bismillah[144]!" at every stroke, till every one had eaten his five lashes.

There were agonising shrieks and grunts as well from the spectators as the actual sufferers. And then the victims were released, a writhing crew. Their relatives rushed forward and sustained them.

"It is against the law! We shall complain of thee, O bloody tyrant! Thou shalt be beaten, thou thyself, and put in prison – that I promise thee!" blubbered Suleymân, supported by his weeping wife and sisters. He alone of all the gang had fight left in him.

"Go, do what pleases thee!" replied the omdeh suavely. "But be polite or thou shalt eat another flogging."

The old man was majestic. None dared meet his eyes. When the victims and their friends had fled, men fell down and embraced his feet, proclaiming him the saviour of the land. His eyes ranged over the inconstant crowd with vast contempt and just a hint of pride, for which he asked God's pardon. He had a strong, half humorous desire to make these also taste the great kurbâg. The English might degrade him now, might cast him into prison, even kill him, if they chose. He was indifferent to life henceforward, having had his hour. Meanwhile Suleymân and his supporters, with a crowd of sympathisers, boys and girls, had rushed out of the village, mad with rage and grief, and taken refuge in a field of sugar-cane.

"O Lord, befriend us!" wailed their leader. "We are dishonoured, flouted, in the sight of all. Escaped but yesterday from cruel tyranny, we were rejoicing in the company of those who love us, most peacefully inclined and harming no man, when this shame befell!"

---

143 Heave-ho!

144 In the name of God.

"Wallahi, our hearts bleed," his comrades moaned. "O Allah, witness our extremity! We, the bravest, the most self-respecting of mankind to be so treated! We writhe! We burn! Wâh! Wâh!"

"Now listen, all of you!" exclaimed Suleymân with fierce decision. "I swear that I will never more lie down to sleep nor close my eyes till I have taken steps to humble to the dust this vile oppressor, and have made him taste the pains which I now suffer. He has done a thing illegal. The mudîr allowed it; but the English care no more for the mudîr than for a dung-beetle. I will make petition to the English, who will drag our persecutor to the judge. Then will we testify against him, saying: 'This horrible old man, this worst of tyrants, did seize on us when we were sitting quiet in the shade, and for sheer lust of cruelty did flog us till our blood bade fair to inundate the village.' When they behold him in the culprit's place, degraded, spat upon, all people will support our tale with acclamation."

"And I will say," chimed in another, weeping lamentably: "O judge, so cruel was that causeless flogging that one man of our number died. I am that man. I feel it certainly. God knows I shall not live another day."

"We must be careful what we say before the judge," exclaimed the sister of Suleymân, a girl renowned for wit. "Our stories must agree at every point. Every word must be made true beforehand by rehearsal, for judges and the people of the courts are cunning devils, who catch poor righteous folk in nets of questions."

At once, and weeping though they all still were, the mournful group assumed the likeness of a court of law. The sister of Suleymân became the judge, and one by one the witnesses appeared before her and were questioned. She prompted their replies, corrected, schooled them, weeding out discrepancies, until she had their testimony solid as the testimony of one man. By then their tears were dried and hope prevailed.

"I hasten to the capital this night," declared Suleymân Derwîish. Some of the girls returned into the village to fetch food. They brought back news to their companions waiting in the patch of cane. The omdeh, being asked point-blank by what authority he had ordained the flogging, had confessed that he had acted on his own responsibility, against the orders of the governor, whom he had seen that day. The tidings were received with howls of joy.

"Then I will go to the mudîr," declared Suleymân Derwîsh with satisfaction. "It is much nearer, and our vengeance will be felt at once. Come with me all of you and bear the witness we have prepared and verified!"

They waited in the patch of sugar-cane till it was night, and then set out with song to keep up their courage in the darkness, the men repeating doggedly the name of Allah.

It was still night when they reached the chief town of the province, but the muezzins were already calling up the dawn, which soon appeared. They went into a mosque to rest awhile, partaking of the food which they had brought with them. Then they repaired to the government offices, where Suleymân inquired for the mudîr. He was told that His Excellency was busy for the moment, being closeted with the English inspector. At that the girls trilled forth their joy-cries; all was glee. The degradation of the omdeh was assured.

The sentries and attendants, judging from their noise and numbers that the matter was important, sent in word to the mudîr, who soon received them.

"What means this concourse? What is your complaint?" His Excellency asked, in some dismay as they poured in.

"A terrible complaint, O lord of justice! The law is set at naught; oppression has come back upon the land; poor honest men are flogged to death, impaled and mutilated daily. In our village, in Mashrûtah . . ."

At mention of that name the mudîr exchanged portentous glances with the Englishman who sat beside him; while Suleymân went on to tell his story. No sooner had he finished, than another of the suppliants took up the parable in order, as had been arranged. But the mudîr commanded silence.

"What is thy name, O buck?" he asked of the first speaker.

"Suleymân Derwîsh, thy servant, O my lord."

Again the governor exchanged glances with the Englishman.

"What is thy calling?"

"I am a farmer."

"Thou liest, dog, thou art a brigand! We keep the record of such persons. Turn it up!"

A scribe, who sat beneath His Excellency, at that command produced a monstrous book, opened it at a certain place and laid it before the governor for his perusal.

"Here are some hundred charges to thy name. For three years thou hast been a scourge and nuisance to the countryside. Thou art yesterday but returned from prison, and to-day thou comest hither with complaints! What means all this?"

"It is some other, surely, O my lord. The name is common. I am not a malefactor. The omdeh beat me near to death without a cause."

Suleymân Derwîsh began his story once again with fear of death upon him from the great man's frown. The others as a chorus whined their preconcerted testimony, till soldiers came and laid hands upon some of them, when there were howls of fear and bitter wailing.

The omdeh of Mashrûtah sat that evening in the courtyard of his house watching the antics of his little grandson, who was playing with some discs of cow-dung, calmly expecting the conclusion of his dignified, respected life. He knew that his enemies had gone to the mudîr; and conscious as he was of disobedience to the code, conscious as he also was of rectitude, he never thought of moving to defend himself, but merely waited for the soldiers who should take him to the gaol. He felt no fear, indeed looked forward to his trial with a sort of eagerness, meaning to speak his mind upon the state of Egypt once for all in public upon that occasion. He was thinking of the very words to be employed when certain of the elders came in and told him: –

"Our enemies return. They seem dejected. Suleymân Derwîsh is not among them."

The mudîr neither moved nor spoke. He waited. Presently the sound of wailing grew apace, the courtyard was invaded by a crowd of men and girls, dusty and footsore, most of them with tear-stained faces. A girl – it was the sister of Suleymân Derwîsh – stood forth and said: –

"We have a grief against thee. Hitherto we had esteemed thee as a just man, if stern; but now we know thee for no better than an infidel. Thou wentest yesterday to the mudîr and he informed thee of a new device for getting rid of brave, unruly youths out of the villages. Thou camest home and thou didst cause Suleymân and his companions to be flogged. But thou didst not inform them of the reason of thy sudden confidence. Thou didst lie to them for their destruction, saying that the flogging was against the will of the mudîr; luring them on to make complaint to the authorities. They went to the mudîr, and as a consequence Suleymân Derwîsh, my brother, Mahrûs and Hamdi, sons of Musa Yûsuf, Mustafa the hunchback, and young Ali are banished and enslaved for life. Hast thou acted justly? Was not the flogging quite enough without the banishment?"

"By Allah, the right is with her," cried the elders of the village, while the common crowd gave forth an ugly snarl.

The omdeh knew he was in danger of his life. Once before – and only once – in all the years of his long pilgrimage on earth had he heard a village murmur as one man with rage, and then a family of twenty souls had been exterminated. Still he felt no fear, although the crowd was surging forward, and men were shouting: –

"Drag him out upon the dust-heaps!"

He drew his little grandson to his side and held him close for safety while he gazed hard at the sky between the palm-trunks, blue-green above the dark mud wall, and tried to realise exactly what had happened.

"Answer, O Sheykh," the people yelled at him. "Answer the charge or we will kill thee like a fly."

His family and the more zealous of the watchmen gathered round for his protection. Already they were struggling with the foremost of the crowd, while he reviewed the wonders of his life. He had seen with equanimity the spread of Frankish influence in the valley of the Nile. The train, the telegraph, the telephone – he had beheld them all without the least surprise. What had surprised him was the atheism of the Franks in the face of such discoveries, which made him all the more extol the Power of God. It was this atheism only that he hated in the works of Europe. When the English came he had perceived their good intentions, but shuddered at their errors, the result of atheism. They seemed to think it more important that the people of the country should resemble them in haste and greed of gain, should be governed in their manner and adopt their tricks for saving time than that they should lead the life of thinking and believing men. He had deplored but not resented all their interference with the villages. But now, as he surveyed their latest blunder, the life-long patience of his soul gave way, and from his heart he cursed them. He scarcely heard the clamour of the crowd, though men were shouting: "Kill him!" and a fierce fight was raging close at hand. His sole defenders were the people of his household and three watchmen. The elders of the village, his old cronies, were among the crowd. All at once his mind returned to earth. He stood up and demanded silence. There came a hush of curiosity. He cried: –

"I swear by Allah, before all here present, by the beard of the Prophet, by my life, by my salvation, that I knew nothing of the thing with which that girl has charged me till she spoke of it. I flogged those youths because I could no longer bear their insults to my old grey beard. I knew that in so doing I transgressed the law, but was content to bear the punishment of that transgression. I never dreamt that they would banish men for life without a trial – they who prate of justice and equality. Alas, that I should live to see such tyranny! I go to-morrow early to the mudîriyeh, and if the youths are not released on my petition, I shall at once resign the post of omdeh of this village."

"Our Lord reward thee and prolong thy life, O Sheykh!"

The crowd surged forward, friendly in a trice. The elders of the village stood once more beside their chief, trying to look as if they had not left him. One of them whispered in his ear: "It is enough, O dear one! Thou hast cleared thyself.

Pledge not thy soul too far, I do beseech thee. We do not want those devils back a second time, when Allah in His mercy has relieved us of them. Praise be to Him who made the English think of something sensible at last! Those malefactors ruined business in the district."

"You are pupils of the English!" said the omdeh grimly. "As for me, I am old-fashioned. Let me go my way."

BETWEEN OURSELVES

This story first appeared in the collection, As Others See Us, published in October 1922.

Most of the Egyptian stories are located in the rural Delta. When the British appear they are marginal and are perceived from the point of view of the Egyptian villager. This is unusual in that the Egyptians are seen from the point of view of the grand British official. It is also a first person tale, and it could be Pickthall is recalling and quoting the long narrative of Sir Charles Duclay, who bears a resemblance to Sir Ronald Storrs (1881-1955) in his elegance, his sympathies for individual Egyptians, and the implied affection for and familiarity with the country.

Pickthall draws a picture of the disillusioned Egyptian who has been a supporter of the British occupation but, after snubs and indifference from the British, is driven into political opposition. Indeed, in anticipation of twenty-first century politics, it shows how a Muslim is radicalised to contemplate acts of terrorism. In many ways it tells a tale similar to the first in this collection, Karàkter.

There are many Pickthallian touches. He describes the dress of people and it is significant when Abbâs, the central Egyptan character sports a bowler hat rather than a fez, or dons a "formidable pair of gold-rimmed spectacles". There is also a deeply ironic line, the last words of Duclay's narrative when he says Abbâs from his prison cell suggested he become a Muslim – "It made me wince as if I had been stung." Pickthall had openly declared his conversion to Islam five years before the publication of this story.

The P. & O. steamship *Marmora* was half-way on her voyage from Port Said to Naples. I lay in a deck-chair in the shade with a book upon my knees, between Tom Harris, a young cub in the Irrigation Department, and Sir Charles

Duclay. K.C.M.G., one of the rulers of Egypt and a famous Orientalist; each of whom likewise lay in a deck-chair and had a book upon his knees. We were all three tired of reading, yet found nothing in particular to say to one another at the moment. Beyond the awning under which our chairs were stretched there was nothing to be seen but burning sky and tumbled sea – a sea which seemed opaque in its commotion and very nearly black as I surveyed it out of half-closed eyes, beneath the brim of a straw hat tipped forward till it touched my nose. Not far from us two groups of men and girls were playing at deck quoits. Behind us somewhere, a seemingly exciting match at bull-board was in progress. Coming from Egypt, we were out of all the fun; the Anglo-Indians quietly ignoring us, looking right through us when we moved within their range of vision, and generally seeming to regard us as some kind of "natives". We lay and read and sauntered up and down and talked, with thought of the next meal as of a coming great event.

We were lying side by side in silence, blinking at the restless sea, when an Anglo-Indian lady, neither young nor lovely, came along the deck. She seized upon an empty chair not far from us and began to fold it, evidently wishing to transport it to some other place. Duclay, as swift and graceful in his movements as a panther, was beside her in a trice. He was carrying the chair in the direction pointed out to him, she seeming much embarrassed and, I thought, annoyed at his politeness, when an elderly man in khaki supervened and took it from him, with a curt: "Thank ye. Much obliged. . . . Where do you want it put, my dear?"

"Over there by Mrs Mallinson, if you will be so good, dear."

The couple took no further notice of Duclay, who instantly rejoined us, chuckling.

"That was pretty cool, I must say," murmured Harris drowsily.

"They thought I wished to scrape acquaintance with them," explained Duclay. "They're old inhabitants, and we're new-comers. It's the same wherever there are English people."

He was silent for a minute, then remarked abruptly: –

"We are a lot of priceless hypocrites, we English! –"

"Speak for yourself," growled Harris, half asleep.

"We ourselves are so accustomed to swallowing the grain of salt which makes belief in our perfection possible that we forget to warn the peoples before whom we pose of the need for that facilitating condiment. The mind of Orientals – of Egyptians, anyhow – is as literal as A B C – intensely and enthusiastically literal. Our mind, on the other hand, is hyperbolical, doggedly and duly so, so much so that we go through life without an inkling of it. Imagine a man gassing about generosity, the abstract virtue, to another man who thinks he means to give him money in a minute! It was all right while we simply took and held by force. That was a simple proposition understanded of the Oriental. But when we got on to the magnanimous lay: 'conquest for the benfit of the conquered,' 'government for the benefit of the governed,' and began this preaching and protesting business, our literal-minded friend began to worry. His bright and singularly knowing eye was on us. He was perplexed and in the end enraged by our hypocrisy; more particularly since we joined with Russia[145] – a move which gave the show away completely. I can tell you the story of a man I know – a native – who was sentenced the other day to ten years' penal servitude, which illustrates exactly what I mean. If it won't bore you?"

"It will," snapped Harris, who had turned his back to us. "Don't talk of Egypt. I want to wipe out the whole beastly country for the next three months. Oh, for a good Scotch mist and heather under me!"

But Duclay had addressed himself to me, and I was glad to listen. He turned half over towards me in his chair, was restless for a moment while he sought a comfortable pose, and then began.

Two years ago I spent the whole of April at the Mena House, recovering from an attack of sunstroke, the result of my own carelessness when up at Halfa on a visit. My wife had gone to England to her mother, who was ill, leaving me practically homeless for the time. I was fit for nothing, and forbidden by the doctor to do more than sit about and blink at life; which made me irritable. The everlasting sunlight was a nightmare. I hated that damned sand and those confounded pyramids as something that was driving me insane. If it had not been for an American woman, unattached and skittish, who happened to be staying in the hotel, I should probably have died of simple boredom. She chose to play the ministering angel, and did her best to keep my pulses going. I was sitting out with her one afternoon in the veranda when one of the sufragis[146] came and handed me a visiting car. It was that of a native professor in the School of Law – a very intelligent man whom I had known for years. Above his name was scrawled in English: 'To introduce Abbâs Lutfi Suleymân, my pupil and your very great admirer.' It was not the first time he had sent promising young men for my inspection, knowing as he did my curiosity about young Egypt.

"Excusing myself to Madame, I dragged myself along the veranda, meaning to have the interview indoors, but I had not got half-way before the same sufragi

[145] An allusion to Anglo-Russian of 1907.

[146] Waiter or barman at a hotel or restaurant.

met me, followed by about the finest specimen of Eastern manhood that it has ever been my luck to meet. Even a Frangi[147] suit of cheap material, a high collar, a garish tie and a pair of yellow boots too large for him, could not disguise his fine proportions and his grace of movement. Though his colouring was rather dark for an Egyptian, there was no reminder of the negro in his face. His lips were not too full, his nose was aquiline, his eyes were large and really beautiful. He seemed to me the pure Arabian type, entirely nervous in the same way that your thoroughbred Arab horse is nervous. The finest of those horses always strike me as alight. Well this man seemed alight as he ran forward and tried to kiss my hand.

"'I am so happy, sir,' he said in tolerable English. 'This is the brightest day in all my life. At last I am permitted to be near to one of those noble and good men who have brought civilisation and all blessings to our poor dear Egypt. I am but a young student, sir, but I do love the English more than I can tell. I think, sir, I would gladly die for them.'

"He said this with a beatific smile as, having put a stop to the hand-kissing business, I made him take a chair beside me at a little table; tapping on which I ordered coffee to be brought at once. You know what a fool one feels when slapped in the face with compliments of that description. Many men I know get downright rude on such occasions, thinking it all humbug, which it seldom is. Any one can tell the ring of a false compliment. We fail to make allowance for the capacity of young people of these sunstruck races for enthusiasm over anything and anybody. It always seemed to me a cruel shame for us to snub and terrify our wild admirers. Still I feel as foolish as another under admiration, and that man's admiration was a scorching fire.

"I laughed and said that we had tried to do a little for the good of Egypt, not at all for the *beaux yeux* of the Egyptians, but because it suited our ambition and convenience.

"'Ah, don't say that, sir!' he cried out ecstatically, with tears of real enthusiasm in his eyes. 'I know well the generous work which you have done here. In my childhood I did learn it at the school from books, and since then I have seen it with my eyes – the noble work. You make everybody be polite to everybody. You say, there shall be no more rudeness, no more beating, no more fighting and low insults; if anybody rude he shall be punished. Civilisation. So we all become as brothers; so we go ahead. Many people do not understand your gracious goodness. I teach them that the English are their noble friends. It is in my thinking' – here he touched his forehead – 'to write one mighty book in

[147] Frankish, European.

praise of all the English, that those fools may learn how devilish silly they have been.'

"I objected that our praises could not fill a book, that criticism of our conduct would be more acceptable. He did not seem to hear my interruption, but went on exclaiming: –

"'They shall see and know! I will instruct them. It is in my thinking to devote my life to this great service for my country: to extol the English!'

"From his coming to me with an introduction I at first supposed that, like every other student, he was after government employment. I presently remarked as much; informing him that the only way of gaining such employment was the high-road of competitive examination. With another beatific smile, he answered: –

"'I have no desire for an employment. All I wish is to write the beautiful sweet thoughts which come into my mind about the English, our too noble benefactors. I will write them and make everybody glad, and so grow famous.'

"I was in the presence of a genuine enthusiasm – one might call it mania, for I suppose a clever doctor could have cured him of it. As a child at school he had learnt by heart those text-books, inspired by adulation of the conqueror, which glorify our work for Egypt, conveying the idea that we are angels sent from Heaven to benefit the world in general and the Nile valley in particular. Regarding education as a magic thing, and everything he saw in print as gospel truth at that age, he accepted that ideal view of us without the grain of salt desirable, and preached it to his parents and the other villagers who, not having had the benefit of modern schooling, hung for instruction on his infant lips. What strikes me as most wonderful – indeed miraculous – is that, as he grew up, his enthusiasm did not weaken. It was doubtless owing to the circumstance that he had not personally had to do with any Englishman until the day he came to me, except Vardon of the School of Law – a weak-eyed and benignant creature. Thus he had reached the age of two and twenty, in a country overridden by the English, without a doubt of our angelic character!

"I asked if he was going to practise law. He answered, No. His one idea was to present his radiant vision of the English and their way of progress intelligibly to his fellow-countrymen. He was writing for *El Balad*, a new journal founded by a friend of his, and hoped that I would condescend to read his articles.

"We had got to this point of the conversation when the American widow – I say 'widow', but believe she had a husband somewhere – came up and rather coolly took a chair between us. My visitor sprang up and executed wondrous bows. 'An English lady?' he inquired with his ecstatic smile, as if the joy of presentation to an English lady would instantly have cut the thread which bound him to this earth.

"'No; American,' I answered rather curtly, for I was irritated by the way she smiled upon my dark Antinous[148], already dazzled by her blond effulgence. I dismissed him quickly, much to her disgust. She declared him afterwards to be the 'sweetest thing' that she had ever seen.

"Next day he came again, bringing samples of his journalistic work for my inspection. As it happened, I was in my bedroom, so kept him waiting. When I went out at last to the veranda I found my fair friend sitting with him at a table, head to head over a newspaper spread out between them, her auburn chevelure in contact with his fez.

"'I'm having my first lesson,' she called out to me as I approached. 'You never mean to say that you can read this script quite easily? Mr Abbâs is teaching me the letters. It's too fascinating. I guess I'll have real lessons when I come back here next winter.'

"She then got up and left us, Mr Abbâs protesting that there was no need for her departure, which I, however, expedited with a frown.

"The articles he showed me had a certain eloquence, but did not touch this earth at any point that I could see. In one of them my name was mentioned with encomiums. He watched me while I read it, all on tenterhooks for my approval. I did my best to look extremely gratified, rose, bowed to him and murmured of unworthiness. He literally crowed for joy, and swore, I recollect, by Allah to write articles, a many, about nothing but my goodness. I had to speak to him severely to preserve my name.

"After that he came out by train two or three times a week to spend an hour at my instructive feet. If I encouraged his visits it was in order gently to deflate his too embarrassing illusion with regard to us. I took the American woman into my confidence about him, and found her sympathetic at the time. Though I now know she was playing her own game. As I recovered and was able to get about, I found myself let in for various excursions, with Abbâs for guide; and in a few days saw more of Cairo and its neighbourhood than I had seen in all the years which I had spent in Egypt. At last I went into harness, the fair American retired to Switzerland, and Abbâs vanished from my ken until the following winter.

"Then – it was in December; my wife was back; we had taken a new house on the Gezireh, and I was basking in the atmosphere of domesticity – he came to me one afternoon in great distress. The newspaper – *El Balad* – for which he had been writing, a pro-British organ, had been suppressed for no good

[148] A Greek youth, the lover of the Emperor Hadrian.

reason. Would I bring the matter to the notice of the British Agency, and use my influence to put things right? I made inquiries, and was told that the newspaper in question had uttered an atrocious libel on a high official of the Khedive's entourage. I handed on this information to Abbâs when next he came to see me, and presented him with the report of the case, consisting of fifty typewritten pages of dog French, which had been furnished by the Egyptian authorities on my demand. I have a lively recollection of the scene. It was late afternoon, and we were sitting in my garden by the Nile, where there was shade. Through the yellow blaze above the river we could see the masts and tumbled buildings of Bûlâc, and hear the hammering from the boat-builders' yards. The gardener was busy with a hose deluging each individual plant and blade of grass. My wife was up in the veranda at a table, reading.

"Abbâs, who, as I said before, was uncommonly good-looking, had that day chosen to disfigure himself by putting on a formidable pair of gold-rimmed spectacles – of which he seemed absurdly proud – though he was not short-sighted. It is queer how Orientals, when they imitate us, invariably pitch on something which we think unlovely. A man I know – young Farrow – had an accident which obliged him for some time to wear a kind of iron apparatus like a cage on his right leg. The notables of his district were always asking him how much it cost, and where they could buy one like it. Because some learned men have spoilt their eyes with reading and so take to glasses, glasses have been adopted as the symbol of a serious mind. I noticed that Abbâs removed them when he wished to read.

"'But,' he exclaimed, after studying the papers I had given him, 'they speak untrue. It was no libel which we made. The case was so, as we declared to be. The gentleman of whom we wrote had persecuted righteous people, and stolen money from them with great wickedness. He leads, moreover, a most filthy, vicious life in private.'

"'A libel need not be a lie,' I told him. 'It is an attempt to injure some one's reputation by malicious statements."

"'But, sir,' he wailed, 'by God, I beg you, look! All which we wrote was only to seek justice for men wronged most beastly, to call the attention of the English to a case of very horrid wickedness. It was for that they did destroy our journal. Will you not protect us from injustice? We love the English very much indeed.'

"He had resumed the gold-rimmed spectacles, which hid the childish candour of his eyes and made him an unlovely object. I grew impatient and spoke testily, telling him that, so far as I could see, the matter had been properly investigated; and that it was not our English custom to interfere high-handedly with the course of law, nor to support our partisans through right and wrong. I then laid my hand upon his shoulder and suggested we should go and have some tea. I was afraid that he was going to cry, he seemed so crestfallen. However, by dint of talk on general subjects, and flattering up a bit, we managed to restore his spirits. My wife gave him a rose when he said good-bye. I escorted him a few steps, and he went away as happy as a king.

"Two days later, in the afternoon, he called at the house, but went away again on being told that we had visitors. He left word with the doorkeeper that he had serious news for me, and would seek the favour of an audience on the following morning. In fact, next morning, when I got down to my office, he was in the ante-room among the usual crowd of suitors; and hardly had I sat down at my desk and begun to glance over the pile of correspondence there awaiting me, when my secretary came to tell me that a young effendi was clamouring to see me instantly; which young effendi, so the watchman told him, had been hanging round the place since early dawn. To have done with him, I ordered him to be admitted. He seemed terribly excited, and at the sound of his own voice saluting me, burst into tears. He cried: –

"'It is a libel, sir, and not one word is true. What shall be done to those who work such beastliness?' With that he handed me a sheet of notepaper covered with his careful English writing.

"'That,' he said, 'is the most true translation of what those devils write against me in that wicked journal.'

"I kept the document as a rare jewel of Egyptian journalism, and generally carry about with me in a pocket-book. I may have it on me at this minute. Let me look."

"You made too much fuss of the fellow," growled Harris drowsily. "It doesn't do to let 'em hang around. They get swelled head. I should have choked him off at first, and saved a lot of trouble."

"It would have been more merciful," said Duclay gravely.

"Ah, here's the document I was looking for.

"'From the Arabic journal (*Nîl.*[149])

"'THE MALODOROUS EVIL-LIVER.

"'There is a youth well known to all of us, the son of a dog, a pimp and lickspittle, who gives himself grand airs towards his fellow-countrymen while gluttonously devouring all the dirt of all the English. Anyone would think when they do hear him talk that he was the son of noble and illustrious people. That

[149] The journal has the Arabic name for the river Nile.

is not the case, by God alive. His father was a dog who fed on carrion, his grandfather and his ancestors were pigs most perfectly defiled and damned with very wonderful complete damnation. All of us know his mother. His sisters are much loved by us, but not respected. Therefore we have little veneration for this child of shame and product of disgusting sins. Therefore we urge and importune all honest people to beware of him because his contact and his conversation bring defilement. He is well known to the police as thief, spy, evil-liver and suspected atheist. We ourselves beheld him lately seated with a pompous air among the infidels – himself the worst – on the terrace of Shepheard's Hotel in the company of an English lady, one of those who are renowned for the impartial distribution of their favours in return for gold. Whence does he derive his wealth? Nobody knows, but it is very certain that his wealth is gained by some obscene, nefarious traffic. We have written to the English woman he frequents, warning her to guard her jewellery when that low thief is near. Do you inquire his name after this full description? His name is Abbâs Lutfi Suleymân. We hereby call upon all true believers and Egyptian patriots, and adjure and entreat them, to spit in his face whenever they encounter him, and also to chastise him with a perfect beating; and hereby furthermore declare that we ourselves will bear the legal cost, if any, of such righteous action.'"

"Abbâs was sobbing and exclaiming in my office all the while I was deciphering this gem of literature. When I had finished, he cried out: 'Oh, sir! What shall I do to come to justice? Is this not a libel greater far than that for which they have suppressed our journal? If they did suppress our honourable journal on account of publication of the hidden truth, will they not suppress this filthy one for publication of so many open falsehoods detrimental and disastrous to my reputation?'

"He went on to point out that the libel was not directed only at himself (Abbâs) but also at 'that gracious lady, the companion of Your Honour in your time of illness', who had shown the wonderful and splendid kindness to allow him to approach her. An English lady! – (It was of no use my insisting that she was American) – a sweet, amiable lady! – a gentle, civilised, delightful lady! – to be so insulted! It made him shudder for his country. It was execrable! He asked me to take vengeance upon her traducers and expel them from the land.

"I had heard that the American widow had returned and was at Shepheard's, but had not seen her. My wife had called, but did not seem much pleased with the acquaintance, and I had cause to feel offended with the woman. She had written a book – But more of that anon. It seemed that she was playing the same sentimental game with poor Abbâs which she had played with me. I washed my hands of her; and felt not at all concerned for her share in the libel, though I was extremely sorry for her victim upon all accounts. I had read as bad things often in Egyptian newspapers, had come indeed to view them as mere commonplaces of the vernacular press; but I had never before encountered one of the victims. The spectacle was really harrowing. I told him that he had his remedy at law, advised him to consult a lawyer and then closed the interview.

"From that day onward for about a month he was my bugbear, haunting my house and office, dogging me in the street. He was having a rough time of it, and looked on me as his protector. You know the ragging spirit which takes hold of the Egyptian at the sight of any one bewildered, especially a simple soul revolted and demanding justice; how they send him from pillar to post, hustle and bedevil him. Well, poor Abbâs made such a cry about his wrongs, betrayed so candidly his fool's belief in abstract justice, that the Arabic press received him as a godsend, and the various legal lights whom he consulted held their sides. When he made his application to the *Parquet*[150] he was assured with seeming gravity that the libels of which he complained – they were now legion – were not aimed at so respectable a man, but at another and ignoble person of the same name. He paraded his despair through all the cafés of the town, meeting everywhere with a delusive sympathy, which urged him on to fresh exertions for the town's amusement. His one relief was in the society of the American, who made him welcome, being glad, I fancy, to get the services of a good dragoman for nothing. With her he for a time forgot his anger and perplexity, and felt himself a highly favoured individual. One afternoon, when I was down at Shepheard's calling upon some one else, I saw him with her at a table on the terrace. Old Jones was there. He came across to me and growled:–

"'That woman ought to be shot. Ought to be kicked out of the country! Never would have been allowed in Cromer's time! In front of everybody! It degrades us all!'

"I was too vexed, but my annoyance was for the Egyptian, whom I judged more likely to get harm from her than she from him. I had sized her up pretty completely since our tender parting at the Mena House. She had published a book in which I figured as the lovesick hero – a book full of our conversations, which she must have noted at the time. She was what she called 'studying Egypt'. Having dealt with the English official side through me, she was working at the young Egyptian through Abbâs Effendi, inducing him to take her to all sorts of dreadful haunts he would never have gone to by himself, and making love to him

[150] Term used in occupied Egypt for all public prosecutors.

in her desire for Oriental 'atmosphere'. A dozen such as her come out to Egypt every winter; women who make fools of men for copy; modern vampires; may the devil fly away with the whole breed of them!

"I tried to give Abbâs a hint of her true character; but he, poor fellow, was beyond the reach of hints. At mention of her name he grew delirious. It was more on her account than on his own that he demanded justice on the authors of the libels; for all his outings with her were reported in the native press, and special correspondents watched the steps of Shepheard's day and night.

"I did my best for him in high official quarters – gave him a note of introduction to old Puffing Billy; the case being more akin to his department than it was to mine. I had a line the self-same day from Puffer. Telling me that my protégé was mad. Abbâs had mentioned that he 'loved' him (Puffer). I was begged to keep the ruffian to myself in future.

"'I fear, sir, that His Excellency was intoxicated,' was Abbâs's version of the interview. 'He talked to me exceeding strange, exceeding different from a noble English gentleman.'

"He had, in fact, advised my injured friend to go to hell and afterwards to punch the heads of his insulters severally – a proceeding which, as Abbâs very justly pointed out, was quite uncivilised and quite against the law which Puffer and the rest of us were there to see enforced. I told him that old Puffer was the best of men, but irritable, and having very great affairs to manage for the public good, might reasonably feel aggrieved at being bothered by an individual. But my pacific explanations were becoming threadbare.

"One evening our friend came out to my house in desperation. My wife, who caught a glimpse of him, was quite alarmed. He had, it seemed, approached a high official of the Khedive's household, to whom he had been introduced by one of his admirers – for it had transpired from all this pother of his persecution that he had a following – a score or so of real disciples who admired him blindly. The said high official, instead of giving him a serious hearing, had laughed aloud, advising him to go and make it up with all his libellers. Worse still, he had indulged in rude remarks about the English.

"'Surely,' Abbâs pleaded, 'you will now take my part against these wicked fellows who wish to weaken your authority in Egypt.'

"Then at last I saw that it was necessary to expound to him the real nature of the British Occupation and its history; how we were there for our own ends, and not the good of Egypt, in the first place; how in Cromer's time much good had been achieved, chiefly because the Khedivial Court had been kept under and no British official thought of playing to the gallery; but how at length, when all was going well, the authorities at home, scared by the outcry over the Denshawaî executions[151], had handed back official patronage to the Khedive as the easiest way of quieting the situation; since when, though we had ostensibly reversed our policy at the command of Mr Roosevelt[152], we had continued playing to the gallery both in Egypt and in England; whence these tears! The real power in purely native matters, such as complaint of libel, was now with the Khedivial Court.

"'But do the noble English nation bear such things?" cried out Abbâs in horror.

"The English as a race, I said, knew nothing of them.

"'Then I will go to England, I will teach them,' he exclaimed, jumping up like one demented. 'They shall no longer be maintained in ignorance by the wicked and malevolent Foreign Office.'

"He seemed resolved to start that very minute.

"'But the journey will cost money.' I objected, 'and life in England is as dear as here in Egypt.'

"'No matter, I will get the money,' he cried out in Arabic. 'Upon so holy and humane an errand, what can stop me? The English shall no longer be deceived. I will instruct them!'

"I let him rave, fully expecting that his resolution would go off in words. In point of fact he started that same week, without seeing me again. I got a letter from him some days later from Marseilles, in which he praised my candour and my magnanimity in letting him into the secret of events which had long puzzled him. He was going, he declared, to make the English understand, and so save Egypt from complete destruction. The money for his journey was subscribed by his disciples, but the American woman also gave him fifty pounds, as he himself informed me afterwards, in order to get rid of him, as I suppose, for she was talked of in connection with a Russian prince who had turned up at Shepheard's.

"Well, I forgot him until we were at home last summer, when he called on us at a hotel in London. His brown complexion had then lost its clearness and the kind of healthy glow I had admired in Egypt. It looked muddy. He still wore gold-rimmed spectacles and was as talkative as ever, but he struck me as discrowned, degraded. It was the first time I had seen his face without a fez.

---

[151] In 1906, a dispute between British soldiers and the people of a village in the Delta led to the death of one British officer. The British authorities responded by a trial and execution of some of villagers. Pickthall actually defended the action of the occupation.

[152] Theodore Roosevelt, former President of the United States, in 1910 visited Cairo and spoke favourably of the British occupation.

"I took him out to lunch and let him talk. He showed me cuttings from a number of strange periodicals which I had never heard of, containing articles which he had written since he came to England, and repeatedly assured me he had not been idle. 'Very good and noble people' had received him; he had lectured on the state of Egypt before various crank societies, and was in a fair way to become renowned as an authority. He had grown conceited, I observed incidentally, and very domineering in his tone. In conjunction with his down-at-heels appearance it was quite pathetic. He gave me his card, on which was printed: 'Representative of the Egyptian nation', together with an address at Bayswater; whither I went one afternoon to see him.

"It was one of those streets of fairly decent-looking houses which have fallen almost into slums. A barrel-organ was in full blast when I turned into it, and swarms of noisy children were at play. Arrived at the house, I was shown by an impudent-looking, rather pretty girl with dirty hands, up to a room upon the second floor, which evidently served Young Egypt's representative as bedroom, smoking-room and hall of audience, and had not been swept, I should opine, for several days. The girl went in without knocking, and I heard her cheeky tone towards Abbâs. She addressed him, I remember, by the name of 'Monkey-fice'.

"He had been sprawling on a squalid bed, but sprang up as I entered, and made me welcome, quite without embarrassment. He apologised for his surroundings, which, he said, were temporary. He was moving to more suitable apartments in a week or two. 'Congratulate me!' he exclaimed. 'I am invited by a lord to dine with all the high nobility and to instruct them.' No end of newspapers were scattered on the floor. He picked up one of these, exclaiming: 'I see that that most admirable lady has arrived in London, at the Piccadilly Hotel. I think to visit her this afternoon. Will you come too? She loves you very much. It will be like the old days.'

"I should have scouted the suggestion pretty certainly but for his mention of the old days, which conjured up the vision of his natural surroundings. He had come from blazing sunshine and clear air to that vile hole. Poor wretch! I went with him to call upon the vampire lady.

"The visit was a failure, as far as any hopes Abbâs may have had of it were concerned. The lady smiled on me, but positively scowled at him; asked me in an aside where his good looks had gone to, and told me for the love of all things reputable to make him burn his bowler hat and wear a fez. She had lost all interest in Egypt, it appeared, discoursing much of Russia and the Russians – her new field of 'study'. Just as we were going Abbâs murmured something, and she went apart with him. I don't know what they said, but she looked quite uncompromising, and Abbâs emerged in tears from the short interview.

"'The English are not altogether as I thought,' he told me. 'They are, I think, too cold and cruel and too selfish ever to be sympathetic to the generous Egyptian people.'

"That was his first confession of a disappointment. I guessed he was in straits for money, and had hoped for something from the generosity of the American. When I asked him, in the street, if he had any pressing need, he burst out sobbing and confessed that he owed more than twenty pounds to his landlady. But that was not what made him so unhappy. His landlady's daughter, the saucy girl who I had seen, had loved him at the first, but now despised him. Poor fellow, he was amorous and trusting – defenceless as a kitten against English avarice. The lodging-house damsel had taken him for a prince at first. Well, I got him away from the Bayswater slum into a more cheerful bedroom down at Chiswick, at the same time doing my best to persuade him to give up the conversion of the English and return to Egypt.

"He replied that he had written much too freely of the powers that were in Egypt to find any comfort in the prospect of returning thither. He hung great hopes on the dinner at Lord Vereling's house, to be followed by a sort of drawing-room meeting at which he was to speak. I've known Vereling well for years – we were at school together – a well-meaning crank who always picks up the lost dogs of politics – and drops them. I was not at the dinner, but I heard about it afterwards from Vereling and some others who were present.

"Abbâs, as I have told you, called himself the representative of the Egyptian nation. Now, as it has happened in most summers of late years, there were three or four such self-styled representatives in England, each of them claiming to speak from the great heart of Egypt, and anxious to indoctrinate our politicians with his private views. All of them by misfortune were at Vereling's dinner or the meeting afterwards; and as the others were superior to poor Abbâs in age, rank, wealth, and everything you could mention, they all made common cause against him as a bumptious puppy, when they heard him laying down the law about the state of Egypt. One after another they took Vereling aside and very gravely warned him that the young man was a rank impostor of no influence whatever; one who would not be received in any good Egyptian house, proclaimed him *homme néfaste!* and *canaille premier ordre!* And bade the noble host keep watch upon his silver. Vereling, with his nervous dread of being taken in, took fright and washed his hands of poor Abbâs. Then one of those other representatives replied to a letter which Abbâs had written in a daily paper, flatly contradicting every statement of the hapless author, whom he declared to be 'not in the position to know anything whatever of affairs in Egypt.'

"Abbâs had sent to every Englishman who seemed inclined to help him copies of the various libels which had appeared against him in the Cairo press. His enemies got hold of some of these and published extracts from them, when replying to Abbâs's article, to show the kind of character he bore at home. On a frantic appeal from Abbâs I wrote a letter to the same newspaper, in his favour. But it came too late. By that time he was catching it all round from people who had once been kind to him. He was scouted as a rogue and an impostor.

"'Can I not get justice even here in England?' he asked me when he poured his troubles in my ear. 'Is not what these devils say about me shameless libel? You say that to get justice costs much money? I – I have no money. What then must I do? The English are then wicked. It was false all which they taught me in the school. They have no love of justice. They care nothing for the good of Egypt.'

"I did my best to calm him, but without success. He sat quaking like a person in an ague fit, and moaning: 'I cannot get justice – I cannot get justice,' till my nerves were all on edge.

"'My mind is quite distraught,' he gasped at length. 'I wish to vomit. I greatly fear that I shall hate the English, who are one hand with the bad people of my country. I fear that I shall be compelled by my conscience to join the violent section of my young compatriots.'

"I told him not to lose his head and be a fool; told him that we had all been young and too enthusiastic; had all been through our period of disillusionment. To all that I could urge he only shook his head.

"Inquiring at his lodging two days later, I heard that he had left without a word, and having to some extent stood surety for him, I paid his bill.

"I saw him once again before I went to Egypt, quite by chance. I was staying for a night in Paris, and I happened on him in the street. He was walking with two other young Egyptians. As I was quite alone and rather dull, I asked them to come back with me to my hotel, where I ensconced them in a quiet corner of the lounge, with cigarettes and plenty of black coffee. Abbâs then thought it necessary to inform me, in a set speech, that he was thenceforth a relentless enemy of British rule in Egypt. The Balkan raid on Turkey was beginning, and already there were Christian war-cries in the London press[153]. He said that it was clear to him that the English, as a race, were foes of El Islâm. His two companions murmured their applause at intervals, showing their teeth and the whites of their

[153] This refers to the Balkan wars of 1912-13. It was this trend that led Pickthall to be strongly pro-Ottoman in the First World War, and to declare his conversion to Islam in 1917.

eyes. The English had beguiled the Children of the Nile with talk of justice and civilisation into a bondage far more dreadful than the mere subjection to a foreign yoke, secretly undermining their religion and their nationality. We were great and powerful, but God was greater, he informed me. He and his friends were the servants of God, pledged to frustrate our evil purpose and destroy us. The two others, his companions, chimed in eagerly with stories of the treatment they had met from certain Englishmen.

"Not to be outdone, I also told them stories of the way I too had suffered from my own compatriots, admitting that we were a stiff-necked, uncouth crowd. They laughed at my remarks and got quite friendly. In the end they were polite enough to say that, if only all the Englishmen in Egypt had been just like me in all respects, there would have been no need for any Nationalist movement; every one would have been happy as in Paradise. I watched Abbâs, who looked much better than in London, but had become extremely grave and taciturn. I really was intensely sorry for the fellow, and could not get away from an unpleasant feeling that his misfortunes were my fault to some extent.

"Two months ago I went to visit him in prison, where he lay awaiting trial. He and one of the young men whom I had seen with him in Paris had returned to Egypt as the agents of that great conspiracy, whose aim – as the police reports asserted – was to blow up simultaneously the Cubbeh Palace, Casr ed Dubbâreh[154] and the Savoy Hotel. Abbâs did not at first seem pleased to see me.

"'You deceived us,' he said gloomily in Arabic – 'like all the others, you deceived us! You did not mean the half you said, and yet you spoke so earnestly – like all the English! The curse of God upon them – liars! hypocrites! All your civilisation, all your comforts and mechanical contrivances are false as are your words! God knows that there is nothing steadfast in this world but suffering. Your purpose is to wipe out all the Muslimîn. But you are of this world; while we are God's, and unto Him we shall return.'

"I tried to say some cheering words to him, and he responded with a sudden burst of tears. He fell upon his knees and then began appealing to me in heart-broken tones. At first I was too much astonished at the outburst to hear distinctly what he said; he spoke in such low tones. I imagined he was asking me to intercede for him. He seized my hand and kissed it, seeming very eager. Then I found that he was urging me to take some step for my own safety, was warning me apparently of some great danger. What was it? I bent down my head to listen.

---

[154] Two palaces belonging to the khedival, ruling, family.

Then I realised that he was adjuring me, for my soul's sake, to leave the English and become a Muslim and an Oriental. It made me wince as if I had been stung."

For some time we were silent, staring at the sea. Harris, whom we had imagined to be fast asleep by that time, cried indignantly: –

"I don't like your story – not a little bit! I wonder Duclay has the face to tell it in that cool, complacent way. None of the bigwigs strike me as quite honest nowadays. They hobnob with the natives and don't care what becomes of 'em. They only want to make a good show for themselves, are ready to enter into any dirty compromise to make things last their time; and after that the deluge. What we want is straight men."

Duclay seemed astonished by this outburst. Under his breath I heard him murmur: "Balaam's ass[155]!" "I'm glad you see the point," he answered blandly. "But will you tell me how I personally – ?"

"Oh, you're hand in glove with all the others," answered Harris vehemently; "you let things go on. A chap in my position can't do anything to stop them; but you could. What are you doing, I should like to know? Studying the torture of a wretched Arab – like your vampire woman! Why couldn't you have kept the fellow at a distance or, if you liked him, taken up his case? The Anglo-Indians you were sneering at just now are quite all right. They may be stiff and rude, but they are honest. They don't profess affection for the East. You, Duclay, with your knowledge and your understanding, could not be in Government service now if you were honest."

"The sense of your remarks is not quite clear, my too excitable young friend," said Duclay smoothly vicious. "But in so far as I can grasp it they seem quite uncalled-for." He was going on to murmur something very cutting when a sudden clangour near at hand made speech impossible. At once his frown relaxed. He stretched himself and yawned luxuriously. The same good-temper came on Harris and myself. It was the luncheon-bell.

[155] A Biblical allusion to Numbers 22: 22-36. It means that an otherwise insignificant and overlooked person comes out with a remark worthy of attention.

TURKEY

AN ORDEAL BY FIRE

This story first appeared in the collection, Pot au Feu, published in February 1911. It is the first of his tales located in Turkey.

It is not easy to locate Deramûn, the town where most of the action takes place. It is important enough to have a British Consul, and has a mixed community of Turks, Greeks, Kurds and Armenians – and at least one Indian. It was by the sea and could have been a port on the Marmara Sea or north or south of Izmir on the Aegean coast.

The story was published in 1911, four years before the Armenian massacres. But there had for a generation been a build-up of tension targeting the Armenians, with an outburst of massacres near Muş in the 1890s and in Adana in 1909. During the First World War Pickthall's championship of the Turks led him, in his journalism, to be critical of Armenian claims and even either qualify or to justify the measures taken against them. This story shows how his imaginative creativity and humanity offset any vicarious chauvinism. He is describing atrocities committed against unarmed Armenians without any special pleading.

None of the Armenians, with the possible exception of one girl who can speak English, has any developed personality. And Nora, the British wife, is – unusually for Pickthall's female characters – devoid of much personality.

His portrayal of the British couple, James and Nora, could be from his British short stories. Just as he was conscientious in getting the dialogue right with his Arabs and Turks, so he is similarly painstaking with the language of the bigoted James (who, in spite of himself, plays a heroic role) and of the Consul, Davis.

For various reasons, it is one of the most interesting of Pickthall's stories.

Standing with face very close to a high wall of glass, with hands clasped at his back, James Pope stared wrathfully out upon the charming prospect of blossomed heads of fruit-trees, white and pink, seeming afloat like summer-cloud low down in the vast sun-filled hollow of sea and sky. Behind him, in a shady hall so big that full-sized carpets looked like rugs upon the floor, his wife sat at a table, letter-writing, with every appearance of perfect calm. Never turning, he declaimed:

"A miserable race, I tell you, Nora! One Kurd is worth the blessed lot of them. They're either cringing or offensively familiar – damnable! Of course you take your notions from your father and his silly friends, mere theorising Radicals. They don't know these people; I do; and I tell you I could massacre them myself."

Nora laughed at him with a suggestion of impatience. For nearly two hours she had been constraining herself only to laugh at his ill-temper, while he had seemed to take a deliberate pleasure in giving her cause for anger.

"Please say no more," she told him, closing down an envelope. "The Armenians may be all you say; it is still no excuse for butchering them. You got out of bed the wrong side; nothing I say or do is right this morning. I shall ride up to Deramûn, and lunch with Mrs Ellis. It seems a sin to waste this lovely day. Hasan will do for escort. The steamer must be in by now, there'll be letters to occupy you. If you go into the town, post this for me."

By the time he turned round, meaning to visit her with fresh reproaches, she was gone. Well, since she could find it in her heart to go off like that, coolly, in mid-quarrel, before they had arrived at an understanding, he was not going to hang about and say good-bye to her. In petulant haste he snatched up her letter, found his hat and stick, and, going out, took a path which ran cascading down the terraces, under flowery orchards and grey olive-groves, preferable to the dusty highway as an approach to the town.

"Lord, what rot one talks in anger," he thought when he had gone some distance, the folly of his late tirade appearing plainly. Nora might have started, it was no use going back; but he registered a vow to ride in the afternoon to Deramûn and bring her home with honour.

Near the foot of the tree-clad hill his house surmounted, the orchards fell away, and he surveyed the town. It covered all the narrow plain between hill and sea with a serried growth of flat-topped dwellings, from which some red-tiled roofs devoid of chimneys stood out, shining, like huge carbuncles. Here and there among the houses rose a distaff cypress, and these trees crowded round the principal mosque of the place, so that a single minaret was visible. From time to time a sound of desultory firing shook the sunlight. Having learnt to associate that sound with rejoicings, Pope supposed it was some holiday of Greeks or Armenians, the Muslim feast-days being few and unforgettable.

The sight of unusual animation in the streets presently confirmed this theory, and finding a concourse of Armenians at the French post office[156], whither business took him, he supposed it was they who were keeping festival. But going out again, with eyes alert, he counted in a short while more white turbans than he ever remembered to have seen in this town before. And all these Muslims moved about in troops, some chanting, some invoking the Most High. Passing the mosque, he saw a train of dervishes come out, bearing in their midst a fine embroidered banner. The mosque, from the glimpse he got of its interior, seemed full of turbaned heads. A murmur as of hornets came from it.

It must be a Muslim feast-day after all, he considered, and called at the English consulate for information. There, too, he found the approaches choked with a herd of excited Christians. The cavasses[157] had to clear a way for him to pass to the consul's room.

Davis the consul sat at his desk in council with three Europeans and a dozen Turks, when James Pope entered. "What the devil now?" he shouted as the door opened. "Ah, Pope!" he added, with but little change of tone, "you've heard rumours, I suppose? They aren't exaggerated. There was a preachment in the mosque this morning by one of the softa[158] from the capital; it was followed within an hour by twenty murders. They're not warm yet; you wait! We had not an inkling till this morning, when the thing was on us. Where's your wife? At Deramûn? The best place possible. They're all Muslims there. Join her yourself at once, and stay there, both of you, for the present. The governor and the mosque authorities assure me that there is no danger for Europeans; but the place isn't fit for a woman. Now go, there's a good man; I'm most awfully busy."

Out in the streets once more, among the merchants' awnings, Pope felt the tourist instinct to see all there was to see before retiring. His spirit craving shocks to sight and hearing, he was impatient of the usual movement of the streets, the well-known cries and odours. There was an Indian curiosity-dealer, in the Kurdish quarter, with whom he had struck up something of a friendship. The man spoke English, so could give him all the news. He walked some distance towards the Hindi's shop, then changed his mind and took another road, with back to the sea, and face towards the orchard hill, which was visible from time to time where roofs were low. Of course the fun would be in the Armenian quarter.

[156] In late Ottoman times, foreign companies had the franchise of postal services.

[157] The cavass was a junior official – sometimes a messenger – of a consulate.

[158] Muslim student.

He called it "fun" in thought without brutality, so little sense of tragedy was in his mind. In front he heard the sounds of firing, shouts and screams; behind him bugles sounded in the Turkish barracks; but the street in which he walked was quite deserted, the dogs slept undisturbed along the sunlit wall. Excitement took the place of curiosity. He was going simply to traverse the quarter, as he had often done before, in his way home; but to-day he ran a risk which stirred his blood; if he got through scatheless, he would have a tale to tell.

Suddenly wild shrieks assailed his ears; a group of children running for their lives were seen for a minute. A side street engulfed them. The pursuers followed close – a rabble of small boys armed with long knives, some of which ran blood, calling on God, and shouting out obscenities. At the next turning Pope was in the thick of it, actually jostled by the murderers and their victims, some of whom clutched at him for help. Shots were being fired from upper windows; on the thresholds of some houses fights were raging; but most of the lower storeys had been broken into, and their inhabitants were being butchered in the sunlight. For a moment Pope felt terror on his own account till he saw that the slayers paid not the slightest heed to him. It was as if his English hat had been the helm of Perseus, he moved unseen among them, a most strange sensation. The butchers went about their work methodically, much as the priests of old performed a sacrifice, beginning with "Bismillah[159]", and ending with the death-thrust. They killed a woman close to him with all this ritual, the officiators being three old men with long white beards and anxious, kindly faces. "Pigs!" Pope yelled at them. They saw him then and smiled one to another, saying, "He knows no Turkish." One of them stooped down and, ripping open the body of their victim, tore something out and beat it on the wall. The ground rose up with Pope, then yawned beneath him, like a ship at sea. It brought on actual sickness. A kind arm supported him, leading him clear of the tumult, the while a friendly voice discoursed as to a child: "Efendim[160], grieve not for them, they deserve to die. It is known they have invented a kind of ball – so big! – which goes off like a cannon, killing everyone. With it they hoped to destroy us Muslimîn and all the world except their shameful selves. Efendim, it is justice; but best keep away. The sight affects thee strongly, and our younger men might take offence. Excuse me now, I must return to work. The way lies clear before thee."

Alone once more, and in perfect surroundings, James Pope strode homeward fiercely, with a throat full of sobs. Breasting the orchard hill, he kept waving his stick about and talking to himself like a lunatic. What devil had made him seek

---

159 In the name of God.

160 Term of courteous address.

that sight of horror. But for an impulse of curiosity, which now seemed brutal madness, he could have ridden after Nora with clean hands. Now, from head to foot, he felt defiled. He had seen poor people killed – women and children too – his co-religionists, and here he was going home to lunch without a scratch. In vain did his reason plead that interference by an unarmed man was useless, that actual nausea had at the time disabled him. He felt himself unfit to be alive.

On the terrace of his mansion on the hill he was met by Abbâs, the negro doorkeeper, whose services went with the house. The old black smiled in welcome.

"Hast heard the news, my master? They are punishing the Armenians – a just punishment. They had hatched a plot, it is known, to slay all true believers from the sultan down. And moreover, it is said – I know not how truly – that they have invented a hellish implement – a kind of ball. They throw it and it bursts, and kills as earthquakes do, the just with the unjust, thousands at a blow. Allah is merciful! They deserve to be slain, everyone of them."

Pope passed by him without an answer. He went into the great reception-hall and wrote to Nora, bidding her stay where she was, and also to Mrs Ellis, the missionary's wife at Deramûn, imploring her to detain his wife for a few days. These two letters he confided to the Greek cook, who, both the horses being out, went off to borrow a neighbour's mule for the journey. That done, he tried to eat some lunch, and, failing, took a chair out to the terrace, and lolled there in the shadow of the house, feeling but half alive.

Why had he ever come back to this accursed land? Why had he brought his bride here on her honeymoon, and hired a house for six months? His father had been consul here, he had known the place as a child and loved its memory; he had wished his wife to know it too, and love it. Before that beastly sight two hours ago he would have called the place as safe as Regent's Park. . . . If only his brain would devise some plan by means of which he might hope to rescue one – only one – of those poor wretches! If only his nerves would suffer him to go down again into the slaughter and get a wound in an attempt at rescue! It was in the hope of some such prompting to retrieve his honour that he hung here inactive instead of joining Nora in a safe retreat.

The best thing he could think of, after hours of cogitation, was to go down to Davis at the consulate and volunteer for any rescue work that might be going forward. Already the afternoon was well advanced. He would have a cup of tea at half-past five, and then go down in the cool, prepared to work through the whole night through if necessary. At present he was overwhelmed with lassitude.

It was five o'clock, and he still lounged in his deck-chair, too sick to smoke, disgusted with the flowery tree-tops and the sea before him, when he was disturbed by the crack of a rifle close at hand. It was followed by a volley. Men were fighting. Alive in a trice, he ran in the direction of the noise.

The house stood on the summit of the hill. Behind it, as well as in front, the ground fell away in a succession of steep terraces. Half-way down this inland slope, on a projecting knee, a small Armenian village hung like an eagle's nest. It was thence that the warlike din proceeded. The male inhabitants were checking the assault, for Pope saw only women and children in the stream of fugitives already scrambling up the hill. It was marvellous how they covered the rough ground, springing like wild goats, clambering like monkeys, though some carried babies, and had other children clinging to their skirts. Thank God! They were making for his house. A child fell and screamed, the mother kicked it and dragged it prostrate for some yards ere it regained its feet. The foremost drew quite near. They howled to him. He knew not what they said, but called, "Come on!" A girl said, "Thank you, sir! Thank God!" in quite good English. He herded them across the terrace into the house and left them in the big reception-hall, telling the two Armenian maids to look well after them. As soon as their breath returned they started wailing, and the maids, their co-religionists, wailed with them, useless thenceforth.

Pope went back on to the terrace, pacing up and down. He took a cigarette from his case and smoked quite happily. He saw Abbâs the negro looking sullen, and asked to know what ailed him.

"Are you sorry we have guests indoors?"

"Eyvet, efendim[161]. Such guests bring danger on the house that shelters them."

"But the Kurds will not attack an English house."

"Efendim, if God wills."

"But you would not let these women and children die. They have done no wrong."

"Efendim, they have made a kind of ball –"

"Be silent! They are guests, we must defend them."

"Hâzir, efendim[162]. Am I not thy servant?"

Abbâs sadly resumed his seat upon the ground. Pope finished his cigarette, then went all round the house, securing every aperture as far as possible. But the place remained far from impregnable, the Greek owner, wishing his abode to

[161] Yes, Sir.

[162] Literally: Ready, Sir.

make a show in the sunlight, having assigned too much space to glass in his plan of building. The terrace, however, made an outer rampart hard to scale, and only one stone flight of steps led up to it. It intoxicated Pope to recognise that he was entirely free from fear.

Presently Abbâs summoned his attention by a low call, and pointed down the terraces. Men were climbing swiftly, flinging themselves from point to point rather than leaping, now erect, now sprawling, never stopping for an instant. It was dusk down there under the trees, whose tops were warm in the sunset. Pope turned his field-glass on the climbers. Five more fugitives! The face of one was bloody, another's arm bled; all carried knives in their mouths, and two had pistols. As they mounted his last terrace he could hear their heavy panting. "Where is the entrance?" cried the foremost rudely. Pope let them go indoors.

"Efendim!" cried Abbâs beside himself. "Make them give up their arms. If they fire a shot or strike a blow when the pursuers come, it means the end of us."

Pope followed them indoors, and with the help of the girl who spoke English, persuaded them to give him all their weapons. They said they were the sole survivors of their village; which proved untrue, for in the course of the next half hour, as many more, all badly wounded, straggled in. The wailing of the women got on James Pope's nerves. He told Abbâs to go and make them stop their noise, himself continuing to pace the terrace. What with the long suspense and the approach of night, he found his courage ebbing; and felt fear, less of a possible danger, than of his own nature, lest he should again be seized with nausea, and incapacitated.

At length a murmur of voices rose in the still air – a peaceful sound it seemed. The pursuers, if it was they, were in no haste. They had come by the easiest route, a long way round, and were now moving leisurely up the broad high road. Abbâs, invoking the Supreme Protector, went off to his proper post outside the carriage-gate. Pope's heart beat in his head; he strode to and fro like a caged beast; and in truth suspense encaged him as with bars of iron. He heard much shouting at the gate, where the expostulations of Abbâs, a fellow Muslim, detained the killers for five minutes. Then came a mighty shout of "Dîn Muhammad[163]!" and he knew that the mob was coming towards him slowly as before. "O infidel!" a man cried out, as preface to a long harangue, of which Pope could make nothing, the language being high flown and religious. He was aware of many swinging blots of light down by the ground, the light from lanterns carried in men's hands. Those lanterns made it black night all at once, though the windows of the house still felt the sunset.

---

163 "The religion of Muhammad"; a call to arms.

Abbâs came up the steps to join his master. He interpreted:

"They have sworn a solemn oath to slay these people. Against thee, they have nothing. Do but stand aside!"

"Didst thou not tell them that they are our guests, that the honour of our house is their protection?"

"Of course I did; it is the proper answer. But might it not be well to reconsider?"

"No, by Allah."

"Then they will storm the house."

"No, that they dare not. I am an English subject. They know too well what follows. Tell them that if they use the slightest violence, they will every one of them be hanged in a month's time."

Pope soon saw that his boast had not been empty. They were unwilling to assault a British subject. Abbâs became the centre of a long discussion, to which Pope tried to listen. Would no one silence those mad women there in the house? Their screams, distinctly audible now there was a hush, were bound to excite a mob whose love was murder. He leant over the parapet and called, "Abbâs."

"Here, efendim."

"We have said our last word. Come indoors with me, and bid these people go their way in peace."

This speech, intelligible to the crowd, evoked a perfect storm of execration. Many shots were fired, to scare the Englishman. Abbâs came slowly up the stairs to join him. Together they were entering the house, when a shout went out from the outskirts of the throng below, spreading rapidly till it became a roar of triumph. Abbâs started, and then trembled violently.

"Efendim, their cry is, they have caught our lady."

"They lie; she is at Deramûn. Go and demand some proof of what they say. Let me speak with her, or I shall know her words are lies."

Abbâs was absent but a minute. "They refuse to bring her to thee, fearing some stratagem, but they will give thee proof that it is really she. There is no doubt, efendim."

He stood a moment by his master's side, then went indoors. Someone in the crowd cried out to Pope in English:

"Do hear reason, sir. Armenians wicked fellows. Fifty thousand Armenians not be worth the memsahib."

It was his friend the Indian curiosity-dealer. Had Pope wished to reply, there was no time, for just then a man ran up the steps and fell at his feet, blubbering. It was his own Greek cook.

"O Holy Virgin! Saints beneficent! They have caught our gracious lady. I gave her thy letter, but she would not tarry. Hearing there was trouble, she came back to thee. Now they have caught her, and will harm her unless thou speak some word of power to save. Speak that word, my master, ere we die of fright."

Pope's purpose was completely overborne. What was his duty towards these howling, mad Armenians to compare with that which he owed to Nora, his own wife? She was an Englishwoman, quite alone and innocent, and he had brought her to this country, exposing her to perils, simply for his own whim. He went to drive out the Armenians.

In the great reception-hall he found Abbâs before him, explaining to its inmates that the lady of the house was captured by the enemy. Of course all they, being folk of no account, must go out to their death that she might live. Bad luck for them, but so it was written on the tablets of destiny.

The despair of those poor wretches at his words was dreadful to witness. Women rolled and grovelled on the floor in anguish, tearing their bosoms with their finger-nails, pulling out their hair by the roots. One wounded man was licking the negro's feet. A woman, like a fury, tore his sleeve. The girl who spoke good English ran to Pope and flung her arms round his neck. "Kill us yourself, dear sir!" she shrieked. "In mercy, kill us!"

The nausea of the morning came again upon him; he could not do as he desired.

In a voice quite strange to himself he told Abbâs to let the poor things be.

"You do not deliver them up; our lady suffers?" questioned the Muslim, paralysed with horror.

"It must be so. The lady is myself. She would not wish our house to be dishonoured."

Immediately he repented of his words; they were heroic, and his motive was pure cowardice. They had a strange effect on Abbâs. The negro stared at him a moment, taking stock of his emotion. Suddenly he put out both his hands and touched him, then drew the said hands slowly down his own black face. It is the way Muslims handle holy marvels.

"Get out, old fool!" Pope thundered in a fury.

"Could we not fight our way and rescue her?" he asked after a while with sudden brightness. "These men would help, and there are arms for all."

"Efendim, it is useless. What would happen? While yet we fought our way, they would remove the lady, and those behind would break into the house. Only thy presence stops them."

The crowd outside were clamouring for his answer. "My God, how can I speak to them!" cried Pope, despairingly.

"Move not – I am thy mouthpiece," said Abbâs, and left him. Pope followed from sheer weakness. With a disgust that was near to hatred he heard the negro calling for admiration for an act of heroism worthy to be written in gold in the noblest annals of hospitality. Pope caught the dotard by the arm and dragged him back.

The crowd expected him to say something, he supposed; but at the moment he could think of nothing in their accursed jargon, except some foul expressions which he hurled at them. Abbâs, from behind him, reminded them that the English government would have every one of them hanged, if they should harm the lady.

"Thou hast said, O infidel!" The crowd laughed viciously. Again some shots were fired. A bullet whistled past Pope's cheek, and struck the wall. He wished to God that it had stretched him out. Then they were gone – in a flash, it seemed to him. The stars throbbed tranquilly above the silent trees. A dog was barking somewhere not far off. But for the ceaseless lamentations of the Armenians, he could almost have enjoyed the tragic calm. It was but charity to kill such shrieking brutes. Their presence made the house obscene; he could not enter it, but paced up and down the terrace under the stars.

A sound of hoof-beats on the road brought hope again. It might be they had led her off simply to frighten him. She would come riding back with Hasan in attendance, laughing at her adventure. But presently his ears assured him that a troop of riders was approaching. Perhaps she had been rescued by the garrison. The horsemen came in at his gate; there was no longer any doubt as to their destination. He vowed to lead a stricter life in future, if only they had brought her safe and sound. He shouted something to inform them of his presence.

"Is that you, Pope? What is this about your wife?" The speaker was Davis – foremost of a troop of horsemen, it might be ten or twenty; Pope was quite past counting. The consul sat his horse squarely. Pope cowered in spirit as before a judge. In a toneless voice he made confession of his shame.

"They caught her coming home and held her as a kind of hostage for exchange against the fifty odd Armenians who have taken refuge in my house. I was off my head at the time, and, like a fool, declined to bargain. They've taken her away down there, and I feel like shooting myself."

He expected to be treated like an outcast, a brute beast; but Davis was up the steps in a minute, clasping his hand. The consul wore no hat; his head was bandaged.

"Keep calm, old fellow. They won't dare to hurt her; they know too well we'd make it hell for them. Of course, I throw up all the other work and look for her. These are my helpers, mostly Turks. They know every cranny of the town. We'll bring her back in no time, never fear!"

"Stay, I'll come with you."

"No, you won't, my son! You've got to guard your refugees. Fifty, whew! That's splendid. We've been working hard all day, and so has a French party, and we haven't saved a hundred head, all told. You stay where you are and keep your pecker up. I'll leave two men here. We'll be back directly, in sh'Allah[164]."

Never had Pope known Davis so cordial. The consul's usual manner was almost irritatingly languid and supercilious. The change encouraged him a good deal, marking, as it did, approval of his conduct. He still felt guilty of betraying Nora, but was glad to know his guilt was not self-evident. After a little more than an hour, which seemed a century, he heard again the tramp of hoofs. Going to the edge of the terrace, he strained his eyes towards the carriage gate.

"It's all right, Pope," the consul's voice rang out, and for the first time the howling of the Armenians sounded good to him. "We traced her easily. She's unhurt, we think, but scared to death, poor creature. Quite unconscious. Couldn't wait to get a litter, so put her up before me on the saddle. Hamdi Bey walked alongside and kept her steady. Got any women in the house? They'd be more use than we are!"

"They are damned brutes, these Kurds," he said, ten minutes later, preparing to mount again. "It seems they quite intended to release her, having frightened you, but first – by way of fun, they say – they made her witness a most beastly sight – three women murdered with the usual ritual. Your groom, Hasan, deserves a medal. He stuck to her through it all. I hear he knifed a rascal who was innocent. Your Indian friend, though one of the ringleaders, stood by her too; we found her in his house. I sent a message to the doctor to come up."

The doctor came and spent that night in the house. Early next morning he informed Pope that his wife was conscious, but above all things seemed to dread her husband's presence. Insane aversions often followed on such shocks as that she had sustained, and must be humoured, or the patient's mind might suffer permanently. He therefore asked James Pope to keep away from her, and to order her attendants never to name his name, nor allude to the disasters, nor let her guess there were Armenians in the house. As soon as possible she must go home to England in charge of a proper nurse. Pope bowed assent, feeling himself justly punished. That Nora knew he had failed her there seemed now no doubt.

---

[164] God willing.

A month later, at her father's house in London, he ventured to transgress the doctor's edict and implore her forgiveness, while endeavouring to give her some idea of the dilemma in which he had been caught on that atrocious night. For some time she appeared not to grasp his meaning; then all at once she seized his hand and stopped him with an outcry of amazement:

"You saved Armenians? . . . . O, why was I not told of this before. You sacrificed even me sooner than give them up! If only I had known, I could have borne everything. I thought you still approved of all that wickedness; you had defended massacres, you know, that very morning; and I remembered your words while I was suffering the intensest agonies through sight and hearing. You came to stand for all the horrors I had witnessed. I dreaded the very sight of you, till just this minute, when all the while you were a hero, if I had but seen it!"

James could not see it himself.

MELEK

This story first appeared in As Others See Us, published in October 1922.

It is, in some ways, a political thriller, revolving round the relationship of a young army officer, who is a conspirator with the Young Turk movement, and his sister, the wife of a respected senior general who is on the wrong side of the emerging conflict.

The date given for the events in the story – May 1908 – is significant. It is not clear at first that the location is Salonika, but it was in this Macedonian city many of the revolutionary army was based. In May the Sultan Abdul Hamid was forced to reinstate the constitution and to summon a parliament. In the following month King Edward VII met his wife's nephew, the Russian Tsar Nicholas II at Reval (modern Tallinn in Estonia) to make contingency plans for the future of the Ottoman Empire.

Pickthall felt passionately about these developments. In his journalism at the time he applauded the reinstatement of the constitution and the Young Turk revolution in which a new generation and new ideas dominated the politics of Ottoman Turkey. Pickthall echoed some of the revolutionaries – as in this story – arguing that it also saw the regeneration of Islam.

The character of the sister and wife is compelling. She fervently believes in the revolution and is ready to facilitate the assassination of her much older husband. But when the assassination attempt is foiled and he is later posted (exiled?) to "Arabia" – presumably Yemen – she declares her love for him and readiness to go with him to his new posting. In contrast to E.M. Forster's ideal, she was prepared to betray her husband before her country, but when the crisis of choice was over, she resumed the role as loyal partner.

The story is discussed by Professor Afra S Al-Shiban in Ebtisam A Sadiq, Marmaduke Pickthall Reinstated, Partridge Publishing, Singapore, 2016, pp 153-55.

Behind the city[165] on the shore of the blue gulf there is a hill of cypress-trees, where in mysterious shade amid the gnarled gray stems the tall, slim headstones of the Muslim dead, inclined this way and that, are like a natural undergrowth. On sunny afternoons the glades are populous with groups of shrouded women like white ghosts, and separate groups of fezzed or turbaned men seated around the sepulchres of their relations or walking slowly in the shadow of the trees. Within the grove among the tombs, itinerant coffee-makers and the men who sell salt-nuts and sweetstuffs do a thriving trade, and on the summit of the hill from which the trees recede, affording a wide view of sea and mountains, stands a small kiosk with many stools and tables set around it where coffee and all kinds of sherbet can be had.

At this spot, on an afternoon in May of the year 1908, five Turkish officers were seated with their swords between their knees around a crazy wooden table on which stood a carafe of water, five tumblers and five coffee-cups, long-footed and devoid of handles, on as many plates. It was a Friday, and the space before the tavern was well filled. From time to time one of the officers half rose and laid his hand to his lips and brow, smiling in response to some acquaintance who had caught his eye. The group of five appeared quite gay and careless. They sat outside the throng, upon the brink of the descent. The whole vast panorama of the gulf with all its guardian mountains lay before them in strong sunlight. The leader in their conversation was a captain of dragoons – a blue-eyed, weather-beaten man of dark complexion – who kept one hand upon his heavy black moustache. He wore an Astrakhan cap and a light blue tunic much befrogged; the others wore the scarlet fez and dark blue uniform. They kept their smiling faces turned towards him, laughing but occasionally; and yet the matter of their talk was very grave. The captain of dragoons, with a slight smile, was saying: –

"He is doomed. The duty of removing him is laid upon us five here present."

There was a moment's pause while all gazed out over the sea, striving to realise the news in all its bearings, for the man to be eliminated was the military governor.

"He has somehow got to know of our arrangements, as the capture of the secret post to Smyrna indicates; for the messenger was faithful to his charge; of that the proof is that he died defending it," pursued the captain with affected carelessness. "It is to assign positions in this patriotic task that I have summoned you. According to our rules the actual slayers must be people unacquainted with the victim in order that their action may be quite impersonal. Rustem Bey, as his near relative, is thus excluded; and so am I, who know and love the man,"

[165] Salonika, modern Thessoloniki in Greece, but then part of the Ottoman Empire.

he hesitated, with a look of great compassion in his eyes, before he added: "But Rustem Bey must frame the project, for he, alone of all of us, frequents the house."

Rustem Bey, a youth with face of Grecian beauty, olive-skinned and brown-eyed, threw away the cigarette he had that minute lighted and took another from the silver case which lay before him on the table. For a moment his set face betrayed his anguish. Then, controlling his emotion by an effort, he said:–

"Ready."

"It is the cause of Allah," said the captain gravely. "The Lord of Right have mercy upon him and all of us."

"Allah have mercy upon him!" murmured all the others.

Then, for the benefit of any one who might be watching, the dragoon gave a guffaw and slapped the shoulder of his neighbour, a young gunner, half a negro, who responded with a grin of teeth and eyes; and, pushing back his stool, declared:–

"We must be going."

Amid the compliments of parting he contrived to whisper in the ear of Rustem: "Walk with me to my horse down there among the trees," and murmured to the others: "Leave us." The remaining three then mingled in the crowd of pleasure-makers, seeking out acquaintances, while the dragoon and Rustem Bey descended to the cemetery.

"My soul is grieved for thee," the former said, laying his hand affectionately on the young man's shoulder; "and those above me in the work would fain have spared thee this great ordeal; but the need for action is immediate, and there is no other way. Of one thing I am glad on thy account; it is that he is what he is, a man of noble character, who fears not death. So there will be no meanness in the tragedy."

"One thing perplexes me," said Rustem Bey with studied coolness. "I do not see how I can well perform my portion of the task without confiding our design to one who is not under vows as we are. . . . I mean my sister," he concluded after a long pause.

The captain frowned and tugged at his moustache.

"She might reveal the secret," he said dubiously.

"She will reveal no secret; I would answer for her with my life! But it is likely that she will oppose us in this matter, since the man we have to kill is her own husband."

"Well, if there is no other way, inform her; we must take the risk. But bind her by an oath of secrecy."

"Accept my warmest thanks. May Allah guard thee!" answered Rustem, as the captain of the dragoons sprang up into the saddle.

Left alone, the young man wandered in the shade among the crowded headstones, pausing to decipher an inscription here and there.

"'The rose is circumscribed, a simple flower-ball, but its perfume fills the room. Brief is the life of roses, yet their scent survives them for a day or two. Such is the power of kindness, such its memory."

"In life he praised the Lord continually, and by the blessing of the Lord his death was sudden, without fear of grief, caused by the bullet on an enemy."

"Hast set thy heart on any thing of earth? Know that that too will pass away, O man!"

For the Turk there is no horror in the thought of sudden death: it is desirable. The society of devotees to which young Rustem Bey belonged "died daily", having dedicated all that they possessed; their life, their dear ones, to a sacred cause. The death in contemplation for his brother-in-law was that which every brave man would desire to meet. If Rustem shuddered and was filled with horror at the thought of it, it was from doubt of his own fortitude rather than compassion for the victim. Ali Haidar Pasha was not to be pitied, even in imagination; his manly figure faced the world too squarely. But Rustem Bey was called for the first time to take a leading part in the great work which had for object the creation of a free and happy people and the liberation of Islam: and the call was of a kind which he had not expected. He was sad; so sad that he was loth to quit the cypress-grove at length and face the town.

Upon his way to Ali Haidar Pasha's house, as he was passing by a café in a fashionable street, a hand was thrust out to detain him, and a jolly voice exclaimed:-

"'Haste is from the devil', say the Arabs. Come, sit down! Rash counsels always go with hurrying feet."

Half-angry, the young man was dragged into a chair, and found himself confronted with the laughing face of Dehli Reshid Bey – "mad" Reshid Bey, so called from his eccentric manners – a man of wealth and high connections, who made mock of everything – the last man Rustem wished to meet just then.

"It is a bad thing, soul of mine[166], to hurry in these days," began the joker, "because it is the mark of certain people who are not in favour."

"I ask your pardon. I am very busy," pleaded Rustem, trying to escape; but Reshid Bey prevented him, exclaiming: –

---

[166] A literal translation of the Turkish affectionate address.

"Stay with me but a minute! Hear a story! . . . I had noticed how it was the way of certain people to walk about with rapid steps and with a look of business, and how other people, soldiers for the most part, seeing them of that demeanour, ran and whispered in their ears and were despatched on errands."

"The truth is you have noticed nothing of the kind," cried Rustem irritably.

"By Allah, I have seen it! But first hear my tale. One day I walked precisely in their manner, for experiment. A kind of beggar-man came up and whispered: 'Let what will be, be!' I caught the vein and answered: 'If what will be or will not be may be, then let the form of being of what will or may be, being alone what it can be, be.' He raised objections, saying: 'But the Powers of Europe . . . ?' I answered: 'May they burst!' That gave him comfort, for he smiled and blessed me, and departed quickly as if reassured. . . . And that, my friend, is what you call new light! . . . . Nay, stop a minute, mannerless! There is much more!"

But Rustem Bey had made good his escape and was already many paces distant, fleeing desperately from that nonsense which annoyed his brain. Even the usual traffic of the streets, the careless common life, was jarring to him.

In a deep lane of high blind walls he stopped before a gate and rang a bell which hung there. After a while a negro opened to him, and he passed into a flowering garden, where he had to wait until some women, who were visiting his sister, chose to go. He waited for an hour in agitation, pacing a length of path between two judas-trees; and then his sister came to him, a slender figure veiled in white, emerging from a thicket of white lilac. Her eyes grew bright at sight of him; she hardly smiled. He noticed the accomplished ease of her demeanour, the grace of one accustomed to command as to obey; beheld the wife of Ali Haidar Pasha, a great lady, in one who until now had seemed his girlish sister.

She led him towards a bower of wistaria, which was her summer-house, while he, to break the subject of his visit, assumed so sad an air that she was forced to ask what ailed him.

He answered: "I have serious news," and then he paused, uncertain for a moment what direction to pursue. The nonsense uttered by mad Reshid Bey kept running in his head like a refrain, distracting him.

They sat together in the arbour, the long tassels of wistaria hanging as a coloured fringe between them and the evening light.

"My sister," he began at last, "dost thou remember our old talks together there at home, beside the Bosphorus, and how we longed for the regeneration of our country and, through our country, of Islam? I told thee many things in those days, and thy heart was with us."

"I have forgotten nothing," said his sister, motionless.

"The matter has gone forward since our talk of those days; and the end is near. The King of England meets the Czar at Reval, which means that our old friend among the Christian Powers will soon join hands with our relentless enemy. The condition of our country seems indeed past hope. All is corrupt and rotten, in the tyrant's hand. The nations, gazing at us, see no sign of life; they hear no cry. What wonder then, that they account us dead, and now take measures to divide our heritage? We must arise at once, or all is lost."

The girl's hands, clasping and unclasping nervously, alone betrayed her interest in what he said. She watched her fingers, keeping her eyes hidden.

"My sister, is thy spirit with us?" he inquired, with anguish.

"Aye, to the death!" she answered, with a husky voice, raising her eyes to his. They spoke a passion which amazed him.

"My errand is no less than death," he murmured; "and we crave thy help."

"Command, say rather!" she replied with fervour.

Rustem's lips were dry. He moistened them awhile before proceeding: –

"We are in great danger from the efforts of a certain personage, who is a strong supporter of the tyranny. By some means he has come to knowledge of our methods. The secret post to Anatolia has been seized, our agent slain; another of our messengers has been arrested on the road to Seres. We know the man who ordered those arrests. What must be done?"

"He must be killed at once," she answered.

Young Rustem hung his head, and murmured: –

"Thou hast said it! The doomed man is no other than the master of this house."

"Allah have mercy on him!" muttered Melek Khanum, and after that sat silent a long time.

"Dost that disclosure alter thy resolve?" he asked at length.

"By no means," she made answer in a dreamy way. "It is impersonal. His body stands between our land and a great light. Let the light shine! . . . . Who kills him? Is it I?"

"No, praise to Allah! But the slayers are appointed. They require thy help."

The lady sat immersed in thought awhile before she said: –

"To-morrow night he sups with certain friends, not in the selamlik out of doors, but in the house. The room in which the supper will be laid has three large windows looking on this garden. The shutters of the middle window will be open. My lord the Pasha sits quite close to it. My own slave Ali, whom thou knowest, will keep the garden gate from sunset onward. He will have orders to admit the man or men who, asking for admittance, say 'For freedom'. He will show them where to wait concealed, until the time arrives."

"I offer thanks, my sister," murmured Rustem miserably, her calm arrangement of the work of slaughter having chilled his blood. How she must hate her husband, was his thought. But something new and stern in her demeanour forbade confidences; and while he still sat wondering what next to say, a shadow fell upon the path before them, and Ali Haidar Pasha came into the arbour, bowing his head beneath the blossoms of wistaria.

His wife rose up to welcome him with seeming pleasure, while as in duty Rustem sprang to the salute. He was preparing to depart immediately, but Melek by a secret gesture bade him stay.

"We were discussing the new revolutionary ideas, Pasha Effendim," she said casually, while Rustem wished the ground would open and engulf him. "What may we ask in confidence, is your opinion of them?"

"The question is soon answered," replied Ali Haidar Pasha pleasantly, tucking one foot beneath him on the sofa which was in the arbour, and playing with the chaplet which he always carried. "I think these young men – I suppose them young although, for aught I know, there may be greybeards among them – build all their hopes upon a fallacy. They think the Powers of Europe are sincere in their expressed desire to see our land reformed by us upon the model of their institutions. I know that they are not sincere, and I can prove it, for wherever any one of us has worked resolutely for the improvement of the administration or the good of the inhabitants, one or other of those Powers has vexed him and procured his downfall. In my opinion the one way to foil him is that adopted by our Padishah[167] (whom God preserve!) – namely, to keep up an appearance of corruption and decrepitude while striving to increase our fighting strength by every means, and fostering a fierce Islamic spirit in the ranks."

"But we were saying that, by all accounts, these young men are good Muslims, and are seeking the same object, only by another way?"

"I do not doubt it. And their way is more desirable and would be better if our plight were other than it is, and if the Powers of Europe were not watching us like beasts of prey, content to wait while they suppose us dying. At a sign of health they will assail us all together."

"That, I hear, is what they say will happen as things are," sighed Melek Khanum. "The King of England goes to meet the Czar at Reval."

---

[167] That is the Sultan Abdulhamid II.

"Allahu Akbar[168]!" said the Pasha, with a shrug. "If danger threatens us from any quarter we shall not face it better for a change of institutions which, for a time at any rate, must make us weak."

"I am glad to know your true opinion," answered Melek sweetly.

"They may be right, I quite admit it," added the old soldier. "I mean they may have power to work a miracle. God may be with them, which would alter everything. But I personally, with the wit entrusted to me, think them wrong. And if I thought them right in their conclusions, my plain duty as a soldier, bound by allegiance to the person of the Padishah, is to oppose them – aye, and crush them if I can." He held his right hand clenched a moment, laughing lightly. "Art taken with their flaming doctrines, soul of me?"

"Greatly, I confess," said Melek thoughtfully.

And Rustem left them arguing the subject amicably, as something purely academical, remote from both.

"She hates him and desires his death," he thought, with horror; then, with a glow, exclaimed: "He is a noble man! There is no baseness in him for a cause of fear. May I be just as he is when I come to die!"

He met the captain of dragoons that evening, and made full report. His portion of the work was thus completed.

That night he could not rest at all, and all the following day his brain was in a whirl. He shunned his friends, and did his duty as a Muslim thoroughly, praying at the five appointed hours in private and in congregation. After nightfall he could bear anxiety no longer, and went out from his lodging to the crowded main street of the town, where cafés were ablaze and strains of music floated. After walking up and down awhile, he entered a gay haunt, full at the moment of the blare of "Hiawatha"[169], played inaccurately, but with gusto, by a band of Greek performers. Looking around him on the seated crowd, he caught a glimpse of Dehli Reshid sitting at a little table in a corner all alone, and went to join him.

"Why thus solitary?" he inquired as they saluted.

"I had a crowd here but a minute since," replied the joker, "but they retired because my madness came upon me, drawing too much attention to our table. That was because they bored me with their 'Deign to consider, Bey Effendi!' and

---

168 God is greatest!

169 The music of the cantata "Hiawatha's Wedding Feast" by Samuel Coleridge-Taylor, composed between 1898 and 1900 was an extraordinary hit, popular around the world in the following decade.

'Bey Effendim, if you will but condescend to look with leniency on your slave's opinion!' Braying asses!"

"What news is there to-night?" asked Rustem eagerly.

"The King of Greece, they say, devoured a fragment of dead pig for supper!"

"But seriously?"

"I have sat here since the hour of sunset surrounded by the kind of imbeciles I have described – Waiter, bring coffee, and those cigarettes – What tidings should there be? The world goes on."

"That too will pass," said Rustem, with a shrug.

He did his utmost to seem careless both in speech and manner, but all the while his ears were strained to catch the sound of any outcry or disturbance in the street. His eyes kept furtive watch upon the door. At length he saw a man he knew, an officer of the police, come in and look about him as if seeking some one. Rustem stood up and beckoned to the man, who came then to their table, but would not sit down.

"Thy looks are grave," said Rustem. "Is there any news?"

"There is," was the reply, "but if I tell thee, for Allah's love do not divulge the matter till to-morrow. Ali Haidar Pasha has been shot at, while he sat at supper. By good luck His Excellency happened for some reason to lean sideways suddenly. Thus the first bullet only grazed his cheek. It broke a glass thing in the centre of the table, and some fragments flew into the face of hunchbacked Hasan Bey, who sat upon the other side. A second shot was fired, and then a third in quick succession, but those were intercepted by young Hilmi Bey, the aide-de-camp, who rushed to screen the Pasha with his body. He is severely wounded and, they say, will die. May Allah heal him!"

"May Allah heal him!" muttered Rustem Bey and Dehli Reshid in a breath.

"The leaving open of the window and the private door into the garden," pursued the captain of the police in the same tone, "points to the complicity of some one in the house with the assassins, who made off immediately. One of the haramlik[170] slaves is missing, and we have to find him. I come from thence, and, as you can imagine, I am worried, since the burden of the whole affair is laid on me. I am at present looking for Huseyn Effendi. Have you seen him?"

"No, by Allah," answered Dehli Reshid. "He has not been here. . . . And if he had been here I should not have informed thee," he murmured amiably to the back of the departing gendarme. "I would not help that treacherous spy to earn a beshlik[171]."

---

[170] The women's quarters of a house, in contrast to the selamlik, the male and public quarters.

[171] A five para coin – a very small denomination.

"Allahu Akbar!" murmured Rustem in his soul. He saw the cause to which so many lives were dedicated in the greatest jeopardy, for Ali Haidar Pasha would take vengeance certainly, not for himself, but for his loyal aide-de-camp. His face and hands betrayed his agitation.

"My soul," said Reshid in a meaning whisper, laying a hand on his companion's arm. "I have a great advantage in my house – a most commodious cellar with a secret entrance, ever at the disposal of those friends of mine who cannot hide their feelings in a public place. Such persons should not live above the ground. Forget not what I tell you; you may find it useful. I greatly fear you have embraced the creed of 'Let what will be, be!'"

"I know not what you mean," said Rustem hastily, annoyed that anybody should have guessed his secret. But Dehli Reshid Bey, with all his oddities, was not the type of man to be distressed, so his wrath expired.

"Nay, slay me not!" replied the joker coaxingly. "Truly, my cellar is a cool and pleasant place. It is good for men to go beneath the ground occasionally, in order to get used to it before they die; and – tell it not to everybody! – there is wine there."

Rustem was forced to laugh. He lingered a few minutes, for politeness, before taking leave.

With mind a prey to harrowing anxiety, he went back to his rooms, deeming the hour too late for him to call at Ali Haidar Pasha's, although he doubted whether he ought not to do so, whether it would not be thought the duty of so near a relative. He lay awake all night debating the small question whether his going would have roused or lulled suspicion, while his heart was heavy with the dread of ruin for the cause he served. Early next morning he repaired to Ali Haidar Pasha's house, and found his sister walking in the garden. The Pasha, she informed him, had already gone to the seraï[172]. She too, it seemed, had had no sleep that night.

After describing in impressive tones the whole fiasco, she went on to discuss their present plight.

"Yesterday afternoon," she told him, "I despatched a slave of mine in haste to Monastir, unknown to any other of the household, bidding him travel thence by devious ways to Stamboul, and thence to Geykos, to our father's house. This I did in order that suspicion might be led astray. The police to-day are seeking that man only. But Ali Haidar Pasha is not thus deceived. He knows the real nature of the deed, and will not rest until he has taken vengeance for the hurt done to

---

[172] The government offices.

poor Hilmi Bey, who yet may live, we hear this morning, though his wounds are bad. The one way to forestall his vengeance is to poison him."

Her brother made a gesture of extreme repugnance. Melek noticed it.

"Nay, I should be the one to do it!" she remarked with a peculiar laugh. And Rustem, knowing that it must be done, was forced to acquiesce in the disgusting project.

He went off to his military duties. Returning to his lodging after noon, he found a man from Ali Haidar Pasha's household waiting at his door, the bearer of a note from Melek Khanum: –

"Be good enough to come to me without delay."

He went with fear, supposing all was over.

He was shown into a little ante-room of the haramlik, and waited there for some minutes ere his sister came.

She told him in a weary tone: "We are recalled. My lord is summoned to Stamboul immediately. Already he has gone on board the steamboat. I and the household follow in a day or two. The news of an attempt upon his life alarms the despot, who greatly values his devotion and integrity. I sent for thee to tell thee. Nothing can be done at present."

"Since he departs, we have no grief against him. We all respect him as an individual," said Rustem gladly.

"Is he able to disturb our project from Stamboul?" she questioned earnestly.

"Not more than fifty or a hundred others! It was here, in the position which he filled, that he was dangerous. This is the heart. . . . . My sister, I beseech thee, speak no more of killing. It is horrible. By Allah, I cannot endure to hear thee name the deed."

Rustem showed great emotion. She observed him curiously, giving a little laugh, it seemed, of some contempt. He supposed that she had expected him to be as heartless as herself.

But as she stood before him in the middle of the little room, stroking some roses in a bowl with nervous fingers, he noticed that she was a lovely woman in the flush of youth; and found excuse for her. Young as she was, the marriage with a man so old might well have seemed to her a gross indignity. He remembered now that he had felt a wave of pity when first he heard of the betrothal to the great field-marshal. Yet Ali Haidar Pasha was a figure in the world, and the position of his wife was reckoned enviable. She might, he thought, have taken that into account.

Upon the following day he went again to tell her with authority that the doom against her husband was revoked. She seemed indifferent; and when he saw her for the last time on the day of her departure she spoke of nothing but the journey and her troubles over luggage.

She and her husband filled his mind for a day or two, and then were driven from it altogether for as many weeks, for a little after their departure it was rumoured that the King of England and the Czar together had determined to destroy the Turkish Empire, the former moved by indignation at the despotism which disgraced that country, the latter by his ancient greed and wickedness, or so the revolutionaries thought. The word went forth to strike at once.

Niazi Bey and Enver Bey, young officers till then unknown, took to the mountains with a few devoted followers; and so did Rustem and the blue-eyed captain of dragoons. From place to place they went among the Muslim and the Christian villages, announcing a new era of fraternity and winning thousands of adherents from the men of both religions. The fedaïs[173] never doubted of success; their faith spread through the mountains like a wind-borne fire. In less than three weeks they had forced the Sultan to restore the Constitution, and the guns of Monastir and Salonika thundered to salute their victory. But in the first week Rustem Bey was taken prisoner, having ventured all alone into the town of Resna to get news. Against his expectations, he was not shot there and then, but sent to Salonika for examination, under guard. There must have been some friends among his escort, for at the Salonika railway station there was some confusion, and a soldier told him to escape into the town.

But he was still in danger. He dared not go near any of his former haunts. The mountains where the Revolution spread triumphant were a long way off. Choosing deserted alleys in the poorer quarters, he wandered for a long time aimless, racking his wits to think of some safe place of refuge when, by strange good fortune, he ran straight into the arms of Dehli Reshid Bey, emerging from a doorway, who asked no questions, but led him in and exchanged clothes with him. The house, it seemed, belonged to one of his dependants. That done, he led the rebel to his own kiosk, down to the famous cellar, which was furnished like a room.

In spite of the precaution taken in the change of clothes, some word of Rustem's place of refuge must have got abroad; for that same night the house was searched from ground to roof. The cellar only escaped notice, the entrance to it being cunningly disguised. Two hours after midnight Reshid came and told his friend that all was well. Among other merry jests, he had induced the searchers to crawl upon their bellies down a filthy drain. He gave a lively imitation their spluttering and cursing, and of the zeal with which the slaves had squirted water

[173] Soldiers pledged to sacrifice themselves for a cause.

on them in the garden court. He clapped his hands, calling for lights and eatables; and the two friends sat and feasted until day returned.

Rustem remained in hiding till a certain morning when the city shook with the report of cannon fired at intervals. He was wondering greatly what the noises meant, when Dehli Reshid burst into his dungeon and embraced him in a comic rapture, crying: –

"'Let what will be, be.' It is the Constitution! Liberty, Equality, Fraternity, Justice for all, and general imbecility. Come out, my son, and drive with me and see the joy."

The fugitive emerged once more into the light of day. The carriage was already at the door. They drove through the main streets, beflagged and crowded. Soon Rustem Bey was recognised. A surge of shouting, happy people stopped the carriage, dragged the young man out and raised him shoulder high, amidst a roar of acclamation. Dehli Reshid became anxious for the safety of his hero-friend.

He stood up high upon the box beside his coachman, and thus conspicuous – a small, fat man of middle age – commanded silence.

"My friends," he cried, "and brothers in delirium, this creature, Rustem Bey, whom you exalt so highly and acclaim, has all this while been hiding in my cellar. By Allah, that is all he has been doing these two weeks. If I had known that it conduced to such tremendous honour, I also would have hidden in my cellar. I would have that known."

The people laughed aloud and cheered him madly, and in so doing they let Rustem go. The towzled hero scrambled back into the carriage, saluting right and left as it moved on.

"How dare you talk like that about my hiding? It was downright insult," he exclaimed, "why did you say it?"

"To save your life, my lamb," said Dehli Reshid drily. "A little more, and they had torn you limb from limb. . . . Be calm. . . . And now our destination is the steamboat office, where we shall book your passage on the first boat to Stamboul. I wish you well, for you are not devoid of amiable qualities, and the flavour of my cellar is upon you like a charm. I would not have you absent when they dole out honours. Some of the 'let what will be, be'– ites are much worse than you."

The first thing Rustem heard upon arriving in the capital was that Ali Haidar Pasha had been exiled to Arabia. The news did not affect him as it would have done a month before, for in the frenzy of the Revolution he had seen so many fall, and in the last few days had witnessed such surprising changes, that he had acquired the feelings of a mere spectator of men's fate.

“My sister will be glad,” was all he thought. “She will divorce him, and will marry some scapegrace.”

Going in course of time to visit her, he found her cheerfully engaged in packing a great trunk, surrounded by a group of servants, who were all in tears. These fled at his approach[174].

“What means all this?” he asked. “Art moving house?”

“Hast thou not heard, beloved? We are exiled.”

“Ali Haidar Pasha has been exiled, but thou wilt not follow!”

She turned on him, erect, with flashing eyes.

“Dost think I would desert a man of his distinction, in such misfortune, and already old?”

“But thou art young. It is too much to ask!”

“He begs me to remain behind, but I say no. What should I do or think or say alone? I love my husband more than anything. What made thee think I should desire to leave him?”

“What else was I to think, when thou didst scheme to kill him!” her brother faltered in complete bewilderment.

“That was in a cause for which men’s lives were given freely, for which I would have killed myself if needful. It was my sacrifice.”

“Still . . . thou didst show no pleasure when informed that he might live!”

“How could I feel pleasure while as yet I knew not whether the light would shine or be extinguished. Now that the light has come I am no more divided . . . . Beloved, I was willing thou should be deceived. I do not care to show my heart when it is torn and bleeding. And I think I was then child enough to feel ashamed of ever owning that I loved so old a man. I was relieved to have thee think I hated him, and yet I hated thee for the mistake. I now confess . . . . Swift death was nothing dreadful for a man like him, so upright, so unstained. My one thought was to make it swift and easy for him. The sorrow would have been for me, and with God’s help, I should have borne it. I told him lately the whole story, and he did not blame me.”

Her brother only bowed his head and kissed her hand.

---

[174] They would have fled because they were women.

UNOFFICIAL

This story first appeared in As Others See Us, published in October 1922.

It is another story that is strongly influenced by Pickthall's own political interpretation of the events in Anatolia before the First World War. It is a fictional representation of some of his journalism.

Pickthall is punctilious about the dates of happenings in the story, which were the spring of 1913. At this time Pickthall was himself living in Istanbul. The Grand Vizier who was assassinated in June was Mahmut Şevket Pasha. The location of the story is a city in eastern Anatolia. It could be Van, ten miles or so from the (then) frontier, by a lake fringed with snow-capped mountains. Pickthall never himself went to Van.

Pickthall's championship of the Young Turks made him sympathetic to the Ottoman case against Armenians. The Armenians constituted a third of the population of the provinces of eastern Anatolia that were adjacent to the Russian-occupied provinces of Kars and Ardahan. There the population was also mixed and the Russians who occupied the territory of today's Republic of Armenia used Armenian grievances to provoke and undermine Ottoman authority. There was a range of Armenian political feeling from allegiance to the Ottomans to revolutionary Armenian nationalism. Before 1914 there were numerous outbreaks of communal violence throughout eastern Anatolia.

Pickthall's sympathies also colour his portrayal of individuals. The provincial governor is idealised and humane in a difficult situation, a conscientious public servant. He refuses a bribe, though Pickthall notes he has in the past taken backhanders.

The characters are undeveloped and represent Pickthall's own stereotypes: noble governor, duplicitous Armenian merchant, prejudiced and uncomprehending English travellers.

After dark one winter's evening two muffled figures stole forth from a town of Eastern Anatolia, through the orchards to the house leased by the Turkish governor. The leader, a tall servant, bore a lantern to show up the path. All day long it had been raining, but by then the sky was clear. Great winking stars looked down through leafless branches, which took fantastic forms like stretched-out arms and heads of human hair erect in terror. There was no sound except the sighing of the wind and an occasional dog's bark out of the distance. They met no one till they drew quite near to the Pasha's residence, when a soldier sprang out of the shadows and inquired their business.

"It is very private, very urgent," said the man who walked behind.

"My master is familiar with His Excellency," said the lantern-bearer.

"Vouchsafe the name!" the orderly insisted.

The servant whispered it. It was the name of the most wealthy and respected of Armenian merchants. The soldier, deferential in a second, led them up to the selamlik – a kiosk-like building separated from the house. The place was dark. The soldier brought a lamp, and then a vessel of glowing charcoal, closed the shutters of the windows, and retired.

After a quarter of an hour of waiting, during which they risked no word above the breath, the Pasha came to them. He was a man of fifty, iron-gray and upright, with keen blue eyes and a commanding air. Before him, the Armenian merchant, who had now thrown off his wraps, looked like an aged walrus blinking at the light, his servant the same creature in the prime of life. The governor sat down on the divan and made the merchant sit beside him.

"What is your business?" he inquired after the formal courtesies.

"Ah, Vâh! Vâh! Vâh!" (Woe! Woe! Woe!) the merchant blubbered, flinging up his arms; and "Vâh! Vâh! Vâh!" intoned the servant, squatting down beside the door. And then the merchant broke into a tale of fear, speaking as one who seeks protection and advice, the servant at each pause ejaculating: "Vâh! Vâh! Vâh!"

The Armenian revolutionary committees were once more active in the province – worse than ever! They were creatures of ill-omen. He, the merchant, could remember their iniquities of old, which drew down punishment upon the whole Armenian nation. He, Grégoire Aramîan, the most respected merchant, had been threatened by them, forced under pain of dreadful tortures to subscribe to their accursed funds. A friend of his, who had refused to do so, had been killed, but not till he had seen his daughters ravished and his sons impaled. That happened years ago. And now the menace was renewed, with greater violence! What was a man who had a wife and family, for whom he was responsible to

God, to do? The whole Armenian population was completely terrorised. They knew that if they disobeyed those men's injunctions they would die a hideous death, and on the other hand they knew that the design of the committees was so to rouse the anger of the Mussulman majority as to bring about a general massacre of the Armenian Christians, which would serve as an excuse for the advance of the detested Russian armies, already gathering, he heard, beyond the frontier. It was a chain of misery without an end.

"All this I know," replied the governor, with some asperity, the note of lamentation growing tedious to his ears.

"They boast that the whole force of Russia is behind them, that the Czar, who is become their father, will establish an Armenian empire extending from the foothills of the Caucasus to the Cilician gates. It is incredible, of course. But unwise people will believe them!" The merchant Grégoire wrung his hands and wept real tears. His servant, by the door, cried: "Vâh! Vâh! Vâh!"

"Allah is greater!" said the governor. "And you subscribed to their demands."

"What was I to do, Effendim?"

"Ah, what else, indeed!"

"Your Excellency is aware of my devotion to the government, and that of thousands of my people – the immense majority."

"Of course; but it surprises me that the immense majority should be intimidated by so few – so very few – incendiaries."

"But they are armed."

"If only the bad characters of the Armenian nation possess firearms, then we have only to consult the list of those who hold gun-licences," remarked the Pasha drily. "I did not know the question was so simple."

"Your Excellency is pleased to jest," replied the merchant sadly. "But for the rest of us it is a serious matter. Only think, a Russian army gathered near the frontier, and the revolutionaries urging people to rebellion, at a time when all the garrisons are much depleted, and the Sultan is engaged in a disastrous war in Europe!"

"We have thought of it enough," replied the governor. "In future we intend to think no more, but act."

"But the means at Your Excellency's disposal are inadequate. The troops are few."

"Vâh! Vâh! Vâh!" the servant interjected.

"I do not count upon the troops alone, but on the loyalty of all those thousands of Armenians of whom you spoke just now, who, like yourself, profess devotion to the government," exclaimed the Pasha, rising.

"I would not count on them too much," muttered the merchant gloomily, "for, as I told Your Excellency, they are much afraid."

"At least, I count on you," the Pasha said, with a most friendly smile.

"I am your servant," murmured the old man with some emotion, but he shook his head. The servant having then prepared the lantern, the pair took humble leave and passed into the night, exclaiming: "Vâh! Vâh! Vâh!"

The Pasha crossed the courtyard to the house. All that the Armenian had told him he had known before, and yet the interview left in his mind a sense of evil tidings. Perhaps it was the spectacle, which it revealed, of a great multitude intimidated by the antics of a few banditti and driven towards a course which every one of them was loth to take. Most of the Armenian folk at heart were loyal, as that man had said; most of them hated and distrusted Russia; but they all distrusted one another, and yet held together weakly like a flock of sheep; easily controlled by any one who shouted orders in Armenian. Inquiring of a servant if the ladies of his household were at leisure, the governor was told they also were receiving visitors. The news surprised him greatly, for the women of the town were not accustomed to go out at all at night.

He turned aside into a kind of office bare of furniture save for a desk and chair, and a divan against one wall. When lights were brought, he told his orderly to hasten to the barracks in the town and call the commandant; and then sat down and did some work upon a long report to his superiors, till the clank of spurs and sounds of salutation in the vestibule informed him that the commandant had come. Even then he went on writing for a moment, being at a crucial point.

The commandant, an old man with a white moustache, strode in, saluted with a smile and, seeing that his chief was busy, took a seat on the divan and, pulling out a chaplet from his belt, began to tell the beads. The governor at length laid down his pen, and went and sat beside him. He inquired: "What news?"

"Nothing particular to-day, Effendim, except the usual rumours of disorder and the spread of treason."

"What can be done?"

"Nothing, Effendim, while the trouble is thus scattered, for our force is much too small to be dispersed. Wait till it reaches something like a head, then I will strike with all the might available."

"No good," replied the governor decidedly, "for that would be to play into the hands of Russia. Be good enough to listen, soul of mine!" He laid his hand on his companion's arm and lectured him in a low tone. Their conversation lasted about half an hour. In the end the commandant sprang up and, standing to attention, said: –

"Effendim, let me recapitulate before I go, to ascertain that I have everything quite clear in mind. I send this telegram in cipher to Stamboul at once. I circulate an order to the troops and frontier-guards to keep strict watch for arms of all descriptions, to report their passage and, where possible, their destination, but to avoid collisions which might make a noise; also to report all movements of banditti or suspected rebels. Upon news of any wrong committed on the Muslim population, I am to make haste to the scene of crime with force sufficient to prevent attempts at vengeance by the population which might furnish an excuse for interference to a foreign Power. Say, is that all, Effendim?"

"That is all."

The commandant saluted and withdrew.

The governor resumed his writing for a while. His chief anxiety was for his wife and daughters, for the Armenian revolutionaries, if successful, were sure to massacre the Muslim population, and a Russian army was not likely to restrain them. He wished that he had never let his household leave Stamboul; but at the time of his appointment to this mountain government, the guns of the barbarians were thundering on the Chatalja line[175], and he had thought, when granting their request to bear him company, that there would be less danger for them in the East.

The Ottoman Power was not at war with Russia. That ancient enemy had not come forward openly as instigator of the Balkan States in their combined attack. But everybody knew how her designs had been frustrated by the independent spirit of Bulgaria; and so, desirous always of despoiling Turkey, she now was trying to provoke a cause of war in Eastern Anatolia by favouring Armenian anarchists and other malcontents. The Russian armies in the Caucasus were much superior to any force that he and all his colleagues on the frontier could at that time hope to raise; and in his case the frontier was but ten miles off. He was going to do his duty to the utmost; but the task seemed hopeless, death the best reward.

Inquiring once again about the ladies, he heard that they were now at liberty and went to join them. Their visitors, like his, he learnt, had been Armenians, who had come to warn him of the trouble brewing in the land. The girls were pleasantly excited, and the mother sad.

---

[175] The defensive line, a dozen miles from Istanbul, between the Black Sea and the Sea of Marmara, serving as the outer defences of the city.

"They say the Russian army is advancing," cried the elder daughter. "Well, we will drive it back, we Muslim women, with our teeth and hands."

"I have a pistol," said the younger, "and have practised shooting. I will cut my hair and dress up as a man."

The governor smiled sadly at their foolishness, thinking that, if the worst came, he would kill them both.

That was on the fifteenth of March.

On March 17th, the governor received a telegram from Stamboul, from the best friend he had at court, the secretary to the Grand Vizier, assuring him that the attention of His Highness had been called to his report of troubles.

On March 18th the commandant reported the capture by some frontier-guards of fifteen hundred Russian rifles packed in bales like cotton goods and carried on the backs of mules. According to a muleteer's confession, they were destined not for the Armenians, but some disaffected Kurds.

"Aha!" exclaimed the governor within himself. It is not enough to provoke vengeance; they must also, to make altogether sure, provide the means by which that vengeance shall be executed." He told the commandant to keep the matter secret.

On March 21st a secret agent of Armenian birth, who had been sent three months before to Tiflis to spy out the land, craved audience and informed him that the well-known Kurdish brigand, Kara Ahmed, who, for his crimes, had long been outlawed by the Turkish government, had been received with princely honours by the Russian viceroy, who at the same time was exciting the Armenian revolutionaries with hopes of independence to be gained by Russia's help.

"How can they be independent while they live as a minority among a warlike Muslim population?" mused the governor. "Their aim is to exterminate the Muslims with the help of Russian troops."

He sat with eyes cast down, telling his beads.

"What were the tidings in the villages through which you passed?" he asked aloud of the informer.

"The Armenians hear a rumour that the Muslims will rise up and slay them suddenly, and the Muslims hear the same of the Armenians. It is said in Tiflis that the Russian army only waits for some occurrence which can be made to justify invasion in the eyes of Europe."

Acting upon this and other similar reports, the governor convoked a general meeting of the Ulema[176]. It took place three days later in a hall adjourning the great mosque. The governor explained to the Mohammedan divines the delicacy

[176] The Muslim religious leadership.

of the whole position and its danger, and begged them, in the interests of El Islâm, to keep the Muslim population calm whatever happened. They all replied: "To hear is to obey."

On March 28th a Muslim family, inhabiting a lonely house some two hours' journey from the town was massacred. So lonely was the spot that the atrocity was not discovered until thirty-six hours after it occurred. On March 30th, in the early morning, the governor himself rode over to inspect the scene of the crime. The cottage of the murdered family stood by a lake. Beside it was an orchard, and behind, a wooded hill. It was a sunny day. The waters of the lake were brushed by a light breeze, which troubled the reflection of the great, blue, snow-capped mountains on the farther shore. The peaceful beauty of the place enhanced the tragedy.

When he had seen the mutilation of the bodies the Pasha cursed the murderers beneath his breath. The well-trained soldiers of his escort murmured vengeance. What would have been the conduct of the Muslim rabble of the town? He caused the corpses to be covered up and buried quickly, bidding the soldiers speak to no one of their mutilations. Among the troops detailed to hunt the murderers the tidings spread, however, and increased their zeal. A little company of five Armenians – who, strange to say, were men of education – was surrounded in a wood. Things taken from the cottage of the murdered Muslims were found upon them. They were brought back to the town in bonds and, one by one, interrogated by the governor. Each, when he found himself alone, in peril of his life, confessed the plot, which aimed at far more than the slaughter of a simple family. Upon the information thus obtained a raid was made upon a certain villa in the suburbs, where a whole armoury of bombs and other weapons was discovered, including two machine-guns sent from Russia.

There was no doubt whatever of the guilt of the five men in custody. By all the laws of nations they were Turkey's prisoners. The Russian consulate, however, denied Turkish jurisdiction upon the claim that all the five were Russian subjects. This seemed to be the case with only two of them, upon inquiry; but the consulate upheld its first demand. The governor refused to give them up until he should receive instructions from Stamboul; agreeing in the meanwhile to proceed no further with the charge.

On April 3rd came news that some Armenian brigands near the frontier had burnt a Muslim village, Kizil Tepeh, and exterminated the inhabitants. The place was distant, and the governor, conscious that his presence was most needed at the centre of affairs, sent a commission with an escort to inquire into the crime.

This commission was composed of two Armenian bishops, a Muslim judge and his own aide-de-camp.

Two days later he received a deputation from the Muslims in the district where the outrage had occurred, asking that soldiers should be sent for their protection, and another, representing the Armenians of the town itself, asking for a special guard against the Muslims who, they said, were going to take vengeance indiscriminately for crimes which were the work of thieves and outlaws. He did his best to reassure both parties. Soldiers he could not send, for he had none to spare. He felt exceedingly despondent till, on that same evening, he got a telegram in cipher from Stamboul. It was from no less a person than the Grand Vizier himself. It ran: –

"Highly approve your report of policy. Have sent two regiments, as an earnest of my strong support. Till they arrive, do nothing vigorous, avoid all acts that could be construed as offence to Russia. Am dealing with the embassy about the murderers you have in hand. Send them hither under a safe escort. We give them up; but it is more politic to do so here, before the representatives of all the Powers, who thus must take some cognizance of the affair, however loth, than in your province, where our yielding would be reckoned a great Russian victory. Thanks for your despatch, which has enabled us to question accuracy of a memorandum recently put forth by the Armenian patriarch. Another Russian move – stopped dead, by Allah's mercy. We learn that they are now on a fresh line of action. Beware the Hamidian Kurds. Watch Kara Ahmed. There are hopes of English help, if we can stave off actual war."

This message gave the governor new life. The sender was the man he most respected on earth, a strong man capable of saving Turkey. It was true that almost all the European provinces had been wrested from the Muslim empire in the last few months, with circumstances of unheard-of cruelty. It was true that his own birthplace was in hostile hand. His spirit often yearned for the green hills of Resna, the blue-eyed lake of Ochrida, his childhood's home. But the body of the empire still remained. The Muslims still possessed a splendid heritage which, by reforms and education, with the help of Allah, might yet be made a model for the world. The hope of the Grand Vizier expressed of England cheered him greatly; for England, the traditional friend of the Osmanli, the founder of the great progressive movement in the Muslim realm, had not been friendly since the Revolution. The Turks, who looked to her for active help, had been perplexed and disappointed by her attitude. Doubtless the English people had been misinformed. The Russian agents and their lies were everywhere. If England were once more prepared to give them aid, there was a hope, to match their courage, for the Turks.

The Russian consul, calling on the governor soon after he had read that missive from the Grand Vizier, was much astonished by his cheerful looks and firm replies.

On April 8th a messenger arrived in town with news that the commission delegated to investigate the massacre of Kizil Tepeh had been attacked by a strong force of brigands and annihilated. Late in the same day a more trustworthy report declared that the attacking brigands had been routed, but the governor's aide-de-camp and three soldiers of the escort had been killed, and the Armenian bishop wounded. The Pasha loved that aide-de-camp as his own son. He had, indeed, been plighted to his elder daughter. "Allah have mercy on him!" he exclaimed, with aching heart, hearing sounds of mourning from the women's portion of the house.

On the next day he learned that three of the assailant brigands, wounded in the fight and captured, were being brought into the town for judgment. He deferred their trial till the popular excitement should to some extent subside.

On April 14th came a telegram from the Ministry of the Interior, asking for immediate information on the measures which were being taken to secure the punishment of the Kurds who on the 5th of April had murdered an Armenian bishop at the altar. The Russian embassy demanded satisfaction. He replied that the usual search was being made for the Armenian brigands who on the date in question had attacked a government commission, killing a Turkish officer of distinction and three private soldiers, and wounding, among other persons, an Armenian bishop, on the open road. The said bishop, he subjoined, was far from dead, and had recovered from the trifling injuries he had received.

In reply to this despatch he got an unsigned message which, when deciphered, read: –

"Have Kara Ahmed watched!"

He had already taken steps to have that done; and as good luck would have it, while still he waited for some certain tidings of that outlawed chief, the regiment promised by the Grand Vizier arrived. At once the aspect of the town was changed as if by magic. People who had hardly ventured out of doors for months now filled the streets with talk and swaggering laughter. The peasantry poured in to market as of old. Armenian notables, who for a long while past had shunned the Turkish governor and, if they met him in the street, had slunk by with hurried salutation, as if afraid of being seen to pay him reverence, now fawned upon him. Grégoire Aramïan, that wealthy merchant, called on him in broad daylight at the office of the government and, kissing his hand repeatedly, exclaimed: "The praise to Allah for those soldiers! Praise to Allah!" It was at the very height of this enthusiasm, when the troops had been assigned by companies to all the districts where most disorders were feared, that the governor got word that Kara Ahmed with two hundred of his men disguised as learned clerks and dervishes and simple peasants had come into the town. Their leader, in the garb of a Mohammedan divine, with hennaed beard, had been already to the Russian consulate, where he had spent two hours.

The watch upon the town was strengthened to a half battalion; and on the early morning of the 21st of April, Kara Ahmed and the leaders of the band – thirty-five men in all – were surrounded by the soldiers in a yard where they were holding council, and after their deliberations had been overheard by many witnesses, attacked and overcome. They put up a brave fight. Ten of them broke away, their chief among them, and fled for refuge to the Russian consulate.

The governor, elated, took the liberty to telegraph the news directly to the Grand Vizier. In course of time he had an answer: "Praise to Allah! I shall have a statement of the facts prepared and make a solemn protest to the Powers. Do thou, meanwhile, demand the head of Kara Ahmed, who is unquestionably an Osmanli subject, and was taken in rebellion."

The governor was greatly flattered by this private message. The friendly "thou" especially delighted him, as showing that His Highness was sincerely pleased. He did as he was told, calling repeatedly upon the Russian consul, who was evidently much embarrassed to invent new reasons for evading a demand so manifestly just and reasonable. At last, on the 29th of May he finally admitted, with expressions of profound regret, that the miscreant in question had escaped he knew not whither. The governor was perfectly aware by then Kara Ahmed had been safe in Russian territory for at least three weeks; but he of course pretended ignorance of such a fact, confining himself to an expression of surprise that so notorious a wretch should not have been more strictly guarded, and a regret that the respected consul had not seen his way to deliver up the miscreant at once to Turkish custody. The consul's manner at this interview was abject, and with reason, for he had been sternly reprimanded by his government. He even uttered an apology to the Turkish governor for his refusals to give up the outlawed chief. He had, he said, been misinformed as to that person's character.

The fact, not known till later by the governor, was that a tremendous storm has risen from that local incident. The Grand Vizier was threatening to call the attention of the whole civilised world to an affair so typical of Russian methods in regard to Turkey. What made it look the worse for Russia was the fact that the Russian and Armenian newspapers at Tiflis had published full and horrible accounts of massacres of Christians alleged to have been committed by the Muslims in that very district and on the very day which had been fixed for Kara Ahmed's rising. These showed what would in fact have happened if everything had come to pass as Russia wished. The Grand Vizier used his advantage boldly; and infinite was the embarrassment in all the embassies.

The governor, perceiving that his enemy was silenced temporarily, had the houses of reputed revolutionaries searched, all on one day. Abundant evidence was found of Russia's guilt. On the day after these discoveries, as he was driving from the government building in the city to his private house, two shots were fired on him from a window. One of his fingers on the left hand, which was resting on the carriage door, was shot away, and that was all. The coachman lashed the horses to a furious gallop. The Pasha wrapped his hand up in a handkerchief, assisted by an officer who sat before him in the carriage. Both praised God for their escape.

Outside the town His Excellency noticed white pavilions in a leafy orchard by the river bank and, leaning out, inquired their meaning of the driver.

"Some English travellers, Effendim," the man answered. "Lovers of the Armenians, who desire to see them lords of everything. They do not know them, it is evident, so well as we do. The English used to be considered sensible, but these are friends of Russia. So it is said," he added, with a shrug.

"Impossible," replied the Pasha, drawing in his head.

At his own door, a servant met him with the words: –

"Two English beys await Your Excellency in the garden house."

"I go to them at once," replied the Pasha, and he strode towards the selamlik gaily. He liked Englishmen. But before he reached the door he noticed that the handkerchief on his left hand was soaked with blood. He turned back to the house to get a proper bandage, and it was quite ten minutes ere he could appear before his visitors.

He offered them a cordial welcome to the town and province. But their demeanour chilled him at a glance. One was clean-shaven, of a monkish gravity. The other wore a thin moustache and beard, red turning gray.

Dismayed by the severity of their appearance, the Pasha kept his eyes downcast while they explained the purpose of their visit. It was not, as he had thought, the simple compliment of persons of condition to the local governor. They had heard, it seemed, from some Armenian friends of theirs, of a poor lad who had been kidnapped by the Turkish soldiers and was being kept in prison for no reason; and had come to make a protest in the name of justice. Both spoke intelligible French; and their denunciations of the Turkish mode of government, which they judged upon the surface only with no knowledge of the depths, distressed the governor because the speakers happened to be English, the people most beloved of the Osmanlis[177].

He tried to make them realise the difficulties of which the government of a wild Anatolian province had to fight, speaking his mind more earnestly and freely than he would have done to chance acquaintances of another race, being sincerely anxious to convince them that they had been misled. They listened with apparent incredulity, and, when he paused, returned to the Armenian youth who was in prison.

The Pasha asked to be excused a moment and, going out, made some inquiries of his secretary. When he came back after a few minutes, he was able to assure his visitors that the person in whose case they took an interest had not been "kidnapped", nor arrested by mistake, nor kept in prison without valid reason. The youth had been arrested in connection with a certain outrage, because two bombs were found in his possession. His trial would be public, and would take place in the coming week. If any one had any evidence to give on his behalf, they would have the opportunity to state it then. It was not possible for him, the governor, to interfere in such a case before the judgment.

And then a strange thing happened. The clean-shaven visitor, who was, if anything, the sterner of the two, suddenly flushed up to the roots of his grey hair and, with a face of righteous indignation, blurted: –

"If a reasonable sum of money will facilitate the matter, I will pay it."

The Pasha felt exceedingly disgusted, yet he had to laugh. Although he had accepted presents in his time, he had never known them offered in that manner, nor for a matter which concerned his honour as a servant of the State. Attributing the rudeness to a total ignorance of Turkish customs, he tried to change the subject of the conversation. But they would not, reverting always to the misdeeds of the Turkish government, particularly in regard to the Armenian Christians. The governor, dismayed to hear such unfavourable judgments from the lips of Englishmen, spoke to them of the wildness of the people in those provinces, and of the evil influence of Russia, quoting instances. But, far from sympathising with him, they grew only more indignant.

"Russia is right to protect these unfortunate Christians," remarked the bearded one, with icy vehemence.

"The Czar's yoke, however heavy it may be, will still be preferable to the Sultan's," said the other. "You cannot blind us to the truth. We have been

---

177 Ottomans.

travelling for weeks among the people. We have heard the stories which all classes have to tell of massacre and persecution."

"Are you acquainted with their language?" asked the Pasha, curious.

"No, but we have with us a good interpreter."

"An Armenian, possibly?"

"Certainly, an Armenian."

"Well, we could tell you stories on our side," remarked the Pasha, laughing.

"No doubt," said the clean-shaven one, with nose in air.

"Well, we could tell you stories on the other side. You should go and talk to some Armenians in this town – without your dragoman. There is M. Grégoire Aramïan, our greatest merchant, to whom I can introduce you if you like."

"It would not be worth while, for we depart to-morrow."

It was at that moment of the conversation that a soldier entered with a telegram.

"Excuse me for one moment," said the Pasha, opening it. The message was in cipher. He had to leave his guests a while and go into his private room, to make it out.

"The Grand Vizier was assassinated before noon to-day, as the result of a plot for the extermination of the government. Praise be to God, the government holds firm. The conspirators are known familiars of the Russian and British embassies."

The Pasha tore the paper into little bits, as he strolled back to the selamlik, where he resumed his conversation with the Englishmen. With amiable bows and smiles he placed his judgment at their service. Everything was as they wished. Now that he came to think of it, he might perhaps do something to befriend that young Armenian since he was their protégé. Of course, the Ottoman régime, though much improved, must seem firm and antiquated to their Western eyes. Doubtless the Russian government was more efficient, and so on. He no longer offered any opposition to their point of view. He did not think it worth his while to waste his breath in seeking to dispel the prejudices of known enemies.

A MATTER OF TASTE

This story first appeared in As Others See Us, published in October 1922.

Pickthall's enthusiasm for the Ottoman Empire was for the Turkish Muslim element. He deplored what he called the Levantines, the mixture of communities, Armenian, Jewish and Greek, some of whom had acquired a European nationality. His feelings affected the coloured way he described them, introducing them as "parasites upon the noble Turk". In the text it comes across as irony, but it reflected his actual opinions. His prejudice comes across when he describes the Greek mother and daughter as they are shopping in the Grande Rue de Pera; the central character was "threading his way among the over-dressed, unwholesome crowd of Levantines, when a woman dressed as only harlots dress in England, smiled and bowed to him. It was Molly Alamatapoulo, out shopping with her mother, a huge sallow woman in a purple gown, low-necked and trimmed with artificial pearls, white gloves, white boots and an enormous hat with feathers."

The story is focussed on a young Englishman and his relationship with a Levantine family. There are no significant characters who are Turkish, Arab or Muslim. The story could be classed with his English fiction, for there is the same sensitivity to social position and appropriate English dialogue.

If Stanley Jackson wished to travel, it was more from youthful energy, the desire to move about and overcome new obstacles, than from any curiosity regarding foreign peoples and their habits. These he knew beforehand, with the firm conviction of religious faith, to be inferior. Happening to hear of a vacancy in a mercantile house at Constantinople, in the spirit of adventure he applied for and obtained the post, thinking himself lucky to escape the tame existence of a bank clerk in a little country town. On the journey which he made from Marseilles by a steamer of the Messageries Maritimes service, he gravitated naturally towards the only other Britisher on board, a taciturn and rufous[178] Scot, to the extent of walking up and down the deck with him for hours on end, or lolling by his side in canvas chairs; not that he found this individual at all attractive, but because he held out that any native of these isles, however surly, must in nature, be preferred to any foreigner.

The Scotchman evidently thought the same. They exchanged remarks about the steamer's build and speed with wholesome pity for the French as seamen; grumbled about the food occasionally, and wondered who had won the Rugger Match. At Naples, where they went on shore, it was their one desire to get an English newspaper; at Athens, to devour an English steak. And on the quay at Ghalatah one sunny morning they parted with a casual nod on either side, never to meet again. The Scotchman was employed on some new railway, at that time pushing inland from the Black Sea coast. Jackson instantly forgot him, to attach himself as conscientiously to the next compatriot with whom he happened to be thrown. This was his new employer, an old gentleman who had lived too long abroad to take an interest in current football, the subject on which Jackson talked with most enthusiasm. He atoned for this deficiency, however, by his general kindness, introducing the newcomer to the English colony – hospitable, homely people, if a thought behind the times – and found him lodgings in a "pension" at Cadi-keuy[179], kept by an Englishwoman married to a Greek. He and two older Englishmen – a Mr. Jones and a Mr. Pilling – both like himself employed in commerce, formed the aristocracy of this establishment, though they recognised the presence of some dozen foreigners and even on occasion spoke to them. From his bedroom window high up in the building, Jackson could see, between the high-pitched, old tiled roofs of Cadi-keuy, Seraglio Point, the Mosque of Sultan Ahmed and the lighthouse, steadfast amid the dance of azure sea.

He mentioned this look-out in his first letter to his people, observing that it was as pretty as a painting – an artist could make something of it, he opined. But every morning when, in company with Jones and Pilling, he went by steamer to the bridge which joins Stamboul to Ghalatah, the glorious city with its mosques, the shifting panorama of the Bosphorus, the crowd composed of all the nations of the earth, impressed him as mere background to the life of Englishmen. Among the shipping he looked out for English craft; among the crowd he noticed only English faces; and the sycophancy of the Levantines of his acquaintance confirmed him in this good opinion of his race.

---

178 Reddish faced.

179 Kadiköy, on the Asian side of the Bosphorus.

Pilling was the oldest of the three – a man of forty, with amorous and social inclinations which made him tolerant of Greeks and nondescripts to a degree which struck his younger companions, who pitied the attachés at the Embassy for being forced to mix up with a lot of foreigners, as hardly decent. It was he who, when they would have sat indoors each evening, smoking their pipes and talking of the things of home, dragged them out sometimes to the social gatherings which he frequented; and it was on one of those reluctantly endured occasions that Stanley Jackson met the girl who was his ruin.

There was resident at Moda near to Cadi-keuy a family of wealthy Levantines, the Alamatopoulos; of which the father had, by one means or another, become a British subject in his youth. The family was thus classified as English among the medley of commercial tribes and nations which live as parasites upon the noble Turk. The children were called Percy, Jack and Molly Alamatopoulo, and, if asked their nationality, made answer: "Eng-leesh". The boys, both in the twenties, were short, dark, strongly perfumed, and obsequious in manner. Molly, the girl, was a resplendent beauty of the Eastern mould. At the age of eighteen, when she first met the shocked and frightened eyes of Stanley Jackson, she was as near to perfection, both of form and features, as a girl can be. Jackson, on his side, was a personable youth enough, though very gruff and awkward in society. It was his uncouthness which at first attracted Molly Alamatopoulo. It was so English.

"Why do you stand there all alone, Mr Jackson?" asked the hostess of the evening, coming on him in a corner of the long veranda, where he stood smoking a cigarette and staring at the lights across the Bosphorus. "Come, I will introduce you to an English girl who dies to know you."

The English girl was Molly Alamatopoulo. Had she been introduced as Greek he might have borne with her contemptuously. The cool assumption of the English name by that dark, lissom creature, demonstrative as no English girl could ever be, abounding in soft gestures and alluring glances, aroused in him an indignation which dispelled reserve. Her loveliness, compact of light as were the fabled sylphs, a light for ever being reborn out of darkness, offended Stanley Jackson's native prejudices.

"Come, I say now, you're not English really!" was his first remark after their introduction.

"Yes, I am English real-lee," she replied, with glance and smile so shamelessly seductive that he blushed for her. "Let us sit down somewhere where we can talk comfortabl*ee*. It is so long a time since I have talked of dear old England."

She went and found a seat and beckoned to him. What could he do but follow and sit near her?

"But I say! You aren't English, you know! You can't be, really!" he cried out in anguish.

"If you mean that I have never been myself to England; that is true, alas! My father is an Englishman of Greek descent. My mother also is an Englishwoman, though of Greek descent."

"Well, that isn't the real thing, you know. You're only naturalised. You shouldn't call yourself English, when you're really Greek."

They argued on the subject for quite half an hour; she, in the sweetest manner, trying to coax him to allow her point of view, not caring what they talked about if only they were together; he, earnest in his efforts to convince her that she had no right to call herself an English girl.

"Then you do not wish me for your compatriot?" she asked at length, pouting, and with a sidelong glance that made him hate her.

"That's not the point," he said severely. "A fact's a fact, you know. You can't get round it."

"Well, tell me about England; tell me what you do at home," said Molly, with a shrug of absolute good humour.

Of course, at the command to talk, his tongue grew heavy; but by dint of many questions, which made him laugh in pity of her ignorance, she led him on to speak of his beloved football. She hung upon his every word with breathless eagerness. When they were disturbed by the call to join in a round game, she murmured as she rose: –

"Some other time you must continue teaching me. I am so interested. You will make me reall*ee* Engl*eesh*, will you not?"

And when they joined the party gathered round a table for the homely pastime of "Up, Jenkins", she was at his side. He felt her soft warm hand upon his own, and shrank away as if a snake had touched him.

"You seemed to get along all right with that Alamatopoulo youngster," said Pilling as they went back to the boarding-house. "I admire your taste, my boy. She's a real beauty."

"She had the cheek to call herself an Englishwoman," explained Stanley Jackson in accents of profound disgust. He did not like Miss Alamatopoulo at all; he did not even think her pretty; she was not his sort. Her image in his mind possessed indecency. It should have been the image of a practised siren, and not the image of a girl; which made it enigmatical and in a curious, unpleasant way attractive to his secret thoughts.

Between their first and second meetings he was half afraid of her. Their second meeting turned his fear to pity. It happened in the Grande Rue de Péra[180], as he was coming from the office one fine afternoon. Some people up at Bibek had asked him to play tennis, and he was clad in flannels, with a racket in his hand, threading his way among the over-dressed, unwholesome crowd of Levantines, when a woman dressed as only harlots dress in England, smiled and bowed to him. It was Molly Alamatopoulo, out shopping with her mother, a huge sallow woman in a purple gown, low-necked and trimmed with artificial pearls, white gloves, white boots and an enormous hat with feathers. The daughter wore an equally enormous hat, a pale pink gown and black gloves to above her elbow. Both carried frilly parasols. Stanley Jackson, blushing to the eyes, not for himself, but for them, stopped and allowed them to shake hands with him.

"When weell you come to veeseet us?" cried Madame Alamatopoulo. "I have heard of you so much from Moll*ee*. You must know her father, Meester Alamatopoulo, and her brothers, Jack and Perc*ee*. Verree pleased to see you. Can you come to-morrow afternoon? Without ceremon*ee*?"

"Oh, please do!" murmured Molly, with her killing smile.

He agreed in order to be rid of them, and strode off with a flourish of his hat. Faugh! He blew a great breath to be rid of their besetting perfume, and returned to thoughts of tennis with relief. The girl had rouge on her cheeks, and something beastly on her eyelids, in broad daylight! The observation laid the phantom of desire which for five days had haunted him to his defilement.

It was without fear, and therefore without much embarrassment, that he called upon her people the next day, a Sunday. The Alamatopoulos lived in a pretty villa on the rock of Moda with a garden looking on the Sea of Marmora. He found them very hospitable and polite – much too polite, as he confided afterwards to Jones; it was his complaint of all these people, they made a fellow feel an ass by fussing round him. Old Alamatopoulo, extremely fat and brown, with a walrus moustache and gold-rimmed spectacles, kept in the background with his no less portly spouse, allowing the young people to do all the talking. Jack and Percy, black-avised and sleek, with very high shirt-collars and a taste for jewellery, were duly deferential to the real Englishman, while Molly put on pretty airs of comradeship as if she and Mr. Jackson had been quite old friends. There was no rouge on her cheeks, nor antimony round her eyes, on this occasion. The impression which the visit left upon his mind was mildly favourable, near indifference. After that he did not shrink from meeting Molly.

---

[180] Istiklal Caddesi today.

There was something finished and complete about her manners and appearance which had made him think her older than she really was. It was quite a shock to him when Pilling, upon some one's wondering whom Molly Alamatopoulo would choose to marry, said: "She's only just eighteen. There's loads of time."

"You don't mean that?" cried Stanley Jackson in amazement. "I thought she was at least as old as I am."

"Fruits ripen quickly in the sun," was Pilling's answer. "As for you, you young barbarian, you'll always be green and sour, like a Scotch fig."

"I should never have dreamt it," Jackson muttered.

He had another shock in the discovery that she played tennis well, although with too much exclamation and self-consciousness. This raised her in his estimation a good deal. She remained, of course, a hopeless little "dago". Attractive in a way which he thought reprehensible; but he no longer thought of her as quite impossible, nor much resented her decided liking for himself. She was just a kid.

This was the state of his affections after some six months, when Pilling said to him one evening: –

"I wouldn't go too far, if I were you. People soon start talking, and before a man knows what he's doing he's let in for something which he never contemplated. I don't believe in marrying out here."

"Marrying? Oh, Lord!" cried Jackson wildly. "What have you gone and got into your head?"

"Well, yesterday, when we were at the Alamatopoulos, and you were out with Molly in the garden picking cherries, Madame was careful to explain to me that she would not allow her daughter to pick cherries with just any one, but with an English gentleman she felt quite safe."

"Well, what of that?" said Jackson, with some heat. "The sort of men they know – these beastly Levantines – are utter blackguards. You couldn't trust a girl like Molly out of sight with them."

"A girl like Molly! – eh?"

"I mean . . . . Oh, hang it all! Say, any girl."

When speaking of "a girl like Molly" he was thinking of her tendency to snuggle (so to speak), to lay her hand upon a fellow's sleeve, to touch his hand and so on; which he ascribed to the effusion of her southern nature. But it had occurred to him that it was no affair of Pilling's.

"Say, any girl!" he cried defiantly.

His mentor shrugged: "Well, have it as you like. I've warned you, and I think I know my ground."

Jackson thought the warning nonsense at the time, but when he pondered it alone, misgivings came to him. He remembered that her parents and her brothers had left him rather pointedly to Molly, seeming eager to secure him opportunities not usually allowed to simple friendship in the south. Alarmed at the suspicion of a project to inveigle him (a true-born Briton) into an unthinkable alliance, he determined (as he put it) to cool off. But he had already accepted an invitation from the Alamatopoulos to join a picnic party they were organising for the coming week. Having himself proposed some expedition of the kind, and having taken charge of some of the arrangements, he could not get out of it.

The party of some forty persons – mostly Levantines, elaborately dressed as for a garden party, the men all wearing gloves, the women their best hats – set out at six one morning from the quay of Cadi-keuy in a procession of six country carts devoid of springs, each with a canopy and flapping blinds of red or yellow, each with two horses and a Turkish driver. The coachmen cracked their whips, the horses galloped, the ladies grinned self-consciously at the attention they attracted, till they passed the suburbs, when their pace subsided to a steady trot. It was a three hours' journey over roads so execrable that at times the elegants were thrown a foot into the air, returning violently; were tumbled all together sideways and narrowly escaped an overturn. They did not seem to mind it in the least, though Stanley Jackson was at times alarmed for them. He was far from comfortable. Beside him in the cart sat Molly and, whether from the jolting or her own desire, she was continually leaning up against him. He could not actually push her off, nor was he able to withdraw his person any distance without indenting the soft mass of Madame Alamatopoulo, who sat upon his other side.

So he bore with the inevitable, sitting stiff and ill-at-ease, while the procession of rude vehicles with their fashionable occupants jogged through meadow valleys or jolted over rocky slopes, traversed a village of gray wooden kiosks wreathed in wistaria, clustering round a white mosque, and, crawling up a long and rough ascent, approached its destination. This was a grove of noble, ancient trees, knee-deep in fern and wild flowers, high up on a mountain side. Here, in the shade, the carts stopped and disgorged their inmates. Between the outer columns of the forest loomed the sea, uprising like a wall, as blue as ink in contrast with the sun-bleached land. After an hour of screaming preparations, a place of rest was chosen, and the luncheon spread. Stanley Jackson showed a feverish zeal in these arrangements, glad of a respite from temptations which alarmed his soul.

But after luncheon, when the elders rested and the younger members of the party wandered off in groups, he once more found himself alone with Molly. She had whispered: "Come, and I will show you where those lilies grow", and he had followed weakly, lacking the presence or strength of mind to feign fatigue. In truth, his feelings were divided in that languid moment. He saw an opportunity to "choke her off" (as he expressed it); at the same time, he doubted his own courage, his own will to do so. The day was warm, the scene doubtful, and he had eaten well and drunk his fill of country wine. He vowed that, if he got through that one day without disgrace, he would throw up his position in Constantinople and go home for safety. Never had he been so tempted in his life before. His very thoughts, his very blood, were traitors.

They sat down on a rock among the lilies, when she had picked a bunch of them, and after that were silent for some time. There was a singing in his ears. Suddenly she turned and laid her hand upon his arm.

"Why are you so silent? Don't you like to be with me?"

"Oh, Lord!" groaned Jackson in his inmost soul. His limbs were palsied, quaking, his mouth dry. She was looking at him with her great soft eyes which seemed of power to melt the marrow in his bones; he breath was on his face; she took his hand and pressed it.

"Will you not tell me what has made you sad? For you are sad to-day. Have you some trouble?" she inquired, with friendly earnestness.

Never had she seemed so lovely in his eyes, or so un-English. The attraction and the impossibility appeared to him together, alike threatening. He felt as helpless as if he had been actually pulled with equal force in two opposite directions.

"What is it, tell me! I am frightened for you," she went on insisting.

"It's nothing. Only that I am afraid that I may have to leave this country in a week or two, and I've grown fond of it."

The lie had slipped out unawares – without his will, it seemed, against his judgment; yet it struck him as about the best thing that he could have said. Her bright face clouded instantly. Tears sprang into her eyes.

She moaned: "I am so sad. How I shall miss you!"

He got up.

"I shall be sorry, too," he said with studied coolness. "Hadn't we better go back to the others? They'll be wondering where we are."

He felt an utter brute. The youngster's smile, the joy suffusing her dark beauty like an inward light, was gone, and he had killed it. And she was but a kid, after all – the thought tugged at his heartstrings – as good, perhaps, as any English girl, only so different!

Molly was very silent on the homeward road, and so, for the matter of that, was almost everybody, for the spirits of the party were not proof against fatigue. She sat against him as before, he could feel every movement of her body, and once or twice, when it grew dark, he fancied she was crying. At length, as they drew near their journey's end, jogging along a straight paved road, the lights of Cadi-keuy rising up before them, she clasped his arm and for a moment laid her head upon his shoulder whispering: "Take me with you!" His brain swam. He all but hugged her in his arms. Saving himself in time, he touched her hand, and murmured: –

"Don't make it harder for me than it is already."

She was sobbing.

"I must get away at once," he said to Pilling at the boarding-house, after confiding to the older man as much as he thought fit of the day's story. "I must get away at once," he said to his employer, on a similar confession, the next morning. Both recognised his need to fly, but the old merchant said: –

"I shall be sorry if you left us altogether. From what you say there's really no harm done. The whole thing will blow over in a month. I'll tell you what I'll do. I'll transfer you to our Egyptian house for half a year. Some one reliable is badly needed there. How will that suit you? You can start next week."

"That suits me down to the ground. I'm very grateful to you, sir."

The news that Stanley Jackson was to go to Egypt travelled quickly through the British colony and its adherent circles, and also, as things secret will leak out, the fact that he had wished to leave Constantinople. He had arranged to start on a Tuesday by the Austrian Lloyd steamer. On the Sunday morning he was sitting in his own room at the boarding-house, packing his belongings in a leisurely way, when the man-of-all-work of the boarding-house, a Laz[181] called Mukhtar, brought a card to him. It bore the printed legend: "M. Jack Alamatopoulo", and underneath, hand-written: "M. Percy Alamatopoulo". He coloured up as he made Mukhtar understand he was to show them in. He felt he was behaving shabbily towards the family, but did not see how, as an Englishman, he could have acted otherwise. They had all been so devilishly polite and hospitable, had always seemed to like him so much more than he liked them; and now they came so decently to say good-bye to him, that he felt an utter worm, as he himself expressed it. He met them with a shameful cordiality, exclaiming: "I was

[181] People of the north east Black Sea coast.

meaning to come and see you this very afternoon," before he noticed that their looks were not as usual.

They were little men, with thick black hair much greased and slightly waved – rather ridiculous little men, he had once thought them. But now they had acquired a certain dignity. Both stood bolt upright with chins held at an even higher angle than that which their shirt-collars made obligatory; both frowned like the recording angel. Jack, who was short-sighted, fixed his gold-rimmed pince-nez and observed: –

"We wish for ver*ee* serious conversation."

"Well?" asked Jackson.

"What, may I ask you, sir, are your intentions with regard to our beloved sister, Meess Mollee Alamatopoulo?"

"That is what we come to learn," emitted Percy.

"What do you mean?" asked Jackson rather crossly. "We are just good friends."

"Friends!" bellowed Percy with extreme ferocity. "You call it friends to tamper with the feelings of a girl so young and innocent? We are an honourable famil*ee*, and we do not want your friendship until we know that you are honourable like as we are. You have dragged my sister's reputation in the dirt, in the mire, with what you call your friendship. Father and mother had no fears. They thought: 'An Englishman is honourable. When he behaves to a young girl in such a way that no one after him would wish to marry her, he will not leave her there to die of shame.'"

"You're talking nonsense. You know perfectly well that there was nothing of the sort between us. We were only friends."

"Nice friends! And she is now in tears with broken heart, because you go away and scorn her after too much friendship! Nice friends, when every one has seen your conduct both at our house and also at the picnic, and every one has thought you were engaged to her!"

"That's not my fault!"

"Not your fault, sir? Not your fault?" repeated Percy, with terrific mildness.

Jack cut in: –

"I put a question to you, Meester Jackson: Will you marr*ee* my sister, Meess Moll*ee* Alamatopoulo? We stop here till we have your promise in handwriting signed and witnessed."

"Then you'll stop here till the Day of Judgment," answered Stanley Jackson.

"Then we will thrash you like the dirty leetle dog you are!" cried Percy. He struck at Jackson with his cane, but missed the stroke. Jack then attacked.

They both ran in on him. But both were mad and nearly blind with rage, while Jackson at the first blow had grown cooler than he had been since they came into the room. After some three minutes of excited struggle, he pushed them both outside the door, which Mukhtar, by good fortune, had that minute opened, coming to see what the commotion meant. The Laz took part with Jackson, and accelerated their departure down the stairs.

But the victor in this battle knew no joy. He saw the scandal which the news of such a brawl was sure to raise, and felt that it was hard on little Molly. More than ever he was anxious to be gone. He wished he could have gone that very minute. However, he must grin and bear it until Tuesday.

In the farewell visits which he had to pay he was received by the women with marked coldness, by the men with sly hilarity.

"It's all right, old fellow; it'll all blow over," Pilling told him, when his face betrayed dejection. "No Englishman of any sense will blame you. One must keep clear of dagoes, in that way. To-morrow when you're safe on board the boat, with Stamboul sinking in the sea astern, you'll thank your stars and feel a different man."

"I don't know," muttered Stanley Jackson miserably. "It's pretty beastly. I never thought of anything, that's the hard part of it."

Struggling with deep thoughts and new emotions, he was scarce articulate.

With feelings of immense relief he found himself at last upon the Austrian steamer, the centre of a little crowd of English who had come to say good-bye. And his sensation of relief increased when the ship moved at last and, standing by the bulwarks, he kept waving to his friends on shore. He watched the glorious city gliding by – the quays, the bridge, the panorama of great mosques, the palace, Sultan Ahmed and the light-house; then turned to gaze upon the other side, at Cadi-keuy and the point of Moda where she lived; and then with a deep sigh he cleared his mind and sauntered down to the saloon to have a drink. There, at the bar, he happened on a fellow-countryman, a talkative old man upon a tour around the world, with whom he stayed in conversation for some time.

When he returned on deck, the sun was setting; Stamboul had dwindled to a streak upon the far edge of the purpled sea, a mere appendage of the hills of Asia. His shadow stretched before him on the deck as he strolled towards the stern for a last look at it. A girl already stood there watching the receding coast. Her head was hooded in a white veil such as Turkish women in the country wear, her figure wrapped in a black satin cloak. She turned as he drew near. Not thinking of her, he continued to advance, until he realised that he stood face to face with Molly Alamatopoulo.

"You here?" he murmured in amazement.

Strange to say, his first sensation was of unmixed gladness at her presence. Then, as he suspected that it was a plot, that her parents or her brothers were on board with her, that he might not escape, he added in the coldest tone at his command: –

"What are you here for?"

"Don't stand like that, or people will be staring at us. Let us walk about. Give me your arm."

She took command of him, and he submitted, although his face preserved a look of obstinate distrust.

"You ask me why I am here. I wished to speak to you, and so I came."

"How many of your people are on board?" he questioned, with a savage grin.

"What do you mean? Oh, do you think – you cannot – think! Oh, I am ashamed!"

For a moment he was much afraid that she was going to cry. The plain white veil ennobled her appearance, which he had generally seen degraded by some monstrous hat. After a moment's silence, she resumed: –

"It is the fault of my brothers. They have made you think such things. They went and tried to frighten you – the fools! – on Sunday morning; and now you think that we are all alike, both they and I, and would do anything. Believe me, I knew nothing of their going to you. If I had known of their design beforehand, they should not have gone. I would have killed them sooner. Oh, and I was so glad you overcame them both and drove them out. I thought: 'My Stanl*ee* is so strong; he knows no fear.' And I was glad; but then I thought, 'he does not love poor Moll*ee*, he is flying from her', and I was so sorr*ee*. At last I thought of this which I am doing now: to come on the same ship and speak alone with you, that we may understand each other clearl*ee*. Once for all. 'Perhaps', I said, 'He does not know how much I feel.'"

"But how did you ever get here? Have you got a berth on board?"

"Yes, Stanl*ee*." Her lips parted in a childlike smile.

"But a berth costs money. Then your parents know?"

"No, Stanl*ee*. They know nothing. I just stole the money and gave it to our Muslim gardener, who bought the ticket for me."

"But what possessed you? What good can it do, your talking to me?"

"This good it can do, Stanl*ee*. It can put an end to what has so much troubled me. My talk with you is this: I ask you, will you take me with you where you're going? Yes or No? If you say yes, I shall be very happ*ee*. If you say no, I throw myself into the sea."

"You're not so mad!" cried Jackson horrified. Like a person in the act of drowning, he had the vision of his whole past life, beheld his parents and his home surroundings, his comrades, and the cool ideal of girlhood which he had always cherished in his bosom until now.

"No, Stanl*ee*. I shall do exactly as I say."

He met her eyes, and knew that she was speaking the truth.

"Well, Stanl*ee*, is it Yes or No?"

"Oh, yes, then, since you put it that way."

She pressed his arm and leaned against it lovingly.

"Thank you so much," she sighed. "You give me life. You will not regret what you have done. I swear to God."

He, though assuredly enamoured, had grave doubts of that; but it was now too late to air them with advantage. It was agreed that they should meet on deck as mere acquaintances until the boat reached Alexandria, where Molly had an aunt and uncle who would take her in while Stanley made arrangements for their marriage. The bridegroom's heart was heavy on the voyage and in the days and nights he spent at an hotel at Ramleh. He had to write the startling news to his home people and, which was worse, to people at Constantinople, where he knew that it would raise a storm of mocking laughter. But he did his best to keep a cheerful face before the girl. It was therefore with dismay that, on the day before the wedding, he heard her say: –

"I think I know what you are feeling. You are afraid, because I am not quite an English girl. I asked you – did I not? – to marry me. That you think shocking. But it was to save my life. You do not know how girls not English suffer when they love in vain. Dear Stanl*ee*, this I know: that you will not regret it."

"Of course I shan't!" said Jackson manfully. "The prettiest girl in Constantinople! I'm a lucky dog."

"You never thought me prett*ee*!" she asserted boldly, putting her face close to his. "You do not think me prett*ee* even now!"

"Oh, I do!"

"You don't. But I will make you think me prett*ee*. I will drive all that you have thought against me from your mind. I will make you love me better than an English girl, so that you shall never in your life regret that you said yes to me."

And so it may seem, she kept her word.

When after six months' absence the young couple came back to Constantinople, Stanley Jackson was already a changed man. Instead of coming shamefaced to the place where the wretched circumstances of his marriage were well known, he returned triumphant, proud of his young wife. He manifested not the least repugnance for the Alamatopoulos and all their tribe, seemed even to prefer them to his English friends. Molly might wear the most outrageous hats, might perfume her white skin or touch her cheeks with rouge, he never noticed anything amiss with her. And his delight in her increased as time went on.

His English friends observed the process of degeneration. He grew fatter every month, and less inclined for manly exercise. On the other hand, he was now making money with the assistance of the Alamatopoulos, who knew the ins and outs of all financial ventures, and was a great deal more polite and amiable than of yore.

"He's just a dago!" exclaimed Jones disgustedly, one evening after he and Pilling had met and talked with Jackson on the Cadi-keuy boat. "Whoever would have thought a decent Englishman could change his skin like that?"

"He's happy," answered Pilling, with a shrug. "There's only one thing English girls are bad at – that is, love. They think too much about themselves. They keep a man in a perpetual state of irritation, which produces energy. Now little Molly has made Jackson happy. He's content to be a dago – any blessed thing – with her. You mustn't blame him. It's a question of supply and demand."

"I call it a question of good taste," said Jones fastidiously.

THE MARSEILLES TRAGEDY

This story first appeared in As Others See Us, published in October 1922.

It is located first in a village on the Marmara Sea, and then in Marseilles. The time is 1908, after the reissue of the Ottoman constitution and after the Austrian annexation of Bosnia and Herzegovina. These events made Pickthall strongly committed to the Ottoman Muslim view. The Young Turk Revolution was a promise of a reinvigorated Islam. The different elements of Ottoman society were being brought together.

Pickthall was rarely fair to the Christian communities of the Eastern Mediterranean. His Christian characters are murderous fanatics and his Muslim characters liberal and noble. It is true that elsewhere in his fiction, Pickthall creates plenty of Muslim villains, but in this story the ethical contrasts between the Ottoman Greeks and Ottoman Muslims could not be greater.

As always Pickthall is excellent in setting the scene, describing the physical appearance of the village and the behaviour of the people. There is also a good section on Marseilles, how a naïve Greek from Turkey would see the city, and how poorer migrants were treated in Europe. They were herded into quarantine camps on an offshore island, and then exploited by a bullying Syrian who rented out rooms.

In the drink-shop – a kiosk on a little pier built out into the water of the inland sea, an old man full of arak wept continuously, while those around him offered words of sympathy and plied him with the potent liquor, drinking too. Among these sad carousers was a priest, a little fierce-eyed man whose speech consisted of appeals to God, the Virgin and the saints. The sea laughed in the splendid sunlight under a light breeze, lapping the pebbles of the beach with a refreshing sound and moving a few boats about the landing-stage; while from the hill of houses interspersed with gardens came peaceful human noises and the coo of doves.

The old man, with mouth hanging open, and tears running down his wrinkled cheeks, sobbed: –

"May my right hand wither if I go not now to kill her."

"Wait for the deputation," growled his son, who sat beside him. The young one had been drinking quite as freely as the old, but the result in him was grim excitement and not weakness.

"Aye – Lord of Heaven! – that is good advice," put in the priest. "They may restore the girl – the Holy Virgin grant it! – when thou and Dmitri here can kill her quietly."

"My father and my mother are to blame. They spoilt her with indulgence," said the young man, Dmitri.

At that his father's grief became convulsive. He wailed out: "Woe the day! The sun is blackened! Holy St. Michael, save me, for I burn in hell, and naught can quench the burning save my daughter's blood."

"Be patient, Dmitri," said the priest in chiding tone. "Thy father is distraught with righteous grief. – The saints protect us! – It is a sin for thee to vex him in so dark an hour."

"Do not know him?" sneered the young man bitterly. "He weeps and drinks and curses, that is all. I know he will resign himself to this, as to all other ignominy. As for me, I swear to kill my sister, Miriam, sooner or later, though it take me years. God knows how fondly I have always loved her!"

"The Lord give strength to thy right arm!" exclaimed the priest approvingly, and all who heard the benediction said, Amen.

From the place where Dmitri sat between his father and the priest, he could see a good way up a street of steps which cleft the village. There presently he spied a group of men, descending, under sunshades, leisurely. It was the deputation coming back from its long visit to the representative of Turkish government in Merdiven-keuy[182]. Some women from the houses ran out, questioning, and soon the men down in the drink-shop heard distinctly their angry crying of one word: "Refused!" The old man moaned out, "Lord have mercy!" seeming at the point of death. His son shrugged up his shoulders and laughed bitterly.

---

[182] Merdivenkŏy is a suburb of Istanbul, on the Asian side, east of Kadikŏy. Pickthall spend six months in 1913 living in Erenkŏy, between Merdivenkŏy and the Sea of Marmara. But Pickthall suggests that Merdivenkŏy is actually on the sea shore. Merdivenkŏy means, in Turkish, village of the steps, referring to the street of steps.

"Alas, my brothers," said the headman as he, with others of the deputation, joined them, bidding the tavern-keeper bring a whole decanter full of arak with salted dainties to enhance his pleasure in the drink. "All was in vain. I spoke about our ancient privileges, and the law forbidding all attempts at our conversion. I spoke, too, of the Constitution and the promise of improved conditions lately made to us. His Honour called the culprit and his father to confront us. They swore, of course, that they had no intention to convert the girl, nor hinder from practising the Christian faith."

"She shall not have the sacraments in Merdiven-keuy," cried the priest vindictively. "And what said the mudîr himself?"

"He talked," replied the headman, with a shrug, "a long tale about toleration and the blessings of the Constitution, and how the Muslims are henceforth our brothers."

There were loud, scornful laughs. Young Dmitri ground his teeth and cried:–

"She shall not live!"

"Now comes the most important part," pursued the headman. "Although of European education, the mudîr is still a Turk. After talking about brotherhood and progress a long while, just as we were rising to depart, he looked me in the eyes – a tiger-glance – and said: 'If any harm befalls the bride of Mahmûd Agha, I punish the whole Christian commune. So beware!' He is not such a harmless one as he at first appears. He knows our hearts. Therefore it behoves us to move cautiously."

"She shall at least be excommunicated," said the priest.

"Be careful even there," replied the headman gravely.

"Merciful Christ!" arose the general murmur of dismay.

"Thy Englishman might help; he is a sort of Christian," said a fair-haired man to Dmitri privately.

"I am going now to try him," was the answer of the angry youth, who soon departed from the drinking-shop without a word to any one.

The trouble had originated on a summer's day of the preceding year, when men had come by boat to Merdiven-keuy from the chief town of the coast, and had proceeded up the street of steps with banners; pausing before the church to make harangues in Greek and Turkish, pausing again for the same purpose underneath a mulberry-tree half up the hill, and then again in the wide open space before the mosque; announcing that the day of brotherhood, of equal rights and justice had dawned at last for all the human race. It took time for the simple folk of Merdiven-keuy to grasp the meaning of the learned words, but when the Muslim khoja kissed the Christian priest upon both cheeks, hailing him brother, there were shouts of praise to Allah, and the town went mad. Christians were made welcome in the mosque, and Muslims in the church, at the thanksgiving services; and all that day and night the two streams in the population, which had flowed apart for centuries, mingled and ran together in a single flood.

It was towards morning that Dmitri, going homeward with a lantern through his father's orchard, espied a Christian girl in conversation with a Muslim man. He did not recognise his sister; but his soul was angered, and in the morning he informed the priest, who preached upon the next Sunday. Still the goodwill continued till the day when it was known in Merdiven-keu that Austria had annexed two Turkish provinces[183] and Bulgaria had thrown off the last scrap of allegiance, with impunity.

The men who had harangued them on the day of liberty had said the Christian Powers were all in favour of the new ideas. They, who had long looked forward to a Christian conquest of the country, enabling them to extirpate and spoil the Muslims, had thought their hope of domination at an end. They now beheld the talk of equal justice as a mere device to rob them of those ancient privileges by means of which they could embarrass and obstruct the government; a plot to level them with Muslims and submerge them quite. They thus became suspicious of the new arrangements; resisted a proposed improvement of the education in their school, quarrelled with the appointment of votes for the new parliament and regarded military service for the Christians as a cruel outrage, finding in every new proposal food for hate. And now, as the result of the new-fangled nonsense, a Christian maid was taken by a Muslim man!

That Miriam had left her parents of her own accord, and after persecution, made no difference. No Christian girl must look with favour on a Muslim. The punishment for such a crime in decent families was always death, the task of killing being on the next of kin. If she remained unpunished, all her race would be ashamed, and Muslims would be always after Christian girls.

The sunny day was dark in Dmitri's eyes as he passed up the staircase street into the Muslim quarter with its latticed windows and walled gardens imparting to each house a look of proud reserve, past the white mosque with minarets like candlesticks, to open country where, beneath a pear-tree, the Englishman had pitched his little camp.

This person, though apparently a man of wealth, had the peculiar madness of wandering around the world with guns in chase of birds; and, still more strange to say, his wife accompanied him. Dmitri was their guide on more than one

[183] This was the annexation of Bosnia and Herzegovina, Ottoman territories but administered by Austria.

excursion and, when a servant of their camp fell ill, he had replaced him. They had been at Merdiven-keuy now for several weeks and as they knew some Greek but little Turkish, he had contrived to interest them in the Christians of the place. The priest, the headman and the schoolmaster had been to visit them, and told them many things about the Musulmans.

The pair, though odd, were Christians of a sort and so would shudder when they heard of the choice of Miriam. But Dmitri had sufficient doubt about their Christianity to recognise the need of caution in approaching them with such a tale. Their talk was sometimes almost indistinguishable from the talk of Muslim rationalists. Once or twice it had inspired him with an inkling that they might be freemasons[184] – a kind of persons whom he classed with Muslims in imagination– people who deny the efficacy of the priesthood and the sacraments and all the magic proofs of Christianity. He was therefore full of thought as he approached the tent.

"What is it, Dmitri?" asked the Englishman.

"I come to beg your help, sir," he exclaimed dramatically, wringing his hands. "My best beloved sister has been taken by the Muslims and put in a harem. The Christians all are grieved and very angry."

"You don't mean that they took her from your father's house?"

"No, but they tempted her – a girl so young, and knowing nothing of the kind of people that they are, nor yet the kind of place to which they take her."

The Englishman went to the tent mouth, calling "Grace!" on which his wife appeared from the adjoining tent and, having heard the tidings in her turn, expressed deep horror. She was a champion of her sex and in her calls at Christian houses, gave strange counsel to the women, who pronounced her mad.

"All that we wish," said Dmitri, sobbing, "is that they give her back to us, that she have time to think. She does not know the wicked thing that she is doing. They will make her curse our Lord!"

"I don't suppose that they'll do that," replied the burly Englishman; "but I think it likely she will suffer for her foolishness."

"It is horrible enough in any case," exclaimed the lady. "The Muslims take so low a view of women."

"There is another thing which hurts us," put in Dmitri eagerly. "No Muslim girl is free to wed a Christian – no more since the Revolution than before. When one poor Muslim girl did do it, in Constantinople, all the Muslims rose and killed her and the man together very cruelly."

"The savages!" exclaimed the English lady, with clenched teeth.

[184] Pickthall was a Freemason.

She and her husband strove to comfort the young man. They spoke of going straight to the mudîr and threatening, in the case of a refusal to restore the girl, to bring the matter to the knowledge of the British Embassy. Dmitri was then dismissed, a little reassured, with orders to return at night and hear the news.

But when he did return, he found them changed. The lady, it appeared, had seen his sister, who declared herself quite happy with her Muslim lord. She had been astonished by the courtliness of her reception and by the fact that Miriam's husband had no other wives. Too late, Dmitri realised that he had been unwise to rouse false expectations with his talk of harems; for the mudîr, who spoke good French, had told the Englishman with hearty laughter that no such luxury existed at the present day. When he spoke against the law forbidding Muslim girls from marrying Christians, the Englishman had been informed that Christians thought it necessary to convert their spouses, whereas Islâm allowed full liberty of conscience. And when he argued on this point, maintaining that the Christians were more tolerant, the mudîr answered: –

"That may be the case in England; it is not so here. Here they do not think at all of Christos and his teaching, which we also venerate, but only of the priests' inventions and their magic tricks. Do you know why they wish to have this girl restored to them? It is because they wish to kill her, they are so fanatical."

The Englishman reported this to Dmitri with a laugh, observing: –

"So you see, they think of you as wrongly as you think of them. However, I am glad my wife has seen your sister. You will now be able to assure your parents that she is not unhappy."

"Ah, sir, you do not know the half!" Dmitri wailed, and fled from consolations which increased his grief. As he strode back through the village in the dark, he swore that he would taste no joy till he had knifed his sister.

This oath he kept repeating in the days which followed, even after his mother had paid Miriam a visit, and his father had tamely accepted bounty from the Muslim bridegroom. His vow of sacrifice became the common talk; till one day he was called by the mudîr, who thus addressed him: –

"Thou art the person named Dmitri, son of Jurzi?"

"Yes, Effendim."

"Thou hast threatened murder to the wife of Mahmûd Agha?"

"No, by the Holy Name," gasped Dmitri, but the mudîr went on, unheeding the denial: –

"If harm befalls her anywhere within these realms by any hand, thou wilt be held responsible."

Dmitri's mouth and throat had suddenly become so dry that he could make no sound in answer to this solemn warning, so with a rough salute, he slunk away. He went straight to the priest and told his story. The priest at once absolved him of his vow, exclaiming: –

"It is now too dangerous. It might bring penalties upon the whole community. That brute beast has also spoken to the headman and to me. I have agreed against my will to let her come to church. Do thou, for thy part, lay aside the thought of vengeance."

Dmitri bowed his head as if assenting, though in his heart desire to kill his sister burned as strong as ever. It was a holy and a sweet resolve, for he still loved her more than any other creature, and by that sacrifice alone, it seemed, could she be his once more, her soul reclaimed from everlasting torments, her name redeemed from a dishonour which was poison to his brain.

A few days later it was known that Mahmûd Agha and his wife were going to remove their dwelling to some other place.

"Thanks be to God!" exclaimed the Christian villagers. "A stinking corpse is taken off our doorsteps."

But Dmitri, the devoted brother, was oppressed with grief. When Miriam was gone he knew no peace of mind. So long as she remained in Merdiven-keuy she had not seemed altogether lost to him; he had been able to observe her from a distance sometimes, and refresh his spirit with the thought that he could kill her when he liked. Except for his attendance on the English travellers there was nothing left to interest him in his native place; and when, as happened in the natural course of things, those travellers departed, he resolved to follow Miriam to her new dwelling place. The threat of the mudîr had taught him that he could not hope to gratify his longing with impunity in a country ruled by Muslims. In dreams – and he was always dreaming when alone – he saw a Christian country, with vast herds of swine feeding upon a plain, and church spires in the distance; and a great crucifix, at the foot of which lay Miriam dying, while he himself knelt by her weeping passionately. Around them was a crowd of Christian people, who applauded his devotion while they wept for him.

All Christians, of whatever country, hate the Muslims, he considered, and would rage to think of any Christian girl in his profane embrace.

At the end of a week's journey, made on foot, he stood before his sister in her new abode. Her joy at seeing him relieved his mind, as showing that she had not grown forgetful in her new surroundings. At the same time he began to wonder if the Englishman had not been right when he declared on one occasion that his (Dmitri's) horror of this Muslim marriage was in part imaginary.

She spoke with deep affection of her husband, but betrayed some disappointment at their way of living. It was dull. The Muslim women round about were shy of her because she still remained a Christian; though her husband told her that in cities they had no such prejudice. She would have liked to live in Brusa or Constantinople! But to do so in a pleasant way required much money; and so Mahmûd, who tried to give her all she wanted, talked of going to America to try his luck. She could not quite make up her mind to let him go, though sometimes, through desire for money, she was sorely tempted; and he said that after he had found employment, she might go and join him. It would please her well to see that rich, new country. And. even if he had to be away a year or two, she would not feel so very lonely if her brother was at hand. She hoped that he had come to stay with her.

Her husband, when he came in, was as cordial in his hope that Dmitri would not think of going back to Merdiven-keuy. In private, he informed him: –

"I have not yet told her that I start next week. A friend of mine, who knows America, is then returning, and I should be a fool to miss the chance he offers. I never thought of money till I married Miriam, but she, like all you Christians" – here he chuckled – "worships it. By choosing me she has estranged her old friends without gaining new ones, a state of things which wealth alone can remedy. And so, to save her from a life all disappointment, I am going out to seek my fortune in the world, with Allah's help. If thou art here, my mind will be at peace concerning her. Remain then, I beseech thee, for her sake."

Dmitri agreed. He journeyed back to Merdiven-keuy to tell his father of his purpose and to say farewell. When he returned to Miriam, she was alone, and saddened from parting from her husband. He found a small employment in the place, and cultivated certain fields belonging to Mahmûd, on behalf of Miriam. So happy and so tranquil was their life together that for months his mind was free from the desire to kill her; till one day she informed him that she was with child, mourning anew the absence of her lord. He nearly swooned with horror at the tidings, which reminded him of the dishonour of his race acutely. The child his sister bore would be a Muslim! The horror preyed upon his mind continually. He renewed his vow. The fierce desire of sacrifice once more consumed him, and he cast about for some safe way to gratify it. At length one day, returning from the market-town, he told her: –

"I have made inquiries and I find that we can journey to America for much less than the money which we have in hand."

She clapped her hands for joy at this assurance. Mahmûd had written to her of success, suggesting that he might invite her to rejoin him before very long; and ever since the coming of that letter she had been building palaces upon the hope it held for her. A month passed busily in preparations and farewells. Before they started Dmitri went to Merdiven-keuy on purpose to be shriven by the black-browed priest who knew his story.

From the place upon the lower deck of a great steamer where he and Miriam sat upon their heap of bedding, amid the crowd of steerage passengers, most of them with eyes screwed up against the glare of sea and sky, Dmitri saw more lucky people, clad in European clothes, moving upon the first-class deck above. Occasionally some of these would lean upon the railing and gaze upon the humble crowd a moment with disdainful eyes. Once a man and woman from that upper world came down to walk among them, out of curiosity. Dmitri, who was at his dinner of dry bread and olives, took no notice of the couple till they came abreast of him, when he recognised the English who had camped so long at Merdiven-keuy.

They recognised him too, and stopped before him, when Dmitri introduced his sister and explained that he was taking her to join her husband in America.

"What a pathetic face!" exclaimed the lady, who straightway entered into talk with Miriam; while the gentleman, apart with Dmitri, asked facetiously: –

"Is that your sister who was in a harem? I am glad to see that you are reconciled to her."

After that the English people came down every day from their superior deck to talk with Miriam and Dmitri.

"Marsilia[185], sir? That is a Christian country?" Dmitri asked the Englishman on one occasion.

"Yes, I suppose so," was the dubious answer. "Why do you ask?"

"Because I shall be glad to reach a country where the Christians rule," said Dmitri, smiling.

From the talk of other steerage passengers he gained the notion that Marseilles was truly Christian. These spoke with smacking lips of shops quite full of pork, and how the pious people of the country lived on pork and arak. By contrast with a Muslim country it was Paradise.

The English gentleman and lady stood by the rail and waved farewell when Dmitri and his sister with the crowd of emigrants were taken off in boats to the quarantine island. They were pleased to notice the young Greek's attentions to his sister, the way he lifted her into the boat, and then arranged their baggage as a throne for her, taking no thought whatever for himself. As the last boat-load of poor Orientals left its side, the ship steamed on into the harbour of Marseilles.

[185] Marseilles.

The crowd of emigrants from Turkey, mostly Maronites from the Lebanon, remained three days upon the island, sleeping in long huts, and guarded by French soldiers. Miriam consorted with the other women, and Dmitri thus had time for lonely thought. He found a spot whence he could see the outline of Marseilles, and even hear the murmur of the seaport when the wind was right. The streams of many coloured smoke arising constantly, the sheaves of masts, the high suspension bridge of which he could not guess the purpose, filled him with vague alarm, which was at once allayed when his gaze came to rest upon the church of Notre Dame de la Garde, alone upon its height, its tower surmounted by a golden statue of the Holy Virgin.

"A Christian country," he would then assure his soul.

One early morning, when the waves were sparkling under pearly haze, the emigrants, after having been examined for the last time by the doctor, were driven from the huts on to a little steamer black with coal-dust, which conveyed them quickly to the town. The noise and bustle of the arrival stupefied them. Dmitri, in despair, set down his luggage on the quay, and sat upon it with his sister, opposing every one who wished to seize it. The sunlight shimmered upon everything, a strong wind blew; from time to time the notes of bugles rang out above the other noises of the port.

Dmitri, seeing that his sister's face was sad – he had till then been too distraught to take much note of her – inquired the cause.

She said: "I had a dream last night. I saw Mahmûd, and he was weeping bitterly. Then I knew that I was dead and should not see him more, until we meet again in Paradise."

"Mahmûd is not for Paradise," said Dmitri sternly. "He is a Muslim, food of fire hereafter."

"That I will not believe!" exclaimed his sister. "Much that we learnt in childhood must be false, or how can God be just or merciful?"

"Her mind is tainted with Islâm," Dmitri thought with horror, "which gives salvation to all kinds of men regardless of Redemption by the Sacred Blood." But his answer to his sister was: "God knows the truth."

From where they sat upon the quay, resisting the attention of a crowd of harpies, he could not see the Virgin's church upon the hill. But when a man who spoke their language found them and they went along with him, he saw it once again with great relief. It was a Christian land!

In a squalid back street of Marseilles there is a row of houses kept as a caravanserai for Eastern emigrants, numbers of whom are always passing through the town on their way to the United States or South America. There, for a trifling sum of money, they may occupy the bare floor of a room, and have the food they choose to buy prepared for them, upon condition that they pay respect to the proprietor, a heartless Maronite, who orders them about like dogs and even whips them. Then Dmitri and his sister sought a lodging by their guide's advice and, having money in their hands, were well received. They hired a small room for themselves alone, which gave them standing, and the Syrian landlord, who had made a fortune by this traffic with the very poor, called them his children.

Dmitri, leaving Miriam and their luggage in their room, went out to a church and prayed, then to a pork shop, where he purchased pies and sausages, then to a café where he bought two bottles of strong drink, laden with which he went back to his sister. It was a festival day, he told her; since it was the first that either of them had spent upon the soil of Christendom; and they were going to have a feast of Christian food. He crossed himself devoutly and then set to work upon the victuals, bidding his sister do the same, for it was pork, which Christians of the East regard as sacred meat, because the Muslims and the Jews abhor it. She did at length obey, but with reluctance. Her Muslim husband had corrupted her, he thought with rage and anguish, watching her with the corner of an eye. He ate till he could eat no more with any pleasure, and then he fell to drinking, still observing her by stealth, and every now and then exclaiming in a kind of ecstasy: "Thanks be to God that we have reached a Christian land!"

"Why talk of Christians and of Muslims?" sighed his sister. "This country is less peaceful than our native land. I feel that no one could be happy here."

Then Dmitri told her of the glories of the land of Fransa, its wealth, its commerce, the conveniences of railways, tram-cars, banks and telephones. And all the Christian countries of the world had these advantages. Could any Muslim country boast the like? He argued with her fiercely, making it appear that she maintained the Muslim to be better than the Christian countries; deliberately working himself up to frenzy, and gulping down raw spirit in the pauses of his talk. His sister answered gently for some time; but when he grew abusive in his speech and cursed all Muslims, she became angry in her turn and cried:–

"Would God that I could see a Muslim in thy place, thou evil-speaker! Mahmûd is not a drunkard; he is kind to all. I think that he will go to Heaven before thee, defiled one!"

"Thou speakest blasphemy!" cried Dmitri, springing up and glaring at her with wild, drunken eyes. It is not thou that speakest, but the Muslim babe within thee."

He drew out of his girdle a long knife.

"Sit down!" she urged. "Be not so mad, so foolish!"

But he had seized her by the head-veil and the tail of hair beneath. "O Lord, accept the sacrifice and save her soul from hell." He mumbled piously; while she, struck dumb by terror, stared into his face. With his left hand upon her hair he dragged her backwards while with his right he struck down with the knife, then dragged it upwards. She gave one piercing shriek, so like an infant's that he believed it was the death-cry of the Muslim babe, and then pitched sidelong on the floor, which soon was reddened.

He stood and watched her with regret and satisfaction queerly mingled, till all at once the room was full of hostile shapes, and he was struggling with a man who seemed intent to kill him. It was the Syrian owner of the hostelry, who with the help of others flung the murderer upon the ground, and beat and kicked him, calling him evil names in Greek and Arabic. Then soldiers came and asked him strange questions, which the master of the house translated for him in insulting tones. He answered dully: –

"Is it not a Christian country? I am a Christian. I can clear myself."

Then suddenly it struck him that he had no witnesses to prove that Miriam had really been disgraced by marriage with a Muslim man. There was but one in Europe who had knowledge of the facts – the Englishman who had camped at Merdiven-keuy. So when the landlord, speaking for the soldiers, asked him: –

"Is there any one who knows thee in this land?" he answered dully: "Meester Clark, the Englishman who travelled with us on the steamship *Niger*.

Then he was handcuffed and led out through gibbering crowds to an automobile, which wafted him and his tormentors as by magic to a building like a fortress kept by many soldiers. There he was shut up in a white-washed room without a window. Still he assured himself: "It is a Christian country. When they know that she was married to a Muslim and with child by him, they will respect me."

And when the warder came into his cell with food and water he asked again for "Mûsiû[186] Clark, the Englishman".

As luck would have it, Mr. Clark had not yet left Marseilles, and as the best hotels are few in number, a gendarme detailed for the purpose found him easily. That very evening he was ushered into Dmitri's cell, together with a brisk, frock-coated French official who had long been waiting for him in the corridor. The prisoner fell down upon the floor and tried to kiss his feet. The French official said: –

"It is an Arab, is it not, monsieur?"

"No," replied the Englishman, "it is a Greek from Turkey."

---

186 Monsieur.

The Frenchman shrugged as if to say it made no difference, and then resumed:–

"A tragic case! The man has murdered his own sister; she was enceinte[187], as you doubtless know. The man was drunk, and in so far as we can gather from the master of the lodging-house, who speaks his tongue, he fancied that the babe she carried would become his enemy. He has declared repeatedly, we understand, that you, monsieur, can show that he was justified in what he did; or at least that he is justified according to the law of his own country. Does any law of any country sanction such a crime? I ask myself! I am most curious to know the facts."

But the Englishman was once again in Merdiven-keuy – the little climbing town of gardens by the inland sea. He saw once more the face of the mudîr who had annoyed him by maintaining that the Christians wished to kill the girl now lying dead; while Dmitri, clinging to his feet, implored him to assure the Frenchman that the victim had in truth disgraced the Christian name.

"She had submitted to a Muslim. A Muslim babe was in her; so she had to die . . . . It is a Christian country. There is a great church with a golden Virgin on it, on a hill. These men are Christians; they eat pork, drink wine. I also am a Christian. They will let me go. I slew her to avenge the honour of the people of the Cross."

"They will not let thee live," replied the Englishman.

Then Dmitri uttered shriek on shriek of rage and horror, calling his captors freemasons and atheists, to take the side of unbelievers against Christian men.

"This is no Christian land. God's curse be on it!" he shouted in a final paroxysm ere, foaming at the mouth, he swooned away.

[187] Pregnant.

BIBLIOGRAPHY

Claire Chambers, *Britain through Muslim Eyes, Literary Representations, 1780-1988*, Palgrave Macmillan, London, 2015

Peter Clark, *Marmaduke Pickthall: British Muslim*, Quartet Books, London, 1986: reissued by Beacon Books, Manchester, 2016

Anne Fremantle, *Loyal Enemy, the Life of Marmaduke Pickthall*, Hutchinson, London, 1938

Ahmad Yahya al-Ghamdi, *Marmaduke Pickthall (1875-1936) and the Literature of Transition*, PhD thesis, Michagan State University, 1995

Jamie Gilham, *Loyal Enemies, British Converts to Islam, 1850-1950*, Hurst, London, 2014

Andrew C Long, *Reading Arabia, British Orientalism in the Age of Mass Production*, Syracuse University Press, New York, 2014

Geoffrey P Nash, *Marmaduke Pickthall, Islam and the Modern World*, Brill, Leyden, 2017

Marmaduke Pickthall, *As Others See Us*, Collins, London, 1922

Marmaduke Pickthall, *Pot au Feu*, John Murray, London, 1911

Marmaduke Pickthall, *Tales from Five Chimneys*, Mills and Boon, London, 1915

Ebtisam A Sadiq (ed), *Marmaduke Pickthall Reinstated*, Partridge, Singapore, 2016

Lightning Source UK Ltd.
Milton Keynes UK
UKHW041626120619
344250UK00001B/96/P

9 781912 356027